THE SEASIDE ANGEL

Margate, 1884: When seventeen-year-old Hannah Bentley fled the family home, she never dreamed she'd find her feet working as a nurse on the children's ward at the Royal Sea Bathing Infirmary. She adores her patients and the sea air, and looks forward to a time when she'll have put away enough money so her younger sister can join her. But when her sister suddenly turns up unannounced, she brings more trouble than Hannah bargained for. As Hannah is forced to risk everything to keep her sister out of trouble, she must somehow find the strength to save herself too . . .

EVIE GRACE

THE SEASIDE ANGEL

Complete and Unabridged

MAGNA
Leicester

First published in Great Britain in 2019 by
Arrow Books
an imprint of Penguin Random House UK
London

First Ulverscroft Edition
published 2020
by arrangement with
Arrow Books
Penguin Random House UK
London

ISBN 978–0–7505–4810–6

Published by
Ulverscroft Limited
Anstey, Leicestershire

Set by Words & Graphics Ltd.
Anstey, Leicestershire
Printed and bound in Great Britain by
T. J. International Ltd., Padstow, Cornwall

This book is printed on acid-free paper

To Laura

Acknowledgements

I should like to thank Laura and everyone at MBA Literary Agents, and Cass and the team at Penguin Random House UK for their continuing enthusiasm and support.

1

White Aprons, Collars and Cuffs

London, May 1884

'How are you today, Davy?' Hannah asked the boy who was sitting up in his cot. He was playing with a tin toy train that one of the lady volunteers had brought into the ward the day before.

'Much better, Nurse.' He looked up with a toothy smile on his face. He was nine, quite scrawny for his age, but he had an air of toughness about him.

'I believe the doctor has said you can go home today.'

His expression changed. 'I don't wanna go 'ome.'

'Your ma and sister will be pleased to have you back.'

'I don't think so — Ma says she's goin' to give me a good 'idin' for what I done.'

'I'm sure she didn't mean it. She was upset.'

'I was nearly a goner,' he said earnestly.

'At least you've learned your lesson — don't eat things when you don't know what they are.'

'I thought it was treacle. It looked like treacle and tasted like it too.'

'Never mind. I'm glad you're well again. That's all that matters.' When he'd been admitted a few days before, Davy had been suffering from delirium, shouting out and screaming, his eyes flicking from side to side, having consumed deadly nightshade mixed as a physic for horses.

Hannah turned to her next patient, a boy of eleven who was lying on his side in the adjacent cot. He'd had a stroke after being struck down with scarlet fever two months before.

'Good morning, Joe.' She reached for his uppermost hand and gave it a gentle squeeze. He squeezed back. 'Let me sit you up so you can see what's going on. Nurse Huckstep ... ' She looked past the nature table of greenery and pebbles, to where Alice, wearing a dark dress like hers, with a white apron, collar and cuffs, and with her blonde hair tucked neatly beneath her cap, was changing the sheets on an empty bed.

'You wish to move this patient, Nurse Bentley?' Alice stepped quickly across the ward to help her roll Joe on to his back before sitting him up, arranging the pillows to hold him in position.

'One more.' Alice picked up a bolster, and Hannah lifted Joe's limp arm to let her slide it underneath. 'Thank you.' The corners of Alice's bright blue eyes creased as she smiled. 'We make a good team.'

'The best.' They'd been friends since arriving at the Hospital for Sick Children to begin their training as lady probationers two years previously. Hannah had been eighteen at the time, and Alice twenty-one.

'There you are.' Hannah lowered Joe's arm on

to the pillow. 'Would you like something to drink? Perhaps some beer?'

Joe smiled and nodded his head.

'Did you take your cod liver oil?' Alice asked, at which he frowned.

'You did, didn't you?' Hannah said. 'I gave it to you yesterday evening and you had extra sugared toast for being a good boy.' Joe didn't respond this time and she followed his gaze towards the entrance to the ward where Sister — they called her the General behind her back — was standing with her hands on her hips.

'Nurse Bentley, you're to go to the lady superintendent's office forthwith. Immediately!' she added when Hannah hesitated. 'Today, not tomorrow. One mustn't keep Miss Russell waiting.'

'What is it about?' Hannah asked tentatively.

'I don't know — I'm merely the messenger. Hurry along!'

'Yes, Sister.' Hannah glanced towards Alice who mouthed, 'Good luck.'

What had she done, or — just as likely — forgotten to do? She hurried along the corridors, aware of the prickly scent of carbolic mingling with the smell of overcooked cabbage from the hospital kitchens, and the sound of chatter, the thin wail of an ailing infant and a mother singing a lullaby.

Once outside the office, Hannah took a deep breath and knocked on the door.

'Do come in.' The lady super's mellifluous tone was deceptive, reminding Hannah of the first line of a poem she sometimes told the children: *Will you walk into my parlour? said the spider to the fly.* They had crossed swords on many occasions: she had broken a thermometer; miscalculated the amount of medicine required to mix into a poultice; told one of the surgeons that she was a nurse, not his maid. Miss Russell had hauled her over the coals for the last, saying that although Hannah had expressed the sentiments shared by others, she should have bitten her tongue.

She pushed the door open and Miss Russell looked up from her desk, the furrows in her brow deepening, the careworn lines on her face the result perhaps of the burden of running the hospital and managing everyone within it.

'Nurse Bentley, take a seat.' She smiled — she actually smiled — and Hannah felt a little better about being summoned from the ward. She fiddled with her cuffs, glad that she had changed them for a freshly laundered pair. Having overslept that morning, she'd put her copper-red hair up in a bun without bothering with hairpins, and long ringlets were escaping from under her cap.

'This won't take long,' Miss Russell went on. 'Mrs Knowles, Matron at the Royal Sea Bathing Infirmary in Margate, is looking for staff — I recommended you to her, and she's keen to take you on. What do you think?'

'You want me to go to Margate, ma'am?' Hannah said, surprised at the turn of events. She liked living in London; loved the hospital and had friends here, Alice especially.

'The infirmary is well thought of and there are

4

opportunities for advancement. At your interview, you told me in no uncertain terms of the extent of your ambition. You were forward and rather presumptuous considering you'd had no experience on the wards, but I put that down to your youth and family situation.'

It had been difficult, Hannah recalled.

★ ★ ★

She'd been about to turn eighteen, and her stepmother had been preparing her to attend her first ball which was being held at a country house near Faversham. On the evening before the great event and having enjoyed a final lesson with her dance master, Hannah had hurried to join her father who had called her to his study.

'You're late,' he observed as she entered his den.

By a minute, she thought, glancing at the marble clock on his desk. His mane of red hair was tousled and his face scarlet, as though he'd partaken of a drop too much of madeira before dinner.

'Sit down.'

'Thank you, Pa.' She took the seat opposite him and waited for him to speak.

'I understand that you had a dress fitting earlier this week — I'll be awaiting the dressmaker's bill with interest and a little trepidation.' His smile didn't reach his eyes — it never did. He was an actuary who had been promoted to top-hat at the Canterbury agency of the Wessex Union fire office, an expert in statistics, life expectancy and losses, a highly intelligent man who could make money, but had no idea how to inspire happiness in those around him. He'd made Cook cry again that morning because the cream for his coffee had been on the turn, and she'd been unable to supply an immediate replacement.

'I'll keep this brief,' he went on eventually. 'I have excellent news that will be of great delight and satisfaction to you. I've secured you an offer — '

'I beg your pardon,' Hannah interrupted, a pulse of doubt beginning to throb at her temple.

'Of marriage. To my dear friend, Mr Edison. Why do you stare at me like that? He's no stranger to our family.' Pa's elderly and widowed acquaintance had been invited to the house in Dane John many times, and as Hannah had grown older, she'd come to dread his presence at dinner. Recoiling at the memory of the wiry touch of his whiskers against her cheek as he'd pressed up against her on the staircase, she shuddered.

She'd always known that one day she would marry, but not Mr Edison with his pale, pink-rimmed eyes, white hair and long, claw-like fingernails.

'You could express at least an ounce of gratitude. You caught his eye some time ago and he's been patient, waiting for you to come of age. He's a decent man, a gentleman.'

'He's very old, Pa . . . '

'A significant age gap makes for a better marriage,' her father said. 'A younger woman has

6

an endearing naivety about her which makes her more likely to acquiesce to her husband's wishes when it comes to her manners, mode of dress and friendships. She's easier to command and mould into the perfect wife and mother.'

As he'd done with her dear Ma before she'd been cruelly snatched away from them? Hannah wondered.

'I don't want a husband — I don't want to be married.'

'There's a poem by Coventry Patmore which sums up the balance of the sexes in a nutshell. *Man must be pleased; but him to please / Is woman's pleasure* . . . I can't quote the rest — it's completely slipped my mind, but that is the essence of it.'

'Stepmother doesn't seem to find pleasure in pleasing you,' Hannah blurted out.

Pa frowned. 'I'd suggest that you think twice about challenging your father. Suffice to say, the values I hold have been the foundation of society for many generations. They've served us well, and I don't see any reason to change them now. A man's role is to provide for his wife and family, something Mr Edison is more than capable of. A man requires purpose, the acquisition of wealth, while a woman should be content to stay at home, spending his money to make it a haven of tranquillity.

'Your stepmother needs reminding of her duty sometimes. Anyway, I'm talking about *your* future. May I remind you that it's your destiny to marry well — there's no getting away from it.'

Glancing towards the window, Hannah noticed

a few raindrops glittering against the darkness outside. She felt trapped, hardly able to breathe.

'May I remind you that you're a very ordinary woman with the prettiness that comes with youth and fades soon after. You'll never receive a better offer, so I suggest you accept Mr Edison as your husband — willingly.'

'And if I don't?'

'Oh, you will. I can't see you giving up your comforts for a life on the streets.'

'I shall go out to work,' she said, shocked at her father's suggestion.

'You aren't going to work for your living. I absolutely forbid it. Labour of any kind cuts women off from their family and social circle. What's more, it makes them appear masculine and coarse.'

She wasn't sure that she believed him — Cook, their maid and the private nurse who had attended to the twins all looked perfectly feminine. She wondered if it had more to do with making Pa look less of a man.

'Your obligation is to care for your husband and bring up the children of the household. That is what the female brain is uniquely suited to, being inferior to a man's in every way, apart from their instinct for understanding an infant's needs and their generosity in satisfying their husband's demands.

'What would it look like? That I couldn't afford to keep my daughters in the manner to which they've become accustomed? That I cared so little for them that they turned their back on me? Hannah, a woman is only forced to work when she can't find a husband to support her.' He stood up. 'What on earth would you do anyway?'

She hadn't had to consider finding a suitable occupation before, but the choice seemed obvious. 'I'd be a nurse.'

'Don't be ridiculous — there's no way I'd let you follow in that Nightingale woman's footsteps.'

'The work she's done has been nothing short of miraculous — I've read about her.'

'Nursing is best left to the lower classes, as it's always been. You would hate it.'

'You find great satisfaction in your work,' she countered. 'Isn't it reasonable that a woman should find the same?'

'You're beginning to sound like your mother, expressing these delusions and irrational thoughts.' Her father rested his hands on the desk and leaned across it until she could see the bloodshot whites of his eyes and the spittle on his lips. 'This discussion is irrelevant, and a waste of my precious time. You will not insult my name by taking paid occupation, or embarrass me by turning down Mr Edison.'

'I won't have anything to do with him.'

'Then I will have you horsewhipped to within an inch of your life! You will marry my friend. Is that clear?'

'Perfectly,' she snapped, getting up and straightening her heavy skirts, before rushing away in a fit of fury and resentment. Upstairs in her room, she pulled out her case and hatboxes from under the bed and opened her trunk. She started packing her belongings before realising that she could never carry it all by herself.

'Where are you going?' she heard Ruby ask as she sat on the rug, wondering what to do.

'Grandma's, if she'll have me,' she said through a flood of tears. 'I'm sorry — I can't stay here any longer.'

'Why? You're supposed to be going to the ball tomorrow. What's happened?'

'Pa has told me that I must marry Mr Edison. It's impossible. It makes me sick to think of it.'

'Oh dear. Cook calls him a lecherous snake.'

'Ruby!' Aghast at her sister's frankness, she looked up.

'Shall I speak to Stepmother on your behalf?' Ruby's eyes were dark and beseeching. 'I can explain that you aren't happy with our father's choice.'

'It will make no difference. Pa's mind is made up, and besides, when has he ever taken notice of his wife?'

'Perhaps he would agree on you settling for somebody else, a gentleman nearer your age, and of a fairer countenance?'

'Ruby, I shall never marry anyone. I've seen and heard enough to know that marriage is more a bed of thorns than roses. But I don't know what to do because Pa says he'll have me whipped if I disobey him — I have to get away from here.'

'How will you survive?'

'I'll work for my living — as a nurse who cares for children.'

'That's a noble sentiment, if ever there was

one.' Ruby frowned.

'It isn't a sentiment. I intend to act upon it.'

Ruby plunged to her knees on the rug, her skirts billowing out around her as she flung her arms around Hannah's neck. 'Please, don't go. Don't leave me with Pa and Stepmother.'

'I'll write every day, or as often as I can,' Hannah said, extricating herself from her embrace. 'You can visit me too — Grandma isn't far away.'

'It won't be the same. You'll forget about me.' Ruby started sobbing.

'Don't be silly. Of course I won't. You're my sister, my best and only friend.'

It was true that they were very close, kept isolated from society except when Pa had dinner guests, or Stepmother decided she wished to show them off: Hannah for her reading voice, and Ruby for her beauty and doll-like appearance with her long, dark hair and full lips.

She kissed the top of Ruby's head, her heart breaking at the thought of leaving her behind.

'I wish I could take you with me, but I can't until I start earning enough money to support the two of us. I promise I'll send for you as soon as I can. You know how much I love you, and if you're ever in any danger, you must come and find me straight away.' Hannah was afraid for a moment that Pa might press Mr Edison's suit upon her sister, until she remembered that Ruby was only fifteen.

'Thank you.' Ruby brightened. 'For your sake and that of the little children who are suffering, I give you my blessing,' she said bravely. 'Shall I help you carry your boxes?'

'No. Go down to dinner as usual. Tell them I'm indisposed. I'll speak to Grandma when I get there — perhaps she'll arrange to have my belongings sent on later.'

'You don't think Pa will come after you?'

Hannah shook her head, recalling one of his favourite sayings: boys are a blessing sent from Heaven, while girls are the devil's spawn. 'You know how it is — he's always been too busy to bother with us. I don't think he'll waste his time trying to persuade me to return.'

As soon as she'd uttered these words, the door banged open, rattling the window, and Pa came striding in.

'You can both go to bed without dinner,' he thundered. 'I'll decide what to do with the pair of you in the morning. I heard you plotting against me.'

'Ruby has nothing to do with this,' Hannah said protectively.

'I have no doubt that it's six of one and half a dozen of the other — you're your mother's daughters.'

'Promise me you won't punish her. This is all my doing,' Hannah insisted, getting up at the same time as her sister.

'Run along, Ruby.' Pa gestured to her to leave the room, which she did after glancing at Hannah who nodded, praying that this meant that Ruby would escape uncensured. 'Now I can deal with you, you insolent and disrespectful young woman,' Pa said when she had gone.

'I wish to leave this house,' Hannah said.

12

'You aren't stepping outside this room until your engagement to Mr Edison has been announced in the newspapers. You'll be kept under constant supervision until it's recorded in black and white for all to see.'

Hannah tried to push her way past him, but he grabbed her by the wrist, holding it so tightly that her hand turned white from lack of blood. With great effort, she tore herself away, and having dodged past him, she ran down the stairs with the sound of her breathing harsh in her ears, and his heavy footsteps in close pursuit.

She raced out on to the steps down to the street, turning and slamming the door in his face, before heading towards the centre of Canterbury, running along the pavements and cutting left and right, hardly knowing where she was going, but intent on getting away. Having turned a corner, she ducked into an archway where she stopped, pressing herself against the wall with pain searing through her lungs, and her limbs frozen to the bone.

'Show yourself!' she heard her father bellow. 'I'm losing my patience with you!'

Without moving a muscle, she waited for him to go, his shadow retreating along the dark street to the corner where a gaslight briefly illuminated his figure in the falling rain before he disappeared.

Although her satin slippers were wet through and she had only a shawl for warmth, she remained in her hiding place until the cathedral bell tolled eleven o'clock. Only then did she hasten across the bridge over the stinking black waters of the

Stour and past the looming Westgate. Having reached her grandmother's house in St Dunstan's, she hammered on the door.

'Let me in!' she begged when her grandmother's maid opened it. 'It's me. Hannah.'

The maid frowned. 'I di'n't recognise you.'

'Who is it calling at this time of night?' her grandmother said, hurrying across the hall in her nightgown.

'It's Miss Bentley, lookin' like a drowned rat.'

'Oh? Come in, quickly. You'll catch your death.'

'I'm sorry for bringing trouble to your door,' Hannah stuttered, her lips numb with cold, as she stepped inside. 'I didn't know where else to go.'

'Don't worry, my dear,' Grandma said. 'Let's find you some dry clothes and brandy. Elsie, stoke the fire in the parlour. Hannah, you can tell me exactly what's going on.'

'I'm afraid he'll come after me.' Hannah glanced back at the door where the maid was turning the key in the lock. 'It's Father . . . He's in such a temper.'

'You're safe here and welcome to stay for as long as you need.'

'He'll drag me home and keep me locked up until I agree to marry his friend, Mr Edison.'

'Over my dead body! I won't let him make you do anything. That man won't dare cross me, not after what he did to my daughter . . . your blameless and loving mother.' Her grandmother wiped a tear from her eye as she led Hannah into the parlour.

'What exactly did he do?' Hannah muttered.

'He treated her most cruelly, but that's all I wish to say on the matter for now. You've been through more than enough for one day.' Grandma took the woollen shawl from Hannah's shoulders and placed it on the fireguard where it left a gleaming puddle on the floor. 'All I will say is that it will give me great pleasure to tell your father that you're staying with me from now on.'

Hannah hardly slept that night. She was up at dawn when she heard the knock at the door announcing her father's arrival, raised voices and harsh words.

'If she doesn't come back with me, I'll sever all ties. Mr Edison won't want her when he finds out she's a wayward, disobedient and foolish young woman, just like her mother.'

'You know what you did to my daughter — you drove her to it,' Grandma said angrily, 'and I won't stand by and let history repeat itself.'

'Then tell Hannah that she's cooked her goose. As far as I'm concerned, I no longer consider her my daughter. She's on her own, and good luck to her. I hope she has plenty of time to dwell on the consequences of her stupidity.'

Staring down at the bruises on her wrist, Hannah realised then what her father was capable of, and that she couldn't possibly turn back from the path she had chosen. She didn't have much idea about what being a nurse involved, but she was certain it couldn't be worse than continuing to live under the same roof as her father.

It was her grandmother and Miss Russell who had given her the chance to experience life on the wards.

* * *

'I seem to have caught you by surprise. Are you listening to me, Nurse Bentley?'

'Yes. Yes, of course,' Hannah said quickly, remembering where she was.

'There are others whom I could put forward, but I'm asking you first.' Miss Russell gave her a hard stare, making it clear that turning the offer down wasn't what she wanted to hear.

In a way, Hannah felt obligated to the woman who'd admitted her for training at a younger age than was customary. It was certainly an honour to have been chosen, and one of those chances of a lifetime that should be grasped with both hands. She pictured herself as ward sister, then — though it seemed an impossible dream — matron. She had a long way to go, but, having found her calling, it was no time to sit back.

'I'm very grateful for your consideration,' she said. 'I'd be delighted — '

'That's excellent. I would have made the same decision if I were in your shoes. You will leave tomorrow morning.'

'That soon?' Hannah suppressed a gasp of shock.

'I've been notified of two poor boys who have been chosen by the governors — under the instructions of Mr Piper, medical officer at St Pancras, and Mr Willis, our resident surgeon

16

— to spend time at the infirmary. Usually one of our volunteers escorts them on the journey, but there's no one available. I thought that this would kill two birds with one stone: the boys will be safely delivered, and you'll be in Margate, ready to start work. You have time to pack what you need and say your goodbyes. I'll arrange for the rest of your belongings to be sent after you. Is that clear?'

'Yes, thank you.'

'The infirmary helps the incurables and long-term sick, the old and young, and those in between, using thalassotherapy to treat chronic diseases like scrofula. They have several children's wards and they're short of trained nurses. I wouldn't have suggested it otherwise, knowing how good you are with the little ones. You'll like Margate — I spent a few days there last summer.' Miss Russell put on her pince-nez and opened a ledger on her desk. 'That is all. You are dismissed.'

Hannah walked back to the ward with a spring in her step and joy in her heart because it seemed that her conviction and dedication to duty had been vindicated. There had been times when she'd had doubts about whether she was really suited to be a nurse, but Miss Russell's recommendation proved that she had made the right decision.

She'd soon realised after starting work that a nurse's wage wouldn't provide food and lodgings for her and Ruby, but she hadn't forgotten her promise. She had saved every penny she could and put the small inheritance she'd received when her grandmother passed away to one side, but it still wasn't enough. If she was promoted to ward sister — which seemed more likely now — she would help Ruby get away from their father and any plans he might have to marry her off. She resolved to write to let her know about her move to Margate, as soon as she could.

★ ★ ★

As Hannah entered the ward, Alice looked up from where she was attending to one of their patients: a boy with a shock of red curls and more freckles than Hannah. Alice raised her eyebrows in question. Hannah shook her head. It would have to wait until they found a quiet moment out of earshot. But it wasn't to be, because the General sent Alice to assist on another ward for the rest of their shift.

'What did Miss Russell want with you? I've been on tenterhooks all day.' Alice fastened her cape as they headed to the district home in the twilight of the cool May evening. 'Are you in trouble?'

'It's quite the opposite. She's sending me to Margate.'

'It's a little early for a summer holiday, isn't it?' Alice smiled. 'How long will you be away for?'

Hannah's throat tightened. 'I'm afraid it's permanent — there's a position available there.'

'You're going to take it without a second thought?'

'Miss Russell's recommended me to the matron

at the Royal Sea Bathing Infirmary where they treat their patients with thala-something. Oh dear, I was too overwhelmed to ask her what it was.'

'Thalassotherapy,' Alice finished for her. 'Saltwater treatment.'

'Thank you. I don't want to leave you behind, but Ruby's seventeen. It won't be long before my father finds her some old man for a husband, like he tried to do with me.' Hannah had felt uneasy about her situation ever since she'd left home. It was more precarious now because with their grandmother gone, Ruby had nowhere to run to. Their uncle — Ma's brother — would offer her a place to stay for a while if life at home became unbearable, but it wouldn't be permanent as he had a large family of his own living under the one roof at the maltings.

'You don't have to explain,' Alice said. 'This brings you one step closer to freeing your sister from your father's control — as long as it's what she really wants. I'm not trying to stop you going to Margate, but Ruby may have changed her mind by now.'

'It's true that she doesn't complain about her lot — her letters are filled with stories of how she and our stepmother spend their time together. However, when I see her — which isn't often — she always begs me to take her back to London with me. Pa is the same — mean and bad-tempered — a leopard doesn't change its spots.'

'Then I wish you all the best. Oh, I don't know what else to say, except that you deserve it. Congratulations! But I'm going to miss you.'

19

Alice put her arm through Hannah's. 'You're my best friend, my confidante . . . '

'I'll miss you too. We've been through a lot together. Do you remember our first day on the wards?'

'How could I forget? You caught me when I fainted — I thought that Miss Russell was going to send me packing because I couldn't stand the sight of blood, but you asked her to give me a second chance.'

'She would have done anyway,' Hannah said. 'She's very sharp — she recognises potential when she sees it.'

'You know, I envy you in a way. I'd love to spend some time at the seaside — my lungs do suffer so in the smog — but I don't think my Tom would like it if I suddenly upped sticks.'

It was no secret that Alice planned to give up nursing when she got married, not that her sweetheart, a banker who was rising through the ranks, had made any suggestion of it, even though they'd been walking out together for several months.

'There's no sign of an engagement yet?' Hannah wasn't sure about Mr Fry being a gentleman — they weren't well acquainted.

'There's no hurry, and besides, he's working all the hours God sends to make his mark, which means he doesn't make any fuss about the time I spend at the hospital. He's thoughtful and handsome . . . '

He wasn't quite as wonderful as Alice made out, in Hannah's opinion. She pictured the skinny young man with his sparse, curly beard, the rash on his neck and his badly cut coat. They had first met him while walking along Regent Street on a rare free afternoon, entering into conversation with him when he saw off a scoundrel who'd had the audacity to follow them into a milliner's shop and make an ill-judged remark on Alice's voluptuous appearance.

'Leave these young ladies alone or I'll turn you into a skinful o' bones,' he'd said, and the miscreant had backed down at the sight of this unlikely hero, while Alice had fallen in love with him.

'Every cloud has a silver lining — I reckon your leaving will inspire him to offer his hand,' Alice said.

'I don't see why that will make any difference.'

'Well, of course it does! It changes everything. We won't be able to meet without you.'

It was true. Without a chaperone, Alice would find it much harder, if not impossible, to meet her beau. If they became engaged, they'd be permitted to walk out together, but as soon as she found out, Miss Russell would encourage them to wed as soon as possible, and Alice would have to leave the hospital. Nursing and marriage were not compatible bedfellows. When a nurse married, she was obliged to leave her post and turn her hand to motherhood and running her household, as society expected. Hannah felt it wasn't entirely fair that a man could continue his career when he married, while a woman was condemned to make a choice.

'Write to me,' Alice went on.

'I will. I promise.'

'And you'll come back to visit us, and one day, my husband and I will come to see you in Margate.'

Hannah smiled ruefully. She knew very well that Alice would use her precious annual week's holiday to visit her mother, while she would stay with her uncle in Canterbury, where Ruby would join her for a few days. With the hours they worked, they couldn't often get home to their families, even if they wished to. Eating cake was their only vice. They took little alcohol, had to behave in the way expected of refined young ladies, and were forbidden to have visiting gentlemen — not that Hannah had any interest in the male sex, thanks to her father's domineering ways.

They had walked in Hyde Park where they'd stopped to stare at the statue of the Iron Duke, hero of a hundred fights. They had skated on the frozen Serpentine while the men employed by the Royal Humane Society and the Met Police had stood watching, waiting with hooks and ropes. They had seen the Queen and her carriage, and waved flags at the Boat Race. They had shared laughter and tears, joys and sadness. They had kept each other going, and now it was over.

'Don't look so downcast, Hannah. The next time we meet, I'll be Mrs Thomas Fry, you'll be Sister Bentley, and Ruby will be safe and happy, living with you in a cosy house beside the sea. Everything will work out. You'll see.'

22

2

The Margate Hoy

Having packed the essentials in a small carpet bag and said farewell to Alice and her patients on the ward early the following morning, Hannah went to meet the two poor boys whom she was taking to Margate. They were waiting in the hospital entrance hall where the porter was already directing a stream of visitors to the outpatients' department.

''Ere, miss. They're all yours,' the young man standing with them said roughly. 'I'll be glad to get 'em off my 'ands. I didn't know what I was lettin' myself in for when I offered to bring 'em 'ere.'

Hannah knew that boys were troublesome creatures, but she couldn't see either of them having the strength to say boo to a goose. They appeared very similar, no more than ten or eleven years old, and dressed in tatty caps, dirty brown shirts and shoes that were falling off their feet. She was sorry to see how sickly they looked.

'Have you brought their paperwork and boxes with you?' she asked.

'The medical officer at St Pancras gave me this.' He pulled a wad of papers from his jacket pocket. 'They don't 'ave much, not even a change of socks — they're carryin' all their

23

worldly goods about their persons. I 'ave to go.'
He spun on his heels and hurried away.

'Oh, wait,' she called after him, but he was
already halfway through the door.

'You're too late, Nurse Bentley,' the porter
observed. ' 'E's gone.'

'Mr Glanvill don't like us,' one of the boys
piped up. He prodded the other boy who
muttered in agreement. 'We're nothin' to 'im.
Can we get goin' now? I'm lookin' forward to
seein' the sea.'

'Be patient — I need to check our
instructions.' Hannah opened the paperwork and
read the letters of recommendation from their
sponsor, and the doctor who'd examined them.

Dear Doctor Clifton,

*I have here two boys with tickets for the
Royal Sea Bathing Infirmary. Both are of
poor families condemned to the St Pancras
poorhouse who have no means of paying for
their treatments.*

*Peter Herring, aged 11 (approximately),
is suffering from scrofulous glands in the
neck, general malaise and a worrying
reluctance to eat.*

*Charlie Swift, aged 10, is suffering from
scrofula of the knee joints.*

*In my opinion, both boys would benefit
from a stay at your establishment.*

*I trust you are well, I remain your humble
servant etc.,*

J. H. Piper

24

There was another envelope containing money for tickets on the hoy — not enough for passage on a steam-packet, she noted, which would mean their journey would depend on the weather and tide.

She looked up on hearing the porter clear his throat.

'On learnin' that you were leavin' us, I took the liberty of askin' Cook to make up a basket of provisions for you. There's a letter with it too — it arrived in the second post yesterday.'

'Thank you, Mr Featherstone. That's very kind.' Hannah touched the corner of her eye, suddenly close to tears, as he picked up a basket covered with a gingham cloth from the side table in the hall and carried it over to her.

'You've always treated me with the greatest of respect, and you cheer me up with your ready smile.' He and his wife had had a bad time, losing their first child to the palsy soon after Hannah had started her training. 'I'm going to miss you.'

'I'll carry it for yer, missus,' the shorter of the two boys offered.

'It's Nurse Bentley to you, young fella,' Mr Featherstone said. 'You'd better act like a gentleman when you're with 'er, or you'll 'ave me to answer to.'

The boy's eyes opened a little wider as she let him take hold of the basket.

'There's a lot o' wittles in there,' he marvelled.

Hannah could only flinch as she caught sight of his grubby hands.

'Good day, and give my regards to Mrs

Featherstone,' she said, before shooing the boys out of the hospital on to Great Ormond Street. 'I don't think we've been properly introduced,' she went on as they began to make their way slowly along the pavement which was glistening in the hazy sunshine after a brief shower. 'Which one of you is Master Herring?'

'I'm Charlie, missus. I mean, Nurse.'

'Then you must be Peter,' she said to the other.

'No, 'e's Charlie,' the first boy said. 'I'm Peter, same as my ma's always called me.' His mouth curved into a small smile. His brown sandy hair was crawling with nits and his legs were bowed. 'That's right, ain't it, Peter?'

The other boy nodded. His hair was darker, almost black, and he had a smattering of freckles across his upturned nose. She could see the scrofula around his neck, the swollen glands, one suppurating and half covered with a dirty bandage.

'You're beginning to try my patience,' Hannah said lightly. 'At this rate, we'll miss the boat.'

'I'm sorry, Nurse,' they said in unison.

'I'm Charlie,' the bigger one said — she already knew that the size of a child didn't necessarily correlate with their age. 'And so is 'e.' He chuckled, but she remembered the details in the letter.

'Oh, you two are incorrigible,' she sighed, playing along because Peter — the boy with the scrofulous glands in the neck — didn't look as if he'd ever had any fun in his life. 'Come with me — I shall call you both Charlie.'

They were smiling as they made their way along Gray's Inn Road towards the Old Bailey. Their minds were lively enough, but they struggled to walk. Charlie winced with every stride he took, and Peter dragged his feet with each step, as swarms of people hurried past them, their heads down, barely looking at where they were going.

'Mind your backs!' Hannah stepped aside as a carriage pulled by a pair of bays flew past, followed by a rider on a grey cob, then a horse and cart loaded with barrels of ale.

'Why is everyone in such a tearing hurry?' she muttered. 'Boys, you must stay close. Don't touch that, please,' she went on as Charlie stopped to pick up a small stick from the pavement and began digging around in a heap of dirt.

'You never know what you might find that you can sell for a farthin' or two.' He slipped the stick into his pocket. 'I've found bones and rags, even an 'a'penny once.'

Hannah thought of her younger half-brothers at Charlie's age — they would never have thought of grubbing around in the gutter looking for treasure. They hadn't needed to.

She recalled the day the twins had been born. She and Ruby had been upstairs in the nursery, playing with a doll and a fine china tea service in miniature, when they'd heard the first cry which meant that their lives had changed for ever: the arrival of not one, but two much-wanted sons. There had been visitors, celebrations and two strapping young wet nurses — women from the slums of Canterbury whom Pa would never normally have allowed anywhere near the house, let alone inside it. The twins had been reared in the nursery under controlled conditions like pineapples in a pinery, and Hannah and her sister had been put aside. No longer interested in the minutiae of their lives, no longer asking them to show him their drawings, or recite poetry in front of his guests, Pa had virtually ignored them.

A fire had burned in the grate all that summer, keeping the babies snug while the laundry was sent out daily and the windows left open to allow fresh air into their bellowing lungs. Within six months, the wet nurses had been dispensed with. After that, there had been a grand christening for the two chubby cherubs.

Plans had been made for their golden futures and they were given everything they could have possibly wished for, while these two poor boys she was with now had nothing, except for an apparent acceptance of their lot. They had no hesitation about walking through puddles and they didn't care that their nostrils dripped snot almost constantly.

Hannah directed them along Newgate Street where they were distracted by the costermongers, hawking their wares.

'Penny pies, all hot, hot, hot,' sang the pieman.

'Milk below, milk belooow,' came the sweet voices of the milkmaids.

'Pots and kettles to mend!' called the tinker's boy.

'Come along,' Hannah urged as they loitered on the pavement, and eventually, having passed St Paul's and made their way along Cheapside,

28

they reached London Bridge where a bell chimed the quarter-hour.

'Look at all 'em boats.' Charlie pointed to the hundreds of masts and funnels of the vessels moored at the wharves along the river. ''Ow do we know which of 'em's ours?'

'There are signs, look,' Hannah said, before realising that they were of no use to him. 'I've been told that the Margate hoy leaves from Blackwell Pier, which is this way.'

'It's an adventure, ain't it?' Charlie went on, and, caught up in his anticipation of the journey as they found the hoy and embarked, her heart began to beat faster.

'When are we going to get there?' Peter muttered as the hoy moved into the river and floated down towards the estuary, joining the fleet of steam packets spewing smoke, the cutters and broad-bottomed barges with their rust-red sails and cargo of London dirt destined for the brickfields of Faversham.

'I don't know,' she said, suspecting it would take longer than they would wish.

'Excuse me.' One of their fellow passengers, an elderly woman in a bonnet adorned with frayed feathers, stopped sucking on her brandy bottle for a moment. 'Those boys shouldn't be on deck — they are an offence to my eyes.'

'Look at 'em,' said another, a maid off to spend the season working in one of the guest-houses along the coast, Hannah guessed. 'Look at the girt lumps on that one's neck.'

Peter tugged at his bandages to try to cover them.

29

'The other couldn't stop a pig in a passage with legs like that,' the elderly woman jibed.

'I'd be grateful if you'd leave them alone,' Hannah said crossly. 'They can't help what they look like, no more than you can with your beak and your fleshworms.' The woman touched her nose, and the maid was blushing at the reference to her pimples when she turned away.

'That's 'er been told,' Charlie said.

'Well said,' commented a large gentleman who was perched on a trunk nearby. He looked like an invalid too, red-faced and perspiring in a greatcoat on a warm, sunny day.

'I don't like the way people stare at me, like I'm a freak,' Charlie observed mournfully. 'I'm missing my ma — she'd give 'em what for.'

'You're being very brave,' Hannah reassured him. 'Your time in Margate will pass in the blink of an eye.'

'Peter's an orphan — at least, 'e don't know for certain what 'appened to 'is parents. They left 'im at the poor'ouse, so he says. Ain't that true, Peter?' Charlie gave him a nudge.

'Me ma's dead,' he said, yawning and rubbing his eyes.

They had that in common, Hannah mused, thinking of her own mother who had died soon after Ruby was born. Hannah had been three at the time — her memories existed in fragments: Ma's long, dark hair; soft hazel eyes; the faint scent of roses and lavender; the lilt of her voice as she sang. The pain of loss, of not having a mother's love, lessened, but her anger over what her father had done to her remained.

A few days after she moved in with her grandmother, Hannah plucked up the courage to ask her exactly what had happened to her mother.

'I'm sorry that it's painful for you, Grandma, but I won't have any peace of mind until I know,' she said.

'Sit down, dear,' Grandma said. 'Elsie, fetch the brandy.'

'Are you sure we should have any more?' Hannah said. 'We must have had half a bottle between us the other night.'

'It's for medicinal purposes, no other reason.'

'I don't need any medicine.'

'It's a restorative — it maintains one's strength when one is receiving unsettling news. The story of your mother's passing is most disturbing, and one which should have been told before.' Grandma's voice wavered. 'You were inconsolable when we lost her — I couldn't bring myself to upset you further. And your father wouldn't say anything that would incriminate him and cause his daughters to hate his very bones. You will take a little brandy?'

'Yes, thank you.' She heard the chink of the decanter clipping the glasses as the maid poured two generous measures, then left the room.

'Your father treated your mother very badly and I will never forgive him for what he did and the way he took up with your stepmother in such indecent haste afterwards. When he met Mercy — my daughter — he was besotted. He would

31

have her and nothing would stand in his way.'

'Did she love him back?' Hannah enquired.

'Oh yes. She did — very much. All should have been well, but your mother was a fragile young woman, far too delicate for a boor like him. I'm sorry — I forget he's your flesh and blood.'

'He's nothing to me,' Hannah said quietly.

'He made her life a misery when she gave birth to girls, not the sons he wanted. Feeling trapped and helpless, your mother began to suffer from long spells of sadness when she wasn't herself. Your father blamed me for duping him, inducing him to marry my daughter without warning him of her changeable moods.

'He banned me from the house, claiming that my presence made her worse, but after Ruby was born, I insisted on seeing her. I hardly recognised Mercy — ' Grandma bit her lip before continuing. 'She just stared out of the window, completely uninterested in her darling infant who was squalling to be fed. I wanted to take them home — Mercy, Ruby and you — but there was no way he'd let me. Instead, he had your mother put away in the asylum — for a rest, he said.'

'That's terrible!' Hannah exclaimed. 'Poor Ma. She must have been so frightened.'

'It isn't uncommon for mothers to suffer from melancholia after they've birthed a child, but I'd never heard of anyone being put away for it.' Grandma took a gulp of brandy before going on, 'You must have wondered why you've never been taken to your mother's grave.'

'I assumed that it was too upsetting . . . for you, Pa, everyone . . . '

'There is no grave, nowhere we can go to pay our respects, lay flowers in her memory or just sit quietly with her.' Grandma started to cry. They were both crying. 'Hannah, this is painful to say, but your mother died at the asylum. She was working in the laundry . . . '

'Go on,' Hannah said, her heart in her mouth.

'She took some sheets . . . she hanged herself.'

Dumbstruck, Hannah pictured her dark-haired mother, racked with grief at having been torn away from her daughters, knotting freshly laundered sheets together to make a noose for her neck.

'Why?' she whispered. 'Why did she abandon us like that?'

'That's a question I've asked myself many times over, but I've never come up with a satisfactory answer. There is no answer, Hannah. As far as I'm concerned, she didn't deserve to die — your father's cruelty drove her to it and I shall never forgive him.

'It's a sin in the eyes of God to die by one's own hand — that's why there's no grave. I'm sorry. She was a loving mother who did her best to be a good wife.'

They sat for a while, watching the embers in the grate gradually flicker and die.

'If you're sure about pursuing your choice of vocation, I can help you,' Grandma said. 'I'll do it to honour your mother's memory, and I confess, it will give me great pleasure to spite your father. I have some money put by and I'd like to use it to put towards your training.'

Hannah's spirits lifted a little after the shock of her grandmother's revelations. 'I'm very grateful, but how will I repay you?'

'I will find satisfaction in your achievements. That will be reward enough.'

★ ★ ★

Determined not to let her grandmother down, Hannah had taken up her offer — which was how she'd ended up on the hoy now with Charlie and Peter, all this time later.

'What about you, Charlie?' Hannah asked. 'You mentioned your ma. What about your pa?'

'I don't know who 'e is and I don't think Ma knows either. It weren't 'er fault — she's a dignified and respectable woman who got taken advantage of.'

'I don't think you should be talking of your mother like that,' Hannah said gently.

'I have three sisters an' they don't know 'ow many fathers they 'ave between 'em.'

'I see.' There was a time when she would have been outraged, but she'd learned a lot about human nature since she'd started nursing.

It wasn't long before they were past Canvey Island and into open water where the wind grew stronger and whipped up a swell. Poor Charlie was seasick and Peter rigid with fear. Their travelling companions turned morose and green around the gills, but Hannah was hungry. She took the letter, addressed to her in Ruby's copperplate hand, from the top of the basket, and tucked it inside her bodice before eating some bread and cheese washed down with a little small beer. She would read her correspondence later when she was no longer obliged to keep watch over the boys.

'I've never seen the sea before' — Charlie held his hand up to shade his eyes — 'and I wouldn't be sorry if I never saw it again. You must 'ave a cast-iron belly.' He fell silent, but it wasn't long before he started talking again.

'Nurse, am I goin' to die?' he asked in a small voice.

An icy finger traced a path down her spine as she wondered how to reply.

Her half-brother had told her he was dying, and out of fear, she had denied it.

It had been the fourth of January, and everyone in the Bentley household except for Hannah seemed to have forgotten that it was her sixteenth birthday. Nine days before, the twins had been sent home from the cathedral school in Canterbury where they were choristers, and Doctor Crossley had been called for.

Not only that, Stepmother had cancelled a soiree to which she'd invited a phrenology expert to impress her guests, and she'd sent the butler to call Pa home urgently from the agency.

'It's scarlet fever,' Doctor Crossley opined, having run through the symptoms. Ten-year-old Christopher had been irritable and keen to eat, but Theo had a high fever and couldn't stop shivering. The doctor advised Stepmother to put them to bed and offer them whey or broth with Epsom salts to fight the poison that came with the fever. He told Pa that he should employ a barber to shave the blonde curls from the twins' heads, but Pa had insisted on doing it himself, then wrapping their bald pates in cool rags, before leaving Hannah to watch over them until the private nurse arrived.

Gradually, Christopher had begun to get better — his rash faded and the skin on his tongue peeled away. Theo was slower to improve, but when they reached the eighth day of their illness, the doctor pronounced that they would both make a full recovery. The very next day, Theo had gone, carried up to Heaven by the angels.

Hannah cuddled up to her sister that night, afraid to fall asleep in case Ruby stopped breathing and she lost her too.

'I will always be a twin,' Christopher said, 'and when I sing again, I will sing for my brother.'

Stepmother hadn't been able to stop crying. She said that she wished it had been Hannah or Ruby who had died, and Pa didn't stand up and tell her to take it back. He was colder than he'd ever been, any warmth he'd had buried beneath the smooth, white marble memorial he'd had erected in memory of their son.

He had sent her and Ruby to stay with their grandmother for a few weeks where they'd worn their lilac and white mourning clothes, played hopscotch and gone out for walks every day. Hannah hadn't wanted to go home, but eventually, they'd had to return to the house in Dane John where they'd lived quietly, cocooned indoors by their father's and stepmother's grief and resentment, while Christopher went back to St Edmund's and continued to sing until his voice broke.

Hannah looked at Charlie and forced a smile.

'I think you have as good a chance of living to a ripe old age as anyone else, having enjoyed the benefit of a few weeks of fresh air and saltwater baths.'

'Baths? Oh no!' he exclaimed. 'I never go near water — it's cold and wet, and you can die from it.'

She wished she hadn't mentioned it — his expression of alarm had woken Peter, who had fallen asleep against her skirts.

'Where am I?' he said, looking befuddled.

'On a boat,' Charlie informed him. 'Peter, they're going to dunk us in the sea for a cure.'

'That isn't what I said,' Hannah pointed out.

'I suppose medicine 'as to taste bad to do a body any good,' Peter said with an old man's wisdom. 'I thought we'd be there by now . . . '

'It can't be much further . . . '

'We've passed Whitstable.' The large gentleman who'd spoken to them before gestured towards the coast. 'It won't be long before the Reculver Towers come into view over Herne Bay.'

At about four o'clock when a strong breeze came sweeping across the deck, the town of Margate appeared behind a vast expanse of beach and scrub, the buildings burnished gold by the afternoon sun.

'Look at all that sand, Nurse,' Charlie shouted, 'as far as the eye can see.'

37

'Hush, Master Swift. You're drawing attention to yourself.'

'I can't 'elp it — I've never been to the seaside. It's much bigger than I thought it would be. Peter, look at all the people!'

Peter dragged himself up to look.

'What are those carriages doin' on the beach?' he asked.

'They're bathing machines, designed with a hood to protect the modesty of ladies who wish to bathe in the sea,' said the gentleman who had adopted the role of their guide. 'We're almost there — we're going to stop at the stone pier, the one with the lighthouse at the end of it.'

The captain turned the hoy towards the harbour and the crew took down the sails. He brought it alongside the pier and the sailors prepared the gangway for the travellers to disembark.

'Boys, look away,' Hannah said quickly as the ladies' petticoats billowed in the wind, revealing their stockings. 'Charlie,' she went on, admonishing them as they continued to stare, but she couldn't help smiling to herself as she stepped out on to the pier, the stones solid and still beneath her feet. Despite her regrets about leaving London, she had a sense that Miss Russell could be right. Perhaps Margate would be the making of her.

3

A Place for Everything and Everything in its Place

Hannah took a deep breath of sharp sea air and strawberries as they passed the hokey-pokey men from Sicily who were selling their penny licks. She was sorely tempted, but — she glanced at the boys who were struggling, wide-eyed, along Marine Terrace with her — she wasn't here for a holiday, more was the pity.

Even though it was early in the season, there was an air of gaiety and abandon among the wandering crowds: children frolicking like lambkins, running along the pavements without looking where they were going; pretty misses and foppish striplings walking brazenly arm in arm; people stopping to buy from the brightly coloured stalls and barrows along the front.

They made slow progress.

'Charlie, where are your shoelaces?' Hannah asked.

'Which Charlie are you talkin' to?' Charlie said.

'The one without his laces,' she responded.

'I ain't got any and I'm glad 'cause I was always trippin' up.'

'Those shoes will hinder you — they must be four sizes too big.'

'Ma says I'll grow into 'em.'

'Mine are too small,' Peter commented, reaching down to press on the gaping toe of his boot. 'This is all Mr Glanvill 'ad.'

Having reached the Hall by the Sea, they took the Canterbury road which turned away from the main sands near the railway station, before finding the infirmary on their right. It was an imposing building nine bays wide and two storeys high, its design reminding Hannah of a drawing of a Greek temple she had once seen in a book in her father's study.

'I don't like it,' Peter announced, seeming overawed as he gazed up at the massive stone columns on either side of the main entrance. 'I'm not goin' in there. Mr Glanvill says it's the gateway of death.'

'I shouldn't listen to him — what does he know? Take Charlie's hand if it makes you feel safer.'

'No way. I'm not 'olding on to 'is 'and,' Charlie argued. 'We aren't babies.'

'Then you must behave like young gentlemen and walk in side by side, quietly, behind me. Do you think you can do that?' she went on more gently, not wanting to make Peter cry.

'Yes, Nurse,' Charlie said.

'Yes . . . ' Peter echoed weakly.

Inside the reception hall, the porter, an elderly gentleman with spectacles, stained teeth and a twinkle in his eye, introduced himself.

'My name is Mr Mordikai. You must be Nurse Bentley with the boys from St Pancras. We've been expecting you. Welcome to the house.'

'Thank you.' Hannah glanced from the oil

40

paintings on the walls to the rug on the floor, a Turkish carpet that had seen better days, and suppressed the thought that she'd have burned it if she'd been matron. 'I'd be very grateful if you could direct me to the ward, so the boys may be admitted — they're tired after a rather trying journey.'

'Ah, leave them with me. I'll take them along to meet Sister Trim.'

Peter slipped his hand into Hannah's, whispering, 'Don't leave me.'

'There's nothing to be frightened of,' she began, before recollecting how she'd felt as a probationer walking on to a ward for the first time: the stares, the stink of sickness, the uncertainty. 'I'll stay with you until you're admitted.'

'Sister won't like that,' Mr Mordikai said.

'I'll speak to her. I'm sure she'll have no objection.'

The porter raised one thin eyebrow — a sign of doubt, perhaps — but Hannah was undeterred. Having made sure she had the letters, including the one from Ruby, she watched him put her bag and basket behind his desk, then followed him, a hefty figure dressed in a bowler hat, waistcoat and striped shirt, into a wide corridor. There were doors leading off from one side, into examination rooms, bathing rooms and sluices, with the wards coming off the other.

'You will notice that the house has undergone much building work. This is the older part of the infirmary.' The porter stopped beneath a sign above an open door. It read, *The Lettsom Ward*

41

1858, in gold lettering.

'I'd be much obliged if you'd wait here while I find Sister,' he said, before proceeding to look for her.

Hannah took in her surroundings. The tall windows were wide open, and the beds — iron cots like those at the Hospital for Sick Children — were occupied by boys of various ages, some sleeping, some looking at picture books, some playing quietly with toy boats and spinning tops. There was a nurse, wearing a dark blue dress with her white apron, cuffs, collar and cap, pushing a trolley of dressings and medicines along the ward, and a lady on a chair reading to two boys who were sitting cross-legged at her feet.

There were more doors opening on to a balcony which overlooked the sea, where a fishing skiff with seagulls circling above it was tacking towards the harbour.

'This ain't nothin' like London,' Charlie breathed.

'It's a wonderful view, isn't it?' Hannah said. 'I think we'll be very happy here in Margate.'

'This is most irregular.' A woman about ten years older than Hannah, with an angular nose, pale lips and a widow's peak of dark hair emerging from under her cap, came marching up with the porter. 'There's no need for you to remain on my ward, Miss Bentley.' She emphasised the word 'Miss', and Hannah, realising that it was a deliberate slight, didn't try to correct her. 'Mr Mordikai will fetch the duty physician to admit the boys.'

'I'll wait with them, if you don't mind,' Hannah said firmly, as Peter clung to her hand

and Charlie hid behind her.

'I do mind. Visiting hours are from two until four on Mondays, Wednesdays and Fridays, and the same on Sundays for the sake of the fathers who are at work during the week.' Sister Trim looked past her. 'Ma'am?'

'I'd reconsider if I were you.' Hannah turned to face the speaker, an older lady dressed in royal blue and white, her grey hair up in a bun. 'One can always use an extra pair of hands when one is short-staffed. I'm Mrs Knowles, matron of this house.' She smiled. 'Welcome to Margate.'

Hannah thanked her, aware of Sister Trim's sullen glower.

'As soon as the boys have been admitted, come along to my office.' Mrs Knowles turned from Hannah to Sister Trim. 'Nurse Bentley will be joining you on the Lettsom after she's completed her orientation.'

'Yes, ma'am,' the sister said in clipped tones, before directing Hannah and her charges to sit on a bench at the far end of the ward to await the doctor. Hannah overheard her muttering to the porter, 'I wish Mrs Knowles would stop meddling, taking on nurses who aren't trained in our ways. It's a recipe for disaster.'

'I believe that it's unwise, but it isn't my place to take it up with her,' Mr Mordikai agreed. 'Let me go and find the duty physician.'

After an hour of being seated, Charlie began to fidget and Peter to flag. Hannah was just beginning to wonder if she dared ask Sister Trim if they'd been forgotten, when a tall, broad-shouldered gentleman wearing a plaid waistcoat, white shirt and cravat, with dark, high-waisted trousers, strolled into the ward.

He greeted every patient by name as he passed by.

'How are you today, Johnnie?' he asked, pausing beside one of the boys whose left leg was immobilised in a cast.

'A little better, thank you, but my plaster — it does itch so,' he replied.

'I'll bring you a knitting needle next time I'm on the ward — don't tell Sister, though.'

'Oh, I won't,' the boy grinned.

'What was that, Doctor Clifton?' Sister Trim's voice carried along the ward.

'I'm afraid I cannot say,' the doctor said with humour. 'I have taken the Hippocratic Oath — *whatever, in connection with my professional service, or not in connection with it, I see or hear, in the life of men, which ought not to be spoken of abroad, I will not divulge, as reckoning that all such should be kept secret.*'

He continued along the ward, like a breath of fresh air, Hannah thought, comparing him with the rather stuffy doctor who'd carried out the rounds at the Hospital for Sick Children in London. He had been an elderly physician who'd failed to move with the times: his tie always looked as if he'd dipped it in a bowl of soup, and his cuffs were often spattered with blood. His examinations were perfunctory, and he did little to put their young patients at ease. Doctor Clifton was quite another kettle of fish.

Well-spoken and youthful, he couldn't have been more than twenty-eight years old. His light brown hair was run through with strands of gold as if he'd been out in the sun, and he wore it short, to just above his collar, with a side parting and swept back. His sideburns were neatly trimmed.

'Good afternoon,' he said, joining Hannah and her charges.

'You must stand up when addressed by your elders and betters.' Hannah gave Charlie a nudge.

'You may remain seated,' the doctor said kindly.

'This is Miss Bentley with the two boys for admission,' Sister Trim said, scurrying up alongside him. 'Nurse Finch will be with you shortly.'

'Thank you, Sister,' the doctor said. 'Please accept my apologies for keeping you, Miss Bentley. The infirmary is always busy — we have over two hundred patients, three-quarters of them children — but the extra visitors coming to Margate for the summer put even more pressure on our resources. I have patients queuing up for beds.'

The boys were staring at him warily, their eyes on stalks, like wavering snails ready to duck back inside their shells.

'I have the paperwork for Master Swift and Master Herring.' Hannah handed over the letters from her pocket.

He read them, then looked up. 'These are all in order. Where is Nurse Finch to take the notes?'

'I can do it,' Hannah said, noting that his eyes were blue with a hint of green, like the sea, one slightly darker than the other.

'I don't think so.' He raised one eyebrow. 'There are certain medical terms — '

'She's a nurse,' said Charlie.

45

'Hush,' she said softly. 'One mustn't speak unless spoken to.'

'It appears that I must apologise for a second time. Sister Trim didn't say so and Mrs Knowles hasn't seen fit to mention it.'

It seemed that the doctors and nurses were locked in conflict at the infirmary, just like they were at the Hospital for Sick Children.

'I trained as a lady probationer in London and I've been offered a position here.' It had crossed Hannah's mind that she would be in a pickle if Mrs Knowles took against her for any reason.

'Forgive me for the misunderstanding.'

'Of course.' She noticed the dimples in his cheeks, which gave him an air of boyish charm. 'You weren't to know.'

'Ah, here is Nurse Finch,' Doctor Clifton said as the other nurse she had seen on the ward turned up with a trolley, neatly organised with pens, ink and paper, boards and board-clips, flannels and soap, and two pairs of pyjamas. 'Nurse Finch, this is Nurse Bentley — she will be assisting me.'

'Yes, Doctor.' Hannah noticed the warmth in the nurse's striking grey eyes when she gave Hannah a brief smile. She was a handsome young woman, tall and elegant, with brown hair and a clear complexion. 'Matron's given me orders to take you under my wing later.'

'Nurse Finch, there's no time for gossip,' Sister Trim called. 'Benjamin has been sick, and his sheets need changing. Mattie's wound is weeping — it needs a dressing to keep off the flies.'

Nurse Finch left the trolley and returned to her work. Hannah wondered how long she'd been working at the infirmary — she was a few years older than her, in her late twenties perhaps.

Hannah pushed the trolley along behind the boys, who followed Doctor Clifton to one of the examination rooms across the corridor, like lambs to the slaughter. The doctor held the door open for them, catching Hannah's eye.

'It will soon be dinnertime. The food is excellent — I can thoroughly recommend it,' he said cheerfully. 'Now, which of you two young gentlemen is going to be first?'

'Not me,' Charlie said quickly.

'Peter, then.' Hannah pushed him gently forward. He didn't resist, seemingly reassured by the doctor's manner as he removed the filthy bandages from his neck and poked and prodded the scrofulous lumps. He measured his temperature and listened to his chest with his stethoscope, while Hannah took down his observations.

'Are you keeping up?' he asked.

'Yes, Doctor,' she said, although her hand was aching and the pen was scratchy, leaving blots of ink across the page. She didn't like to delay him — his time was precious.

He moved on to Charlie and, at the end of his examination, summed up his plans for them.

'Gentlemen, you'll receive a nutritious diet as prescribed, daily saltwater baths and as many hours as possible in the open air. Mr Anthony, the house surgeon, will discuss the options for surgery in the morning. Nurse Finch will take over now — one of the conditions for admittance is a thorough scrub to remove any unwanted visitors. I'll see you on our rounds tomorrow morning.

'Thank you, Nurse Bentley,' he added with a smile, before he left the room.

'I won't 'ave a bath of any sort,' Charlie said.

'Doctor knows best,' Hannah said, ushering them back towards the ward. In her experience, they thought they did anyway.

'I told you, I can't 'ave a bath.' Charlie brushed back tears.

'Cry baby,' muttered Peter.

'Leave him alone,' Hannah scolded as she steered them back towards Nurse Finch who was putting bandages away in a box. 'It'll be your turn soon enough.'

Peter fell silent. She feared that he was about to face something far worse than a bath, but it was better he didn't know about it until the last minute.

'Trimmie's asked me to take them now,' Nurse Finch said. 'I mean — Sister . . . Sister Trim.'

'What's for tea?' Charlie asked her. 'The doctor said it was nearly dinnertime.'

'It's mutton and potatoes today. Come along. Let's get you settled in.'

Charlie and Peter seemed to have no qualms about going off with Nurse Finch while Hannah made her way to Matron's office.

Mrs Knowles called for tea and Florentines. 'I won't keep you long,' she said. 'I'm delighted that you've agreed to take up the position here. There will of course be a month's probation, but it's only a formality. I'll have a contract prepared for you to sign in the next few days. You'll spend a week in various departments — outpatients, the splint room, theatre and the wards before you take up your position on the Lettsom. You'll find that Judith Trim is an excellent sister, strict but fair.'

'Thank you, ma'am.'

'I've asked Nurse Finch to look after you. She'll meet you in the dining hall at six. I've also arranged for one of the maids to see what you require in the way of dresses and aprons, and tell you about the arrangements for laundering. You may wait in the reception hall until Nurse Finch is ready.'

Hannah didn't like having to wait — she would much rather have started work straight away — but she filled in the hour meeting with the maid, then sat and read her letter from her sister.

Dear Hannah,

I have had to resort to subterfuge to send this letter because Pa has decided to censor all my correspondence. Although it is an inconvenience to her, dear Miss Fellows at number three has agreed to post and receive letters on my behalf until the storm dies down. I expect you are asking yourself why, and the only way I can respond is to say that there was a misunderstanding. I admit that I did play a part in it, but Pa has blown it out of all proportion.

I hope you are well and happy in London.

Do send me your news.
 Yours affectionately,
 Ruby

Hannah frowned as she put the letter away. What had Ruby done to raise their father's ire? She felt a little frustrated that she hadn't gone into more detail, but she guessed that she couldn't reveal too much in case Pa happened to intercept her post. Who knew what he would do if he found out that Ruby had gone against him?

She was still worrying about her sister when she and Nurse Finch took their places in the dining hall later.

'Ignore Trimmie,' Nurse Finch said. 'Matron told her that you were coming here highly recommended, and she's afraid that you'll be favoured over her. My name's Charlotte, by the way.'

'I'm Hannah. Thank you for looking after me. It all feels rather strange after London. I'm sorry about Sister Trim — I have no intention of treading on her toes.'

'She has her eye on the prize: the position of matron one day,' Charlotte said.

'Mrs Knowles didn't give me the impression that she was planning her retirement.'

'Well, Trimmie has expectations, whereas I would hate to be in Matron's shoes — she always seems to be stuck between the devil and the deep blue sea. If she isn't fighting a running battle with the doctors, she's under siege from Mr Cumberpatch, the superintendent, who's in charge of maintenance. As you may have noticed, there's been a lot of building work over the past two or three years, although we still haven't got a purpose-built nurses' home. Never mind, the house that the infirmary rents for us is only a short walk away.'

'How long have you been working here?' Hannah asked as they tucked into their mutton, peas, carrots and bread, served with part of their daily ration of ale.

'Five years — I was twenty-three when I started nursing. Before that, I was engaged to be married, but the man — he was no gentleman — in question jilted me three days before the wedding.'

'I'm sorry,' Hannah said quickly.

'Don't be. I was distraught at the time, because I really did believe that I loved him, and he felt the same about me, but I reckon I had a lucky escape, because a year later, he eloped with my younger sister. I was shamed and humiliated by my own flesh and blood. Imagine that!'

'I can't.' Hannah was shocked, thinking of Ruby's letter and the concern she felt for her. 'Why would a sister do such a thing?'

'I think she was jealous of my good fortune and set out to seduce him. Anyway, I've never asked her — we haven't spoken since. After that, I needed occupation and an income, not wishing to impose on my parents any longer — my father is a bookseller who retired through ill health. To that end, I spent three months volunteering here before applying for a place on the wards. Anyway, that's enough about me. What about you?' She gave a wry smile. 'Don't tell me you became a nurse for the money.'

'Everyone knows we work for nothing in return but God's favour.' Hannah smiled back. 'No, I ran away from home to escape my father and the threat of a forced marriage to a man who was more than twice my age.'

'Then it's my turn to be sorry for being flippant.'

'I turned to nursing because it was the only respectable occupation I could think of, having met a private nurse, an admirable woman who was taken on to care for my half-brothers when they had scarlet fever.' She lowered her voice. 'One of them — Theo — was taken up by the angels, but Christopher survived. I thought I could care for children like them and earn a decent living at the same time, enough to rent a small house and bring my sister to live with me, but it turns out that one can only do that when one's been appointed to manage a ward.'

'It's a shame, but that's the way it is. Marriage is the only other way out of this life of drudgery.' Hannah wasn't sure if Charlotte was being serious. 'It's all that I ever wanted until my fiancé broke my heart. I'm not sure I could go through with it again.'

'I intend to hold on to my independence to my last breath,' Hannah said. 'I've seen the way my father has mistreated my stepmother and kept a tight hold on the purse-strings. He's been violent to her, too, and she has no redress.'

'You mean he beats her?'

'He's hurt her,' Hannah responded.

It had started not long after Theo had passed

away. She and Ruby had been upstairs in their room when they'd heard a crash and the sound of breaking glass, followed by an eerie silence. Hannah had stared at her sister as the shouting began.

'You are my wife, my property, and you'd do well to remember it! Get out of my sight before I do you an injury.'

'You hit me,' Stepmother had cried.

'I did nothing of the sort. You walked into the door. Oh, look at you, you miserable, snivelling whore. There was a time when you wanted nothing more than to be with me. Now you can't wait to get away.'

'What shall we do, Hannah?' Ruby had whispered.

'I don't know. Pa will take it out on us, if we go down . . . ' Hannah's heart had pounded as she'd heard her stepmother's footsteps and the banging of doors. 'We should find out if she's all right, even though there's no love lost between us.'

They had crept downstairs, following the sound of Stepmother's sobbing to her boudoir where they'd knocked softly at the door, Hannah praying that their father wouldn't turn up. 'It's me and Ruby,' she'd said and after a while, their stepmother had opened the door and, keeping her face half covered, reassured them that all was well. There had been a minor disagreement over her plan to order a new coat for a special service at the cathedral where Christopher would be singing in the choir. Pa had knocked over a candlestick, breaking a pane of glass in the dining room. In her hurry to fetch the maid to clear it up, Stepmother had walked into the door, bruising her eye.

'You see, it's all my fault. I've always been prone to accidents.'

'He called you a . . . ' — Hannah couldn't bring herself to echo Pa's exact words — ' . . . an unfortunate woman.'

And Stepmother had deliberately misunderstood her. 'I certainly am — I can't possibly go and hear Christopher sing, looking like this. Go to bed, you two. It's kind of you to come and find me, but there's nothing to be done.'

Hannah shuddered at the memory

'Then your stepmother has all the disadvantages of marriage and none of the benefits.' Charlotte sighed. 'What do you think of Doctor Clifton?'

'He seems very professional.'

'Oh, come on. He's like a god. Everyone says so, except Trimmie.'

'I can't say. I've only met him once.' She had steeled herself against taking any significant notice of members of the male sex for some time, and it had become a habit. The doctor had a stirring voice, deep and authoritative with a lilt of tenderness when required, which she had observed when he had been examining Charlie's knees. His countenance, eyes and smile were pleasing, but not excessively so.

'I've seen him go beyond the call of duty many times, but he's set far too high above the likes of us,' Charlotte went on.

'You would entertain another engagement?' Hannah enquired.

'I didn't think I would, but now that a decent

amount of time has elapsed, I would consider it.'
Charlotte chuckled. 'I'm not interested in
Doctor Clifton, if that's what you're thinking.
Watch out for Mr Anthony, the surgeon — he's a
most disagreeable man, but very good at his job.
And then there are the medical students who
come here two or three at a time to see what we
do at the infirmary. What else can I tell you?'

'How were the boys? Sister Trim said she
didn't want them disturbed when I stopped by to
see them.'

'Charlie was none too keen on having a bath
— Mrs Merry, the bathing attendant, had a devil
of a time with him — but you should have seen
the way his eyes lit up when he saw his dinner.
He devoured the whole lot, but Peter hardly
touched his, the poor little mite. I'm afraid he's
completely lost his merriment.' Charlotte wiped
her mouth with a napkin. 'If you're ready, I can
show you where you'll be sleeping. You're
sharing my room.'

'I hope you don't mind,' Hannah said.

'Not at all, as long as you don't snore like
Charity used to. She's gone to run a private
convalescent home nearby — working on the
wards left her almost worn out. Shall we go? Mr
Mordikai said he'd arrange to have your boxes
left outside the door.'

'I haven't brought much with me. The rest of
my things are being sent on.'

'I expect there'll be a uniform waiting for you.
Mrs Knowles is good like that — she looks after
us.'

Hannah followed Charlotte out of the dining

hall and they made their way out of the infirmary and along the road to a terraced house overlooking the sea.

'This is it,' Charlotte said as she opened the front door, letting Hannah inside. 'Our room is on the top floor. It's a little cramped, but it's home.'

It was cosy and well-appointed with two beds, a washstand, table and rickety chaise. There was a pair of drapes in a heavy, blue brocade, and a striped rag rug.

'Of course, the views are much better in daylight.' Charlotte smiled as she showed Hannah the sights from the windows: a moonlit courtyard garden and other houses to the rear; the sea to the front. Hannah unpacked her few belongings, then turned in. Having assumed that she wouldn't be able to sleep, she didn't remember a thing from when her head hit the pillow, until the rattling of windows, laughter and the deep, throaty yells of masculine voices disturbed her. They began to sing,

'If any sick they bring to me,
I physics, bleeds and sweats 'em.
If after that they choose to die,
What's that to me? I Lettsom.'

'What on earth's going on? Is there a fire?' Hannah leapt out of bed, but Charlotte was already at the open window, gazing into the darkness.

'Gentlemen! That's quite enough. There are ladies trying to sleep.'

'Sleep? Oh, come down here, beautiful creatures . . . '

'Who are they?' Hannah clutched the collar of her nightgown, holding it across her throat, as she looked past Charlotte's shoulder to find three faces looking up, their features illuminated by the moon. They were louche young men with trimmed beards and crumpled shirts. One had a tie dangling around his neck. Another carried what looked suspiciously like a tankard, and the third smiled inanely, flashing his white teeth.

'You are like angels,' he said, but Hannah didn't think he was addressing her — his gaze lingered longingly on Charlotte.

'Henry, they are angels,' said one of his companions. 'They are too good for the likes of us.'

'For goodness' sake, go home to bed!' Charlotte said, half scolding, half laughing. 'We have to be up at the crack of dawn tomorrow. And you're making yourselves look ridiculous.'

'You heard what the lady said.' Henry's companions lifted him under the arms and dragged him away protesting, before he called back, 'Goodnight, my darlings.'

'They're going to have sore heads tomorrow.' Grinning, Charlotte closed the curtains. 'They're the latest crop of medical students who've come to make the most of what Margate has to offer. They get in the way on the wards, but I don't mind — they liven the place up.'

'I've met their kind before,' Hannah said. 'It never ceases to amaze me how they suddenly transform from boorish louts to respectable physicians, like butterflies emerging from their cocoons.' She returned to bed and heard nothing more until Charlotte woke her.

'Morning,' she said brightly. 'It's time to rise and shine.'

'That felt like a very short night,' Hannah sighed, but she didn't take long to get ready, eager to find her way around the infirmary. However, Matron's plan for her orientation fell apart as staff shortages meant that she was sent straight to the Lettsom, where Sister Trim gave her a lecture to start the day.

'I expect you to turn up on my ward smartly presented and clean to honour the memory of our founder, Doctor Coakley Lettsom, gemmologist, philanthropist, botanist . . . '

As Sister Trim listed his interests — apparently, he had even introduced the mangelwurzel, whatever that was, to England — Hannah wondered how on earth he'd had time to be a doctor as well. She could only deduce that he must have had the support of an obliging wife and a multitude of servants.

'He made a fortune from his private patients, but he used it wisely, endowing this infirmary to the residents of Margate and beyond. Now, I don't know how you were taught, but we have our own way of doing things around here.'

'I understand,' Hannah said.

'A child's prattle is wearying and sometimes the parents are horrible. They can be uncivil and treat you like a servant, but you have to bear their ingratitude and do your duty without complaining.'

Hannah had to bite her tongue as Sister Trim continued, 'Always speak in a low and gentle voice. Walk carefully — I hope your shoes don't squeak — and not on tiptoes, for there's a sham quietness that disturbs the sick more than the loudest noise.'

'Yes, Sister.' She heard a water closet flushing and the gurgle and banging of water in the pipes, and the tick-tick-tick as they heated up to provide the day's baths.

'The doctors will stop here on their rounds at about nine o'clock when all the patients should be ready, the bedpans emptied, and the bedsides spick and span. Then it's breakfast time for those who are not nil by mouth. Lunch is taken out on the balcony, come rain or shine. When the patients are outdoors, you will change the beds, dust the ward — including the windowsills — and mop the floors.'

'May I assist with Master Swift's bath?' she dared to ask.

Sister Trim stared at her. 'We don't allow favourites here. Anyway, that's the bathing attendant's responsibility, not yours. Make haste. Nurse Finch will show you where to find the equipment you need: a place for everything, and everything in its place.'

Soon the ward was tidy, although Hannah hadn't got around to attending to all her patients by the time the doctors made their appearance. She heard them before she saw them: the sound of their metal-tipped shoes tapping against the teak floorboards. Doctor Clifton introduced her to Mr Anthony, who was in his forties, and one of those men who made up for their lack of stature by being as disagreeable as possible. He had delicate fingers, a Roman nose and a bald head, and his loud voice alarmed the children.

'Good day, Nurse,' he said gruffly. 'Tell me about Master Herring. Has he complained of pain overnight? Has he evacuated his bowels this morning? Why haven't you removed his bandages in readiness? Even with my excellent vision, I haven't the capacity to see through gauze.'

'I'm sorry I didn't have time to prepare on this occasion,' she said, refusing to be cowed.

'Well, that just isn't good enough, but it's the sort of incompetence I've come to expect from Matron's handmaidens.'

'Nurse Bentley is new to the house,' Doctor Clifton said.

'Excuses, excuses.' Mr Anthony turned on him. 'There's no excuse for laziness.'

Hannah's face burned. He was a bully — she'd met his like before. Whenever there was a foul smell on the ward, the surgeons would scurry past while the nurses valiantly rushed in. Had Sister Trim deliberately tripped her up, keeping her away from her patients while she lectured her? she wondered as Mr Anthony waited, huffing with impatience as she removed Peter's bandages.

Eventually, the doctors finished their round, giving their instructions for each patient. The surgeon rushed off to begin on his list of operations for the day.

'Don't worry about him,' Doctor Clifton said, stepping up beside her. 'He's a brilliant man, but his manner leaves a little to be desired.'

'You mean ol' fly-rink, the one with the bald

60

'ead,' Charlie said, overhearing.

'It's none of your business.' Hannah tried not to smile.

'I don't know 'ow you 'eld your tongue.'

'Charlie!'

'I never knew what nursin' was all about.'

'Never mind,' she said, amused. 'Neither do the doctors.'

Doctor Clifton didn't appear the slightest bit offended. He kept his voice low, so she had to lean in to hear him.

'Would you do me a favour? Give this to Johnnie from me. Remind him to hide it from Sister, or we'll be in the doghouse.' Like a magician, he let a knitting needle fall from inside his shirtsleeve.

'Do you knit, Doctor Clifton?' she asked.

'I undertake a little sewing, although I prefer to leave the suturing of wounds to the surgeons. No, this belonged to my dearly departed wife.'

'I'm sorry . . . ' She felt guilty for asking the question, but how was she supposed to know that he was a widower? Charlotte hadn't mentioned he'd been married. She'd assumed he was one of the luckiest men in the world, born with the proverbial silver spoon in his mouth into a good family, educated at Oxford or Cambridge before registering with the Royal College of Physicians. He certainly had all the advantages that nature could bestow. She glanced from his hands, strong yet gentle, his nails blunt and clean, to the knitting needle. 'I can't take this,' she said. 'It's a danger to the children. They will have someone's eye out with it.'

'Don't you have any compassion for Johnnie's predicament?'

'I have every sympathy for him, but this isn't the solution.'

She realised now why he'd been soft-soaping her, acting on friendly terms — so he could take advantage of her good nature. If he imagined that she would side with him rather than Sister Trim, then he was wrong.

'Good day, Doctor,' she said hotly.

'I'll have to find another way,' he sighed.

'Please don't. If I find that anywhere near here, I'll have to report you.'

He frowned, and she wished she'd made more light of it.

After he had left the ward, she helped Peter with his breakfast, served up in a pewter dish marked '*Margate infmry*' on the rim.

'I'm not 'ungry.' He couldn't swallow even a morsel of porridge. 'Me neck 'urts.'

'He ain't up to dick,' Charlie said from the next bed along. 'He ain't well at all.'

Hannah couldn't help wondering what a bath and a day in the sun was going to do for him. No amount of dressing changes was going to alter his fate. When she left his bedside, Peter lay back on the pillow, his face as white as the sheet which covered his skinny frame.

'Master Swift, you're the first one on my list!' Hannah looked up as a middle-aged woman with roughened hands, plump arms and a beaming smile came across to Charlie's bedside.

'No, Mrs Merry.' He sat up and pulled the sheet over his head. 'I won't 'ave anuvver bath.'

'Come on, Charlie. It will do you good.'
Hannah went across and tugged the sheet away,
much to his annoyance.

'The bath is lovely and warm,' Mrs Merry
said.

'I've seen what 'appens to soap when you leave
it in water. That's what Ma says'll 'appen to me.'

'That's a load of old — ' Mrs Merry broke off
as Sister Trim stalked towards them.

Charlie shrank back at the ferocity of her
stare.

'Rules is rules. You bathe daily, or you leave
the infirmary so that another sickly child can
have your place,' she said.

Charlie looked at Peter whose eyes glazed with
sudden tears.

'It's all right. I won't leave you, my friend,' he
said gamely, and he slipped out of the bed,
wincing as his legs bore his weight. Anticipating
trouble, Mrs Merry picked him up under one
arm and carried him off. A few minutes later,
Hannah heard his howls of anguish echoing
through the corridors.

'My word, it sounded as if someone was being
murdered,' Charlotte exclaimed when Mrs
Merry returned with a dejected Charlie limping
along behind her, shivering in his pyjamas.

'Somebody'll be murdered if they carry on like
that,' Mrs Merry said gaily, boxing Charlie's ear.
'Look at my apron. I've almost 'ad a bath myself.
Get changed, then you can go and play out on
the balcony.'

Hannah helped him — he smelled faintly of
seaweed.

'I ain't feeling no better,' he grumbled, 'and the salt's got into me cuts and grazes.'

'It takes time,' she said, and she sent him out into the sunshine to join Peter, who was already sitting up, watching a steam packet with a long pennant of blue smoke trailing from its funnel, making its way across Westbrook Bay towards the pier.

'Charlie, can you see them angels dancin' on the sea?' she heard Peter say.

'No,' Charlie said. 'Where?'

'They're like lights on the tops of the waves. Oh, look at 'em. There's 'undreds of 'em out there.'

Hannah took a moment to look too, but she couldn't see anything, apart from the sun's rays glittering across the surface of the sea. Both boys seemed brighter and more settled, but she couldn't help wondering if this was simply the calm before the storm.

She wasn't sure if the infirmary was going to suit her either. She missed Alice and the children's hospital, having felt perfectly at home there. However, she had no option but to stay on, no matter how much she wished she could take the next boat — even the hoy — back to London, because this was the only way she could see of bringing Ruby to live with her, something which seemed all the more urgent now, thanks to her letter.

Pa was trying to interfere with her correspondence. How long would it be before he had lined up some unsuitable suitor for her? Mr Edison was long gone, refusing to entertain marriage to either of the Bentley sisters after Hannah's running away from home had shown the young ladies to be flighty and out of control, but there were bound to be others.

Hannah's dearest wish was for them to be reunited, and she was determined not to let her sister down.

4

If in Doubt, Cut it Out

'I hope you didn't come to Margate expecting a rest,' Sister Trim said the following morning, having given Hannah a list of tasks as long as her arm. 'I checked under the beds for dust last thing — you will sweep and mop through again, thoroughly this time.'

'Yes, Sister,' Hannah said.

'You'll help Nurse Finch prepare for the ward round first.'

She followed Sister's gaze towards Peter's bed where a scuffle had broken out between Charlie and Johnnie.

'He snores like a fat pig,' Johnnie shouted as he hobbled towards Charlie, who danced bow-legged, squaring up to him like a boxer.

''E can't 'elp it,' Charlie yelled. 'You leave 'im alone, you stuck-up — I'll give yer a belly-go-fister for teasin' 'im!'

As Peter looked on, Johnnie lunged towards Charlie, pulling something from behind his back and stabbing it at Charlie's face.

'Stop!' Hannah rushed to intercept him, but the end of the knitting needle made contact.

'Ow! 'E's got me in the eye,' Charlie shrieked. 'I'm goin' to get you for that.'

'No!' Peter slid stiffly out of bed. 'Don't rise to

it. 'E ain't worth it.' He glowered at Johnnie who, apparently realising the consequences of what he'd done, backed off into Sister Trim's clutches. She dug her fingers into the flesh on his shoulders and confiscated his weapon.

'You! Go and sit in the corner. Over there! I'll deal with you shortly. Master Herring, go back to bed. Master Swift, show me your eye.'

'I can't open it. I can't see — 'e's blinded me. Ow,' he said, as Sister tried to open it for him.

'The doctors will look at it and decide what's to be done. They'll be here shortly.' Tapping the knitting needle against her palm, she turned to Hannah. 'Have you any idea how this got here?'

'No, Sister,' she said, deciding that she had no way of proving that it had been Doctor Clifton who'd smuggled it on to the ward.

'I'll be keeping my eye on you. In the meantime, you're free to get on with your work.'

The atmosphere was subdued when Hannah went to remove Peter's dressings. This was a painful business, as the dressings were stuck to his neck, and Hannah apologised for making him cry. She then went round the other patients and checked them thoroughly, reading through the notes left by the night staff and making her own.

'The difference between Mr Anthony and Doctor Clifton is that the former thinks he's a god, whereas the latter is one,' Charlotte whispered, cheering her up a little as the doctors arrived on the ward.

They examined Charlie, pronouncing that his eye was undamaged apart from a little bruising. When he mentioned that Johnnie had attacked him with a knitting needle, Doctor Clifton glanced towards Hannah who quickly averted her gaze.

Hannah was ready to give the doctors a full report on Peter's condition, but the surgeon was dismissive, saying, 'I don't need all this detail. Just give me the salient facts.'

She took a small step back.

'He ain't too good this mornin',' Charlie contributed. ''E was sobbin' in 'is sleep.'

'Hush, Charlie,' Hannah said.

'It's quite possible that the tubercular disease in the glands of the neck will spread to the lungs, if they are not removed. I'm of the opinion that surgery is the only option,' Mr Anthony said. 'If in doubt, cut it out. I'll put him on my list for tomorrow morning. You will do well, Master Herring — I have great success with the knife.'

As the doctors moved on, Peter burst into tears.

'What's wrong?' Hannah asked, her heart going out to him.

''E's goin' to chop my 'ead off,' he sobbed.

'No, he isn't.' She hugged him, letting him cry into her apron. 'I'll be with you when you go to theatre, and I'll be waiting for you when you come back. I promise.'

When he'd calmed down, she helped him with his breakfast from the maid's trolley, but all he took was a sip of sweetened tea. Charlie asked if he could have the rest. Hannah didn't see why not. It would be a shame to waste it.

'The wittles 'ere are the best I've ever 'ad,' he said, tucking into a second portion of poached eggs on toast.

After breakfast, Hannah made a start on Sister Trim's list, but as she fetched the dustpan and brush, mop and bucket from the cupboard beside the sluice, Sister intercepted her.

'You'll have to leave that for now. You've had a lucky escape for the moment — Matron has asked me to send you to outpatients. They are overly busy and the staff there are struggling to cope, but don't think for a moment that that's let you off the hook — the chores will await your return.'

On her way to the outpatients' department, she found herself lost in the new wing, where the wards — even loftier than the Lettsom, and with walls tiled in pristine white — were named after the princesses: Alexandra, Louise, Victoria and Maud. Having asked for directions, she turned back.

Outpatients was crowded with people, young and old, waiting on the benches to see a physician for a variety of ailments, some self-inflicted, including a pair of sisters with blistered skin from the sun, and a child who had swallowed a thrupenny bit.

'We've tried tipping him upside down, but it won't come out, even with a good shake,' Hannah heard his mother say.

'You should count yourself lucky that it wasn't a crown, Mrs Rice,' one of the doctors said, as Hannah made her way to find someone who could tell her where she was supposed to be.

She passed the dispensary where the apothecary was pouring physic from a jug, dolling out purgatives, sulphate of magnesia and quassia.

One of the dispensing nurses was explaining to a patient how to take his medicine, but when Hannah noticed him a few seconds later, he was sharing the bottle with his companion.

'Ah, a spare pair of hands at last. Nurse Bentley, come with me.'

'Doctor Clifton.' She couldn't say she was pleased to see him.

'I'm sorry about the incident with the needle. I shouldn't have asked you to break the rules on my behalf. You're new to the house and trying to make a good impression. It was thoughtless and ungentlemanly of me.'

She was grateful and a little surprised at his apology, as he continued, 'I appreciate your not mentioning my involvement in the matter to Sister Trim.'

'I would have said, if I could have proved it.'

'I see.' She thought she saw a flicker of amusement cross his face as he opened the door to an examination room. 'Let battle commence. Call the first one in.'

'Doctor Clifton is ready,' she called, and not one patient, but a whole family came barging through the crowd with a large pram, shoving everyone aside.

'Hey, she's pushing in. There's a queue here.'

'We were here first.'

'Excuse me.' Hannah stood between the pram and the door. 'You must see the inquiry officer first.'

'The babe is sick. We 'ave to see the doctor, I think 'e's goin' to die.' The mother's wails and sobbing were most terrible to hear, and the other

70

patients backed down, muttering with annoyance rather than openly rebelling.

'Let them through,' Doctor Clifton called. 'Out of compassion, allow me to assess the infant's condition. It would be shameful to let him fade in the waiting hall, so near yet so far from medical attention. You would be eternally grateful if it was your child.'

'Listen to the good doctor,' somebody said. 'Ladies and gentlemen, step aside.'

Hannah held the door open for them: the man pushing the pram, and the woman with a babe in her arms and another on her hip. The pram contained a boy of about fourteen — not an infant at all — with his limbs folded up and his eyes rolling in their sockets.

The inquiry officer followed, and Hannah pulled the door to a close behind him.

Doctor Clifton helped the father lift the groaning child on to the trolley, while introducing Mr Taylor, the person responsible for interviewing potential patients and deciding who would be seen.

'Name and profession?' Mr Taylor asked.

'Allspice, ropewalker and travellin' showman, not that it's any business of yours,' the man said rudely. 'This is our son, Alan.'

'Address?'

'We 'ave lodgin's in Ramsgate.'

If she'd seen them on the street, she wouldn't have looked twice, Hannah thought. Mr Allspice was in his forties, with a greying moustache and side whiskers. He wore tight-fitting fustian breeches and a grubby blue waistcoat over a frilled white shirt, while his wife, with her sallow olive skin, her greasy black hair tied back and wearing a torn bottle-green dress, appeared decidedly downtrodden.

Hannah turned her attention to Doctor Clifton who was talking to the boy.

'It's me leg,' he complained weakly. 'Ah,' he gasped when the doctor tried to straighten his right knee and hip.

'These people are not eligible for assistance,' Mr Taylor said.

'For what reason?' Doctor Clifton seemed a little put out. 'This young man has scrofula of the hip — he requires treatment.'

'They're the kind of people who bring this trouble on themselves,' Mr Taylor maintained. 'They have no moral virtue and therefore are not entitled to help.'

'But the child is innocent.' Hannah couldn't hold her tongue. Doctor Clifton and Mr Taylor stared at her in surprise. 'Who are we to make that decision? What moral virtue can we claim if we abandon him?' The poor boy couldn't choose his parents. She thought briefly of her father, and how she'd often wished that someone had walked into her life to tell her that it had all been a mistake and he wasn't her father at all.

'We are superior to these people in every way.' Mr Taylor stared at her. 'If Mr Allspice took up proper employment and provided a settled abode for his family, then I'd deem his son a suitable patient for admission to this house.'

'You can't judge a book by its cover,' Hannah said. 'You can have no idea of this gentleman's virtues, or otherwise. I've seen patients hiring clothes for the day to make themselves look respectable for their visit to the hospital, which makes them appear well off, and able to afford treatment when they can't. There are others who turn up with their servants and letters of recommendation when they could have paid for themselves.' She became aware that Doctor Clifton was looking at her, his head slightly to one side.

'The father is a ruffian who can barely string a sentence together,' Mr Taylor interjected.

'Excuse me, sir. My ma — God rest 'er soul — learned me how to speak the Queen's Hinglish,' Mr Allspice said, his face turning a shade of beetroot. 'It's a cryin' shame that you don't consider ropewalkin' a respectable profession.' He turned to Doctor Clifton. 'I 'ave 'undreds and thousands of people lookin' up to me, like I'm a god, every time I perform.'

'This isn't about the family. 'It's about a poorly boy. Doctor Clifton, you wouldn't allow Mr Taylor to turn him away?' Hannah recalled her training: even when a nurse disagreed with a decision, she should never forget her proper place, interfere with a doctor's duties or set herself above his directions. 'I'm sorry. I've overstepped the mark. It isn't my — '

'I admire you for speaking up when you see suffering and injustice,' Doctor Clifton said.

'Nurse, your sentiments are misplaced,' Mr Taylor said. 'Doctor Clifton?'

'Nurse Bentley is right. We should reconsider.'

'There are at least twenty patients out there,

each one requiring treatment,' Mr Taylor responded, staring over the top of his horn-rimmed spectacles. 'I hope you understand that you're putting me in an impossible position.'

'I need our boy better,' Mr Allspice said. 'I can't afford to keep an invalid.'

'He should be admitted, but he requires a ticket for that,' Doctor Clifton decided. 'I can't promise anything, Mr Allspice, but if you wait outside, I'll see what I can do.'

'Thank you,' Mrs Allspice cried as her husband folded the boy's limbs and lifted him back into the pram. 'People tell me it don't matter if you lose one child when you've got twelve more, but they don't know what they're talkin' about. They're all precious to me and it would break my 'eart if I lost any of 'em.'

'Doctor, you've been here long enough to know how the system works,' Mr Taylor complained when the Allspices had left the room. 'The house has finite resources and the new wards are filled to capacity, therefore there has to be a method of rationing treatment. That family have brought their son's sickness upon themselves with their dissolute, itinerant way of life.'

'Sickness — scrofula in particular — has no respect for wealth or status,' Doctor Clifton said coolly. 'Mr Taylor, please excuse me — I wish to get on. Nurse, call the next one in.'

For the next two hours, she was kept busy, calling patients to the examination room and running errands for the doctor, and even when the queue had dwindled to nothing, it seemed

74

that they were far from finished.

'There's one more asking for you,' Mr Taylor said stiffly. 'A Mrs Phillips. I've put her in the room next door.'

Doctor Clifton thanked him while Hannah packed away the bandages and cleaned up after their last patient, a little girl who'd cut her foot while playing on the beach. 'I hope that Sister Trim can spare you for another half an hour.'

He must have seen her face fall, she realised, when he went on.

'She's keeping your nose to the grindstone?'

Hannah nodded, thinking of the list of chores she hadn't started on yet.

'I don't like to impose, but I have a favour to ask. Don't worry — I'm not asking you to break any rules this time. I'm in need of a chaperone. Mrs Phillips has called at my private practice on false pretences three times in the past week. A doctor without a wife is considered fair game by some women, and I'm taking no chances — I've had ladies throw themselves into my arms, and others set out to entrap me by suggesting impropriety when there was none.

'Listening to a lady's heart and lungs, or examining her ankles, for example, is fraught with potential misunderstanding.'

Hannah blushed furiously as he continued, 'There are some who say that the cure for her hysteria is for her husband to pay her more attention, but I have to be sure that she isn't suffering from some other condition that can be more easily treated. She's a challenging case. This way.' He held the doors open for her on the

75

way to the adjacent room while she marvelled at his shocking frankness. She wasn't sure how to take him.

'Doctor Clifton! Oh?' Mrs Phillips exclaimed, looking from the doctor to Hannah and back. She was in her late thirties, Hannah guessed, and dressed in the height of fashion in a peacock-blue princess-line dress with a high collar, and a narrow skirt which looked almost impossible to walk in.

'Nurse Bentley is assisting me today.'

'I'm sure you're more than capable of examining me by yourself.' Mrs Phillips gazed at him adoringly. 'I'll need help with my dress, though, I suppose.'

'The last time I saw you, you were seeking treatment for inflammation of the tonsils,' Doctor Clifton said sternly. 'There's no need to disrobe.'

'Oh dear, but I'm having terrible pains right here.' She touched her breast, pointing to her heart.

'They've come on suddenly?' he queried.

'Well, yes.' She stood up and swept towards him, reaching for his hand and pressing it to her chest. 'Can you feel it? My heart is racing uncontrollably.'

'Nurse will help you undress. I'll return shortly'

With a sigh, she released his hand and turned to Hannah with a look of resignation.

When he'd left the room, Hannah unfastened the hooks and eyes at the back of Mrs Phillips's dress, and helped her into a gown. Mrs Phillips lay down on the trolley with one arm behind her head and the gown draped loosely across her chest, as though emulating Venus, the goddess of love.

Hannah was surprised at how she was carrying on — she was at least ten years older than Doctor Clifton and married at that.

He came back to check her throat, heart and lungs, and prescribed honey and lemon with a dash of whisky, along with a tonic from the pharmacy, for which he wrote out a prescription slip.

'What about my palpitations?' Mrs Phillips said, apparently not entirely satisfied with his diagnosis.

'How many cups of coffee do you have in a day?' the doctor asked.

'Oh, several.' She waved her arm, deliberately exposing her breast.

'Then I suggest that you cut back — the active component has a stimulatory effect on the heart.' He lowered his voice. 'Do you think you can do that, Mrs Phillips? For the sake of your health.'

'I shall try, if you think it's necessary,' she said, her tone husky. 'I shall expect a house call next time. It can't be good for an invalid to have to leave the comfort of her home to mingle with all and sundry at the infirmary, but I'm teaching you to suck eggs, Doctor Clifton.'

He wished her good day, and Hannah helped her back into her clothes, before showing her to the pharmacy and making her way past the Allspices who were still waiting.

'Has she gone?' she heard someone whisper. At first, she thought she'd imagined it, but the doctor peered out from the shadows of a doorway.

'I showed her to the pharmacy,' she said, frowning.

'I won't be able to relax until she's left the building. Oh dear, you think I'm touched.' He grinned. 'Mrs Phillips believes that we have an attachment when there's nothing of the sort. Her husband — he's elderly, and doesn't please her any more . . . '

'She's pining for you?'

He nodded.

'Why do you humour her? Why don't you tell her to find another doctor?'

'It isn't that straightforward. Firstly, Mr Phillips is Chair of the Board and a major donor to the house, and secondly, ladies like Mrs Phillips are my bread and butter. How can I give my services to the house gratis if I have no income?'

'I didn't realise . . . ' she stammered. According to Charlotte, he spent most days at the infirmary — she'd assumed that he had been taking a wage.

'I wouldn't take advantage of those who give charitably to provide treatment for the poor by insisting on being paid, but' — he quirked one eyebrow — 'I don't do it entirely out of selflessness. I gain experience and make a name for myself, which benefits my private practice. There's little wrong with Mrs Phillips. I believe that much ill health arises from abnormal states of the mind — giving reassurance and offering the simple placebo of a harmless tonic can stop the patient fretting about every ache and pain.'

'She is lovesick, though,' Hannah said. 'I didn't think there was a cure for that, apart from time . . . '

'Ah' — a shadow crossed his eyes — 'they say that time is a healer, but I have my doubts. Thank you for your assistance today.'

She returned to the ward.

'Oh, here comes Nurse Bentley at last, making herself out to be some seaside angel,' Sister Trim said acidly. 'Matron's on the warpath, by the way. She wants to see you in her office.'

'Now?' Hannah's forehead tightened.

'Now,' Sister Trim confirmed, and Hannah felt sick, as if she'd received one of Charlie's belly-go-fisters.

'Miss Russell said that you were outspoken, but I thought you would know your place by now,' Mrs Knowles said, her cheeks pink with annoyance as Hannah sat facing her across her desk. 'However, I have to temper my opinion of Mr Taylor's report of your conduct with the fact that Doctor Clifton saw fit to agree with you and take steps to have the patient admitted.'

'It was an impossible situation,' Hannah said. 'I couldn't accept that the boy was about to be turned away because of his parents' lack of moral virtue. It isn't fair that certain people who have nothing wrong with them are treated like royalty, while those who really need our care are left to suffer.'

'This is about you, not others,' Matron said impatiently. 'In future, you are to think before you speak.'

'Yes, I'm sorry.'

'I appreciate the difficulty in striking a balance between asserting one's authority and keeping quiet on matters which you find hard to accept. Either one is considered a bull in a china shop or a shrinking violet. You demonstrate the qualities of leadership — initiative and the courage to speak your mind — but you also need to learn tact and diplomacy if you're going to progress.' Matron's face relaxed into a smile. 'I'm living proof that it can be done, given time.'

For once, Hannah didn't know what to say.

'Sister Trim and I have managed to organise the rota so that you and Nurse Finch have the same afternoon off this week — I thought she could show you around Margate before you attend church. Off you go.'

As Hannah returned to the Lettsom, she came across Charlotte who was mopping the floors.

'Thank you for making a start on my chores,' she said. 'I'm very grateful.'

Charlotte grinned. 'I can't be seen to be standing around doing nothing. I heard what happened today with Mr Taylor and Doctor Clifton. It's all over the house. You caused rather a stir.'

On reflection, Hannah would do the same again, but as Mrs Knowles had suggested, in a more tactful and considered way.

⋆   ⋆   ⋆

'Nurse Bentley, Nurse Finch, you may go,' Sister Trim said, looking up at the clock. It was four in the afternoon on the Friday, two days after the

80

incident with Mr Taylor and the Allspices. 'I'll see you in the morning at seven o'clock sharp.' Hannah treasured her time off. She had one early finish a week to go to church, one day a week to herself, and one week's annual holiday. She worked from seven in the morning until eight in the evening, taking her meals at the infirmary, and sharing the house with Charlotte and the other nurses.

'We'll be bright and early, Sister,' Charlotte said, beaming.

Light of step, Hannah hurried back with her to the nurses' home where they changed into their Sunday best.

'I don't know about you, but I only go to church on special occasions — Christmas and Easter, weddings . . . ' Charlotte said as she looked for her bonnet. 'I pray every night, but I'm not sure if that makes up for it. The chaplain holds a service in the new chapel every evening, or you can worship at Holy Trinity. Or we can go for a walk along the beach.'

'I'd like to see a little of Margate. I can go to church next week, or the one after.'

'I hope I'm not leading you astray.'

'Only a little,' Hannah smiled. 'Thinking about going astray, what happened to Henry and his companions? We haven't seen hide nor hair of them since their escapade the other night.'

'Someone reported back to Matron — they've been suspended for a week. Apparently, Doctor Clifton was furious. It turns out that Henry is his cousin — Mrs Merry told me. She has her finger on the pulse, so to speak, when it comes to the

81

gossip. I think he's particularly annoyed because he invited Henry here as a favour, to help him with his studies.'

'Henry's interests seem to lie elsewhere,' Hannah observed.

It wasn't long before they were on the beach, paddling through the shallow, foaming waves without their shoes and stockings.

'This seems very daring to me,' Hannah said, burying her toes in the warm sand.

'It's perfectly acceptable. I come down here whenever I can, pretending I'm on holiday. I've heard that Brighton is superior to Margate, but I don't believe it.' Charlotte giggled as the water splashed the hem of her skirt.

'My sister would love it here.' Hannah gazed towards the promenade where the crowds were being entertained by minstrels, Punch and Judy, and a showman with a singing dog.

'She should come and stay for part of the summer. Write to her.'

'I need to buy stationery and stamps, so I can get in touch with her to let her know I've moved,' Hannah said, feeling guilty that she hadn't had a chance to write back before. Ruby would be wondering why she hadn't heard from her.

'I'll show you where the best shops are. Oh, look at all these people. By July, Margate will be crawling with emmets. I wish they'd stay in London.' Charlotte stopped abruptly. 'No offence.'

'None taken.' It was busy, but Hannah liked the way that all classes of society seemed to be mixing together. There were children playing in the sand, building castles with buckets and spades, while their mothers and nannies watched them.

A group of fashionably dressed ladies in straw hats with ribbons streaming in the breeze stood facing out to sea, their eyes fixed on several figures who were cavorting some distance from the shore.

'May I have the glasses now?' one said in a wheedling voice. 'You've had your turn.'

'One more minute,' another said, holding opera glasses up to her eyes. 'Oh, aren't they beautiful?'

'Give me the glasses!' Hannah thought she recognised Mrs Phillips in one of her form-fitting skirts. 'You are being mean.'

'You must bring your own next time.'

'Why are they making a scene?' Hannah whispered as she and Charlotte walked past. 'It's most unladylike.'

'Can you hear the men shouting?' Charlotte asked.

Hannah paused, straining her ears and eyes as she tried to make out what the commotion was about. There were gentlemen splashing and laughing, diving in and out of the water from a pontoon, the rays of the late afternoon sunshine endowing their naked torsos with a coppery glow.

She gasped. 'They aren't wearing shirts, just bathing drawers.'

'That's right.' Charlotte didn't seem at all shocked, merely amused. 'My eyes aren't so good — perhaps I should invest in a telescope.'

'There's no need for that. Really, there isn't.'

'You're sounding like a prude, Hannah. It could be worse. Apparently there are ladies and gentlemen who like to swim in company with each other, in a promiscuous manner.'

'I had no idea.'

'The ladies look even less modest than the gentlemen, the way their bathing costumes cling to their figures.'

'They certainly don't frolic like this in London,' Hannah said, watching two men wrestling on the pontoon: one tall and broad-shouldered, the other equally tall, but bulkier. The former threw the latter into the water.

'I'll get you back for that,' he shouted, laughing as the slimmer one stood brazenly showing off his naked chest, his skin gleaming as he shook the water from his hair.

'Well, that's a treat for you,' Charlotte said.

'If you say so.' Hannah blushed. 'We are all the same, skin, flesh and bone.'

'But we're put together differently, some in a more harmonious way than others . . .'

Hannah couldn't disagree, nor could she stop thinking about what she'd seen, when they put on their shoes and stockings and proceeded to the front to treat themselves to a penny lick.

One of the Sicilians who kept his wares cold with ice from Norway and salt from Cheshire took a glass and dipped a wooden paddle into the ice-cream container on his stall. He took out a lump and smoothed it into the glass, leaving a peak. He added a second on top.

84

'That looks more like a tuppenny's worth,' Charlotte said.

'It's a little extra for you lovely young ladies. *Comu bedda.*' He winked from under his cap.

'Thank you.' Hannah licked the ice cream, savouring the sweet crystalline texture and its vanilla taste, and feeling shy about eating on the street, something that Pa and Stepmother would have frowned upon.

She returned the glass. The Sicilian wiped it with a flannel and put it back on the stall.

'I think he has a fancy for you,' Charlotte observed as they followed the road into town. 'He's never given me free ice cream before.'

'The hokey-pokey man?' Hannah couldn't restrain a chuckle at her companion's outrageous suggestion. 'Oh no, I don't think so.'

'I'm sure he has.'

Hannah turned and looked back. He was watching. Caught out, he grinned.

'You seem surprised. You must have attracted a good few admirers before.'

'There was one,' Hannah admitted. 'He proposed to me, but I turned him down.'

'Was it a romantic proposal? Did you break his heart?'

'It was about six months ago when I returned to Canterbury for a family funeral.'

'I'm sorry — I'm always putting my foot in it.'

'Don't worry. My grandmother — on my mother's side — had been ill for some time. Her death came more as a blessed release than a surprise to anyone, but I was still very upset. It's a long story, but when I ran away from home, I moved in with her. I owe her a great debt for paying for my training.' Hannah smiled ruefully. 'Anyway, Mr Adamson and I formed a friendship. He walked me home from church sometimes — in the presence of my cousins, I hasten to add.' Hannah hadn't encouraged him in the slightest. In fact, his double-edged comments about his attraction to her had put her off, especially when he'd said that he was prepared to tolerate her freckles because he found her figure most agreeable.

'He tried to kiss me once, so I suppose I shouldn't have been surprised when he approached me at the wake,' she continued.

'What did he say?'

'He offered me his condolences, then remarked that I looked more beautiful than ever . . . then he said that he held me in great esteem and admired the way I'd worked to become a young lady of independent means. He told me that it was completely unnecessary for me to continue, that I should give up caring for my patients and look after him instead. Can you believe that?

'I told him that I'd rather be a slave to my vocation than to matrimony, at which he smiled and said that he was prepared to wait until I'd changed my mind.'

'How presumptuous.'

'He said he'd ask again, so I retorted, 'A gentleman would not, sir,' and turned my back on him.' She recalled how her uncle had come to her rescue, then taken her aside to tell her of the small inheritance her grandmother had left her, a nest egg to put away for a rainy day, with a proviso that she would use some of it to help her sister, if she saw fit. With that and her savings, she had just enough for a deposit and a few weeks' rent, not enough to support Ruby longer-term, unless her sister found paid occupation, but, as she and Charlotte wandered through Margate, Hannah made her decision. She would summon Ruby straight away to keep her safe and for her own peace of mind.

'You were very blunt, then,' Charlotte said as they passed W. Tubbs, the tobacconist on Trinity Hill where the scent of cigar smoke vied with the aroma of ladies' perfume from the shop next door.

'I beg your pardon . . . I was miles away.'

'With this Mr Adamson.' Charlotte smiled.

'Oh yes. I had to be cruel to be kind. I could see that my attempts at letting him down gently were only encouraging him. He didn't understand that I couldn't bear the idea of marriage, of being cooped up running a household, like a hen with her wings clipped, and subject to a husband's every whim.' Not only that, if she ever wed, she knew she'd be terrified that her husband would turn out to be like her father.

'Even though we're poorly paid and subject to Matron's orders, we have a certain amount of freedom,' Charlotte agreed. 'Do you think you'll stay on at the infirmary?'

'It'll take me a while to get used to it, but yes, I think so.'

'There's plenty to do in Margate — you can visit the Hall by the Sea, the pleasure gardens and the grotto, and spend time in one of the bathing rooms. Failing that, you can always go window shopping.' Charlotte stopped outside the next shop and pointed to a pair of shoes made of blue French silk, a complete contrast to their plain everyday leather footwear which had flannel linings and stout India-rubber soles. 'Look at those.'

'They'd be perfect for dancing,' Hannah said, coveting the ribbons and silver buckles. 'I've never been to a ball.'

'Neither have I,' Charlotte said sadly.

'If I'd accepted Mr Adamson's hand, I'd have been able to buy any number of pairs of those shoes in all the different colours of the rainbow.'

'Do you ever regret the choices you've made?'

'Not at all. If I had a husband to buy me a new pair of shoes like this, I'd wear them a few times, then put them away in the wardrobe. The rewards from nursing are far longer-lasting.' Hannah thought of the bond she'd made with Peter.

'The glow of satisfaction one gets when one's scrubbed the bedpans, and made the beds, you mean,' Charlotte said with irony. 'Let me show you to the stationer's.'

They headed to the High Street, passing Harlows' Mineral Waters and various other shops: corn chandlers; milliners and dressmakers; fruiterers and greengrocers. Hannah bought paper and ink, before they stopped at the confectioner's to pick up peppermints and fudge.

After they'd returned home, Hannah stayed up late, writing letters to Alice and Ruby by the light of the moon to avoid keeping Charlotte awake with the flickering flame of a candle. She told Alice of the bathers on Margate beach, of Sister Trim, Charlie and Peter, Charlotte and Doctor Clifton, and wrote to Ruby, addressing the letter to Miss Fellows, the Bentleys' neighbour in Canterbury.

Dear Ruby,

Please note my new address. I will not say too much here, but I have very recently moved to Margate to work at the Royal Sea Bathing Infirmary.

Your letter causes me much concern because it appears that our father is turning against you, as he did with me. My dearest wish is that you leave Canterbury and come to live with me so that I know you are safe and happy. Let me know when you will arrive, so I can make the necessary arrangements.

I have been in Margate but a week, and it has exceeded all my expectations. I sign off with renewed hope and optimism for the future,

With love from Hannah

5

Kill or Cure

A week passed and Hannah had heard nothing from Ruby, which was odd, because she normally replied by return of post. Wondering if Pa had intercepted her letter, she wrote again, and waited.

Peter's surgery had been delayed and Alan Allspice hadn't yet been admitted to the infirmary because, despite his best efforts, Doctor Clifton hadn't been able to obtain a ticket for him. On the Monday ward round, though, Mr Anthony had news: Peter was to have his surgery that morning.

'Where is that cousin of yours?' he asked Doctor Clifton.

At that moment, a young man dressed in a dark jacket and tie rushed on to the ward. Running his hands through his hair, which was a darker shade of brown than his beard, he hurried towards them and stopped beside Peter's bed.

'What time do you call this, Mr Hunter?' Mr Anthony enquired.

'My apologies.' Henry bowed his head in front of his superiors.

'I should think so too,' Doctor Clifton growled. 'You're an embarrassment. Hasn't your suspension taught you anything? How will you ever command respect by turning up on the wards in this state?

'It was forever thus,' Mr Anthony sighed. 'Now that you have graced us with your presence at last, perhaps you would like to examine this patient's neck . . . '

Mr Hunter turned to Peter and smiled.

'Good morning, Master . . . '

'Herring,' Hannah said.

'Master Herring, how are you feeling today?'

'I 'ave to say I've felt better, sir,' Peter said solemnly.

'The lesions, Mr Hunter?' Mr Anthony interrupted. 'Focus on the disease.'

Mr Hunter looked closely at the weeping lumps on Peter's neck. 'This patient has scrofula,' he muttered, beads of perspiration forming across his bloodless brow.

'A revelation to us all,' Mr Anthony said with sarcasm.

'Of the glands . . . they are suppurating.' He straightened and stepped back.

'It would serve you well to put your books before ale in future.' Mr Anthony smiled at Mr Hunter's discomfiture.

'Will you allow me to give you my report on the patient's condition?' Hannah said, recalling Matron's lecture on speaking with tact.

'It isn't necessary — I have a gap in my list today,' Mr Anthony snapped.

There was a momentary silence, then Hannah decided she had to speak up anyway.

'Master Herring has shown signs of improvement. The spikes of fever are less frequent, and

91

he's taking small amounts of solid food. Perhaps you would consider delaying the operation for a few more days so he can build his strength up further . . . I fear that he's too weak to withstand surgery at present.' She paused, noticing how the surgeon's eyes flashed with annoyance. 'I know my patients — I'm with them all day, every day. I want the best for them.'

'How dare you question my authority! Who do you think you are?' Mr Anthony said coldly. 'This is an example of exactly what I've been saying: that nurses don't need all this training. As a nurse advances in the scientific knowledge incidental to her calling, she declines in efficiency. It makes her dissatisfied with the drudgery of which life as a nurse is greatly made up, and she becomes argumentative.

'We've shilly-shallied around for long enough with potions and poultices. It's time to go in with curettage, lavage and full excision, if necessary, under chloroform. Doctor Clifton, what is your view?' he challenged.

'I believe that we should listen to the nurse who's in close contact with young Peter here,' the doctor said, to her surprise.

'You would take her opinion over mine!' Hannah thought the surgeon might explode with rage.

'I'm not saying that. I'm suggesting that we acknowledge all the evidence in the best interest of the patient. We shouldn't rush into any kind of treatment which may do more harm than good, out of professional vanity.'

'You are merely a visiting physician,' Mr

Anthony spat. 'I'm going to take this to the Board and make sure you never work in this establishment again.'

'You would sacrifice a patient's life out of pride?'

'And you would not offer him this chance out of jealousy?'

Hannah didn't know where to put herself. She glanced towards Charlotte, who made a gesture, fanning her face with her hand as the medical student looked in her direction with a meek smile on his lips. Was she mistaken in thinking that Mr Hunter was taking more notice of Nurse Finch than the argument going on in front of them? He seemed transfixed.

'Gentlemen!' Sister Trim marched over to join them. 'Not on my ward. Take your argument elsewhere. You're upsetting the boys.'

The medical men left the ward to continue their discussion in the corridor, and Hannah stroked Peter's brow. 'I'm sorry about that,' she said. 'We all want you to get better.'

'My 'ead 'urts,' he moaned.

'I'm sure it does after that little episode,' Sister said. 'They are worse than children. It's a disgrace. I can believe it of Mr Anthony, but Doctor Clifton ... well ... ' Hannah was expecting an inquest, but Sister went on, 'I wish they'd pay more attention to the nurses when we're the ones who know the patients best. We carry out their observations hourly while the doctors see them once a day, maybe twice. As for that student, what does he expect to learn, coming on to my ward, stinking of drink?'

Mr Hunter returned to Peter's bedside a few minutes later.

'Mr Anthony has sent me to tell you that you are to prepare Master Herring to go under the knife, Nurse Bentley.'

'I'd advise you to choose your words more wisely,' she said, upset on Peter's behalf. 'There should be no mention of knives on a children's ward, but I thank you for letting me know.'

When he'd gone, Hannah washed Peter's face and cleaned his neck, then sat quietly, holding his hand.

'You're being very brave,' she murmured.

'I want to get better,' he whispered.

'What will you do when you're well enough to leave us?'

'I'll be a doctor like Doctor Clifton.' His eyes clouded slightly as he frowned. 'I don't know 'ow — I don't think they teach doctorin' at the . . . '

He meant the poorhouse, she thought, her heart breaking for him.

'Oh, it's no use,' Peter sighed. 'I'll never be a gen'leman.'

'You're more of a gentleman than many of the men I know,' Hannah said, thinking of Henry and the other medical students, and Mr Allspice. 'Just you remember that.'

'I will.' He squeezed her hand. 'Thank you for everythin' you do for me, Nurse.'

'It's a pleasure,' she said with a smile.

'I'll be thinkin' of you.' Charlie came to wave him off when the porter came to take Peter to the operating theatre. 'When you're better, we'll go out maffickin' an' — '

94

'Oh no, you won't be going anywhere,' Hannah chuckled. 'It isn't right for boys your age to be out being rowdy on the streets.'

'When we're older, then,' Charlie said, as his friend was wheeled away, 'like that Mr 'unter. Anyone can see 'e's 'alf rats.'

'Don't you say anything against him — he's under the weather, that's all.'

'Yes, Nurse.' Charlie looked up and winked like an actor on stage.

'Outside. Off you go,' she said. 'You're missing out on the sunshine.'

When Peter returned to the ward three hours later, he was half asleep, the circles around his eyes darker than they'd ever been, and his face a luminous shade of white. Speaking softly to him, Hannah changed his dressings as the blood seeped through them, and washed his wounds with carbolic to drive off the flies which made their way indoors in the hot weather. She offered him teaspoonfuls of broth, most of which ended up on his pyjamas, so she changed those too before she dined and sat with him again, holding his hand and mopping his brow.

'Dear boy,' she murmured, but he didn't speak. She didn't think he had the strength.

'We're done here for now,' she heard Charlotte say later. 'Hannah? Oh, he is in a bad way, the poor little mite.'

'I'm going to stay for another hour or two.'

'You'll wear yourself out.'

'I know, but Peter doesn't have anyone else to sit with him.'

'Except me,' Charlie said from his bed. 'I'll

look after 'im for you, Nurse.'

'Thank you.' Her eyes pricked with tears. 'That's very kind.'

She stayed for another hour, then whispered farewell, before going back to find Charlotte sitting up waiting for her.

'There's a letter for you,' Charlotte said, handing her an envelope. 'Mr Mordikai asked me to give it to you.'

'Thank you. Oh, it's from my friend in London.' Her heart sank a little. 'I was hoping it was from my sister.' Hannah had told Charlotte of her plan while they were dining at the infirmary a few days before.

'I know you're worried about her, but I reckon no news is good news.'

Hannah smiled weakly, realising that Charlotte was only trying to cheer her up.

'Do you think Mr Anthony will really take this spat of his and Doctor Clifton's to the Board?' she said, changing the subject, as they shared some of the fudge they'd bought on their shopping expedition.

'I don't know — he's a law unto himself.'

'I'm afraid that he'll drag me into it to make a point. He's stuck in the past, expecting nurses to pay blind obedience to the physicians and surgeons. He's afraid of losing control of his cases to us lady nurses.'

'I'd tread carefully if I were you, Hannah. Things haven't changed that much. Mr Anthony still believes that he has the right to dispose of any nurse who steps out of line — according to his wish, not Matron's. Don't stick your neck on the block for nothing.'

Hannah thanked Charlotte for the advice and retired to bed, more concerned for Peter's fate and what was going on with Ruby than any meeting of the Board.

★   ★   ★

When she came back to the Lettsom the following morning, Charlie was lying on Peter's bed with his arms around his friend. Hannah swallowed hard, not wanting to cry in front of the boys.

'Don't disturb them,' Charlotte whispered. 'Even Sister Trim says not to.'

Peter's condition was worse — his breathing was shallow, and a terrible smell emanated from his neck. When Mr Anthony and Doctor Clifton turned up on their rounds, they frowned and shook their heads. Mr Hunter, who was sober this time, stood quietly at the bedside. It didn't matter who was right or wrong, Hannah thought. Peter had been too far gone when he was admitted for any treatment to have helped.

Charlie looked up when he became aware of her shadow falling across his shoulder.

' 'E's dyin'.'

'We'll pray for him,' Hannah said, pulling the screens around the bed.

'What good will that do?'

'It will be a comfort to him. Keep talking — they say that the sense of hearing is the last to go . . . '

An atmosphere of gloom came over the ward.

Dark clouds converged and spilled their rain, sending the summer visitors into Margate's library, coffee houses and bathing rooms for shelter. As the wind whistled across the balcony, blowing the patients' parasols and umbrellas inside out, Peter took one last rasping breath.

'Sleep tight, little one,' Hannah said, choked with a sudden grief, even though he was at peace, his torment over.

Charlie burst into tears of rage and sorrow.

'They've killed 'im,' he sobbed. 'Nurse, you said we was comin' 'ere to get better.'

'I know, and we tried. Everyone tried — Doctor Clifton, Mr Anthony . . . '

'I told you them baths wouldn't do no good, but you wouldn't listen!'

She leaned across and closed Peter's eyes. 'We must call for the duty doctor — '

'What for?' Charlie interrupted. 'It's too late.'

Nurse Finch came to take him out to the balcony, where the other patients were grumbling at Sister who'd insisted that they stay outside. They'd come to the house for fresh air, and fresh air they would have.

Doctor Clifton turned up to certify the cause of Peter's passing and send for a porter to remove the body to the mortuary, before he rushed away again to attend to a patient who had broken his shoulder, crushed by falling barrels on the wharf.

It was a difficult day, not made any easier by the arrival of Alan Allspice, the boy with the scrofulous hip who took Peter's empty bed as soon as it had been cleaned and the linen changed.

At the end of her shift when Hannah stopped to wish Charlie goodnight, he turned his back to her. She couldn't face anyone either, not yet.

Needing some time to herself, she made her way to the chapel where she offered prayers for Peter's soul, for Charlie and Alan, for the other patients and the staff at the infirmary, for her sister whom she hadn't heard from and her extended family. She gazed up at the stained-glass windows, studying the picture of Jesus restoring sight to the blind beggar. The pain of Peter's death began to lessen slightly with the reminder that they couldn't perform miracles, only do their best.

Someone moved behind her. She turned to find Doctor Clifton walking along the aisle towards the cross on the altar.

'I'm sorry for disturbing you,' he whispered as he stopped beside her. 'I wanted to ask you if you were all right.'

'I'm better now,' she said, standing up. 'I needed to . . . ' She'd been taught to moderate any outward display of emotion, but sometimes it was impossible.

He smiled wryly. 'We wouldn't be human if we didn't feel for our patients. Peter was a young boy with his life ahead of him. He hadn't had much luck before he came here — it seems terribly unfair.' His voice was deep and reassuring. 'We must look on the bright side, though — he had a few days of comfort here, even happiness. I saw it in his eyes when he and Charlie were together, when you spoke to him . . . '

She gazed at him. He was unusual, not

arrogant or mocking, unlike many of the other doctors she'd met.

'I admire your compassion and your ability to express it,' she said. 'It's refreshing.'

'It's sometimes said that a doctor ought to be a nurse before he's a physician. It's a vocation, a privilege to care for the sick and dying, and it pains me to find doctors at loggerheads with each other and the nursing profession. When this matter — the one which arose yesterday between Mr Anthony and me — goes before the Board — '

'He is going ahead with it?'

He nodded. 'The governors meet tomorrow. I don't know if you'll be called as a witness.'

'You can rely on my support, if that's the case.'

'I'm very grateful. I wish that everyone — physicians, surgeons and nurses alike — would put their patients before their professional pride. We can learn much from each other — but that's enough. I've said my piece. How is Master Swift?'

'He's devastated. He places the blame for Peter's death squarely at the door of the house.'

'I'll talk to him tomorrow. There was nothing we could do — Peter's brain was fatally inflamed. I will write to Mr Piper at St Pancras, enclosing the certificate of burial after the funeral.'

'Will he have a proper send-off? He's an orphan.'

'The chaplain will say a few words and he'll be interred here in Margate, his grave unmarked, but recorded.'

Hannah sat down again.

'His memory will live on in my heart,' she said, wiping the corner of her eye. 'Do you know what he said to me yesterday? That he wanted to be a doctor like you.'

Doctor Clifton cleared his throat. 'That's terribly sad — and humbling.'

Hannah took a moment to regain a measure of self-control. 'What about Master Allspice?' she asked eventually. 'You found him a ticket.'

'I asked Mrs Phillips to speak to her husband — he had an unused ticket which he was pleased to allocate to a sick boy from an impoverished yet deserving family.'

'Doctor Clifton, were you being devious?'

'A little,' he admitted. 'May I sit with you? If I'm not intruding, that is. I'm sorry, you came here for some quiet reflection.'

'It's fine. You're welcome.'

'You're missing London?' Doctor Clifton took a seat beside her, stretching out his long legs into the space that had been left free of pews so that patients could be wheeled into the chapel and take part in the services.

'A little,' she confessed.

'You have friends there?'

''Yes, but Charlotte — I mean, Nurse Finch — has been very kind.'

'What brought you into nursing?' he asked.

'It's a long story. I left home at seventeen when my father tried to force me into marriage to a friend of his. Unable to contemplate such a fate, I told him I'd rather earn my living as a nurse, but he was dead set against it. To be honest, I didn't know much about nursing as a vocation back then, only that I remembered the kindness of the private nurse when I lost my half-brother to scarlet fever.'

'I'm sorry to hear of your troubles. You've been through some hard times.'

'I think they're supposed to build character,' she said, forcing a smile. 'It's been two years since I last saw my father. The nurses, my patients and the community of whichever hospital I'm working at are my family now, although I'm still very close to my sister.'

'What about your mother? She must be very proud of you.'

'She died,' Hannah said softly.

'I'm sorry.'

'I was only three — I have very few memories of her.' She kept the details of her mother's passing to herself.

'My father was disappointed in my choice of profession,' Doctor Clifton confided. 'He's a naval chaplain who wished me to follow in his footsteps, but I wanted to heal minds and bodies, not souls.'

'What about your mother?'

'Oh, she was delighted at the prospect of having a medical man in the family. She wanted me for her personal physician. Hence' — smiling, he tipped his head slightly to one side — 'I moved here to put a convenient distance between us. She lives in Hastings, close enough to maintain family ties and offer advice, but too far away to make house calls. One shouldn't treat family or friends — one is too involved to make rational, dispassionate decisions.'

'Do you have any brothers or sisters?' She wondered if she was being impertinent, but it was Doctor Clifton who'd started the conversation.

'I have a brother, four years my junior, who's gone into the Church after my father, then I have three sisters, all flibbertigibbets,' he said fondly. 'Their letters and drawings have been a comfort to me, though, since Suzanna — my wife — passed away.'

It was Hannah's turn to feel sorry for him as he looked up towards the altar, his expression shaded with grief.

'Today is the second anniversary of the day my life changed for ever. When . . . ' — she heard him gulp and clear his throat before he could continue — ' . . . she died in my arms, I not only lost her, but I lost my faith. Why would God cause so much pain and suffering to my beautiful wife whom I loved with a passion? Why would he tear us apart after just a year of marriage?

'I've always strived to be a good man; I didn't understand what I'd done to deserve it. I still don't — it's unfathomable. I tell the relatives of my departed patients that the feelings subside, that time heals, but it's a lie. Nothing heals the wounds. Even though you do your best to cover them, they continue to fester underneath. I've prayed and prayed, and God hasn't answered me.'

'You're an unbeliever?' Hannah recalled how she'd gradually come to terms with the loss of her half-brother, trusting that one day they would meet in Heaven. Not to have that comfort would be unbearable.

'I don't know. I've not been able to move on from those thoughts. I recall the day as if it were yesterday: the sweet fragrance of roses outside the open window; the sound of gulls on the roof; the metallic taste of tea that our housekeeper brought up to the sickroom — she'd forgotten the sugar. Suzanna's death haunts me from the dawn of each day to the next.'

Hannah's heart went out to him. The doctor was in as much need of healing as his patients, but who and what would cure him?

'I also lost faith in medicine. What use could I be when I couldn't save my own? I took a few months away to travel, but when I returned, the doubts remained. Am I really helping these people? Or am I giving them false hope?' His tone was run through with misery.

'Everyone dies eventually,' Hannah said. 'Medicine hasn't discovered the elixir of eternal life on Earth, but we must trust in God and that life goes on in Heaven.' She realised her words would sound empty to an unbeliever. 'Doctor Clifton, you must trust me, too, when I say that you're an excellent physician. The patients not only respect you, they like you. You go out of your way to help them.' She stopped abruptly, remembering the incident with the knitting needle.

'Well, I thank you for your belief in me. Oh dear, I shouldn't have inflicted my sorrows on you . . . You must think me weak,' he muttered.

'Not at all,' she said gently, wondering how much courage it had taken him to talk. She couldn't imagine her father expressing feelings of regret and sadness, if he had any, in such a frank manner.

The doctor smiled sadly. 'I'll be back to my normal self tomorrow.'

'I wish you a peaceful evening,' she said, standing up. He stood too and walked with her to the door.

'Goodnight,' he said, letting her go ahead of him.

She returned to the nurses' home, deep in thought. Having shared in his grief, she felt she had formed a closer connection with him, akin to friendship. She guessed that Doctor Clifton threw himself into his work as a way of coping with his wife's passing. She wished she'd known what to say or do to console a doctor who felt too much.

6

What's Sauce for the Goose is Sauce for the Gander

When she arrived on the ward the next morning, she looked for Peter, but it was Alan Allspice who gazed back from the bed. He was fifteen, older than the other boys on the Lettsom.

'Top o' the mornin' to you, Nurse,' he said politely, recognising her from a few days before.

'How are you today?' she asked.

'I've told 'im, 'e'll only get worse comin' in 'ere,' Charlie interrupted from the bed next door. 'Look at the dirty toe-rag takin' Peter's bed when it's still warm.'

'Oh, Charlie, you can't say things like that.' Hannah moved up beside him. 'Peter was very poorly, and yes, we lost him, and we all feel terrible about it, but life has to go on. There are hundreds, thousands of boys like him — like you and Alan here — who deserve the chance to be well again.'

Charlie fell silent, tears rolling down his face.

A different doctor turned up for rounds, causing some consternation among the nurses. Doctor Pyle, the resident physician, was middle-aged, quiet and efficient. Charlie was to continue with his saltwater baths and daily quarter-pint of seawater, while Alan was to begin a regime of baths and further treatment on consultation with Doctor Clifton, who'd been delayed, preparing for the Board meeting later that day.

Hannah was called at eleven o'clock and shown by Mr Mordikai to the boardroom.

'I don't think you'll be expected to speak,' he muttered, opening the door for her. 'Mrs Knowles wishes to show off her latest protégée.'

She took a seat on one of the chairs beside Matron, and glanced at the lists of governors written in gold leaf on mahogany panels on the walls, and the paintings of Doctor Lettsom and other dignitaries who'd been involved with the infirmary.

Thanks to Charlotte, she had some idea of how the hierarchy worked. Queen Victoria was patron, then there was a Court of Directors in London, and under that, the Margate Local Management Committee. Anyone who gave ten pounds could become a governor and donate a ticket to admit one patient each year. Matron looked after the nurses and patients, while Mr Cumberpatch looked after the maintenance and general running of the house.

'We will reconvene,' the chairman said. 'The next item on the agenda is the complaint raised by Mr Anthony, resident surgeon, against Doctor Clifton, visiting physician.' He peered over his spectacles. 'Will those two gentlemen make themselves known?'

They stood, one at each end of the row of seats.

'Mr Phillips, I'm most grateful to have this opportunity of stating my case to the Board of this magnificent house,' Mr Anthony began.

Hannah remembered Doctor Clifton's patient, Mrs Phillips, and that her husband was Chairman of the Board. They were an odd couple, she thought, certain that Mr Phillips, with his white hair and long salt-and-pepper moustache, couldn't be less than sixty years old.

'Your preference is that Doctor Clifton be removed from his position as visiting physician, due to a disagreement over the treatment of one of your patients, a Master Herring,' Mr Phillips said, reading from his notes. 'Doctor Clifton, what do you have to say for yourself?'

'Only that I apologise if Mr Anthony thinks that I spoke out of turn. We come from different backgrounds and contrasting disciplines, but we have the same aim, to improve the lives of our patients.'

'You did speak out of turn,' Mr Anthony said crossly.

'Please remain silent unless you're spoken to,' Mr Phillips barked. 'The outcome of your preferred option for Master Herring's treatment was unsatisfactory, was it not? What happened to the patient?'

'He ... um, unfortunately ... died post-surgery,' Mr Anthony muttered.

'In that case, I put it to the Board that there is no case to answer, as we can never know if medicine alone would have cured this poor boy.'

The members of the Board voted, and the motion was carried unanimously.

Mr Phillips summed up.

'It's a shame that there's such conflict between

the physicians and surgeons, and the medical men and nurses, for that matter. Gentlemen, shake hands and be done with it. We'll move on to the next item on the agenda, which is . . . the provision of a new Turkish rug to replace the existing one in the reception hall . . . '

'You may leave now, Nurse Bentley,' Mrs Knowles whispered. 'Common sense has prevailed, thank goodness. I wouldn't want to see either of them leave the house.'

Hannah returned to the Lettsom. She asked one of the lady volunteers to read Charlie a story, something uplifting, but she chose a tract from the Bible, being avid in her wish to improve the children's minds. Charlie sat with his arms folded, frowning, as she read. When he glanced across at Hannah, he seemed to frown even harder.

'I sat and listened for you, Nurse,' he said afterwards.

'Did you enjoy it?'

'Out of respect for your feelin's, I'll say that I did.'

After their break, Hannah and Charlotte continued cleaning and tidying until visiting time started at two. Neither Alan nor Charlie received any visitors, and the pitiful expression on Charlie's face reminded Hannah of waiting for her own mother who'd never arrived.

She'd been three years old and, although her memories were vague, the image of Ma's glittering smile, Ruby's mop of dark hair, and Ma's white bed-coat was as vibrant as if it was yesterday. Ma had let her perch on the edge of the mattress and touch the infant's cheek. She'd told her she was proud of her for being so gentle, that she would make the best big sister in the entire world, and then she'd hugged Hannah and whispered, 'I love you, little one.'

That had been the last time she'd seen her.

There had been much discussion behind closed doors, then a nurse had been summoned before Ma had gone away for a rest. A few weeks after that, Pa had called Hannah to his study to tell her that Ma had been taken up by the angels and he was engaged to be married to the woman who would become their stepmother.

There'd been no sugar to sweeten the bitter pill of that loss, but on the ward at teatime, the boys — some of whom had cried when their mothers had gone — were given extra treacle on toast as a treat to restore their spirits.

'I could do with extra treacle to cheer me up,' Hannah said aside to Charlotte as the maid cleared the plates away. 'I'm worried that I haven't received a letter from my sister. I've written to her a second time, asking her to write back by return of post, but I've heard nothing. I hope she isn't unwell.'

'You could write to your stepmother,' Charlotte suggested, 'but as I've said before, you're probably fretting unnecessarily. I expect she'll be in touch soon.'

Hannah changed the subject. 'By the way, I wanted to ask you — do you know what happened to Doctor Clifton's wife?'

'Oh, it was a terrible thing, an accident.' Charlotte kept her voice down. 'Her nightgown caught fire — she was horribly burned and lingered for a long time afterwards. I don't think he'll ever get over it. He hasn't walked out with anyone since — as far as I know, at least.'

'It's no wonder. I can't imagine anything worse.'

Charlotte glanced around. 'Quickly, Trimmie's on the warpath,' she said, moving away.

'Nurse Bentley, Charlie has been sick on his bedclothes,' Sister Trim called.

It was the last thing she needed, she thought, hurrying to his side with a bowl, cloths and fresh linen.

'I got the mullygrubs,' he groaned.

'I'm not surprised you have bellyache — you've eaten too much treacle.'

'Will you call Doctor Clifton for me? 'E'll make it better.'

'I'm not going to disturb him now. I'll give you some gripe water and a wash.' She turned briefly to Alan who had rolled himself up into a ball, like a hedgehog, with just his bad leg stretched out to one side. 'What on earth are you doing?'

'Practisin',' he mumbled.

''E's in the circus,' Charlie said, impressed. ''E's goin' to show me 'ow to be a con-tor-tion-ist.' His complexion paled. She thrust the bowl under his chin just in time. It had been a day of mixed fortunes.

★ ★ ★

Three more weeks passed and, even though she'd written twice more, addressing her letters

111

to the neighbour, Miss Fellows, Hannah still hadn't heard back from Ruby. She did hear back from their stepmother, though, having decided to write to her at Charlotte's suggestion. Her reply had been both reassuring and disturbing at the same time.

Ruby was in trouble with Pa over an incident with the butcher's boy, and that's all Stepmother would say about it, except to add that her sister was well, and accepting of her punishment. She expressed her desire that Hannah would stop putting ideas of leaving home into Ruby's head because she was young and foolish, and it would break Stepmother's heart because she'd grown very fond of her.

Hannah realised that their stepmother — and probably Pa too — must have read her letters. All she could do now was keep writing inconsequential notes to her sister, just to let her know she was thinking of her. She didn't want to cause her any further difficulty with Pa, and she didn't know what else to do.

It was the third week of June and Sister Trim had been pushing her, telling her that if she wanted to be a sister, she'd have to prove she was capable. Hannah didn't think it would go down too well if she asked for unpaid leave so soon to go to Canterbury to speak to Ruby face-to-face.

One morning, the doctors turned up as usual. Mr Anthony and Doctor Clifton had called a truce, and Mr Hunter, who joined them on the ward a couple of times a week, appeared to have taken notice of his cousin's advice and was attending to his studies most diligently, asking questions and taking notes.

'How are you, Master Swift?' Doctor Clifton asked, after he'd greeted everyone.

'I'm feelin' well, but me knee does ache so.'

'Let me have a look.' Charlie had been fitted with a Thomas splint at the beginning of June. An iron ring padded with leather was fitted around the highest point of Charlie's leg, while two iron rods ran down to a ring beneath his foot. The splint was held on by means of a leather strap across his shoulder, while traction was provided by more straps stretched tight between the two rings. 'What is your opinion, Mr Hunter?'

Mr Hunter hummed and hawed for a while. Hannah flashed a glance at Charlotte. She felt for him — the presence of his superiors seemed to have knocked his confidence.

'I think that the splint is in compression,' he said eventually.

'What does that mean for the patient?' Doctor Clifton asked.

'Um, it means . . . '

'Spit it out, man,' Mr Anthony muttered from behind him. 'We haven't got all day.'

'What I mean is that the patient has grown, but the splint hasn't. It needs to be replaced with a larger one, to relieve the pressure on the knee joint which is causing the pain.'

'That's right,' Doctor Clifton agreed. 'Charlie, Nurse Bentley will arrange a time for you to go back to the workshop for a new splint. Mr Anthony, I will write to Mr Piper at St Pancras to request that Master Swift remains here for a further six weeks after his ticket runs out. He has been here a month already and another two weeks won't be long enough.'

'I'd like to go 'ome and see Ma.'

'The next few weeks will fly by,' Hannah said.

'Must I still 'ave a bath every day?' Charlie asked.

'Oh yes,' Doctor Clifton said. 'You may not be going into the sea, but you are benefitting from the saltwater in your baths. I didn't believe in the miracle of a daily dip in the sea until I came to Margate and tried it for myself. The water is most invigorating.'

'What's sauce for the goose is sauce for the gander,' Mr Anthony observed.

'You should try it, Nurse,' Doctor Clifton said, making her blush.

She wouldn't be seen dead in a bathing dress, even protected from view by a bathing machine. As it was, it had seemed terribly daring to expose her ankles while paddling with Charlotte . . . A memory of the men splashing around in the distance came into her head, and suddenly, she didn't know which way to turn. She felt sure that she'd seen Doctor Clifton and his cousin cavorting shirtless in the sea.

'Nurse Bentley . . . Nurse, this is the second time I've asked you for your report on Master Allspice . . . ' she heard Mr Anthony say as Charlotte gave her a dig in the ribs.

Recovering herself, she summarised his vital signs, level of pain and appetite.

'I'm glad to see you're paying attention,' Mr Anthony said sarcastically. 'Perhaps you should consider getting more sleep — you look as if you've been burning the candle at both ends.'

She bit her tongue as she watched the surgeon poke and pull Alan's leg, making him grimace and cry out.

'This patient will benefit from a further spell in traction,' he said, and Alan's face fell. He'd been confined to bed in traction before, and Mr Anthony had decided that he'd shown enough improvement for the splint to be removed, but it seemed that Alan's condition had deteriorated since.

'Doctor Clifton, you'll arrange this for later this morning?'

He nodded. 'Nurse Bentley can bring him to the examination room at eleven. Mr Hunter will seek out the splint we used before, then come and assist.'

The doctors moved on, but Mr Hunter lingered.

'Nurse Finch, where do you think this splint will be?' Hannah heard him ask.

'I don't know,' she said. 'We wouldn't keep it on the ward.'

'Could it be in one of the cupboards or bathing rooms? Perhaps you could help me search for it.'

'I'm sorry — I have work to do. Why don't you try the workshop?'

'Ah, good idea. Thank you. I'm indebted to you . . .'

'Mr Hunter, I have to get on, or Trimmie — I mean, Sister Trim — will be after me.'

After he'd left the ward, Charlotte hastened over to where Hannah was helping Charlie put on the boot she'd borrowed from the infirmary's stores. He wore it on the foot without the splint, so he could walk around.

'Does that man really think I have time to look after him?' Charlotte hissed. 'Honestly!'

'It's so obvious,' Hannah smiled. 'He's taken a fancy to you.'

'No? Do you think so?'

Hannah nodded. 'That's why he asked you to help him look for the splint.'

Charlotte blushed. 'He is very handsome, but he's such a boor when he's with his friends.'

'Haven't you noticed how he's reformed recently?'

'He seems to have taken a special interest in children's orthopaedics,' Charlotte observed.

'Don't be silly — he's taking a special interest in you.'

'As Doctor Clifton is with you, Hannah. It has been noticed . . . There's no point denying it.'

'He treats everyone the same — with respect and kindness. Besides, he's still in mourning for his wife.'

'Doesn't it make a gentleman seem more attractive, knowing he has a broken heart and needs an angel to come along and heal him?' Charlotte mused. 'Oh no!' She squealed and leapt away. 'It ran over my foot . . . '

'What is it? What's wrong?' Hannah exclaimed.

Sister Trim came hurrying up to them, and a bathing assistant who had just come into the ward to collect a patient screamed.

'A mouse!' Charlotte flapped her apron. 'Where did it go? I can't see it.'

'It's all right, ladies,' Charlie said from behind them. 'I'll get it.' Despite his splint, he scrambled under one of the beds with a dish and storybook, then reappeared with the book over the top of the dish.

'Oh well done Master Swift.' Hannah clapped.

'What shall I do with it?'

'Take it outside and let it go,' Charlotte exclaimed.

'It'll come straight back in,' Sister Trim said.

'I wouldn't like any harm to come to it,' Charlotte went on. 'It's one of God's creatures, after all.'

'We could send it to the 'All by the Sea,' Alan joined in. 'They keep lots of animals there.'

'Not mice,' Sister Trim said. 'Who would pay to see vermin?'

'Why don't we ask one of the porters to release it?' Hannah suggested.

The problem was solved. The mouse was carried away to its new quarters, wherever they were.

'Really,' Sister Trim said, losing her composure and allowing herself a chuckle, seeming to break her rule that a moment of laughter would lead to a lifetime of misery. 'Never has something so small caused so much consternation. Back to your work. Immediately. And make sure you clean up thoroughly after that disgusting creature's been in here.'

It wasn't long before Hannah was with Doctor Clifton and Mr Hunter in one of the examination rooms, where Alan was lying on a trolley, his eyes dark with apprehension.

'It'll soon be over,' she reassured him.

'You weren't 'ere the last time Doctor Clifton did it,' he said. 'It 'urts more than anythin', even more than when Pa used to bend me into shape when I was a littlun. 'E used to twist me up and leave me until my bones felt like they were goin' to break apart and I'd spew up with the pain.'

'That wasn't a kind thing to do.' The thought of it brought tears to Hannah's eyes. 'How old were you?'

'Three or four — it 'as to be done while your bones are soft.'

'Did you hear that, Doctor Clifton?' Hannah asked.

'I did. I can assure you, Master Allspice, that this will be painful, but it won't hurt for long. The improvement you'll obtain from a few more weeks in traction will far outweigh a few minutes of discomfort. Henry, you have found the right splint?'

'It's here.' He held out two metal frames, one for each leg, along with a pole and a series of straps.

Hannah held Alan's hand as Doctor Clifton oversaw Mr Hunter applying the apparatus.

'I can see that you need more practice,' he observed as Hannah began to wilt in the heat. She wished she'd thought to open the window. 'The straps must be secure before attaching the end of the pole and ties to the bars of the trolley.'

'Yes, Doctor Clifton, I can see that,' Mr Hunter said.

'Keep talking and explaining what you're doing. Ignorance is often the basis of a patient's fear.'

Mr Hunter completed setting up the splint

before telling Alan that the next step was to apply the traction. Doctor Clifton would steady him while Mr Hunter turned the crank to extend the pole.

Hannah felt Alan's grip tighten on her fingers as Doctor Clifton took his place and Mr Hunter began to turn the crank, a quarter turn at a time. On each occasion, Doctor Clifton checked the angle of Alan's hip before recommending another quarter turn.

'That must be enough,' Alan gasped, as his leg stretched.

'You're doing well,' Hannah murmured. She didn't feel so good, her fingers crushed and perspiration trickling down her back. The room began to spin.

'Let's have another one, Mr Hunter,' Doctor Clifton said.

With the next turn of the crank, there was a horrible crunch of grating bones. Alan screeched in agony, and Hannah swooned.

'Let her have some air,' she heard Doctor Clifton say as she recovered consciousness.

'They are both in a faint,' Mr Hunter said, surprised.

'That's a good thing in a way — it means that the patient won't say anything when he's back on the ward. You won't mention this, will you, Henry? Nurse Bentley will be mortified. Wheel Master Allspice back for me. I'll deal with this.'

Hearing the squeak of the trolley as Mr Hunter steered it out of the examination room, Hannah tried to sit up, but she hadn't the strength.

'Stay there for a while, or you'll be straight

down on the floor again . . . and I'll have to catch you for a second time.' She looked up to where Doctor Clifton was kneeling beside her. A smile played on his mouth as he continued, 'Not that I'd find that too much of a hardship.'

'You are flirting with me?'

'You could say that.' He grinned, and her heart missed a beat and another, until she felt quite faint again. She didn't know whether to be affronted or relieved that he'd caught her — it was the first time a gentleman had laid a finger on her, apart from Mr Adamson's fumbling attempt at a kiss.

The room had stopped spinning, but she was shocked at her own unexpected response. She had considered the doctor quite average in appearance, but close up and having got to know him a little, she found him very handsome.

'I feel such a fool,' she said, scolding herself inwardly for her weakness. 'I've never fainted before.'

'It's the heat, and you've been overexerting yourself. I've seen you. We're both guilty of going beyond the call of duty, but you mustn't do it to the point of exhaustion.' He reached out as if he was going to touch her face, then changed his mind, abruptly pulling his hand away.

'You won't say anything? I don't want to lose my place.'

'I won't breathe a word to anyone, and I'll make sure Henry doesn't either.

'I'd be very grateful.'

'Promise me that you'll go home on time this evening.'

'I'll try.'

'I'll let you into a secret — I fainted when I was training to be a physician. As well as studying in Greek and Latin, we were obliged to observe various operations. The first one I attended, an osteotomy, was so brutal and bloody that I blacked out.'

'I don't believe you,' she said. 'This is but a feeble attempt to make me feel better.'

'It's true. I went to my supervisor and told him I'd have to leave. He persuaded me that I would become hardened to it, and the rest is history. Let me find you some ale and a sweet biscuit before you return to the ward.'

'Don't worry — Sister will be wondering where I've got to.'

'I must insist that you follow my orders — I'm the doctor here.' Chuckling, he stood up and left the room. Hannah picked up her skirts and took a seat on the chair in the corner. She touched her cheeks — they were on fire. Minutes later, her saviour was back. She sipped the cool ale and nibbled at the biscuit as he hovered beside her, his eyes filled with concern.

'There's no harm in letting somebody look after you now and again.'

'I have to confess it is rather pleasant,' she said, revelling in the attention. 'Thank you. I feel much better, but I'm so sorry for putting you to the trouble — '

'It's been no trouble, Nurse Bentley. No trouble at all.'

She stood up and brushed the crumbs from her apron.

'Allow me to hold the door for you,' he said, hastening towards it at the same time as her so they bumped arms.

'I'm sorry . . . ' they both said, making Hannah giggle as he opened the door with a flourish.

'After you.'

'Thank you, Doctor Clifton,' she said, sweeping past.

★　★　★

The sensation that she was walking on air soon turned to a sense of confusion. Every time she saw him or thought of him, which was much more often than could be considered reasonable, she had palpitations. Falling in love with a doctor wasn't part of her plan, and she was determined not to let it go any further.

7

The Parade of the Animals

Hannah sat at the dressing table and gazed at her reflection in the mirror. A week had passed since the embarrassing incident with Doctor Clifton and Mr Hunter, and she'd taken advantage of her afternoon off to go shopping and attend the early evening service at the chapel. She'd also checked the price of tickets and the times of the trains from Canterbury and started to look at how to go about acquiring lodgings in Margate, in case Ruby came to join her sooner rather than later. She shouldn't keep worrying about her, she told herself. Even though Pa had treated Stepmother cruelly, there was no way she'd let Ruby come to harm. As for the incident with the butcher's boy, whatever that was, she couldn't imagine that it was anything so serious that it wouldn't soon blow over.

For now, she had other, more pressing concerns.

'I'm home,' Charlotte called. She came into the room and saw Hannah's face in the mirror. 'Oh, what have you done?'

Hannah felt like a little girl who'd been caught out by her nanny doing something naughty.

'You're bright red!'

Hannah touched the tip of her nose where the skin had blistered.

'Have you been out in the sun all afternoon?'

'I thought I'd try to bleach some of these freckles away,' she confessed.

'Why?' Charlotte stopped behind her and rested her hands on the back of the chair. 'Does it have anything to do with your dalliance with Doctor Clifton? Everyone's talking about it, how he spends an awful lot of time on the Lettsom, and addresses you in preference to anyone else, even Trimmie.'

'This has nothing to do with him,' Hannah retorted.

'If you say so, but seriously, though, what on earth possessed you?'

'It was just that I heard somebody mention that carbolic can get rid of facial blemishes . . . '

'I've heard that too, but one of the side effects is that it causes wrinkles.'

'Then I will look as if I've aged twenty years overnight.' Hannah railed in silence at her stupidity. It had been a moment of weakness, a surrender to vanity. 'What am I going to do?'

'We'll tell anyone who asks that you fell asleep in the sun, and when you woke up, you were burnt to a cinder.'

'I've been trying to tell myself that it isn't that bad.'

'It is pretty dreadful. You look as if you have a high fever.' Charlotte grinned. 'Maybe the good doctor will offer to mop your brow.'

Hannah stood up. 'This is terrible — he'll think I'm a flibbertigibbet like his sisters. What will Trimmie say? And Matron?'

'It'll be all right in a couple of days,' Charlotte

said soothingly. 'Tell you what — let me go and beg some lard from the kitchens. That's supposed to be good for the skin, wrinkles especially.'

'You won't tell them what it's for?'

'I'll say it's for you . . . ' Charlotte's eyes twinkled with humour. 'Of course I won't! I'll be back soon.'

★ ★ ★

The next morning, Hannah went in to work.

'Nurse, there's something different about you,' Sister Trim pounced on her straight away. 'Are you wearing the devil's fakery?'

'I stayed out in the sun too long,' Hannah lied.

'A nurse should be more careful with her health if she's to set an example to her patients.'

'I know. I'm sorry,' she said, blushing. She felt like a freak, her face red and shiny, and smelling of lard which had gone rancid overnight.

The rest of the staff were polite, behaving as though there was nothing untoward in her appearance, but her patients were perfectly blunt.

'What 'ave you done to yer face?' Charlie asked.

'Someone's bin in the sun too long,' Alan said.

'Does it 'urt?' Charlie went on softly.

'A little,' she replied.

'My ma swears by cold cream,' Alan said.

'Or you can eat them wafers like the ladies who come to read to us,' Charlie added. 'Mrs Phillips told us about 'em.'

125

'Did she?' Hannah said, surprised.

'I asked 'er why she looked like a ghost, and she said — what was it?' He looked up at the ceiling, thinking. 'I remember now. She's 'fashionably pale'.'

'That one looks like she should be in 'ospital 'erself for lack of blood,' Alan said.

'Well, thank you for your contributions, but you really shouldn't be talking about the ladies who volunteer their time to entertain you,' Hannah scolded before attending to her duties, hoping that she wouldn't run into Doctor Clifton.

At visiting time, she kept her head down as she had done all day, trying not to be noticed while the mothers and fathers sat with their respective children on the balcony or in the ward. The sound of coarse laughter echoed through from the balcony. Charlie remained in his bed, looking mournful.

'Why don't you go outside for a while?' she suggested. 'The sunshine will make you feel better.'

'It didn't do you any good, did it?' he said, looking at her with a cheeky smile.

She had to smile back, despite his impudence.

'Is there something wrong?' she asked.

'I miss my ma,' he confided.

'I see.' It had to be hard for him to see his fellow patients surrounded by the love of their families while he had no one. 'I'm sure she's thinking of you even though she can't be here.'

'I dunno,' he said, folding his arms.

Hannah reached out and squeezed his

shoulder. 'Keep your chin up, young man. It won't be long before Doctor Clifton sends you back to London.'

'Yeah,' he sighed. 'If only this knee would get movin' like it should, then I could go back to Ma and make sure she's all right.'

Hannah could have cried for him. All she could offer was reassurance.

When the visitors had gone, and the ward was settling back to normal, Sister Trim turned up to inspect Hannah's work.

'You haven't done your corners properly. Do them again.'

Hannah's heart sank. There was nothing wrong with her corners — she could make a bed just as well as any of them. Either Sister had a higher set of standards especially for her, or she was giving her extra work, seeing how far she could push her before she broke.

'Yes, Sister.' She returned to the bed she had just changed and started again, pulling off the freshly laundered sheets which smelled sweetly of soap and the outdoors. As she redid the corners, smoothing and folding them neatly so they enveloped the mattress, Charlotte sidled up with the trolley of clean laundry.

'Did you have the pleasure — I say that with irony — of meeting the dreadful Allspices?'

'I think I heard Mr Allspice laughing out on the balcony, loud enough to wake the dead,' Hannah said.

'That doesn't surprise me. The father wanted to check on Alan's progress, so he started releasing the traction, can you believe it? Sister

Trim had to give him a good telling-off, and then he started arguing with his wife for being on Trimmie's side. Apparently, Alan's booked to perform at the circus very soon, and Mr Allspice wants him out of here in time for it. He's prepared to go against doctor's orders and undo their good work.'

'Then he's a fool.'

'Oh, he's a fool all right. Alan said he wished the ground would swallow him up — I think he meant his father, not himself. Anyway, Mr Allspice did bring exciting news — they're planning to bring the animals from the Hall by the Sea on to the wards.'

'Really?' Charlie was still sitting glumly in bed. Perhaps this would cheer him up, Hannah thought. 'How come?'

'It's a thank you to the infirmary for looking after his boy.'

'I'll tell Master Swift,' Hannah said, but it seemed that he already knew.

'I 'eard you.' He smiled. 'Do you think they'll bring the lions?'

'I doubt it. Mr Anthony will have to sew your heads back on if they do.'

'You're scaring him,' Charlotte said. 'Spare a thought for the night staff. And us, for that matter. Imagine cleaning the floors after a parade of animals. Trimmie's furious — she said they shouldn't come, but Matron's overruled her.'

'It will give the children such a lift to see them, though.' It would brighten their day as well, Hannah thought. Any change on the ward was as good as a rest.

She recalled the day when, having begged Pa in vain to let them go to the circus, Nanny had taken it upon herself to take the four Bentley children out for a walk around Canterbury, an expedition which had fortuitously coincided with the parade as it passed along St Dunstan's to Westgate Towers.

Hannah had been fifteen, Ruby twelve and the twins nine years old, and just about to start as choristers at the cathedral. They had formed a procession themselves, the girls in front, the boys next and Nanny walking along behind, until they'd met with the crowd that was spilling from the pavements and into the street. It had seemed that the whole of Canterbury had turned out to see the spectacle — except for Pa and Stepmother.

'Make way for the children,' Nanny ordered, prodding the people in front of them with her umbrella. 'They can't see.' As a couple parted to allow them through, Nanny pushed through too.

'Now we can't see,' the woman complained.

'I can't possibly let these little ones out of my sight,' Nanny said. 'Hannah, hold Ruby's hand.'

'I'm too grown-up for that,' Ruby hissed, pushing Hannah aside.

'It's Nanny's orders,' Hannah said as they were swept closer to the edge of the pavement, but Ruby ignored her. Hannah turned to look for the twins — Nanny had hold of their hands and they were standing quietly, like little angels — while Ruby bounced up and down on the balls of her feet, her eyes flashing with excitement.

A marching band with drums and trumpets appeared through the central arch of the towers, followed by a gilded carriage drawn by four cream horses wearing state harness. Britannia, carrying a gold shield and trident, sat inside it, with a lion and a lamb at her feet.

'Why don't the lion eat the lamb?' someone said.

'It's a miracle, if you ask me. Look, there's Lord Sanger.' Another pointed at the second carriage which conveyed a man in a top hat, who was waving to the crowd.

'He i'n't no Lord — that's just what 'e calls 'imself. 'E's plain George, and that glamorous wife of 'is, Madame de Vere, is in fact Ellen Chapman.'

'You're jealous 'cause 'e's made 'imself a millionaire out of makin' entertainment for the common people.'

'Oh look, what is that?' Theo said, pointing. The twins were dressed in matching sailor's outfits. They were blonde-haired and blue-eyed with delicate lashes and pouting mouths, not like their half-sisters at all.

'It's a camel — it stores food and water in its humps,' Nanny said knowledgeably. Pa had selected her from the best candidates in London, and she was young and enthusiastic about education.

After the camel, the clowns — in chequered pantaloons with fearsome smiles painted on their faces — came tumbling by, followed by the freaks who looked down from carts pulled along by spotted horses.

'Who are those poor people?' Hannah asked.

'They are the curiosities. Their unfortunate appearances are a consequence of their own sins, and those of their fathers,' Nanny said.

What had they done to deserve their fate? Hannah stared at the Wolf Woman whose face was covered in long, dark hair. Then there was a child — no, twins — joined at the chest, and the World's Fattest Man.

Hannah felt a sense of relief when the elephants came through, ambling along, one behind the other, trunk to tail in order of decreasing size. She was so busy watching the baby elephant gambolling along at the end of the line that she didn't notice Ruby step off the pavement until it was too late. There was a cry of pain as the smallest one playfully knocked her to the ground.

'Oh, Ruby, what have you done?' Nanny stepped forwards. 'Hannah, I told you to hold her hand.'

'It isn't Hannah's fault. I tripped,' Ruby stammered, knowing that she'd done wrong.

'I'm going to be in a lot of trouble,' Nanny said fearfully, her face whiter than Ruby's. 'Perhaps it will be all right. Let me help you up.'

It soon became clear that Ruby's arm had been broken. Within the hour, they had returned to the smart four-storey townhouse on Dane John with its stone parapet and iron balcony. The bonesetter was called for, Nanny sent packing and the girls put to bed. Pa made them both suffer a month of bread, gruel and rice pudding to cure Ruby's intemperate behaviour and violent emotion.

'Your daughters are running wild without Nanny's guiding hand,' Stepmother complained a week or two later, in front of Hannah who'd been doing some embroidery in the peace and quiet of the parlour.

'Why don't you take some responsibility for them?' Pa closed his book and put it aside. 'You complain of having no occupation.'

'I don't know what I can do. Hannah is a strange child — she takes no notice of anyone. I can't believe she sprang from your loins. Perhaps she didn't. Perhaps you were cuckolded. I wouldn't blame her. Mercy must have been driven mad being here with you.'

What was a cuckold? Hannah wondered. She wished Ma was there to explain.

'But Ruby is a sweet girl,' Stepmother continued. 'When she's dressed up, she looks like a tiny doll.'

'That's all very well, but when we married, we did so on the understanding that you would take on the role of mother, looking after the moral education of my daughters.'

'That was your understanding, not mine. Oh, you are so very dull. You promised me dinners, dances and the company of high society, yet I can't remember when we last went out together. I think you would have me locked away and kept prisoner for the rest of my life.'

'We have an invitation to dine at the Mostyns' next week,' Pa said.

'I hope you've declined. I can't bear those people. Mrs Mostyn is always talking about the good she does for the poor, and her husband does nothing but complain about his infirmities.'

'They're friends of mine, and I wish to spend time with them in the company of my wife. Mr Edison from the bank will be there too.'

'Ugh, I detest that man. I wish you wouldn't keep inviting him here — I don't like the way he looks at the girls, Hannah especially. I won't go,' Stepmother said.

'You have no choice. As the head of this household, I have the final word. You will be ready on the allotted day at the required time, dressed in your green gown and with a willing smile on your pretty features.'

'I won't go,' Stepmother repeated, and Pa rose from his seat, his fists clenching as he leaned close to her and growled, 'You are my wife — you will obey me. If you don't do as I say, I promise I'll drag you kicking and screaming to the Mostyns'.'

The blood drained from Stepmother's face. 'You wouldn't?'

'I'm not in the habit of making false promises. Dry your tears, Miranda.' Pa returned to his chair, picked up his book again and started to read, and Stepmother stormed out of the room, slamming the door behind her. 'That woman has no decorum,' Pa muttered, 'no decorum at all.'

* * *

Hannah returned to the present, smoothing the sheet and folding it so it sat flat across the mattress. There was nothing for Trimmie to

133

criticise — gone were the days when her corners had looked like dogs' ears.

*   *   *

Hannah's complexion and her confidence returned to normal quite quickly, and although Alan complained a lot, his hip was improving again under traction. After another three days, he was allowed out of bed on crutches and there was talk of him going back to the circus.

That evening, Hannah walked home with Charlotte.

'It's so busy I can almost believe that I'm back in London,' she said, dodging the families and couples who thronged the seafront, making the most of the warm summer evening. Glancing at the pale blue sky and skeins of pink cloud, she found herself wishing that she could be walking arm in arm with Doctor Clifton.

'I've heard that the wives stay here all week while their husbands join them on Sundays. I don't think I'd like that — if I was married, I'd want to keep an eye on mine,' Charlotte observed.

'Has Mr Hunter said anything to you?' Hannah teased. 'He hasn't asked you to go looking for any more splints with him recently?'

Charlotte didn't reply. She had stopped to look behind her.

'I think someone's stalking us. I've had this feeling since we left the house.'

'You're imagining things.' Hannah followed her gaze back along the road, taking in the horse and carriage moving smartly along the gravel, the group of teetering ladies dressed in straw bonnets, and a man carrying a bucket of herring.

'I'm not. I'm certain of it. Didn't you see her?'

No sooner had Hannah spotted the figure in a hooded cloak, struggling along with a bag and hatbox, than it vanished again behind a haycart. Hannah hesitated, her heart beating faster. There was something very familiar about the young woman . . .

'It's my sister!' she exclaimed. 'She's here in Margate!'

Charlotte slipped her arm through Hannah's, and they hurried back down the road as the figure reappeared.

'Ruby!' Hannah cried as they reached her. 'You should have warned me you were coming!'

Ruby dropped her luggage and pulled down her hood, revealing tears running down her face. Her dark brown eyes were filled with fear, and her hair, in waves the colour of stout, was dishevelled.

'I couldn't,' she sobbed. 'When Pa found out I was sending letters without his permission, he locked me up. He made me a prisoner in my room. Only the maid was allowed in with food and water, and to empty the chamber pot.' She flung her arms around Hannah's neck and clung to her like a limpet.

'Oh, I'm so sorry, Ruby,' Hannah said. 'Are you all right?'

'I'm all the better for seeing you,' she said, growing calmer as she took a step back. Although she was seventeen, the top of her head came less than halfway up Hannah's chest.

Hannah noticed a welt on her sister's arm. 'What's that, Ruby?'

'It's nothing. A flesh wound. I caught it on a nail as I was climbing out of the window.' She was speaking so quickly that Hannah could hardly make out the words. 'I threw my boxes out on to the roof below, then clambered down the drainpipe under the cover of darkness last night.'

'You could have fallen. Ruby, you could have been killed!' Hannah trembled at the thought.

'I was willing to take the risk. The day before, Pa came to tell me that he'd pay two doctors to sign a certificate of insanity, like he did with Ma. He said I was losing my mind. How could I stay any longer?'

'Did you stay out all night?'

'I walked the streets — I had nowhere to go while I was waiting for the trains to start running this morning, and then I didn't like to disturb you at work.'

Hannah became aware that a small crowd was forming around them.

'Let's go somewhere quiet. I don't want all and sundry knowing our business.' She turned to Charlotte. 'This is my friend, Charlotte. Charlotte, allow me to introduce my sister, Ruby.'

'It's lovely to meet you, although it could have been under better circumstances,' Charlotte said. 'Hannah talks about you often. Come home with us.'

'If that's all right with you,' Hannah said. 'It's

rather an imposition.'

'Not at all. You'd do the same for me — not that I shall ever see my sister again.'

Hannah walked along, holding Ruby's hand like they used to when they were little girls promenading along the city wall in Canterbury with Nanny. She wished she could confront their father and tell him exactly what she thought of him. He'd had Ma locked up and look what had happened. He was even more wicked than she'd imagined for him to have incarcerated Ruby after that.

When they arrived at the nurses' home, Charlotte made herself scarce while Hannah and Ruby talked.

'What did you do to upset Pa like that?' Hannah had to ask.

'It was a punishment for something I didn't do ... I don't know — I seem to be a constant irritation to him, like a flea on a dog.'

'You must have done something.'

'I answered back when he accused me of leading the butcher's boy astray, that's all. And I may have lied to Cook a little.' Ruby's lip trembled. 'You have to believe me.'

'Oh, I do. Of course I do. I know what Pa's like. Here, dry your eyes.' Hannah handed her a handkerchief. 'It's done now, and we must think of the future. You'll stay with me in Margate.'

Ruby jumped nervously when the door opened, and Charlotte reappeared.

'Come and join us,' Hannah said. 'We're making plans.'

'Ruby can stay with us tonight, if that's what

you're about to ask, then you can start looking for somewhere to live tomorrow. I'll ask Trimmie if I can swap my afternoon off with you, if it helps.'

'Thank you — that would be a great kindness.'

'We should celebrate. There's fruit cake in the tin and half a dozen bottles of ale under my bed.'

They sat and talked for a couple of hours before retiring. Hannah shared her bed with Ruby who fell asleep, exhausted, while Hannah lay awake, grateful that they'd been reunited.

The next morning, she felt uncomfortable about having to leave Ruby alone and unchaperoned.

'You'll wait here until I get back,' she said. 'There's a lock on the door.'

'I'll have to have breakfast, or I'll fade away.'

'There's more cake. Ruby, I don't want you to feel like a prisoner, but what if Pa comes to find you? I saw you last night when Charlotte opened the door — you're a bag of nerves.'

'I want to go out,' Ruby said softly. 'Even if our father does turn up, what can he do? He can hardly snatch me away against my will, not in front of all those people.'

'We'll have plenty of time to go out this afternoon,' Hannah insisted. 'Promise me you won't leave the house. We'll go and look for lodgings together. I'll use some of my savings, and Grandma's nest egg — she made a proviso that I would use some of it to help you when the occasion arose.'

'Why did she not trust my judgement? No, I mustn't think of that. She meant well, I suppose.'

'What about your belongings?'

'I have my bag and hatbox, and I managed to smuggle a note to Cook who's going to send a trunk of my best clothes to this address in the next day or two, if she can. Hannah, you can't possibly understand how unbearable it's been.' Ruby broke into sobs, and Hannah stayed an extra five minutes after Charlotte had gone to console her, and then she missed breakfast and was late on the ward, much to Trimmie's annoyance and Hannah's discomfiture. Refusing to be cowed by Sister's scolding, Hannah resolved to concentrate on the future. No matter how hard it turned out to be, she would make the best life possible for her and Ruby, something she'd dreamt of since running away from home.

8

A Bitter Pill to Swallow

The sisters walked along the seafront where a horse was pulling a water cart and a workman was hosing the roads to keep the dust down. Hannah had done her best to concentrate on her work that morning, but all she'd been able to think about was whether Ruby was safe. To her relief, she was waiting for her at the nurses' home, looking remarkably cheerful for one who'd suffered so much.

'Where shall we start?' Ruby asked as they walked past Marine Gardens. 'We must have a villa with a sea view.'

'We can't afford to rent a whole establishment. A couple of rooms will suffice, and they mustn't be too far from the infirmary.'

'We must have a parlour at the very least.'

'What on earth for?'

'For receiving callers.'

'I work six days a week, and even if I had the time, the last thing I'd want to do is entertain visitors.' Hannah felt a little sorry for her sister — finding out that she led a quiet life had to be a bitter pill to swallow.

'What's happened to you? You've turned out so very dull,' Ruby blurted out, before quickly apologising. 'You always were the serious one.'

'Somebody has to be,' Hannah sighed.

'We'll go shopping together — it will cheer you up.'

'Another day,' Hannah said, not wanting to dampen her sister's infectious sense of joy. Smiling, she linked arms with her, and they continued along the front, looking at the boats in the harbour where the tide was coming in, lifting them upright, ready to sail out again.

'Fat juicy whelks, a penny a quart . . . Prawns in their shells by the pint . . . ' came the cry of a street-seller. Further along, a band was playing, and a man was showing off his dancing dog, a small white terrier with a patch over one eye and a spotted neckerchief.

'Look at this. Isn't he wonderful?' Ruby said, clasping her hands together.

When his dance was over, the dog picked up a dish and carried it around the crowd, begging for pennies. Hannah gave Ruby a coin for it.

'Thank you for your generosity, ladies and gentlemen,' the man said. 'Mickey'll be able to buy a marrerbone tonight.'

Looking at the man's veiny cheeks and purple nose, Hannah thought it more likely that the money would go on drink than on the dog.

The dog carried the dish back to its owner and put it down in front of him.

'Mickey, that isn't goin' to be enough, is it? You're goin' to 'ave to sing for your supper.' He raised his hand, and the dog sat on its haunches, threw back its head and howled.

'Oh, we must give him another penny,' Ruby said as the dog picked up the now-empty dish and took it around again.

'That's how he makes his money, by tugging on our heartstrings,' Hannah whispered. 'It's the same all over Margate — everyone making hay while the sun shines, because the summer season doesn't last for ever.'

'You would begrudge the poor little dog a bone?'

'All right, but this has to be the last one.' Giving in, she handed her sister another coin. 'We mustn't be distracted from our purpose. I'll be at work all day tomorrow.'

'I wouldn't want to have an occupation. You work too hard.'

'There's no satisfaction to be found in being lazy. Oh dear,' Hannah grinned. 'I'm beginning to sound like Matron.'

'One day, I shall get married, have children and live happily ever after with a rich husband, just like Stepmother.'

'Happily ever after?' Hannah snorted with derision. 'How can she be happy with someone like our father?'

'She doesn't have to work, though, not like you.'

'That isn't the point. She lives under constant threat.'

'Not when he's away at the office.'

'But she doesn't know what mood he'll be in when he gets home. This isn't about our stepmother. I'm talking about you. What if you end up left on the shelf?' It seemed unlikely, Hannah had to admit, because Ruby was a beauty. 'What if your husband falls on hard times? What if he turns out to be a wife-beater? You would be trapped with no means of supporting yourself.'

'Pa's always said that I'm good for nothing except marriage. There's nothing I could do.'

'You have an earnest love of children — I've seen you with our brothers. You can learn to cope with fatigue and control your temper when a sick child wears you down — I've had to.'

'I couldn't be a nurse. I can't imagine attending to the bodily functions of the sick without showing my revulsion,' Ruby said.

'It's a wonderful profession — the children are such fun and it's most rewarding to see them get better. Or you could be a teacher — that's considered to be a respectable profession.'

'Oh, not that. Imagine how dull it would be having to teach the three Rs every day. I'll do the, cooking and cleaning while you're at the infirmary.'

'There's always work at the house — as a bathing assistant or maid. I can put in a good word for you. What do you think?'

'Give me a week or two. I'll need to settle in first.'

'As long as we've found somewhere to live,' Hannah said wryly. 'We're wasting time.'

There were plenty of lodging houses in Margate: in Marine Terrace, Buenos Ayres and Westbrook. They looked at two vacancies, both of which had been advertised on the noticeboard at the infirmary. The first was too expensive as Hannah had feared, and they had to move on to the second: a first-floor apartment a short walk away from the house, with piped water from the Waterworks company, a water closet, bedroom, kitchen and sitting room.

The landlady appeared respectable enough. Slender, grey-haired and well dressed, Mrs Clovis was well spoken and a widow, her husband having made his fortune from buying property and renting it out. Hannah guessed that she was in her late sixties or thereabouts.

'I can supply references and a deposit,' she said. 'I'm a children's nurse at the infirmary.'

'That's wonderful to hear. It's always useful to have a member of the medical profession to call on for one's little aches and pains.'

'I'm not a physician,' Hannah said, quickly making it clear, but Mrs Clovis didn't appear to have heard her.

'My joints are terribly bad on cold damp days.' She unfastened the tiny silver buttons on her cuffs to reveal her misshapen wrists. 'My doctor — Doctor Clifton — tells me I should take extract of willow bark every day and continue with my knitting to maintain strength and flexibility.' She smiled, revealing a set of gold teeth. 'Are the rooms suitable?'

'Yes, thank you,' Hannah said, and they agreed terms before she and Ruby went to fetch a deposit from her savings. They returned with their belongings on a trolley they'd borrowed from Mr Mordikai who had seemed rather taken with Ruby, offering to help them later. Hannah had declined his offer.

'I don't mind too much about not having a sea view,' Ruby said as they started to unpack.

144

'There are glimpses from the sitting room,' Hannah pointed out, as she hung her only picture on the hook: a sketch of the lady with the lamp, walking among the injured soldiers at Scutari. 'It's smartly done out.'

'I agree that it's rather afternoonified,' Ruby said, apparently giving it her approval, despite there being no separate parlour. 'I think we'll be very happy here.'

* * *

Within a few days, they'd settled into their new home and Hannah was getting used to living with her sister again. Sometimes, she felt as though they had never been apart. On other occasions, she felt as though she hardly knew her.

One morning, she got up at her usual time, waking Ruby to let her know she was going out.

'I'll leave my purse and a shopping list for you. I'll be back soon after eight. We can cook together then.'

'What shall I do for the rest of the day?'

'The whole place needs cleaning from top to bottom. There's dust everywhere.'

'I don't think it's anywhere near as bad as you say.'

'It's the nurse in me,' Hannah grinned.

'I'll see if I can get around to it,' Ruby sighed. 'I'm very tired.'

'How can you possibly be tired?' Hannah glanced towards the mantelpiece where Ruby had placed the books she'd borrowed from the library. All she'd done was eat, read and sleep.

'Oh, I don't know. I'm sad about leaving home — it's more of a wrench than I thought it would be.'

'You mean you don't want to be here?'

'I miss Stepmother . . . ' Ruby's eyes glazed with tears. 'And Cook.'

'Oh dear.' Hannah perched on the edge of the mattress and stroked her sister's hand. 'You've had a terrible time, but you'll feel better soon.'

'Let's go out for the day tomorrow — we can visit the gardens to see the animals there,' Ruby suggested in a small voice. 'We don't have to answer to anyone.'

'You have to answer to me,' Hannah said lightly. 'Why not? I've been meaning to go and see if the Hall by the Sea is as marvellous as everyone claims.' She would have gone with Charlotte, but by virtue of working on the same ward, they never had the same day off.

'There are concerts and dances that go on into the evening . . . '

'We'll go early to make the most of the day, but I can't stay out too late.' Keeping Ruby in the manner to which she was accustomed was turning out to be more expensive than she'd imagined. There was always something she needed or wanted, and Hannah didn't like to deny her because she wanted her to be happy. 'I'm not especially well paid — we must remember to cut our cloth accordingly.'

'Thank you. You're the best sister anyone could have,' Ruby said, dragging herself up to give her a hug. 'I'll see you later.'

146

It was half past six when Hannah reached the infirmary where she had breakfast with Charlotte in the dining hall. At seven, she checked on her patients and met with Sister Trim. The doctors did their rounds, and Mr Anthony confirmed that Alan could be discharged that day, having given Mr Hunter a lecture on his reasons for this decision. When the other doctors had gone, Mr Hunter stayed behind.

'Is there something I can help you with?' Hannah asked, as he wandered slowly towards the balcony, his hands behind his back. Charlotte was pushing the dressings trolley along the aisle, and he stepped in front of it.

'Mr Hunter, you are in my way,' she said haughtily.

'I wanted to say something, Nurse Finch,' he said in a low voice which carried along the ward. 'I've never apologised to you personally for disturbing your sleep that night when my friends and I had partaken of too much ale. I'm truly sorry, and I'd like to reassure you that it will never happen again.'

'I should hope not, but I'm a great believer in the principle that the proof is in the pudding.'

'I see.' He smiled. 'You aren't this stern with your patients.'

'They are children. You are a gentleman — I use that word advisedly — and you should know better.'

'I should like to make amends, if you'll allow me. There's a concert at the Hall by the Sea in two weeks' time. I'd be honoured if you and a chosen friend would accompany me for the evening.'

'I'm very grateful for your invitation. I will give it some consideration,' Charlotte whispered as Trimmie came marching along the aisle.

'There's no need for you to be here unless you have business with one of the patients. You're making my ward look untidy, Mr Hunter.' She laid the emphasis on the 'Mr' to emphasise what she thought of him, that he wasn't a doctor who commanded her respect, as yet.

'I am just leaving, Sister,' he said, inclining his head in a small bow. 'Good day.'

Noticing how Charlotte turned to hide her blushes as he left, Hannah sidled across on the pretence of asking her for some dressing materials.

'Will you accept?' she hissed, keeping one eye on Trimmie who was running her finger along the rails of one of the beds, looking for dust.

'I think so. He's very charming . . . ' Charlotte handed her gauze and a bandage, before continuing on her way, and Hannah gave her patients their breakfasts, swept and mopped the floors, and emptied the bedpans. Her hard work earned her a pittance, but the money she stowed away in a box under the bed soon added up, and there was enough there for her and Ruby to treat themselves to a day out.

Matron had a quick word with her when she was returning from the sluice.

'I knew you wouldn't let a change in circumstance affect your work,' she said. 'I've heard about your sister. She's settled in?'

'Yes, thank you.'

'That's all I wanted to say.' Matron smiled.

148

'You'd better prepare yourself for the onslaught.'

'They are mad as 'ops this mornin',' Mrs Merry said, passing them as she returned Charlie to the ward after his daily bath. Hannah knew why — Alan was going home, and the animals were coming to the Lettsom. Not only that, Mr Piper, resident surgeon at St Pancras, was coming to see Doctor Clifton and the patients he'd referred from the poorhouse to check on their progress. It was no ordinary day.

'I should have thought twice about this,' Matron said. 'Anyway, I'd better go and meet Mr Allspice in reception. They'll be here very soon.'

Hannah returned to the ward, where she saw Charlie looking up at Alan who was bouncing on his bed.

'Once they're well enough to cause trouble, they're well enough to go home,' Sister Trim observed, glaring at him.

'Come on, Alan,' Charlie entreated. 'Let's go and laze around on the balcony, like the dandies on 'oliday. It's your last day.'

'I know, and I can't wait to get out of 'ere.'

Charlie's face fell.

'I didn't mean to 'urt your feelin's. You'll 'ave to come and see me at the circus when they let you out.'

Charlie looked more cheerful. 'I'd like that.'

'Here they come!' somebody shouted, and Hannah gazed towards the end of the ward where Mr Allspice was leading a small pot-bellied pony, covered in spots. Its toady eyes peered out through its bushy forelock as the boys, who'd been confined to their beds for their

149

safety, gasped in unison.

'Are them spots real?' Charlie asked out loud.

'Shh,' Hannah said. 'You'll frighten the animals.'

'They're used to a lot worse,' Alan said rather wearily, and Hannah had to admit she was relieved he was leaving. He was more than ready to return to the outside world.

Mr Allspice took the pony to each bedside in turn so the boys could pet its smooth, shiny coat.

'Mind the spots,' Mr Allspice warned. 'It 'urts 'em if you touch 'em.'

Hannah smiled to herself.

''Ere comes the monkey,' said Alan as Mrs Allspice approached with a sorrowful grey creature on her shoulder. It had a red leather collar around its neck and a long piece of fine chain attached. She let it down on Charlie's bed, where it promptly passed water. In the fracas of horror and laughter which ensued, somehow it got away and leapt from the bedrail to the windowsill and across to one of the gasoliers where it dangled by one arm, looking down.

'What are you doing, you silly — ' Mr Allspice exclaimed.

'Ma didn't mean to let 'im go,' Alan interrupted. 'Let me get 'im down.'

''E won't come down now — 'e'll be up there for hours. You know what 'e's like,' Mr Allspice said.

'Where are the lions?' Charlie asked as Alan got out of bed and started to build a platform from a table and chair, while the monkey scratched its hairy belly.

'They aren't comin'. That lazy dolt of a lion tamer is having a siesta, sitting on his fat ass!' Mr Allspice said.

'He means 'donkey',' Sister Trim said, wincing. 'Please, sir, it's lovely of you to do this for us, but you must moderate your language.'

'I can't wait to see the donkey,' Charlie said.

'There isn't one,' Hannah said. 'Look what's next.'

Two birds of paradise were wheeled through in a cage, followed by a young woman in scanty clothing carrying a huge snake across her shoulders.

'Last, but not least,' Mr Allspice said. 'Take a look from the balcony.'

Overcoming their various afflictions, the boys who were able jumped from their beds and stampeded outside.

'Tigers. There are tigers on the beach!' Charlie shouted as Hannah became aware of Doctor Clifton appearing at her side with another gentleman, a stranger.

'That's Lord Sanger 'imself,' Mr Allspice said, dragging the pony out with him. 'When 'e 'eard what I was plannin', 'e insisted on joinin' in. That's 'im with 'is wife and the tigers from the 'all. What do you think?'

'I think you've scared half of Margate away,' Doctor Clifton said wryly.

'They're perfectly 'armless,' Mr Allspice said. 'They 'ad 'alf a lamb each this mornin' so they're no risk to the public.'

Hannah had to admit that she was impressed by the show the Allspices had conjured up as they moved on to the next ward, taking all but the monkey with them. Alan was still trying to coax it down with apples and sultanas from the kitchens while Sister Trim restored order to the Lettsom, when Doctor Clifton called Hannah over to meet the gentleman who was with him.

'This is Mr Piper.' He smiled.

'It's good to meet you.' Mr Piper was an affable man in his forties, with thinning hair and ears like a bat's. 'I'm sorry about Master Herring — I had thought to give him a chance, although the prognosis was poor. However, I hear that Master Swift is showing some improvement.'

'It's slow but sure,' Doctor Clifton said. 'Mr Swift is turning into quite the young gentleman. The governesses say he's very quick to learn his letters and numbers, and it won't be long before he can read to the younger boys.'

Having examined Charlie's knees, the doctors decided that he could have a ticket for another six weeks. They also persuaded him that time spent at the infirmary would be more beneficial than an early return to his mother. When they headed out to the corridor, Hannah followed them.

'May I venture an idea?' she asked.

'Of course,' Doctor Clifton said.

'I've noticed that a patient's recovery often depends on his state of happiness.'

'That's right,' Mr Piper agreed.

'Master Swift has suffered a few setbacks during his time here, his condition always worsening on a Sunday when all the other boys receive visitors. He waits in hope, but nobody comes for him because his mother can't afford to make the journey to Margate. I have a small fund put by, and I'd like Mr Piper to allow me to purchase a ticket for her to visit one day very soon.'

'You think it will make a difference to him?' Mr Piper said.

'I'm sure it will. That boy has been without his mother for far too long, but if it's too much of an imposition . . . '

'No, not at all. It's a kind gesture, but Mrs Swift — well, you must understand that she isn't what you'd call a respectable and refined woman,' Mr Piper explained.

'Does she not wish to visit her son?'

'I'm sure she'd like to see him, but I'm afraid that she'd go and sell any ticket she was given and go out chasing the parrot on the proceeds.'

'I haven't heard that term before.' Hannah frowned.

'He means she will use her ill-gotten gains on absinthe,' Doctor Clifton said.

'Would she really put drink before her son?'

'Nurse Bentley sees only the best in people.'

'Let me see what I can do. If I can coordinate her visit with the next group of patients travelling to Margate, then she will have an escort both ways, someone to guide her.'

'And keep hold of her ticket,' Doctor Clifton added with a smile.

'Then I'd be very grateful,' Hannah said. 'Let me know your address, Mr Piper, and I'll forward the money to you.'

'You're too kind, Nurse Bentley. Doctor

Clifton has my address.'

Doctor Clifton changed the subject. 'I wonder if Sister Trim will allow you to assist me with the outpatients today. There are at least two ladies who have suffered fainting fits, having seen the tigers on their way along the beach, and a young man who's been knocked down by a carriage.'

'You must ask her,' Hannah said firmly.

'I'll do that,' he said, and a few minutes later, Sister came to let her know that she was free to go.

'You can't do much on the ward for now anyway, not with that creature in the way,' she grumbled, pointing at the monkey. 'It's shedding hair and dander everywhere. Off you go. Don't keep Doctor Clifton waiting.'

'I thought you might have had Mr Piper with you,' Hannah said, joining him in the outpatients' department where there were the usual queues with Mr Taylor — the inquiry officer — trying to keep order.

'He's gone to bathe before he returns to London — he never stays for long,' Doctor Clifton said.

'Where do we start?' she asked.

'At the beginning, I hope,' he said, and she couldn't help wondering if he was talking about something else.

'I'll see who Mr Taylor has lined up for you.'

The first patient was one of the ladies who had swooned at the sight of the tigers. Having deemed that she'd made a full recovery, Doctor Clifton sent her on her way with a tonic and instructions to wear looser clothing in future, her stays being too tightly laced for her health.

'I don't think she'll listen,' he said, as he wrote up his notes. 'I hate the way that ladies insist on doing themselves injury for the sake of vanity. I'm sorry, I didn't mean in general terms . . . ' He looked up at Hannah, his brow furrowed. 'Will you forgive me?'

'As long as you promise not to say such things again,' she smiled. 'It's most derogatory to the female sex.'

'I realise that.'

'You are quite harsh when you mention your sisters,' she added.

'They're very vain, but they're also kind-hearted and clever. They've been unfortunate in their lack of formal education. If they'd had the same opportunities, they would have done just as well as Henry and me.'

'You mean they could have become doctors?'

'Indeed. There's no reason in my mind why a woman can't be a physician — perhaps she would have a better rapport with female patients than a man. They couldn't be surgeons — the work is too much like butchery — but to that end, I don't see why men shouldn't aspire to be nurses.'

'I don't think Mrs Knowles would approve, but it is an idea. It turns the world on its head to think of a woman giving a man orders — many men wouldn't take kindly to that.'

'I see no problem with it.'

'Then you are enlightened.' Hannah found herself yearning to feel his touch — his hand on her wrist, his fingers marking her pulse like he did with his patients. Alarmed at the intensity of her feelings, she stepped across and opened the door. 'I'll call the next one in.'

They saw several more patients. Doctor Clifton admitted the man who'd been run over by the carriage for treatment to his broken leg, then sent Hannah to find bandages for a girl who had cut her leg on a knife she'd picked up from a drawer at her lodgings.

When she returned, the girl was sitting up on the trolley with her leg stretched out, the doctor pressing a wad of gauze to her wound, and her mother looking on.

'If you keep the pressure on, Nurse, I'll dress this,' Doctor Clifton said.

She handed him the bandage and safety pins and took his place, their fingers touching each time he wound the bandage around the pad, tightening it to stem the bleeding.

'There,' he said. 'You may let go now. I'll finish the bandage above the ankle and fasten it, so it doesn't fall down.'

It looked terrible, Hannah thought, remembering how Grandma's stockings used to ruckle as they slipped down her ankles during the day.

Once he'd pinned the top of the bandage, Doctor Clifton sent the child and her mother on their way with instructions to return two days later.

'I don't think that dressing will last that long,' Hannah commented as they left the room.

'I'm sorry — I should have let you do it.'

'Yes, you should. I'd have made a much neater job of it,' she teased.

'I've always been bad at delegating,' he sighed. 'Was that the last one?'

'It was,' she confirmed. 'Now I must get back to the Lettsom.'

'Nurse Bentley,' he said quickly. 'May I be so bold as to ask you to meet me today, or at any other time at your convenience?'

'What for?'

'It's rather presumptuous, I know, but there are things I'd like to talk to you about. Not here, and not in front of your sister.' She thought she detected a tremor in his voice, and a catch in his breathing as he waited for her reply.

'It's my day off tomorrow, but I've promised Ruby that I'll take her to the Hall by the Sea. Perhaps, if it won't take long, you could walk me home this evening. This is infirmary business?'

'In part.'

Then it would be permissible, she thought.

'Meet me on the beach at eight,' she said.

'I look forward to it,' he said softly.

'I have to go.' She hurried out of the room, a hot flush spreading across her neck at the thought of seeing him again — and alone — that day.

In a turmoil of uncertainty, she threw herself into cleaning up after the monkey, which Alan and his parents had retrieved and taken away with the rest of the animals. She scrubbed the floors and polished the windows, wondering what Doctor Clifton wanted to talk about. It had to be Charlie, or perhaps his plans for his private clinic. What other interest could he possibly have in asking her for some of her time?

9

The Hall by the Sea

Hannah washed her face and put her hair up again in the sluice room after dining at the house, then made her excuses to Charlotte who asked if she could come and join her and Ruby for an hour or so for company.

'I'm sorry,' she said. 'I'm completely shattered . . . Another time.'

'All right then. I'll see you the day after tomorrow.' They wished each other goodnight, and Hannah headed out of the infirmary and along the front as if she was returning to her lodgings. When she was sure that she was out of Charlotte's view, she turned back and slipped noiselessly down the steps on to the beach where she loitered, gazing out across the water to the far horizon.

'Good evening.' Doctor Clifton stepped up beside her, bent down and picked up a small pebble which he threw out across the breaking waves. 'Thank you for being here — I wasn't sure you'd come.'

A couple walked past, then a family with a line of children trailing along behind them.

'The town is overrun,' he observed. 'With the trains, every man and his dog can afford to come to Margate.'

'You wouldn't begrudge them a pleasant day or two out?' she smiled.

'I suppose I shouldn't. I welcome everyone, except the nose-baggers who bring their own provisions, and those who don't pay their bills in a timely manner. I employ an accountant to manage my financial affairs, and he's been having the devil's own job extracting payment from some of my patients. It's usually the better-off ones who fail to cough up, so to speak.'

'Are you talking of anyone I know?'

He nodded. 'She wishes to delay settlement of her bill until she's certain that she's cured, but I suspect it has more to do with the fact that she hasn't told her husband she's been consulting me about her ailments.'

'Will there be trouble when he finds out?'

'For her, possibly. For me, no. I've had a chaperone present every time, and recorded the details of our conversations in my notes. Anyway, I didn't ask you here to talk medicine. Shall we walk?'

'Which way?' The balmy evening breeze caught the words as they came out of her mouth. What was she thinking of, giving him the option?

'Don't you have to get home to your sister?'

'Not straight away.' She looked up into his eyes, afraid that he would consider her too forward.

'Then we will walk to the far end of the bay,' he said quietly.

They strolled side by side, but apart, along the tideline where the sea had washed up strands of seaweed and shells, a glistening crab carapace and a feather.

'What is it you wished to talk about, Doctor Clifton?' she asked eventually, noticing how he kept his hands behind his back and his body straight. He wore a shirt and silk cravat, dark trousers and black leather shoes. As the evening light caught the angles of his face, he looked more handsome than ever.

He cleared his throat. 'I wanted to say how much I admire you for what you did for Charlie today.'

'Anyone would have organised it, if they could,' she said, her forehead tightening.

'I've paid Mr Piper for the ticket — '

'You've done what?' She turned abruptly to face him as he stopped dead in his tracks.

'I've given him the money . . . ' he stammered.

'I know that, but why? What did you do it for?'

'I did it for you, knowing that you're paid very little for what you do.'

'What right did you have to do that? That was to be my gift to Charlie and his mother.'

'I didn't think you'd mind.' His expression darkened. 'It was supposed to be a kindness on my part.'

Hannah took several steps backwards along the beach. Doctor Clifton followed.

'I didn't mean to offend you,' he said, 'but I should have thought — '

'Yes, you should,' she interrupted crossly. 'Or you could have asked me first. Just because you're a doctor doesn't mean you're entitled to take charge of everything. It's demeaning of you to imagine that I can't afford to pay for that ticket. I wouldn't have offered if I didn't have the money.'

160

'I know, I know . . . You've made it clear, and I realise that now. I'm sorry. I went barging in like a bull in a china shop, but I wasn't doing it to gain approbation for myself. My motives were pure — I did it for you.'

On hearing the splash of a breaking wave that rushed across the sand, she dodged away, but Doctor Clifton was too late. The water spread across the tops of his shoes, soaking the bottoms of his trouser legs. As the wave retreated, he looked down, then back up at Hannah who held out her hand.

'Don't just stand there — the tide's coming in. I'm cross with you, but that doesn't mean I want you to drown.' His face creased in a comical grimace as he reached out and took her hand, linking his fingers through hers. 'Oh dear,' she chuckled as she led him a little way up the shore, his feet squelching as he walked.

He stopped and took off his shoes, emptying them of water, before putting them back on again.

'Is this adequate penance for you?' he grumbled.

'Oh yes, I think so,' she said gaily. 'It's my turn to apologise — perhaps I shouldn't have reacted in the way I did.'

'That isn't a proper apology — you said 'perhaps', not that you definitely shouldn't have been so quick to judge my actions.'

'Well, I am sorry. I'm sure you meant well. Shall we go back towards town?'

'I'm happy to walk further — my shoes are ruined already,' he said wryly, and they

161

continued along the curve of the bay. He offered his arm, but she didn't take it.

'I don't want to give people anything to talk about,' she said gently, noticing how his eyes grew hooded and his mouth turned down at the corners.

'I'd never do anything to hurt your reputation,' he said, backing down. 'It's just that I wish . . . '

'What is it?' she said anxiously.

'I'm not very good when it comes to matters of the heart.'

'But you are a physician, and an expert in how the organs of the body work,' she said, trying to lighten the mood.

'Please don't take offence when I say that you sound almost militant when you defend your independence.'

'A woman should always have a means of supporting herself.'

'It's good for her to have something to fall back on, in case her husband falls to ruin, I suppose, but I don't understand why she would place her occupation above marriage when the latter can provide the ultimate in joy and fulfilment,' Doctor Clifton said. 'Towards the end, Suzanna gave me her blessing to take a new wife, but I couldn't do it, not for a long time, because I felt guilty for even thinking about another woman.'

'You have been . . . lucky in a way that you have experienced that joy, albeit cut short in such sad circumstances . . . ' She picked her words carefully. 'I've seen couples such as my

162

uncle and aunt who are content, but my father's attitudes have put me off the idea of marriage. I'll never forget how he took his second, much younger wife, with indecent haste after my mother's death.'

'From what you've said, he had two young daughters who needed a mother's love and guidance. I don't think it's unreasonable.'

'My stepmother rejected me and my sister — we were inconveniences.'

'But was he happy again?'

'She gave him what he wanted: the sons my mother had been unable to provide. After the death of one of my half-brothers, my father reverted to his cruel and abusive ways.'

'I'm sorry to hear that, but every marriage is different — I adored my wife. She was loving, kind, forgiving . . . as I did my best to be towards her. You see, it's about give and take . . . I'm not sure I'm making myself clear.'

'You're a good man, but being a member of the medical profession, you have this knack of making the simplest observations sound rather obtuse.'

'Sometimes I think that nurses were put on Earth only to take the rise out of us poor, naive doctors,' he sighed.

'I speak the truth. You know me by now.'

'You are always perfectly — painfully — frank,' he admitted. 'Anyway, things are different for me now. I've met a young lady — an angel, in fact — who's changed how I feel. She's beautiful, virtuous and kind, and brings out the best in me.'

'Doctor Clifton, I can't possibly advise you,' Hannah said quickly. She wasn't sure how she felt: pleased that he wished to confide in her; envious of the woman in question; hurt that he felt affection for somebody other than her. She took a deep breath, controlling her responses. It was ridiculous to feel this way when she had no claim on him, and no desire for wedlock.

'You are the only person I can talk to.'

'What about your sisters?'

'They'd tease the life out of me. Please . . . '

'Does she love you?' she asked.

'I don't know.'

'Do you love her?'

He nodded. 'My greatest fear is that she'll turn me down, but it's a risk I'm willing to take.'

'She is a lucky lady.'

'I'm talking about you, Nurse Bentley . . . '

'Me?' He had confused her. 'I'll never put myself in the hands of a husband, not having seen the way my father mistreated his wives. I'm sorry — I'm not saying that you're anything like him, but this way, I make my own decisions and I'm free to do as I please.'

'As you would be as my wife . . . '

She stopped and stared at him.

'Your wife? You are making me an offer?'

'Yes . . . yes, a proposal . . . if you wish . . . if you would do me the honour . . . '

Her heart began to pound, her head to swirl like the waves across the sand.

'Oh . . . I'm sorry . . . ' she said in a hoarse whisper.

'I've overstepped the mark. I don't know what

made me think — '

'Let me speak first. I am fond of you — very fond — but I have . . . Oh, it's unfeminine to talk of it, but I will say it. I've worked very hard and made great sacrifices to become a nurse, and I dream of becoming a sister and then matron of a great hospital.'

'I admire you for it,' he said with a trace of bitterness. 'I wouldn't seek to clip your wings when it comes to following your vocation.'

'I hope we can still be pleasant with each other.'

'Of course. Forgive me. Let me walk you home as we agreed.'

'Thank you.'

It felt like the longest walk she'd ever taken, as they strode in silence back to the lodgings house where he left her in the shadows cast by the gaslight outside.

'Goodnight,' he said gruffly.

'Goodnight,' she echoed as she watched him turn and retreat along the road, her heart and soul aching with regret. How could she call herself 'free' when they were all bound in some way — by conscience, social convention and training? She remembered a conversation she'd had with her grandmother when she went into nursing.

'Young ladies may aspire to a love match, but the foundations of similarity and common purpose are more important than the flimsy scaffold of affection,' Grandma had said. 'Are you sure you wish to pursue this course when you could have a life without hardship, being married and bringing up children?'

She'd responded that she'd thought it through

and didn't want to be dependent on a man to keep her off the streets.

'Even if you loved him?' Grandma had asked, making her blush. 'Not every man is like your father.'

'Yes, even if I loved him . . . I would resist those feelings.'

'It isn't as simple as you make out. Oh, to be young again . . . ' Grandma had smiled, and, although Hannah had chuckled at her wisdom then, she acknowledged the truth in it now.

⋆ ⋆ ⋆

'Where have you been?' Ruby said, when she went indoors.

'I'm sorry. I . . . ' She didn't know what to say: that Doctor Clifton had asked for her hand in marriage? It seemed so strange and out of the blue that Ruby wouldn't believe her. 'Doctor Clifton found some work for me, some extra notes to write up before I left.'

'That's odd,' Ruby observed. 'Did you write these notes in the sand? You have half the beach on your shoes. Oh, Hannah, have you been out gallivanting?'

'No, I have not,' she said hotly. 'If you can't say anything sensible, I'm going straight to bed.'

'Hmm,' Ruby teased. 'Methinks one's sister doth protest too much.'

'What did you find to do today?'

'I bought food for breakfast and put out our clothes for tomorrow. Don't tell me you've forgotten! We're going to the Hall by the Sea.'

'Oh yes, I remember now.' She didn't want to go — she would have preferred to sit quietly at home on her day off, reflecting on what had happened between her and Doctor Clifton. He'd said that he loved her. She wished she could have found a way of letting him down more gently, but what else could she have said? How would she face him when they next met? And how could she work with him again?

★ ★ ★

'Grandma would have loved Margate,' Ruby said as they left their lodgings the next morning, dressed in their Sunday best. Ruby's attire was hardly modest, her curves spilling out from her low-cut bodice. Hannah had given her some lace, but she seemed to have forgotten it. 'I wish she could have been here . . . Why did she have to die?'

Because she was old and weary, Hannah wanted to say, but she didn't because Ruby had a tear in her eye. Hannah felt morose too, as thoughts of Doctor Clifton tumbled through her head. She wished Alice lived nearby so she could confide in her. Charlotte was too close to the situation, and she didn't want Ruby blurting out her secrets to all and sundry, including their landlady.

'What time did you say the Hall by the Sea opens?' she asked.

'The gardens at ten o'clock. At half past four, you can watch the animals being fed. There are concerts at three and half past seven, and a ball at nine.' Ruby rattled the times off as though she'd learned them by rote from the posters which had been pasted all over town. 'We must stay for the whole day.'

'We can't be out too late.'

'Oh, you are a killjoy.'

'I don't mean to be.'

'I'm sorry. Do you think we'll see the lions?' Ruby didn't wait for Hannah's answer. 'Mrs Clovis told me that Lord Sanger keeps his circus animals at the menagerie — the old ones and those which are too young to perform. Hannah, make haste.'

They hurried along Marine Drive to join the throng queuing to buy tickets at the arched gateway into the mock ruins of old Margate Abbey, which had been built from rubble and flint at the side of the Hall by the Sea, the site of a former railway station and embankment. As they stepped into the gardens to the sound of a brass band and the sight of the sunlight catching the fountain on the lake, turning the spray into rainbows, Hannah's heart began to beat faster.

She had never seen anything like it before, and neither had Ruby, who darted from one sight to the next like a madwoman.

They passed enclosures of wolves before entering the Round House to marvel at the bears and a giant sloth, then paid for a two-penny bag of food for the birds which flew on to their hands to feed, menaced by diving seagulls, until a small boy blowing a whistle and waving a stick chased them off.

'We must give him a ha'penny for saving our

lives, Hannah. I thought we were going to be pecked to death,' Ruby laughed as she crumpled the empty bag into a ball and put it in her pocket. 'Let's go this way.' Forgetting about the ha'penny, she pointed to a sign: *To the Elephant*.

Hannah hesitated, recalling her sister's accident on the day the circus came to Canterbury.

'Are you sure you want to see it?'

'Of course. I want to see everything,' she exclaimed.

Caught up in Ruby's enthusiasm, Hannah linked arms with her and they hurried past flower beds filled with scarlet geraniums, pink dahlias and carnations, to an area of gravel where an elephant was standing with its handler and a small boy who couldn't have been more than four years old.

The handler tapped the elephant on its shoulder with a short cane.

'Pick 'im up, Charlie.'

The elephant waved its trunk slowly from side to side before reaching towards the boy. It wrapped its trunk around his middle and raised him off the ground. Hannah's heart was in her mouth as the elephant began swinging him from side to side, making him laugh out loud.

'He'll be squeezed to death,' she whispered.

'You see danger in everything,' Ruby chuckled out loud. 'The boy isn't scared.'

'Children of his age don't have any fear.'

'Because there's nothing for him to be scared of. The baby elephant didn't mean to knock me over — it was my fault for stepping out in front of it. Look at this one — he's playing.'

169

Hannah eyed the elephant with its thick, gnarled skin, tiny eyes and sagging sides, as it put the child down at its handler's request. They carried on through the gardens, Hannah trying to keep up with her sister, and thinking that she must remember to tell Charlie that she had seen an elephant named after him.

After passing aviaries with exotic birds, they reached the menagerie where the doors swung closed behind them, trapping them in a humid haze of intense heat. They followed a line of visitors into the Prophet's Cave, where coloured lanterns illuminated the strange forms created by the petrifying waters that trickled and dripped from the ceiling.

'I don't want to look at any more rocks.' Ruby tugged impatiently at Hannah's sleeve. 'I'd rather watch the monkeys.'

Hannah felt uneasy — as though they were spying on the poor creatures, many of which looked sad, locked away in their dank cages. She counted thirty-five, but Ruby claimed there were many more, counting them four times over and coming to a different number each time.

'This way, ladies. Mr Antonio Milani — lion tamer extraordinaire — is about to enter the den.' A member of staff ushered them quickly along past a tigress — *Eugene*, according to the plaque attached to her cage — and leopards. 'Renowned scientist, Professor Thursby Holt, is also with us today, to give a lecture on the nature of the lion, king of the jungle, afterwards.'

'Why do you hesitate, Hannah?' Ruby said very loudly.

'Please, keep your voice down,' Hannah said, not wanting Ruby to attract attention to herself. Recalling Pa's regime of bland food, his idea of a cure for extremes of emotion, she wondered now if he might have had some cause to question her sister's behaviour. Sometimes she worried that something wasn't quite right.

'Don't tell me you're afraid of the lions?' Ruby teased. 'Why, they're just pussycats on a larger scale.'

'Don't you remember Grandma's cat? He used to ambush me at the kitchen door,' Hannah protested, remembering how the giant ginger tabby would run up her dress, clawing holes in it.

'Poor Tibbs. You mistook his affection for aggression.' Ruby reached the rear of the crowd which had assembled in front of the lions' cage. 'Oh, I can't see a thing,' she wailed, making Hannah shrink back as everyone turned their heads to stare at them. 'What a shame.'

'Let the young ladies through please, gentlemen,' called one of the men from the platform in front of the cage which was built four feet above the ground. His hair was dark, almost black, flowing down over his shoulders. He wasn't very tall — perhaps only up to her shoulder, Hannah guessed — but he seemed to be filled with an irrepressible energy. 'Give those who are disadvantaged in height a chance to enjoy the show.'

If it was Antonio, he didn't sound like a foreigner, but after the crowd had shuffled themselves according to his wish, he twirled his

171

moustache and fastened his bright red cloak, then spoke out with an accent that conjured up a vista of olive groves and lemon trees under a cerulean sky.

'I should like to assure you, ladies, gentlemen and *bambini*, that taming lions is the most dangerous occupation in the universe. If I took one of you and put you into this cage, then Duke would most certainly bite your head straight off.' He gazed at Ruby who took half a step back. 'He won't hurt me,' he went on, addressing the crowd again. 'I've worked with him for many years in the travelling circus, but no more. I've rewarded him with a well-deserved retirement, living out the rest of his days in the company of his ladies, our beautiful lionesses: Holly, Penelope, Esther and Pearl. This year he has fathered three cubs — sadly, the mother passed away, and we've had to find them a wet nurse of sorts, not another lioness, but a bitch.'

The crowd gasped, then fell into talking about how this could be, before the lion tamer raised his arm and cracked his whip, bringing everyone to silence.

A young boy unlocked the cage door and let the lion tamer in, before slamming it shut behind him, leaving him to the whims of a magnificent elderly lion and a single lioness, the others being shut behind bars at the rear of the enclosure.

As the great Antonio moved towards them, whip in hand, the lions slunk away.

Hannah glanced at her sister who was looking on, open-mouthed, transfixed by the lion tamer's powers as the crowd applauded his bravery.

Calling the lions back, he threw down his whip and took a rattan stick from his belt. They padded towards him, their bodies low to the ground. At the twitch of his stick, they froze, and Antonio walked between them, stroking their ears and rubbing their faces as they swished their tails. To Hannah, they looked as if they would turn and pounce at any moment.

'He is well formed, don't you think?' Ruby whispered.

'He's a large lion, but I prefer the other one — the female is more lissom and delicate.'

'I'm not talking about the lions. I'm talking about Mr Milani. Don't you think he's rather marvellous?'

'If you're asking me if I admire his skills in training those beasts, then I'm not sure I can give an answer. Does he rule by fear or mutual respect?'

'I'm asking you about his appearance. He's very handsome.'

'Ruby, you are pulling my leg.' If she'd met him on the street, she'd pass him by, hardly giving him a second glance, but she had to agree that he had a presence, an unwelcome one which made the hairs on the back of her neck stand on end.

'I'm not,' Ruby said, looking hurt.

'You're far too young to be having thoughts like that.'

'I'm seventeen. I know ladies of my age who are already married.'

'Pray, tell me who they are.'

'One, then. The butcher's boy told me that his

173

sister wed at sixteen. By the time three years had passed, she'd had three children, and another on the way.'

'That isn't a good advertisement for marriage at a young age, if you ask me.'

'Stepmother is always trying to persuade Pa to marry me off. Or she was . . . ' Ruby corrected herself. 'She would say that Antonio was born under a fire sign: Aries . . . Oh no, it has to be Leo for the lion.'

Although she didn't say so, Hannah was a little sorry that the lion tamer hadn't put his head in the lion's mouth, before he picked up his whip, gave it a final flourish and exited the cage to uproarious applause.

'Thank you. *Grazie.* You are welcome to show your appreciation by leaving your donations in the box over there — all monies received go towards feeding these wonderful beasts. Now let us welcome Professor Thursby Holt who will give what I'm sure will be a fascinating talk.'

There was more applause while the professor took his place on the platform and pulled out a sheaf of notes from his coat pocket. He cleared his throat and started to speak, at which the crowd began to drift away discreetly. Hannah gave Ruby a gentle nudge.

'Let's go and have some tea,' she whispered.

'Not yet,' Ruby said in a low voice.

'Your time is up.' The lion tamer stepped in front of the bewildered scientist. 'We are tiring the lions — look how they yawn,' he added, as the lioness opened her mouth to reveal her curved teeth, perfectly formed for piercing her prey. 'A round of applause for the professor.'

Ruby clapped her hands and as Hannah joined in, she realised they were the only ones left.

'Come on, Ruby. We should go.'

'Ladies, there's no hurry,' Mr Milani called. 'Allow me to introduce you to the cubs.'

'That would be marvellous,' Ruby said quickly. 'We can have tea at any time, Hannah. This is my elder sister, Miss Bentley. I'm Miss Ruby Bentley.'

Ruby seemed so excited about seeing the cubs that Hannah decided there would be no harm in it. They moved to the next cage along where Mr Milani unlocked the door and shut the snarling bitch, a mongrel the size of a wolf, out the back.

'That's Tess. She's very protective of her *bambini*,' he explained. 'Come on in. There's no danger. The cubs are only four months old — their teeth are like needles, but I'll make sure they don't hurt you.'

Ruby followed him into the cage, her skirts rustling along the ground. Hannah hesitated outside. The stench of cat's piss was beginning to get up her nose.

'Miss Bentley?' Mr Milani said.

'I'll watch from here, thank you.'

'Whatever you wish.' He pulled up a chair from the corner and invited Ruby to sit down.

'You have a scar on your cheek, Mr Milani,' she said, taking her seat.

'Ah, I was staying with friends in the Italian mountains when a young girl was snatched from her cot by a lioness. There was screaming, shouting, hollering.' He waved his arms to emphasise the drama of it. 'My friends told me not to go after her, but I did, and I received this' — he touched the ugly mark on his face — 'for my trouble.'

'You were a hero.' Ruby's voice was filled with admiration. 'That must have hurt.'

'I lost so much blood that I was close to death, but the pain was nothing compared with how I felt when I was injured running the bulls in Pamplona.'

Wasn't Pamplona in Spain? Hannah wondered.

'Let me place a cub upon your lap.'

Ruby squealed with delight as he picked up one of the sandy-coloured cubs and lowered it on to her knees. The cub hissed.

'That isn't how one should speak to a beautiful young lady,' he smiled.

'He won't bite me?'

'Oh no. I won't let him.' Mr Milani went down on one knee right beside her. 'Trust me.'

The problem was that Hannah didn't trust him an inch, the way he looked at her sister, like a lion, wanting to eat her up.

'Ruby, we should go now.'

'Not yet. Forgive my sister's impatience.' Ruby turned her attention back to the cub. 'How do I stroke him, Mr Milani?'

'Gently at first, then you can be more vigorous about it. The beasts appreciate a good rub.'

'You don't have to stay,' Ruby called. 'I'll meet you at the tea room.'

'I'll wait.' Did Ruby really think she'd leave her unchaperoned? Hannah thought crossly.

What the lion tamer lacked in stature, he made up for in temerity. How dare he flirt with her innocent little sister! He was at least twice, if not thrice her age, although she had to concede he had the physique of a younger man.

Ruby got to sit with all three cubs on her lap, one at a time. When she was cuddling the last one, a man Hannah recognised came strutting up to the side of the cage.

'Antonio, my friend,' he exclaimed.

'Allspice . . . can't you see that I'm busy?' Mr Milani said.

'Too busy to help your brother-in-law in his hour of need?' Mr Allspice asked. 'May I have a quiet word?'

'Whatever you wish to say, you may say it in front of the young ladies. I would hate to cut their enjoyment short.'

'Mr Milani, my sister and I are quite happy to leave you to your business,' Hannah said quickly, although she was a little curious. When she'd met Mrs Allspice, she hadn't given the impression of having Italian blood coursing through her veins. 'Ruby, please.'

Ruby ignored Hannah while Mr Allspice turned to her, smiling.

'Well I never, it's Nurse Bentley. Antonio, this young lady was instrumental in makin' sure Alan received the treatment 'e was entitled to.'

The lion tamer cast her a glance, seeming unimpressed.

'I know what you've come to ask, and the answer is yes, but I'm not doing this out of charity or the goodness of my heart. It's to help

177

out my poor long-suffering sister and make myself a few bob in interest.'

'As soon as the show's back on the road, me, the missus and the boys will be in clover. I swear on my wife's life that I'll pay you back every shillin',' Mr Allspice avowed.

'And you'll make sure I appear at the top of the bill?'

'I said so before, didn't I? I 'ave friends in all the right places. But the cubs are too young, and I didn't think you were plannin' to perform with these moth-eaten old cats again.'

'I wasn't, but I've had a change of heart.'

It was all very sudden, Hannah mused, when he'd only just told them that the lions had retired from the circus.

'I've never been top of the bill, even though there's no one who deserves it more. Besides, I miss the excitement of being in the ring, the lights, the applause . . . ' Mr Milani stopped abruptly and looked Mr Allspice up and down. 'You're as slippery as a jellied eel. How can I trust you to pay me back?'

'My word is my bond,' Mr Allspice said. 'We're family anyway.'

The two men stepped towards each other, spat in their palms and shook hands, making Hannah recoil in disgust.

'I'll have the money ready for you this evening. I'll meet you at the Queen's Head at seven o'clock.'

'I'll see you there.' Mr Allspice hurried away.

'I must apologise for the interruption, ladies,' Mr Milani said. 'Miss Ruby, I think that's enough for one day, but you're welcome to come back any time. You'll be amazed at how quickly the cubs grow.'

'I'm very grateful for the experience,' Ruby said when he let her out of the cage. 'It's been most enlightening. I'll return to see them as soon as I can.' She pulled a handkerchief from her purse, and dabbed at her cheek as if removing a fleck of dirt. 'Good day, Mr Milani.'

'Good day, ladies,' he smiled.

'The lion tamer is very kind, lending money to his brother-in-law like that,' Ruby observed. 'I love Margate,' she went on as they walked to the refreshment room, having decided not to queue for a carriage ride around the grounds first. 'I never thought it would be such fun.'

While they were drinking tea and eating cake, Hannah kept catching sight of her reflection in the long mirrors set against the fashionably green walls. She looked well, she thought, but she felt hollow inside, wondering if she'd made the right decision in turning down Doctor Clifton's proposal.

Although she enjoyed her sister's company, she would have loved to have shared the experiences of the Hall by the Sea with him. She smiled wryly. She was a fool for thinking that he would have time to enjoy a concert or a few hours idling through the park. He would always be working, attending to his patients, and writing up his notes.

'Hannah, you aren't listening to me,' Ruby said.

'I'm sorry. I was miles away.'

'I said we should have a ride on the merry-go-round next.'

Hannah finished her tea, and they queued up for the huge steam-powered roundabout that had arrived in Margate for the summer season. Having paid for their tickets, they rode side-saddle on wooden horses painted in garish colours.

'Hold tight!' Ruby screamed as the merry-go-round turned faster and faster until Hannah felt that they might fly off.

'I thought I was going to be sick,' Ruby laughed as they descended the steps and walked back on to the grass. She seemed so happy that Hannah decided not to complain about her behaviour and the lion tamer's attention — Ruby deserved a little joy after what Pa had done to her.

As for Hannah, the distractions of the Hall by the Sea had helped a little, but as they strolled home, with Ruby twirling her parasol as she danced along the pavement, she felt ill at the thought of having to face Doctor Clifton on his ward rounds the next day.

10

Hokey-Pokey

The dreaded ward round was imminent. Hannah heard the doctors before she saw them: the tap-tapping of Mr Anthony's shoes, the low rumble of Doctor Clifton's voice, and then a bump and cursing, followed by profuse apologies. Sister Trim greeted the doctors and left her nurses to assist them with their examinations.

Hannah waited at Charlie's bedside and glanced towards Charlotte who was hurrying over.

'It appears that Mr Hunter is with them.' Hannah smiled, watching the colour rush to Charlotte's cheeks.

'Good day, Nurse Bentley,' Doctor Clifton said, but she could barely look at him as the memory of their walk on the beach came flooding back.

'Good morning,' she said.

'Mr Hunter has deigned to join us today — he has had somewhat of a relapse,' Mr Anthony said sarcastically, as Henry stumbled and reached out for the bedstead to steady himself. 'I hear he's had a setback with his application to the Royal College of Physicians. If he spent more time studying medicine rather than the anatomy of the female form . . . '

'It's important that a gentleman receives a

broad education,' Mr Hunter said, turning towards Charlotte who looked furious, as well she might, Hannah mused. She doubted very much that she would accept his invitation to the concert now. It seemed that his lapse had set him back in his pursuit. 'I'm not the only one who's out all hours. My cousin here' — he rested his hand across Doctor Clifton's shoulders — 'came home well after midnight a couple of nights ago, having been walking innocently by the sea. How do I know this? Because his shoes were soaked, and he'd hung his socks on the fire screen to dry.'

'You old dog,' Mr Anthony jested.

'Mr Hunter, I'd be grateful if you'd hold your tongue,' Doctor Clifton snapped. 'Watch, listen and learn.'

'Charlie has had a good night,' Hannah began.

'Thank you,' Mr Anthony cut in.

'I think this young man can speak for himself.' Doctor Clifton smiled, but his eyes were shaded with sorrow. 'How are you today?'

'I'm well, thank you, Doc.'

'How are your old knees?'

He pulled up his pyjamas to show him.

'How straight can you get those legs?'

'Like a soldier.' Charlie grunted as he straightened them as far as they would go.

'This is much better,' Doctor Clifton said. 'If you carry on like this, there'll be no need for any operations.'

'In this case, I concur,' said Mr Anthony. 'Mr Hunter, have you anything to add?'

Hannah looked up at him — he was decidedly

182

green around the gills. He swayed slightly. She hastily handed him a bedpan, in which he was promptly sick.

'Go home,' Doctor Clifton ordered. 'Go home and think about how you have humiliated yourself, and me.'

Henry bowed his head and, still clutching the bedpan, made his way out of the ward.

''E ain't too good,' Charlie commented.

'It's self-inflicted,' Doctor Clifton said. 'I have no sympathy.'

Having completed the ward round, he dropped back to speak to Hannah.

'Just to inform you that a Miss Huckstep has been admitted to the house from the Hospital for Sick Children. She says she's a friend of yours.'

Not Alice. She was too special, too loved to be struck down in her prime.

'Oh no,' she exclaimed, filled with panic. 'I must go to her as soon as I can. Thank you for letting me know . . . '

'I apologise for Henry's behaviour — I despair of him. I've a good mind to send him back to his father.'

'I don't suppose you were ever like that when you were a student?' She allowed herself a small smile.

'That would be telling.' He smiled back ruefully, before going to catch up with Mr Anthony.

Hannah looked for Charlotte, finding her in the sluice, up to her elbows in suds.

'I'm sorry about Mr Hunter,' she said. 'I know you like him.'

'Liked,' Charlotte said, through a mist of steam. 'I'm glad I didn't rush in and agree to go to the concert with him. He's proved himself to be completely immature and unreliable.'

'You won't change your mind?'

'No,' Charlotte said firmly. 'Oh, I don't know why I'm so upset. I suppose I let my mind — and my heart — run away with me. Don't worry, Hannah. I'll get over it.'

Reassured, Hannah threw herself into her work, but her mind was preoccupied with what had passed between her and Doctor Clifton that evening on the beach, and her worries for Alice. Instead of breaking for lunch, she went to find her, hoping against hope that Doctor Clifton had been mistaken.

'Alice, what are you — ' Hannah stopped abruptly, her joy quickly turning to alarm at finding her old friend on the women's ward. She had longed to see her again, but not like this.

'Miss Russell had me sent here,' Alice said. 'I haven't been well.'

'I see.' Hannah took in the delicate translucence of her complexion, the shadows around her eyes and the red spots on her cheeks which matched the rosy hue of her lips.

'Apparently, the way I look is the height of fashion in London and Paris, so that's one thing to be thankful for. Oh dear, you think I look terrible,' Alice sighed.

'No, not at all. You don't look too bad.' Hannah was lying — she looked dreadful.

'I've been told that I have to drink half a pint of seawater every day.' She grimaced. 'I can't

184

imagine that's good for you. Be honest with me. Does anyone fully recover from this ghastly disease?'

'We've sent many children back to London, their scrofula much improved.'

'But not cured?'

'I can't say. You'll have to ask the doctors when they're on their rounds. Let me wheel you out on to the balcony.' She released the brake and pushed the bed out through the doors. 'How about that? The view is wonderful — at least, I think so.'

Alice squinted. 'The sunshine hurts my eyes.'

'I'll ask Sister to arrange for the doctor to come and see you.' Hannah felt more worried than ever. Poor Peter had suddenly developed a headache and sensitivity to light after surgery, and Doctor Clifton had diagnosed inflammation of the brain. Was the same thing happening to Alice? 'I'll fetch a parasol to give you some shade.'

'Thank you. You'd better get on — I don't want you to get into any trouble on my account.'

Alice was the first nurse she had seen arrive at the infirmary to receive treatment for the same complaint as her patients. Was it a coincidence?

'I'll come and sit with you when I've finished my shift.'

'Don't you have a home to go to?'

'I do, in fact — I moved out of the nurses' home not long ago. I'm sharing lodgings with my sister. She's been in Margate for a couple of weeks now, having fallen out with our father.'

'As you did,' Alice said.

'The circumstances were different, but yes.'

'You don't have to entertain me — Ruby will be expecting you.'

'I'll drop by, at least. I'll see you later.'

★ ★ ★

Although it was late and against the rules of the house, Hannah returned to the women's ward after her shift, so they could talk for a while.

'I'm glad to see you again, but don't waste your evening on me,' Alice said.

'I'm not wasting it,' she smiled. 'We have a lot to catch up on. So much has happened since I left London. What about you? What about your ma?'

'She's worried sick — she'll visit when she's free, but she's nursing an elderly invalid at their home in Enfield at present and doesn't know when she'll be able to get away.'

Alice's mother was a widow, and private nurse.

'What about Mr Fry?' Hannah had noticed the likeness of Alice's young man, which he'd had taken at a photography studio, on the cabinet beside the bed.

'He's supposed to be coming to visit soon . . . '

'He hasn't proposed yet?'

Alice shook her head.

'What have the doctors said?' Hannah went on. 'Has Doctor Clifton seen you?'

'They've uttered all the usual platitudes: give it time; you're one of the lucky ones; we've caught it in the early stages.'

It wasn't that early, Hannah thought, recalling

Alice's previous complaints about struggling to catch her breath in the smog.

'Hannah, I'm scared.'

'I'll be with you all the way, I promise.' She was scared for Alice too, but she wouldn't let it show. She sat with her for half an hour while they reminisced about their training, Miss Russell and London, until Alice began to nod off, exhausted.

Hannah wished she could have confided in her about Doctor Clifton's proposal, but she didn't want to wear her out.

★   ★   ★

Before Hannah had met Doctor Clifton, she'd thought of nothing else but her young and vulnerable patients, but as another week went by, she continued to suffer from doubt and regret over turning him down, even though she'd come to the conclusion that she'd made the right decision. With time, her heartache would resolve like a case of measles or influenza.

On the Monday afternoon, she went to fetch the children in from the balcony where they'd been taking the air.

''Ain't it dinnertime yet? Me belly's growlin' like there's a lion in it,' Charlie grinned.

'It won't be long,' she said with a practised smile.

'Is it mutton or beef?' he asked.

'You'll have to wait and see.'

'You seem a bit down in the mouth today,' he ventured.

'I'm fine, thank you.'

'There's somethin' wrong, I know it.'

'I'm a little worried because one of my friends has been admitted to the house for treatment.'

'That's good, ain't it? The saltwater baths'll 'ave 'er as right as rain soon . . . unless she's as bad as Peter was.'

'We'll see,' Hannah said.

''Ere, 'ave this.' Charlie thrust a crumpled piece of paper into her hand. 'I done this for you to say thank you for what you done for me.'

She unfolded it to find a crude drawing of two stick figures at the bedside of another, smaller one.

'That's me, you an' Doctor Clifton,' he said proudly.

'I don't know what to say.' Fighting back sudden tears, she folded it and slipped it into her pocket. 'I shall treasure it for ever.'

'Nurse Bentley!'

Hannah turned. 'Yes, Sister.'

'You're wanted to assist with an emergency — there's a child been brought into outpatients with a broken leg. Doctor Clifton wishes to set the limb, but the boy won't allow it. He's hysterical.' Sister Trim's expression softened. 'We thought you might be able to tame him.'

'I'll go straight away.'

Hannah joined Doctor Clifton in one of the examination rooms where the boy, an eight-year-old with strawberry-blonde curls, blue eyes and a runny nose, was sitting on a trolley, bawling in protest.

'This is Master Sebastian Crowborough,' the doctor said as the boy quietened at the sight of her arrival. 'His nanny has gone to search for his mother who's at one of the bathing establishments nearby.'

'What happened?' Hannah said, having introduced herself.

'He took a flying leap from a wall and landed badly some six feet below.'

'I've broken my leg,' the boy sobbed.

'I need to apply traction to align the fractured ends of the bones — the tibia and fibula — before I can immobilise the break with a splint. He'll be admitted in advance of the application of a plaster cast when the swelling has reduced.'

The boy screamed.

'Now, now,' Hannah said. 'What's all this fuss about? I thought a young gentleman like you would be braver than this. Think of Admiral Nelson who lost an eye and an arm, yet still found the courage to fight on for England.' She glanced towards Doctor Clifton who rolled his eyes as the boy continued to scream. 'Do you like peppermints?'

Whimpering, he nodded.

'The sooner you let us help you, the sooner you can have some from my secret supply on the ward. Hold my hand — you can squeeze my fingers as hard as you like, if you need to.'

Frowning, the boy took her hand.

'We're ready, Doctor,' she said, and Doctor Clifton gripped the boy's ankle and began to pull, stretching the leg, at which the boy squeezed Hannah's fingers so tightly that they turned white.

'That's it. All done.' Doctor Clifton relaxed his grip and stood back. 'Keep still and I'll apply a splint and bandages.'

'I shall tell your mother how brave you've been,' Hannah said.

'Is there a bed available for him on the Lettsom?' Doctor Clifton asked, once he'd finished wrapping the boy's leg.

'We're full to the gunnels. He'll have to go elsewhere.'

Doctor Clifton rubbed the back of his neck, thinking. 'Then we are in a bit of a bind. Isn't there a boy well enough to be sent home?'

'You know very well there isn't,' Hannah chided.

'What about the convalescent homes? Are there any spare beds there?'

'As far as I know, they're full too.'

'Then I don't know what to do. I don't want Master Crowborough going home until that fracture's immobilised.'

'You'll have to speak to Matron and Mr Cumberpatch.'

'I'll do that. Wait here.'

'Where are my sweets?' the boy demanded as Doctor Clifton left the room.

'You'll have them soon enough,' Hannah said. 'Tell me about your family. Do you have brothers and sisters?' she went on, distracting him, and he chattered about his younger siblings, his mother's intention to send him away to boarding school in September, and how he was going to miss his new puppy.

Eventually, Doctor Clifton returned, saying he

had arranged for an extra bed to be squeezed on to the Lettsom.

'As you can imagine, there was much opposition from Mrs Knowles and Sister Trim, but it has to be done.' She frowned, and he went on, 'I can see you don't like the idea either, but what are we supposed to do? We can't turn these cases away.'

He paused before changing the subject. 'Your friend, Miss Huckstep . . . This is confidential, of course.'

'Of course,' Hannah echoed. 'Do you think she has a good chance of making a full recovery?'

'You know what I'll say to that — there are no guarantees. She has tubercles in her lungs, and all we can do is offer the best treatment. She thinks very highly of you — as I do.' His shoulders sagged. 'I'm sorry — I shouldn't have said that.'

'I'm sorry too,' she said.

'You will not change your mind?'

'My decision is final.'

'Then we will try to carry on as if nothing happened. I hope I didn't offend you by raising the subject once more, but I had to be sure.'

'I have great admiration for you, Doctor Clifton, but — ' Her heart felt as if it would break.

'You don't have to excuse yourself. I do understand,' he cut in.

'I want you to be happy,' she went on. 'It would please me greatly if you would put your feelings for me aside. You'll find someone else to love and cherish one day — I'm certain of it.'

'Then I won't talk of this again. Thank you for your assistance with Master Crowborough.'

'I have to go,' she said hurriedly. 'Sister Trim will be wondering where I've got to.'

She rushed off and hid in the sluice to dry the tears that were falling — for herself, for Doctor Clifton and for Alice.

She stopped by to visit her friend before she left the infirmary that evening as had become her custom, finding Alice sitting up in bed.

'How are you?' Hannah asked.

'About the same, thank you. I could get used to this treatment — I've had a warm saltwater bath, a delicious supper and a lovely snooze in the sunshine.' She glanced at the picture of Mr Fry on the bedside locker. 'The only thing I'm missing is dear Tom.'

'When is he coming to visit you?'

'I'm not sure. It depends on when he can get away from London.'

'It isn't that difficult to get here by train.'

'I know, but he works long hours at the bank, and visits his mother at weekends. Anyway, that's enough about him. What about you? What do you think of Margate and the infirmary?'

'I like it here. Ruby is settling in, Margate is wonderful — much cleaner and fresher than London — and the patients are lovely' — she recalled Master Crowborough's howling, and his complaints after he arrived on the ward that day about the hard mattress, the smell of carbolic and the presence of the poor boys like Charlie — 'on the whole. I've made a good ally in Charlotte, Nurse Finch.'

'And Doctor Clifton?' Alice asked slyly. 'You mentioned him in your letters.'

'You know what it's like when you're working alongside someone all the time. Nursing comes first, and as a nurse, I'm telling you to get some sleep now. I'll see you tomorrow.' Alice didn't protest as she stood up to leave.

'How is your friend?' Ruby asked when Hannah returned to their lodgings.

'I can't say. Anything relating to our patients is confidential.'

'Oh, you are a spoilsport. You know I wouldn't say anything.'

'I know, but it's best that I keep my mouth shut. Tell me, what have you been doing today?'

'I've been out to buy food and ale, and I've received a letter from Stepmother ... We became quite friendly after you left. Our mutual interests in fashion and reading drew us together. Anyway, she wanted to know that she found us well and happy. Apparently, Pa is resigned to my leaving home and has no interest in persuading me to return to Canterbury, which suits me fine, although it means I'll have to find my own husband rather than relying on him to do it for me. And Cook has walked out after all those years working for the family. When Pa found out that she'd sent my boxes to Margate, he lost his temper with her, but instead of crying like she normally would, she packed her bags and left with her head held high.'

Ruby jumped up. 'Shall we go out for a walk? It's still light, and the hokey-pokey men will be on the promenade. You're always reminding me of the benefits of fresh air, although you're a poor advertisement for the infirmary — you look terribly washed out.'

'I'm a little tired, that's all.'

'Come on. You'll feel better for it.' Ruby offered her arm.

'You've put up your hair in a different way, and that dress . . . ' Hannah stroked the soft maroon velvet of her sister's sleeve. 'I envy you.'

'Stepmother bought it for me for one of her soirees.' Ruby touched the gleaming red stone suspended on a gold chain around her neck, her inheritance from their grandmother. 'I think it's important to maintain my standards, even though we seem to be at the very edge of society here in Margate, but I'm not complaining. Margate isn't like Canterbury — it's much more interesting.'

'I'll change my shoes and put on my bonnet at least,' Hannah said.

'Ah, I thought you might permit me to borrow your shoes. I have only one pair here — the rest are still to be sent on. Mine have left a blister — I can barely walk in them.'

Hannah gave in and they walked together along the front, Ruby wearing Hannah's best shoes. They stopped for ice cream at one of the stalls.

'That is a beautiful piece of jewellery.' The hokey-pokey man stared at Ruby who smiled and stepped closer to show him her necklace, before buying two portions of Neapolitan ice cream which they unwrapped and ate as they continued on their way.

'If someone wishes to admire your necklace,

194

they're trying to reel you in.' Hannah's teeth crunched on the ice crystals in the striped sweet treat, which tasted as if the maker had mixed in some mashed swede. 'Indulging in that sort of behaviour might lead you to being handled or kissed.'

'It would in Canterbury,' Ruby said, 'but this is Margate. Everyone's far more relaxed in their manners and modes of dress, and it was a perfectly innocent request. Shall we go window shopping?'

Hannah wasn't sure if she should put temptation in her sister's way.

'I really do need new shoes,' Ruby wheedled. 'If we saw some, I could come back and buy them tomorrow.'

'We'll have to save up first,' Hannah said.

'You have plenty of money. I've seen what you've got in the box, the one you've hidden away under the bed.'

'Shh, Ruby. I have enough, but if we spend beyond our means, we'll soon run out. Look, I'm hoping for a promotion which will mean better pay — life should be a little easier then.' Hannah didn't know when that would be, but she was optimistic. There were rumours that Matron was intending to make some changes among the staff.

'Thank you,' Ruby smiled. 'I thought that tomorrow I might go back to the Hall by the Sea. There's so much to see there — we can't have seen half of it the other day.'

'That was a special treat.'

'I know. I'm sorry. I shouldn't have asked. It's

just that Mr Milani said that the cubs were growing and changing every day, and I'd like to see them again.'

Hannah wasn't sure what was the main attraction — the cubs or the lion tamer — but she had an idea that she should keep Ruby well away.

They carried on walking. It was low tide and the sea was miles out, leaving a vast expanse of rippled sand and shingle, and the boats listing in the harbour. The bathing rooms were closing for the night, but the centre of town was still open for business. Hannah heard the tinkling of a piano and loud chatter coming from the Assembly Rooms where one might spot one of the gentry or even a distant member of the Royal Family.

'Look!' Ruby grasped Hannah's arm as they passed through Cecil Square with its shops and mansions. 'Isn't that the famous Doctor Clifton's plate?'

They moved closer to the building in the corner: a four-storey terrace, built of red brick with Bath stone coping, and a slate roof. To the right of the door, five steps up from the street, was a brass plaque engraved with Doctor Clifton's name and professional registration. Above the door was a sign, reading 'Surgery'.

A pulse beat lightly at Hannah's temple. This was where he ran his private clinic. This was where he lived — where she could have lived, if she'd accepted his offer. A tear sprang to her eye, and she turned away.

'I've walked along here many times, but I've

never come close enough to spot his name before,' Ruby said. 'He must be a gentleman of considerable fortune if he can afford this.'

'He works very hard. He deserves it for what he does.'

'And you don't?'

'It's different.'

Ruby didn't argue. She pointed out the posters on the board outside the library: one for the infirmary fête, and one for tickets for the infirmary ball to be held in late August.

'I should like to go to a ball,' she said longingly.

'One day,' Hannah said. 'When I'm a sister, I'll buy tickets and we'll go together.'

'What about the gentlemen?' Ruby asked. 'Won't we have to find someone to introduce us? We aren't allowed to dance without being introduced first. But then you know plenty of people at the infirmary. Oh, Hannah, the difficulty is resolved.'

'It won't be this year.'

'I know. I'll be patient. I wish the library was open — I'd like to borrow another of Mrs Whiting's books. Her novels are filled with drama — love stories, romance and scandal. Pa used to complain that they inflamed passions in a most unnecessary way, so Stepmother and I used to hide our copies in her dressing room. Have you read any books recently?'

'Only Miss Nightingale's *Notes on Nursing*,' Hannah chuckled.

'I might have known.' Ruby grinned at her. 'Shall we go home?'

11

Counting the Pennies

Two days later, Hannah was on the ward as usual, on her knees, scrubbing the floor with soap and carbolic, while the patients chatted outside on the balcony with one of the governesses who schooled them, and a pair of lady volunteers assisting. Without them, Hannah didn't know how they would manage to get all their work done.

She was aware that Mr Hunter was standing nearby with Charlotte, having expressly asked her to help him summarise Charlie's condition and progress for a report he was writing for his studies. Charlie himself was out on the balcony continuing with his education.

'You'd be better off asking Nurse Bentley,' she heard Charlotte say, sounding rather exasperated at having been taken off her duties. 'He's her patient — she's been looking after him the whole time.'

'I wanted to ask you . . . ' Mr Hunter said in a low voice. 'I thought . . . Oh dear, you have a loose thread on your apron — it's about to unravel. Where will I find a pair of scissors?'

'In the trolley over there,' Charlotte said, 'but it really doesn't matter. I'll deal with it.'

'What's the problem? Does Sister Trim object

to gentlemen rifling through her drawers?'

'Mr Hunter, you are a disgrace!' Charlotte hissed. 'Don't you ever take anything seriously?'

'I'm sorry. Sometimes, I don't think before I speak.'

'Well, you really should learn.'

Hannah heard footsteps before Mr Hunter spoke again. 'May I?'

'I'll do it, thank you,' Charlotte said sternly. 'Now, what was it you wanted to know about Master Swift?'

'Everything,' he said.

'Then you must read his notes — they're over there in the box.'

'Why have you suddenly taken against me?'

'Because you're immature and ungentlemanly, and you're wasting my time — and Doctor Clifton's. Leave me alone — I want nothing to do with you.'

'Nurse Finch, you're breaking my heart.'

'Go away and write your report.'

Hannah almost put her cloth down to applaud the way Charlotte was dealing with his unwanted attentions. He might be privileged and handsome, but he was a fool.

As she heard Charlotte stalk away, her ears pricked at the sound of Sister Trim's voice.

'Your son is spoiled,' she was saying. 'He's had my nurses running around like headless chickens, asking them to fetch this and that for him. You might not like this, Mrs Crowborough, but you really should teach him some manners.'

'He says that you lost your temper with him, that you smacked him across the face.' The cut-glass accent belonged to a woman in a sheer silk dress the colour of lilac — Hannah could see her skirts, the lace edging to her petticoat and the toes of a pair of elegant forest-green shoes from her vantage point.

'Whom should you believe: a ward sister of many years, or a little tattle-tale who's made up these lies because I sent his pudding back when he complained about lumps in the custard?'

'How do you explain the bruise, the one on his cheek?'

'He fell from a wall. One would expect a few bruises as well as the broken leg.'

'I'm not happy about this. I'll be raising a formal complaint with the matron here.'

'Do as you wish,' Sister Trim said, her tone like acid. 'The boy is ready to be discharged — his boxes are beside the bed. I'll call for one of the porters to help you. Good day.' A few minutes afterwards, Sister Trim came over to speak to Hannah who redoubled her efforts at scrubbing. 'Did you hear that? How dare she accuse me of assaulting her precious child?'

'I did hear what she said.' Hannah looked up to where Sister Trim was picking at her nails.

'There's no truth in it — you'll speak up for me if it comes to anything?'

'Of course.' Hannah was comfortable with that — she hadn't seen Sister Trim inflict any kind of violence on the boy. She had on occasion seen her box patients around the ears, and yell at them, terrorising them into submission for an unwanted procedure or high-spirited behaviour. Sister was a skilled nurse when it came to dressing wounds and managing a ward, but her bedside manner left much to be desired when it came to offering a few words of reassurance and comfort.

'I'm very grateful for that. Are you done there?'

'Almost,' she said.

'I have some paperwork to complete. You and Nurse Finch will change the bed that Master Crowborough has just vacated. It is to stay in readiness for the next patient.'

'Yes, Sister.' Hannah wrung out her cloth into the bucket and got to her feet as Sister Trim made her way to the end of the ward where she sat down to work. She emptied her bucket, washed out the cloth and put them away, before joining Charlotte.

They stripped and made up the bed and continued with their chores until Mr Mordikai turned up to request Hannah's presence in Matron's office. Sister Trim looked worried when she excused herself from the ward.

'How is the situation on the Lettsom, Nurse Bentley?' Mrs Knowles asked.

'To what situation are you referring?' Hannah chose her words carefully.

'There's more than one?' Matron raised one eyebrow before smiling. 'I want to know how having an extra bed on the ward is affecting you and the other nurses. I need as much ammunition as possible for the next meeting of the Board. Mr Cumberpatch is preparing his weapons and I must do the same.'

'We have coped as you would expect, but this

situation can't continue long-term because it will wear us all out.'

'I have high hopes for at least two, if not three extra nurses,' Mrs Knowles said. 'And I'm about to make some other changes, which I can't reveal at present. Suffice to say that with Sister Murch talking of moving to Brighton to be near her invalid mother, there will be a vacancy on one of the men's wards, and I'm thinking that, after my visit from a rather irate Mrs Crowborough, Sister Trim would be well suited to it . . . Her tact and diplomacy would keep the gentlemen in line.'

She was being sarcastic, Hannah realised, her heart beating a little faster at the prospect of promotion, or was Matron intending to promote one of the new nurses to Sister of the Lettsom?

'Please, don't say anything to her,' Matron continued. 'I haven't quite made up my mind.' She changed the subject. 'How is your sister?'

'She is well, thank you.'

'I don't like to interfere or seem presumptuous, but if she's looking for occupation, we're always in need of lady volunteers here, as you know.'

Hannah wished she'd thought of it before. It seemed the perfect solution to Ruby's complaints that she was alone all day.

'I'm sorry about your friend and colleague, Miss Huckstep. I hope she makes a full recovery very soon.'

Hannah thanked her and returned to the ward where a new boy was already sitting up in the additional bed.

'What was it? What did Matron say?' Sister

Trim asked, rushing across to meet her.

'She wanted to find out how we managed with the extra patient.'

'Why didn't she ask me? I'm Sister of this ward. Oh, don't say — you are Matron's pet.'

'It's to our advantage,' Hannah said. 'I told her what I thought, that we'll struggle if it continues.'

'Oh no, that won't do, Nurse Bentley. That won't do at all. You are making me appear in the worst possible light. I've explained to her that we are coping magnificently. There are moves afoot to bring in new staff, and I don't want Matron thinking that I can't run this ward to the standard she expects.'

Hannah didn't want to argue with her, but she was wrong.

'Hasn't it occurred to you that they're taking advantage of our good nature and willingness to help our patients?' she began. 'If we say everything is well, what is to stop them bringing another two or three beds on to the ward? We should stand up for ourselves, our working conditions and our standards.'

Sister Trim's nostrils flared, and her eyes narrowed. If she could breathe fire, she would, Hannah thought, but she refused to back down.

'We're on the same side,' she added.

'You're right about that,' Sister Trim agreed. 'We shouldn't be standing around here talking politics — as you can see, they've already filled the extra bed. I'll introduce you to Master Darke.'

Samuel was eleven and suffering from scrofula

of the right elbow. Hannah read through the notes that one of the physicians had made while admitting him through outpatients.

'I see you're from Canterbury,' she said when Sister Trim had gone.

'My father has a shop, selling high-wheelers and tricycles — you can buy one, if you like.'

'They are for young men who wish to show off,' Hannah smiled, recalling how she'd seen someone come a cropper, falling from his bicycle headfirst. 'It would be most unladylike and impractical.' How would one stop one's skirt becoming entangled in the wheels?

'What could be better to impress one's friends and acquaintances?' the boy went on, his hazel eyes glittering in his thin, pixie-like face.

'I for one would rather not break my wrists, falling from a velocipede,' Hannah said, 'but I admire your sales patter.

'Charlie,' she called. 'Would you come and sit with Samuel here? Perhaps you'd like to read to him.'

Pleased to be wanted, Charlie came over, carrying one of the books from the bookshelf. He perched on the edge of Samuel's bed and the next thing Hannah heard was the two boys chuckling together, as thick as thieves, while the book lay unread on the blanket.

* * *

The following day, Ruby agreed to volunteer at the infirmary, but her enthusiasm was short-lived. She insisted that children enjoyed being frightened, but boys like Charlie and Samuel didn't want to hear talk of dying when they were trying to get better. They needed tales with happy endings, not to listen to the terrible fate of the gingerbread man crossing the river, only to be eaten by a fox. When Ruby decided after three hours of reading that she wouldn't continue, Hannah had to admit that she was relieved. Perhaps now Ruby would relish the solitude she had when she was alone at home, rather than make a fuss about it.

Having decided to dine with her sister later to make up for her long absences, Hannah called in on Alice before leaving the house that evening.

'Doctor Clifton said that my pulse was steadier and my chest much improved today,' Alice said.

'I'm glad to hear it. Have you heard from Mr Fry?'

'I think his letters must have got lost in the post.'

'He knows you're here — he could have come to see you.'

'Oh, stop this. Why do you always doubt him?'

Hannah shrugged, knowing that any explanation would only hurt Alice's feelings further. Everything felt wrong: the way they'd met; the way they'd had to enlist her in their secret meetings; his claims that he was too busy feathering their future nest to consider an engagement. Six months to a year was more than long enough to wait, in her opinion.

'Write to him again and tell him to come immediately.' These things were not best left.

Better to foment them, apply heat to bring the poison of doubt and uncertainty bursting to the surface, then Alice's heart could heal — with or without Mr Fry.

Alice changed the subject. 'I keep meaning to ask — have you changed your mind on marriage?'

'Oh no. Matron's raised my hopes for promotion, but I'm not going to let myself think too much of it in case it doesn't work out.' It was a fib because she'd thought of little else since her last meeting with Mrs Knowles. 'Alice, I have a confession to make. I haven't told anyone, not Charlotte, nor Ruby.'

Alice smoothed the bedsheet with the palm of one hand. 'Your secrets are safe with me.'

Hannah lowered her voice to a whisper. 'Doctor Clifton asked me to marry him and I turned him down.'

Alice's eyes widened. 'Are you sure you weren't being too hasty? He's a wonderful man — he's been so kind. He's no ordinary doctor.'

'I know, I know. I was torn, but I've made the right decision. I haven't worked this hard only to give up nursing for the restrictions of marriage.'

'I think you've made a mistake,' Alice maintained.

'Nursing is my life.'

'What about love?'

'I love my work.' She had to clear her throat before she could continue. 'I love Doctor Clifton as well, but I can't have both. It's a cross that we women have to bear.'

'How does he feel about this?'

'Hurt and upset, but he understands my situation. He will recover, I'm sure, and eventually he'll find happiness with someone else.'

'What about you?'

'I look upon this as a test of my resolve. I'm fortunate that I find joy on the ward with my young patients — it was enough for me before I met him, and it can and will be again.' She forced a smile. 'When I'm matron of a great hospital, I'll look back without regret. Now, I mustn't tire you. I'll leave you to write that letter.'

Hannah hurried home to find Ruby sitting on the chaise, reading a library book.

'Have you done anything in the way of housework today?' she said, aggrieved as she looked from the basket of rumpled laundry on its side on the floor to the dirty plate on the mantelpiece.

'I'm tired. I've been volunteering all day.'

'Only for a couple of hours,' Hannah pointed out. 'Are you unwell?'

'No . . . '

'Then you must pull yourself together and put your best foot forward each and every day. It's wonderful, when you're feeling a little under the weather, how a change of scene or some physical exertion can take your mind off it.'

'It isn't as simple as that . . . '

She was determined to shake Ruby out of her low mood. Her sister needed jollying along.

'It's bound to take you a while to recover from what Pa did to you — '

'Don't mention it,' Ruby said sharply.

'All right. I'm sorry. You're bound to feel homesick — I was when I came to Margate.'

'What do you know about anything anyway?' Ruby flared up. 'You're just a nurse.'

'I can arrange for you to see one of the doctors if you wish.'

'I don't need a doctor and I don't need you to keep going on at me. I need to rest, that's all.'

It was like they were eight and five again, and arguing over their dolls and the pram, and Nanny would come and separate them and tell them to behave with decorum as young ladies should, not fight like alley cats. Hannah wanted to shout at her little sister and point out that it was her who'd been on her feet for fourteen hours that day, but she took a deep breath and kept her temper.

'I'll do the laundry tomorrow, I promise,' Ruby said.

'Did you go to the market on your way back from the infirmary?'

Ruby shook her head.

'There is nothing for supper?' Hannah's stomach growled as she looked in the meat safe, the tiny larder with the grille across the front where they kept their staples away from the rats and mice. It was empty, apart from a morsel of hard cheese wrapped in waxed paper. 'Is there any milk or bread?'

'I thought we'd go and buy something from one of the stalls, or dine out,' Ruby said, her expression brightening.

'I'm not made of money. Where's my purse?'

'I'm afraid I don't know.'

'I left it here this morning.'

'I've . . . I seem to have mislaid it.'

'You've been out again then?'

Ruby nodded, her cheeks reddening. 'After I got back, I went out to take the air — I thought you'd be pleased that I'm looking after my health.'

'You've lost my purse!' Hannah exclaimed, her blood hot with anger. 'How could you be so careless as to lose my hard-earned money?'

'I didn't do it on purpose.'

'Did you retrace your steps to see if you could find it?'

'I had a look, but someone must have picked it up.' Tears began to roll down Ruby's cheeks. 'Please, don't send me back to Canterbury. Pa will lock me up again.'

At the sight of her remorse, Hannah's fury began to melt away.

'What am I going to do with you?'

'I'll make it up to you,' Ruby sobbed. 'I'll go out to work, so I can pay you back.'

'You'll have to stick at it, not give up on the first day like you did with the volunteering. I'll ask at the infirmary — you could apply for a position as a maid.'

'I don't want to be a scrubber,' Ruby said, aghast.

'What about nursing, then?'

'You're at work even when you're at home, worrying about your patients. You do as much as a doctor, yet you aren't paid like they are. How can Doctor Clifton afford that lovely house while we sit here in rented rooms?' Ruby's words stung like a swarm of angry wasps.

'Doctor Clifton has nothing to do with this. What about teaching, or nannying? You were always good with Christopher and — ' Hannah broke off.

'I'll enquire at the Hall by the Sea and the hotels along the front.'

'I'm not sure about that. You'd meet all sorts at those places.'

'I know how to behave, if that's what you mean. Don't you trust me?'

'I do, but I don't want to talk about this any further tonight. I'm dead on my feet — I'm going to bed.'

'It's early yet.'

'Goodnight, Ruby,' Hannah said firmly before making her way into the room they shared. She sank down on to the mattress and closed her eyes for a moment, wondering if she was going to regret having her sister to live with her. She was being harsh, she thought. They were both weary.

Tomorrow was a new day and they would feel better in the morning.

12

The Summer Fête

'Ruby?' Hannah wasn't sure if she should wake her or not, she was sleeping so soundly with a small frown on her face. 'I have to go now . . . '

Her sister opened one eye.

'I was dreaming,' she sighed.

'Will you come to the fête today?' Hannah asked. It was almost the end of July, and a week had passed since Ruby had lost her purse. They still hadn't found it, but she'd been paid since then, so they'd just about managed to stay afloat.

'Oh, I'm not sure.'

'The other day, you said you were looking forward to it.'

'I was, but I think I'd prefer to stay in bed — I need the sleep for my complexion.'

'How have you become so vain?' Hannah couldn't help grinning, thinking back to the incident with the carbolic and lard: she still had freckles, but the dreaded wrinkles had failed to materialise, for which she was greatly relieved. To her surprise, though, Ruby burst into tears.

'I'm sorry. I didn't mean to hurt your feelings.'

'You haven't. It's me. I don't feel like doing anything.'

'Oh? That's a shame.'

'I don't know what it is, but sometimes I feel

'. . . empty . . . hopeless . . . I can't describe it. I don't see any point in going out when I know I won't take any pleasure from it.'

'I wish there was something I could do to help,' Hannah said sadly. 'I hate to see you like this. Let me give you a few shillings for the shopping, in case you feel up to going out later. I'll hope to see you this afternoon — there's plenty of entertainment, food and drink, and tours of the infirmary. There'll be lots of people about: the great and good of Margate; Mr Fforde, Borough Surgeon . . . '

Ruby pulled a handkerchief from under her pillow and wiped her eyes. 'Will Doctor Clifton be there? I'm yet to meet him.'

'I expect he'll be busy seeing his private patients at the clinic. Sister Trim is going to let us leave the ward to run our stall: guess the number of sweets in the jar. Of course, we might be called away to an emergency. According to Charlotte, last year one of the ladies had to be carted off on a trolley from the splint room in a faint, after watching Mr Brightside demonstrate how to saw through a plaster cast.'

'Do you think Mr Milani will bring the lion cubs?'

'I don't see why he should — he'll be entertaining visitors to the Hall by the Sea today anyway. What a strange thing to say.'

'Not really. I'm sure he'd raise a lot of money, if people paid to pet them.'

'I suppose so. Look, I must hurry.' Hannah said farewell before leaving the house. It had been raining when she'd risen from her bed, but by seven, the clouds had evaporated, the sun was up, and the streets and beach were washed clean. By eight, she had a ward full of excitable children to get ready for the big day.

'This is worse than when the animals came,' Charlotte said, joining Hannah as she arranged fresh roses in a vase to brighten the place up. Their fragrance made her sneeze.

'Bless you,' Charlotte exclaimed.

'Watch out! Nurse Bentley's caught the scrofula,' Charlie chuckled. He was out of bed with one of the other boys — thirteen-year-old Beckett from Deal, who was suffering from a bowed spine.

'Let's have none of your cheek,' Charlotte said. 'Everyone is to be on their best behaviour for Mr Fforde.'

'Who's 'e when 'e's at 'ome?'

'He's our visiting surgeon, here to inspect every patient before he opens the fête.'

'We don't want any nonsense, or we'll lose our places,' Hannah warned.

Charlotte flashed her a glance of amusement as Charlie fell silent.

At ten, the doctors made their entrance: an entourage led by the Borough Surgeon, followed by Mr Anthony and Doctor Clifton, Doctor Pyle, then Mr Hunter and his medical student friends. They looked on as Mr Fforde made his examinations and held prolonged discussions over each patient. Hannah noticed that they were all smartly dressed — Doctor Clifton had made a special effort, wearing a new jacket and polished shoes, and she fancied that he was

213

wearing a different cologne than usual.

As the doctors progressed slowly along the ward, another one appeared.

'That's Mr Piper,' Hannah whispered aside to Charlotte as Sister Trim walked across to greet him. Two boys — one being pushed in a bath chair by one of the porters, and the other walking with a stick — followed him, and behind them came a woman wearing a stained blue dress with a frayed brown shawl over her head. She stopped and pulled it back to reveal her face, the glint of brown hair, and bare shoulders.

'Ma!' Charlie screeched. 'It's you! I can't believe my eyes.'

'My darlin' boy.' The woman hastened over and threw her arms around him. 'I didn't think I'd see yer again.'

A lump formed in Hannah's throat as Charlie's mother stroked his hair and cuddled him to her breast. He was crying. His ma was crying. Hannah noticed a tear rolling down Charlotte's cheek.

'How did you get 'ere?' Charlie said between sobs.

'Mr Piper said that somebody — out of the goodness of their 'eart — 'ad bought me a train ticket. I've never been on a train before — its joltin' and rattlin' put me in a fair state of petrification, but I'm 'ere now, safe an' sound.' Charlie's ma gave a toothless smile.

He reached out and traced the lines on her face. 'How are my sisters?'

'They're the same as ever. June 'as a babe on the way, Ellie's got married over a broomstick for a third time, and Nancy is back in the . . . I don't mind. I can keep a better eye on 'er in there. I'm workin' 'ard in the laundry.'

'I can tell — look at your poor 'ands.'

'At least they stays clean.' She chuckled, then grew serious again. 'I wish I could make enough of a livin' to make an 'ome for us, no matter 'ow 'umble, but there we go. I'm goin' back with Mr Piper later today, so I won't be stoppin' long. When are you comin' back to London?'

'Doctor Clifton says it will be quite soon. I'm much stronger, and me knees don't 'urt like they used to.'

Hannah suggested that they sit out on the balcony while they waited for the fête to begin.

Sister Trim came across to her and Charlotte. 'Mrs Merry will be here at any minute to watch the ones who are confined to bed. Nurse Bentley, you're in charge of the Lettsom's stall.'

Hannah fetched the jar they'd kept hidden in the sluice and carried it outside. It was filled to the brim with sweets: humbugs; pear drops; barley sugar; liquorice and aniseed balls. She put it on the end of one of the trestle tables which some-one had labelled 'Lettsom', and waited with some slips of paper, pencils and a hat. It wasn't long before Beckett turned up and offered to help.

'It's 'Guess the number of sweets in the jar',' she explained. 'It's a penny a go.'

'I wish I had a penny.'

'If you help me, you can have a free turn.' Beckett was one of Nurse Finch's patients, but Hannah had got to know him well over the past two weeks. He was quite a character with his

215

dimpled smile, green eyes and wayward ginger hair, and he'd sold several pennyworth of guesses even before Mr Fforde declared that the day's entertainments could begin.

Hannah looked along the row of stalls: a coconut shy; a 'test your strength' game; food and drink stands selling jams, cakes and biscuits, mineral waters from the local factory, coffee and tea, and sausage rolls from the hospital kitchens. The aromas of hot doughnuts and fresh seafood made her stomach growl.

'Trimmie's let me go,' she heard Charlotte saying from beside her. 'She said I could help you here, so we can take turns looking after the sweets. Have you heard? Mr Hunter has volunteered to be put into the stocks. I'm going to enjoy this.'

'And then you will forgive him?' Hannah asked, smiling.

'No . . . ' Charlotte said hesitantly.

'Oh, you will,' Hannah laughed. 'I can see right through you — you're in love with him.'

'I'm not.'

'If you weren't, you wouldn't be in the slightest bit bothered about what he gets up to.'

'Well, maybe. All right,' Charlotte confessed. 'He has a kind heart, much like his cousin, and he's good with the patients. I think he'll make an excellent physician in time. There he is.'

Hannah could see the stocks from where she stood guard over the sweets with Beckett. A stampede of people came to watch as Mr Hunter took off his waistcoat and tie and handed them to his friend, before kneeling behind the stocks and allowing a helper to trap his wrists.

'Roll up! Roll up! All monies received to be donated towards the work of this great house!' he shouted.

Mr Hunter's friends threw the first wet sponges at him, then Charlotte picked one from the bucket and aimed it at his head, sending rainbow showers of water through the air.

'You could have wrung it out first, Nurse Finch,' he bellowed, but he was grinning from ear to ear.

'Nurse Bentley, I thought it was you.' Mrs Clovis came up to the stand and beamed at her.

'How are you?' she said.

'Not so bad. My joints are creaking a little, but I'm bearing up. I'd hoped I might have a word with Doctor Clifton if he's here.'

'I haven't seen him since ward rounds,' Hannah said.

'Would you like to guess the number of sweets?' Beckett interrupted. 'I've been trying to count them, but there's more in that jar than there are fish in the sea. It's only a penny a go, and it's all in a good cause.'

'Perhaps I will, young man,' Mrs Clovis said, taking out her purse as Charlie and his mother passed by, holding hands. When she'd made her guess, she turned back to Hannah.

'I wished to say something to you . . . I was going to wait for a more suitable occasion, but I can't have it on my conscience to keep it from you any longer. I don't like telling tales, but I think you should know, as a respectable young lady.'

Hannah's heart began to beat faster. Mrs Clovis was an exacting landlady — did she have some fresh complaint about Ruby leaving crumbs out for the mice or letting the doors slam? She drew Mrs Clovis to one side.

'Go on,' Hannah said.

'It isn't right that they aren't married — I won't have my house used as a . . . place for illicit connections.'

'I beg your pardon?'

'You heard.'

'Whatever you're talking about, it can't possibly have anything to do with me.'

'You need to ask your sister what she gets up to when you're not at home.'

Hannah felt her forehead tighten. 'What are you suggesting?'

'I'm not suggesting anything. I'm telling the truth of it.' Mrs Clovis was adamant. 'There have been some considerable comings and goings — the visitor is of the male variety and he's keeping company with your sister.'

'You must be mistaken. I'll speak with her, but I'm sure there's a perfectly reasonable explanation . . . '

'I'm sure there will be,' Mrs Clovis said with irony. 'To my regret, Margate has become a town where anything goes. Men and women don't care what they do, or who sees them do it. We can't let this continue or people will go to Brighton for the summer instead. I'm sorry to bother you with it, but I must look after my reputation. Promise me you'll have a word with her.'

'I will. Thank you,' Hannah said, relieved when Mrs Clovis left the stall on her way for a tour of the infirmary. She tried to put their landlady's shaming and outrageous suggestion to the back of her mind — she would tackle Ruby later and reassure herself that Mrs Clovis was suffering an attack of delirium and would be forced to apologise.

'I'll look after this for a while,' Charlotte said on her return. 'You're white as a sheet. Are you all right?'

'I've just received some rather unpleasant news.'

'What is it?'

Hannah pulled herself together. 'Oh, it's probably nothing, a case of mistaken identity or some scurrilous gossip.'

'I've just seen your sister — she's over by the coconut shy.'

Unsure whether she was relieved or annoyed, Hannah thanked Charlotte and went to find Ruby. When she saw her innocent, smiling face, she found that she couldn't believe their landlady's accusations, but she knew she'd have to ask Ruby for her version of events — later, not in front of the infirmary staff and half of Margate.

'You're feeling better?' she asked.

'Much better now. The weather was so lovely, I thought I'd come and find you. I've done the shopping and the money's all gone. May I have another shilling — I'd like to try for a coconut.'

'I haven't any,' Hannah said, rather more sharply than she intended. 'I'm sorry. There's a music recital in the marquee — we can go and listen to that instead.'

The tent was crowded, but they found seats towards the back. A young woman with blonde hair piled up on top of her head, and adorned with fresh flowers, was sitting on a makeshift platform, her fingers dancing delicately across the strings of a harp. She wore a diaphanous green dress and gold bangles down her arms, her appearance as beautiful as the notes that she played.

The music raised Hannah's spirits. If it hadn't been for Mrs Clovis's accusations, she would say that she was the happiest she'd ever been, with her sister at her side, the camaraderie of the house, and the prospect of promotion. What's more, Charlie had got to see his mother, thanks to her instigation. All was well, and she wished she could capture the moment and lock it away in her heart for ever.

As the performance came to an end with a final pluck of the strings, the lady bowed her head, her cheeks flushed as the crowd burst into applause. Hannah spotted Doctor Clifton standing in the wings with Mrs Knowles and one of the governors.

'Bravo! Bravo!'

'What a treat,' Ruby whispered as the governor made his way across to join the harpist and held up his hands for quiet.

'I'm very proud of my talented daughter, Miss Osbourne-Cole,' he smiled. 'I hope you will dig deep and support our wonderful Sea Bathing Infirmary so that everyone, young and old, can have access to its care and expertise.' Hannah heard the jangling of coins in a bucket as the harpist got up, smoothed her dress and curtseyed, before Doctor Clifton stepped forward and took her hand to help her down from the stage.

'Well done.' Hannah could read his lips. 'That was a magnificent performance, as I knew it would be.'

'I need some air,' the lady said.

'Allow me.' Doctor Clifton led her towards the exit. As he passed Hannah, he caught her eye, gave the ghost of a smile and looked away.

'I should get back to the stall.' She nudged her sister. 'You will come and help.' It was an order, not a question. She didn't want to let Ruby out of her sight.

Ruby was delighted to join in. Beckett and Charlotte stayed on with them, the latter's eyes drifting away to where Mr Hunter was standing at the coconut shy, waiting a turn with his friends. His hair was rumpled, and his shirt still wet, clinging rather indecently to his chest.

'Have you forgiven him?' Hannah murmured, still afraid that he was one of those impossibly handsome and unruly gentlemen whose escapades made them irresistible to certain young ladies.

'I think he's done very well,' Charlotte said, grinning as Mr Hunter cast a smile in her direction. 'He's showing off, of course, but I don't mind that. He's raised plenty of money today, and now he's promised to win me a coconut. If he succeeds, I've agreed to walk out with him — as long as Doctor Clifton and Miss Osbourne-Cole can be persuaded to accompany us.'

'He's walking out with her?' Hannah felt sick when Charlotte nodded.

'Letitia, yes. I'm sorry. I didn't realise . . . If I'd known, I'd have mentioned it before.'

'It seems I was the last to find out,' Hannah said sadly. Why hadn't Doctor Clifton seen fit to mention it to her? Then equally, she reasoned, why should he? He was under no obligation to her — she had rejected him. As far as he was concerned, he was a free man. Taken by surprise by her regret and jealousy, she pulled up one of the folding chairs and sat down.

Charlotte touched her shoulder. Hannah looked up, squinting into the sunshine.

'It's a shock, that's all. I'll be all right.' She could hardly wait to return to the ward where she could try to forget Doctor Clifton and Miss Osbourne-Cole, and her irrational sense of betrayal. What had she expected? That he would remain unmarried out of respect for her, when she had put her vocation before love? Despite the laughter and sunshine, it was turning out to be one of the darkest days of her life.

And here they were coming to rub salt into her wounds, she thought as she saw them walking side by side towards the stall.

'Good day, Doctor Clifton,' Beckett said. 'Come and have a go.'

'I think we will,' he said. 'We've already guessed the weight of the pig and had a turn at hoopla, which I did very badly at.'

'I thought you did very well,' Miss Osbourne-Cole simpered. 'It wasn't your fault that the wind took hold of the rings . . . '

'There's bound to be some simple equation which can be applied to working out how many sweets are in the jar.' Doctor Clifton frowned. 'Has anyone any idea what the volume of a single humbug is?'

'I haven't the faintest clue,' his companion said. 'We should just count them all from the outside.'

'I've done that,' Beckett said, 'and it always comes out different.'

'I'm forgetting my manners.' Doctor Clifton turned to Miss Osbourne-Cole. 'You haven't met Nurse Bentley and Nurse Finch.'

'It's a pleasure to meet you, and can I say what wonderful work you do?'

'Thank you,' Charlotte said.

'I was most impressed with your recital,' Hannah said politely, the words catching in her craw. 'This is my sister, Miss Ruby Bentley.'

Miss Osbourne-Cole inclined her head in acknowledgement.

'Delighted,' Doctor Clifton said, his attention making Ruby blush.

'Have you completed your calculations?' Hannah went on.

'I think so,' he said, a quizzical expression on his face.

'You are to write the number down on the slip.'

'And give us a penny for it,' Beckett reminded them.

'What shall we do next, James?' Miss Osbourne-Cole said.

'What would please you?' Hannah hated the way he deferred to his companion. She would walk all over him, if he let her. 'The tour of the infirmary is very popular. The operating theatre is open for viewing.'

'I'd rather not. I'd find it too upsetting — I have a delicate constitution and sensitive nerves.'

She wouldn't make a good doctor's wife then, Hannah thought bitterly.

'There is an art exhibition — that might suit you better,' Doctor Clifton suggested.

'I'd like that. I do a little painting myself.'

As they turned away, Hannah spoke to Beckett.

'It must be time to see who has won our competition. Would you be so kind as to empty the slips out of the hat?'

'May I count the sweets?' he said.

'There's no need. When I filled the jar, I wrote the number down and put it inside the lid. Let's see who's the winner,' Hannah said, forcing a smile as she watched the happy couple retreating into the distance. She knew it wasn't her — she had most definitely lost when it came to love.

* * *

After the fête and having finished her shift, Hannah made her way back to their lodgings, where she found that their rooms were tidy, the floors had been swept and the kitchen table scrubbed. On top of the table stood two bottles

224

of stout, a small ham and a pan containing parsley sauce. She tasted it — it was still warm.

'You see how I'll make someone a good wife one day.' Ruby was smiling with pride.

'Thank you.' Hannah was touched by her gesture. 'Have I missed something? Is it a special occasion?'

'I thought I'd make up for being a lazy clodpole and show you how much I appreciate your kindness.'

'It isn't because you're trying to butter me up?'

'Why would I do that?'

'Only Mrs Clovis had a word with me this morning — she says that you've been entertaining a gentleman while I'm out . . . Ruby, tell me that it isn't true.'

'I'm not going to lie,' Ruby said. 'I should have told you before.'

'Told me what exactly?'

The story came out in a jumble of words and apology.

'You remember when we went to the Hall by the Sea and saw the cubs?'

Hannah nodded, dumbstruck. 'That dreadful man, the lion tamer?'

'My dear Antonio,' Ruby sighed. 'I promised him I wouldn't tell you, but I can't keep this to myself.'

'How can this be? He has befriended you? How did you let this happen?'

'I dropped my handkerchief and went back for it the next day — he'd found it and kept it for me.'

'You did it deliberately.' Hannah felt sick at the thought of her sweet and innocent sister flirting with a showman.

'He was kind to me. He treated me like I was special right from when he first set eyes on me in the crowd.'

'Why wouldn't he? You're quite a beauty! Ruby, this has to stop — for my sake as well as yours. Nurses are expected to have certain moral standards. I can't be exposed to any scandal — it could ruin everything.'

'I'm sorry, but — '

'How did he know where to find you?'

'I gave him our address — he asked me so amiably that I couldn't refuse.'

'How foolish can you be? Mrs Clovis says she's seen him here on more than one occasion.'

'He dropped by yesterday to give us tickets for the Hall by the Sea. I offered him tea and he stayed for an hour or so, no more. Don't look at me like that — it's very dull when you aren't here, and you don't need to worry about anything because he was the perfect gentleman.' Ruby fixed her with a glare. 'Don't tell me I have to give them back — they were a gift and we should use them with good grace as he intended.'

'Where are these tickets?' Hannah felt the ire rising in her breast. 'Let me see them.'

'They're on the windowsill over there.'

Hannah marched over, picked them up and tore them in two.

'What did you do that for?' Ruby exclaimed, her cheeks growing scarlet with annoyance.

'You mustn't associate with him any more — you'll ruin your reputation and your chances of making a good match to a decent and respectable young gentleman. What man will take you on for his wife in future, if he gets wind of rumours of how you've encouraged the attentions of others?' Hannah was more convinced now that there had been some truth in the story of Ruby and her involvement with the butcher's boy. She was afraid that her sister may well have encouraged it.

'You would have me marry some boring old doctor or engineer? Someone with stiff manners and unable to show affection? Anyway, it's too late — I will not give him up. He's the sweetest, most wonderful man, as well as being the most extraordinary lion tamer in the world.'

'Who says so?'

'He does.'

'I rest my case.'

'Hannah, I pity you for your cynicism. Can't you accept anything at face value?'

'I know enough of human nature to realise that some people present an image that isn't of their true selves, but of the person they aspire to be. What is he to you?'

'I count him as a friend,' Ruby said, frowning. 'I came to Margate friendless. What harm is there in making new acquaintances?'

'You can't be friends with any man, let alone a travelling showman. Even suggesting that you're acquainted with him is too much.' A thought occurred to Hannah. 'Tell me — did you do things when he was here?'

'A lady doesn't talk of such matters.' Ruby gazed down at her skirt and began tracing the pattern of the lace with her forefinger.

Was this her fault? Had she been too trusting?

'You can't possibly imagine that this man would make a suitable husband. How would you live? Does he have his own house?'

'He's settled in Margate for the summer and he has property in one of the Italian states . . . '

'Why are we having this conversation? He can't possibly support you. How old is he?' Ruby remained silent. 'There has to be at least twenty years between you. It's no use — you must put all thought of him aside. He hasn't offered to marry you, God forbid?'

'Not yet, but I have every expectation that — '

'You can have no expectation at all,' Hannah cut in. Lust had taken hold of her sister's senses, awkward as it was to think of it. 'Antonio lacks both charm and charisma. He's trying to buy you. Don't you see? He's trying to prise your innocence away.'

'What gives you the right to judge him?'

Hannah tried another approach. 'A woman's virtue is all she has in the eyes of society.'

'If it will please you, I'll ask him if he intends to marry me,' Ruby said more cheerfully.

'You'll do no such thing!'

'I'll do as I wish.'

Hannah thought for a moment. 'Let's just say that if he did by some miracle agree to marry you, where would you live?'

'He shares a caravan, but it isn't what it sounds like — it's a proper little house on wheels with a wooden floor and shutters.'

'You'd hate it — you'd feel too restricted.'

'I wouldn't spend every day stuck indoors. Antonio says that I'm not tiny enough for a freak, but I'm supple enough to train to be a dancer.'

'You mean, he wants you to make a spectacle of yourself to support him?'

'We'd support each other, Hannah. That's what it means to be in love.'

'You'll promise me that you won't seek him out again. As I've said, there must be absolutely no further association between the two of you.'

'All you care about is yourself.' Ruby's eyes flashed with anger.

'How do you work that one out when I've done everything for you, you ungrateful — '

'You would make me unhappy because you can't stand the thought of telling your friends at the infirmary that your sister is marrying a lion tamer. I'm seventeen, almost eighteen, while you are twenty-one going on ninety. You're jealous because I have an admirer. In fact, I have many admirers — I turn heads whenever I walk along the street. And you have none. You'll end up as a shrivelled prune of a spinster while I delight in marriage and children, lots of them.'

Hannah clenched her fists, furious and staring at Ruby as if she'd just found the maggot in the core of the sweetest apple.

'You know, I think you're losing your mind — if you're not careful, I'll have to lock you up, like Pa did.'

'You wouldn't!' Ruby's complexion paled, and

she sank to the floor in a sobbing, trembling heap.

'I'm sorry. I didn't mean it. It was said in the heat of the moment.' Hannah knelt beside her and reached out to stroke her hair. Ruby flinched. What had happened to her dear little sister? 'All I ask is that you promise me that you won't have any further contact with Mr Milani.'

'You won't have me put away, will you?' Ruby cried. 'I'm not a lunatic, you know.'

'I know,' Hannah murmured. 'Look, all I want is to keep you safe from scandal and ruin. Society — whether we like it or not — judges a young woman's reputation to be irretrievably damaged if she's found consorting unchaperoned with a member of the male sex. It destroys any chance she has of marriage. If Mr Milani had good intentions and any measure of politeness, he wouldn't turn up here and invite himself in without speaking to me first and making sure you weren't left alone with him. Ruby, he's compromised you. It mustn't happen again.'

'I am sorry. I should have thought about how it looked. I should have considered how it would affect you as well; your position at the infirmary; your friends' regard for you if it became common knowledge.'

'Thank you for the apology. It means a lot to me.'

'I wish you'd stop talking now. You're giving me a headache,' Ruby grumbled.

'You'd better go and lie down, then.' Hannah watched as her sister dragged herself up from the floor and headed for the bedroom. The ham and parsley sauce stood forgotten, no longer inviting.

A little while later when Ruby was tucked up asleep in bed, Hannah took a walk down to the beach. She gazed at the water and listened to the sea breathing, the waves washing softly across the sand. What was she going to do? Ruby hadn't actually promised that she wouldn't see the lion tamer again, although Hannah felt that now she had been found out, she would think twice about allowing anyone to ruin her reputation. She needed occupation and distraction, but what would keep her out of trouble? Hannah didn't know. She was afraid she was out of her depth.

13

The Powers that Be

It was a few days after the fête and Ruby appeared to have taken Hannah's words of warning to heart, because she didn't mention Mr Milani once. She devoted herself to reading, writing letters to Stepmother and Miss Fellows, and keeping their rooms clean and tidy. Hannah had taken to returning home during her breaks now and again to check on Ruby's whereabouts, but today, she'd decided to stay at the infirmary for lunch.

'May I have a word,' Doctor Clifton said, catching up with her as she sat on the balcony, eating her food in peace and quiet. 'I'm sorry for disturbing you, but we haven't had a chance to talk.'

She looked up at him. 'Take a seat,' she offered, putting her knife and fork down.

'You haven't finished.'

'I've had enough.' She pushed her plate aside. 'What is it you wish to discuss?'

'I was delighted to see that Charlie's mother turned up with Mr Piper. The boy's health seems much improved.'

'He'll be going home soon,' she said. 'Thank you for the extra donation you made, by the way — I noticed.'

'In for a penny, in for a pound. I heard that Beckett won the prize.'

'He shared it with everyone on the ward, which was very sweet of him, but the boys were all overexcited afterwards.' She smiled fondly at the memory of having to tell Charlie, Beckett and Samuel off for making an effigy of Sister Trim. 'Don't you think he's too well to be an inpatient, taking up a bed?'

'It turns out that his father is paying generously for him to be here, so the powers that be, the ones who hold the purse-strings, are keen to keep him here for as long as possible. Before you say anything, I've already put my medical opinion forward . . . '

'I see. Was there anything else?'

'No,' he said. 'That is all. Um, have you had a meeting with Mrs Knowles yet?'

She shook her head.

'Then Sister Trim is in with her now.' He checked his pocket watch. 'I'd better go — I have a clinic booked for two o'clock.'

Followed by dinner with Miss Osbourne-Cole? she wondered as she watched him go. She checked her thoughts. She had better things to do than mope about like a lovesick ninny.

Back on the ward, she started on the weekly chore of cleaning the windows which involved washing the glass, then polishing it with a cloth dipped in vinegar to remove the smears. She had only washed one pane before Sister Trim came rushing in.

'Nurse Bentley, you are to go to Matron's office immediately,' she said.

'Is it good news?'

'I shall have to think about it before I can decide. Go on.'

Hannah hurried away to meet Mrs Knowles who was sitting at her desk, waiting for her.

'Take a seat,' she said lightly, and Hannah sat down.

'Normally, I wouldn't pry, but I do need to ask you a question,' Mrs Knowles said, making Hannah catch her breath. How could she possibly know about Ruby's indiscretion? 'It's been observed by some that Doctor Clifton pays you particular attention,' Matron went on.

'I can assure you that there's nothing in it,' Hannah said quickly, relieved that she wasn't asking about her sister. 'I believe that he's soon to be engaged to — '

'Miss Osbourne-Cole. I'd noticed their affection for each other and I'm glad you've confirmed my suspicions. I do so hate losing any of my nurses to matrimony. Anyway, Sister Murch has left the house — her mother has taken a turn for the worse, so I've asked Sister Trim to take over responsibility for her ward, which means there's a vacancy on the Lettsom. I'd like to offer you the role of ward sister. What do you say?'

Her heart leapt.

'Thank you, Mrs Knowles. I'd be delighted to accept.'

'Then it's done. You'll start first thing in the morning. Any problems, report to me. Is that clear?'

'Yes, Matron.'

Hannah returned to the ward, her excitement tempered with a little trepidation as she wondered what Sister Trim thought of Matron's changes.

'Congratulations, Sister Bentley,' Trimmie said, somewhat icily.

'Sister?' Charlotte asked.

'That's right — she's only been here for five minutes.'

'Well done, Hannah,' Charlotte said.

'It will all go to pot, you mark my words. You can't treat your nurses as friends — I'll be watching with interest.'

Hannah refused to let Sister Trim's doubts spoil the day. Charlotte was happy for her, and Ruby, who appeared to have stayed indoors all day, was delighted.

'My sister is a Sister at last,' Ruby smiled. 'We should go out and celebrate with ice cream or cake on your next day off. What do you think?'

'That's a wonderful idea,' Hannah said, pleased that Ruby seemed to have seen sense. She didn't mention the lion tamer once, and, she noticed, hadn't suggested that they should celebrate with an outing to the Hall by the Sea. She felt reassured, but not entirely complacent.

⋆　⋆　⋆

The next morning when she walked on to the ward, she surveyed her new kingdom. She would make a few changes; she would make her mark.

She was responsible for two nurses: Nurse Finch and a new member of staff, Nurse May, who'd had little experience of nursing before, having kept house for her father, who was a captain in the merchant navy, while he was away at sea. It meant that much of the hands-on nursing would still fall to Hannah for a while — at least until she'd trained her up in the ways of the house.

She allocated Nurse May three patients and gave her a list of simple tasks to carry out before the doctors turned up on their rounds.

'Do you think she'll be any good?' Charlotte was helping Hannah change Samuel's dressing. 'I can't believe Mrs Knowles sent her to us.'

'I can't speculate on her suitability for the work.'

'I'm sorry — I keep forgetting that you're Sister now. Where is she anyway?'

Hannah glanced around the ward. There was no sign of her.

'Shall I see if I can find her?' Charlotte asked.

'I'll go. You carry on . . . ' Hannah felt mean. She and Charlotte used to use any excuse for a few minutes away from the ward, but she couldn't be seen to be encouraging that now. What was Nurse May thinking of, disappearing when there was work to be done? She began to feel a little anxious, knowing how impatient Mr Anthony was if his patients weren't ready.

She headed into the corridor, where the door to the sluice was open. As she drew closer, she heard sobbing.

'Nurse?' she said in a low voice as she went inside. 'Whatever's the matter?'

Nurse May was standing at the sink, scrubbing her skirt. She turned to face Hannah, her cheeks glistening with tears.

'I tried to carry too much in one go — I dropped the bedpans.'

Hannah couldn't help smiling. 'Never mind. It's happened to us all at one time or another.'

'I stink — it's disgusting. And look at the mess I've made in here! I don't think I'm cut out for this kind of work.'

'Calm down. One of the maids has a store of clean dresses and aprons — go and get changed, take a few deep breaths and come back. Nurse Finch will help you clean this up.'

'Do I have to?' Charlotte complained when Hannah sent her to the sluice.

'Yes, you do.'

'What about the ward round?'

'I'll deal with it. Off you go.'

Charlotte gave a half-smile, saying, 'I think the power is going to your head,' before leaving the ward just as Mrs Merry arrived wanting to take Charlie for his bath.

'You can't have him yet,' Hannah said.

'I can't 'ang about, waitin' for the doctors.'

'I'd be most grateful' — Hannah spoke firmly — 'if you would start with one of the other wards today.'

'Oh, I don't know. I always do 'em in the same order.' Mrs Merry stared at her before going on, 'Sister Bentley, when Sister Trim was 'ere, she let me have free rein to organise the baths as I wished.'

'I don't think she did,' Hannah said. 'In fact, I'm sure she didn't. I think you're trying it on, Mrs Merry.'

'I don't want to go stomping off to the other end of the 'ouse when I'm already 'ere, do I? It's very inconvenient.'

'Then I suggest you have a word with Mr Anthony or Mr Pyle.'

'I don't like to bother 'em with somethin' so trivial. I'll make a start on my ladies instead.'

Hannah smiled to herself as the bathing attendant lumbered away. She knew that Mrs Merry wouldn't brave speaking to the doctors, considering herself to be many rungs below them.

'Good morning, Sister,' Mr Anthony said when the doctors appeared on their round half an hour later.

'Congratulations on your promotion,' Doctor Clifton added. 'You deserve it.'

She thanked them before adding pointedly, 'You're putting us all behind today.'

'There was an emergency,' Mr Anthony said, sounding irritated. 'One of the kitchen maids sliced through a finger instead of the bread.'

'Whereas I have no excuse except that I overslept.' Doctor Clifton turned away and yawned to prove the point, and Hannah had to fight off an image of him sitting up late at night with Miss Osbourne-Cole. 'Where's Nurse Finch?'

'She's showing our new nurse the ropes.' Hannah led the doctors to Charlie's bedside.

'How are you today?' Doctor Clifton asked him.

'Very well,' he smiled.

He was becoming quite a handful, Hannah

thought, running around and disturbing the other patients. Sister Trim had been right — when they were well enough to cause trouble, it was time for them to go home.

'Would you like to go back to London soon?'

'Yes please, Doc,' he said. 'Ma needs me.'

'I hope you thanked Sister Bentley for arranging your mother's visit.'

'I didn't know. I thought Mr Piper did it.'

'Oh no, it was Sister's idea.'

'Was it?' Charlie turned to her. 'I don't know what to say, 'cept for . . . you're the best nurse in all the world. Thank you for 'elpin' me get better, for bringin' Ma to see me and for bein' so cheerful. Thank you for everythin'.'

'I'm very glad that it's worked out for you. You're a dear boy.'

'You have a ticket for a while longer,' Doctor Clifton said, 'but I don't think it's necessary to keep you here. I'll write to Mr Piper.'

Hannah felt torn about sending Charlie back to the poorhouse at St Pancras, but as much as she'd grown fond of him, they couldn't keep him at the infirmary, wrapped in cotton wool for the rest of his life.

★ ★ ★

It was the beginning of the second week in August when arrangements had been finalised for Charlie's return to his mother, and Hannah was busier than ever on the ward.

'It would have been quicker to do it myself,' she grumbled lightly as she helped Nurse May mop up the river of suds which was spreading across the floor.

'I'm s-s-sorry,' she stammered. 'I didn't mean to — '

'I know.' Hannah picked up the bucket and squeezed the water from her mop. 'Finish clearing up here, then you can help Nurse Finch change Samuel's dressings. Where is Nurse Finch?'

Nurse May looked at her as if she thought she was slightly touched. 'It's her afternoon off.'

'Oh yes, I'd forgotten.' She felt rather stupid, but she had too much on her mind, what with the prospect of the weekly meeting with Mrs Knowles and the other ward sisters, a complaint from one of the parents about how their son's coat had gone missing from his bedside locker, and a request to put in to Mr Cumberpatch about a repair. She knew what he'd say, that she was to blame for letting the boys bounce on the beds. 'What are you waiting for?'

'I'd be very grateful if you'd show me how to do the dressing — I haven't done it before.'

'Nurse Finch was supposed to have shown you.' Hannah sighed inwardly. Charlotte hadn't been the same since she'd announced that Mr Hunter had invited her to the infirmary ball. Her head had been filled with her plans for her gown and other adornments, and she'd arranged to call on Ruby this afternoon, considering her the oracle when it came to the latest fashions. 'Let me demonstrate, then you can do the next one.'

They had just finished when Doctor Clifton came to say goodbye to Charlie.

'I have some news for you, Master Swift. I've put a good word in for you with your sponsor.'

'The gentleman who gave me the ticket?' Charlie asked.

'That's right. If you go to school every day — he'll be checking on you — he'll place you with an ostler at one of the coaching inns.' Doctor Clifton smiled. 'I recall how much you liked seeing the animals on the ward, and I thought it would suit you very well. You'll be paid to look after the horses after lessons: feeding them; mucking out; cleaning their harness . . . What do you think?'

Charlie's eyes lit up. 'I'll make yer proud, I promise.'

'I have something else for you.' Doctor Clifton handed him a package wrapped in brown paper and tied up with string.

'What is it? I've never 'ad a present before.'

'Open it.'

He fumbled with the knots, and Hannah had to fetch a pair of scissors so he could cut them away and dive in, tearing the parcel apart.

'Barley sugar! And socks! Thank you!'

'You may put the socks on,' Doctor Clifton said when Charlie had calmed down a little.

'I don't want to spoil 'em — they'll get ruined and go into 'oles like the old ones.'

'Are you sure you won't wear them for the journey home?' Charlie nodded as the doctor continued, 'Promise me you'll work hard and keep your nose clean.'

'Yes, Doc. I mean, Doctor Clifton. I'll make 'em 'orses shine.'

'Perhaps one day you'll come back and see us,' Doctor Clifton said, just as Hannah heard the lady volunteer speaking from the entrance to the ward. 'Time and tide wait for no man — or boy, for that matter.' He smiled as he shook Charlie's hand.

Hannah hugged him, wishing him good luck before they watched him stride out of the Lettsom with his belongings.

'That's what makes all this worthwhile. I can't imagine any better reward than to see him walk out of here like that,' Doctor Clifton said, and Hannah had to agree.

She took her break at midday, having a bite to eat before strolling along the beach to clear her head. It was on occasions like this that she found herself reflecting on her decision to stay in nursing. She'd made a difference to Charlie and would do so for many other children, something she wouldn't have been able to achieve, had she given it up for marriage. She couldn't help thinking about the ball, though. She could have gone dancing with Doctor Clifton as his fiancée, even his wife, but now he'd be going with Miss Osbourne-Cole.

On her way back to the Lettsom, she came across Mr Fry wandering along the corridor.

'How lovely to see you.' He'd forgotten who she was, she thought, as he stared at her blankly. 'I wish it were in better circumstances, of course. You've come to see Miss Huckstep.'

'Ah yes. You're Nurse Bentley.'

'It's Sister now,' she said.

'You've been promoted.' He looked her up and

down again, making her feel uncomfortable. 'My congratulations.'

'Thank you. Alice will be delighted to see you . . . '

'Pray tell me where I can find her.'

She showed him to the ladies' ward. 'She'll be outside on the balcony.'

He hesitated, one hand in his pocket. 'I've come to do the right thing, you know.'

'Then don't waste any more time — go and speak to her,' Hannah said, pleased that whatever she thought of Mr Fry, Alice would get her wish at long last. The prospect of marriage to the man of her dreams would be of much benefit to her health, giving her something to look forward to — for however long it lasted. She headed back to the Lettsom, not wanting to intrude on their reunion.

By encouraging Alice to write again, she had played her part in making sure that the course of true love ran smoothly — she could do no more — but it wasn't long before Mr Fry came and accosted her on the ward, his cheeks scarlet with anger and embarrassment.

'Sister Bentley, I am here to say goodbye.'

'Please, not in front of the children,' she said, leading him back out into the corridor. 'Keep your voice down.'

'Miss Huckstep has jilted me in the cruellest manner, inviting me here to reject and humiliate me. You gave me the impression that she was about to accept my offer — '

'That's what I thought she wanted,' Hannah cut in, frowning.

'I have no doubt that she'll repent of having let me slip, but there's no remedy now. It's too late.' He scratched at his neck, making a pimple bleed. 'I forgot to ask her for the return of my letters and picture. Will you make sure she sends them back to me in London?'

'Well, yes, of course.'

'Good day,' he said. 'I doubt that we shall meet again.'

'Good day,' she responded, suppressing the urge to rush off to ask Alice what had happened.

At last the end of her shift arrived, and she hurried off to see Alice, taking a seat at the side of her bed.

'I heard what you did to poor Mr Fry. I did actually feel a little sorry for him.'

'He left it too late,' Alice said.

'You haven't done this to let him off the hook? I mean, you deserve some happiness, even if — '

'It's short-lived,' Alice finished for her. 'It's true that I don't know how long I have for this earth, but nobody knows when death will come. We've both seen how an able-bodied person can be struck down by an illness or accident and be gone within the hour. No, I wasn't thinking of sparing his feelings in that way.

'If he'd really loved me, he would have put me first. I didn't want him marrying me out of guilt or sympathy. Don't worry — I've had plenty of time to get used to the idea of being without him.' Alice shivered. 'I've made a promise to God that if I should recover from this terrible disease, I'll commit the rest of my life to nursing. I'll be a better nurse for it, because I know how it feels to be exhausted, scared and in pain.'

Hannah reached out and held her hand, waiting until she had fallen asleep, when she pulled a blanket up around her shoulders and whispered, 'Goodnight.'

14

When the Remedy is Worse
than the Disease

Over the next three weeks, there was much debate between the physicians and surgeons about the approach to the scrofula in Samuel's elbow joint. Mr Anthony wanted to amputate his arm while Doctor Clifton wanted to give a longer course of thalassotherapy. On the morning of the ball, they were still arguing over it.

'If the scrofula should reappear in the other arm, then amputation would be a disaster for the boy,' Doctor Clifton said. 'We shouldn't be too quick to chop out the diseased tissue in this case. I don't think we would be able to say with a clear conscience that we'd done right by him.'

'What do you suggest, then?'

'A dose of *Hirudo medicinalis*.'

'Isn't that rather outdated? Gone are the days when physicians let blood.'

'I think it would do no harm and may do much good. If it makes no difference, then we've lost nothing.'

'Except that you will have lost face, Doctor Clifton,' Mr Anthony smirked. 'All right. If you must, but this wasn't my idea, remember? I don't want to be mocked for sending the house back into the Dark Ages, when the afflicted might hug

246

a chicken to his chest to suppress a cough, or hold a hanged man's hand to cure goitre.'

Doctor Clifton turned to Hannah.

'Sister, you will apply' — he lowered his voice so that Samuel couldn't hear him — 'the leech.'

'I'll order one from the dispensary.' They were kept with the other medicines, in ornate jars suspended in murky water and unfed for up to a year. The thought of it made her flesh crawl — she'd line Charlotte or Nurse May up for the task. She smiled to herself — that was one great advantage of being a sister. One could delegate.

Later, a dispensary nurse came in with a tray with a lid on top.

'I have something for you, I believe,' she grinned, as Hannah walked across to take it from her.

'It's just what I've always wanted,' she chuckled. 'Nurse Finch, where are you?'

'She's gone to clean the bedpans with Nurse May.' Beckett looked up from where he'd made a station for the toy train out of boxes and pencils. 'She said it would take them quite some time. Shall I fetch her for you?'

'No, thank you. I'll do it.' Hannah left the ward, keeping half an eye on what was going on behind her, in case the boys took advantage of her brief absence to get up to mischief. She hesitated outside the door to the sluice and listened for a moment. At the sound of clattering and laughter, she pushed the door open to find Nurse May leaning on the handle of her mop, while Nurse Finch twirled across the room from the sink to the cupboard, holding a broom across her chest.

'That, so Henry's told me, is how to dance a waltz!' Charlotte broke off abruptly. 'Sister! Oh dear.'

Hannah didn't need to tell them off for malingering — they knew they'd done wrong.

'I want you, Nurse Finch, to show Nurse May how to apply a leech.'

Their faces fell.

'Ugh,' Charlotte said with a shudder.

'It's for Samuel. Put these things away and come back to the ward.'

A few minutes later, Hannah was supervising her nurses at Samuel's bedside.

'One is supposed to distract the patient by singing a song or telling a story while placing it just behind one ear or on the top of the head, so that it's out of sight,' Charlotte said.

'In this case, it has to be attached to the elbow to do any good,' Hannah pointed out. 'Now, Samuel, the doctor has said that you are to have a leech applied to the swelling on your arm. It's nothing to worry about. In fact, it's one of our little helpers, working to get you better.'

'I don't want a leech,' he cried out. 'They stick on and won't let go — I had one when I fell in the pond at home.'

'I thought boys liked bugs and creepy crawlies.'

He screeched again, loud enough to wake the dead.

'If you don't let Nurse Finch do this, then there's a strong chance that you will lose your arm, and we don't want that, do we?'

'No . . . ' His mouth formed an O, and he

grew rigid with fear.

'There. That's better,' Hannah said. 'Go ahead, Nurse.'

Charlotte rolled her eyes, and Hannah frowned at her with mock annoyance — it hadn't been straightforward being promoted above a friend. Neither of them was quite used to it.

'I thought it would be better if Nurse May actually applied the leech. She needs the experience.'

'I'd rather we stuck to our principles: see one, do one then teach one.' Hannah took the lid off the tray and pushed it in front of Charlotte who grimaced.

'You have to pick it up,' Hannah said with a wicked grin.

'Can't I use forceps?'

'You'll damage it. Use your fingers.'

'What if it sticks to me?'

'It won't, if you're quick.' Hannah turned to the boy. 'Roll your sleeve right up and hold out your arm. That's right.'

'Sister, you'll have to do it,' Charlotte said, after three false starts, putting her hand in the tray and pulling it out.

'For goodness' sake, try again.'

Charlotte squeezed her eyes almost shut, and this time, she retrieved the leech and planted it with lightning speed into the crook of Samuel's elbow. He shuddered as the squirming creature, four inches long and starving, attached itself by its suckers to the vein. Charlotte covered his arm with a canvas frame, so he couldn't watch it swell as it drained his blood.

'Well done, Samuel,' Charlotte said, more cheerfully. 'How does that feel?'

'All right,' he said. 'It doesn't hurt any more.'

'That's good. I'll be along later to check on you. Thank you, Nurse Finch and Nurse May. You've all been very brave,' Hannah said with irony.

Within a few hours the leech had disappeared, and she had to search among the bedclothes to find it. She dropped it back into the tray, so it could be returned to the dispensary.

'My arm's bleeding,' Samuel said. 'Look . . .'

'Don't worry. It'll stop soon.' Having reassured him, Hannah dressed the wound, but an hour later, the blood had seeped through three layers of bandages, so she decided to send for the duty doctor.

'I don't know who it will be,' Charlotte said, overhearing her talking of her plan with Samuel. 'They'll be getting ready to go to the ball.'

'As you will be in half an hour.' Hannah had given her special dispensation to leave work early.

'I expect you'll look like a princess, Nurse Finch,' Samuel said.

'I hope so,' Charlotte smiled. 'It won't be for want of trying. I have a beautiful gown and new shoes, and a ruby pendant that I've borrowed from a friend of mine.'

'Are you goin' with your 'usband?'

'The gentleman is not my husband, not yet anyway,' Charlotte answered, blushing.

''E's your fancy man then,' Samuel chuckled. 'Is it Mr 'unter? We've all been guessin' it's 'im.'

'Samuel, it's none of your business,' Hannah interrupted. 'Nurse Finch, please will you go and find the duty doctor.'

'Of course,' she said.

It was Doctor Clifton who turned up to examine Samuel's arm.

'It's quite normal for it to bleed for hours, even days,' he said, taking Hannah aside.

'Won't it eventually drain the patient of blood?'

'I've seen a case where a nurse mistook the physician's instructions and attached leeches overnight. On removal, she applied warm compresses to the bites, and the patient . . . well, the outcome was not entirely favourable. Apply a pressure bandage, not overly tight, and I'll drop by later to check that all is well.'

'Thank you, but don't worry. You don't want to be late . . . '

He smiled ruefully. 'You won't have heard — I'm not going.'

'Oh?' Suddenly, she didn't feel so bad about missing out on the ball.

'I'm on duty tonight. If you need me, you know where I am.'

Towards the end of her shift, Hannah made sure that her patients were comfortable before handing over to the night staff. It was her favourite time of day, seeing all the boys settled in their beds with everything in its place ready for the morning. She walked along the centre aisle, whispering goodnight to the little ones who were already half asleep, and to the older boys who were lying awake.

'I don't feel too good,' she heard Samuel mutter.

'Let's have a look at you.' Having reached his bedside, she touched his forehead — it was clammy and cool, and his face was pale. 'Have you any pain?'

'No, but it's freezin' in 'ere . . . '

'Let me see your bandage.'

He lifted his arm to show her the dark stain which had soaked through the gauze and into the sheets.

'I'll call for the doctor.' She frowned. 'Let me fetch you another blanket.'

She hurried away to find Doctor Clifton who was attending to a patient on the girls' ward.

'It's Samuel,' she said softly.

'I'll be with you in two minutes.' He turned to the young girl who was wearing a neck brace. 'How is the pain now?'

'A little better,' she murmured.

'Nurse will be with you shortly. In the meantime, I have to go and see another patient, but I can come back at any time, if the pain should flare up again.'

The girl smiled weakly. Doctor Clifton had a way with the children — he would make a wonderful father. Dismissing a pang of sorrow and regret, Hannah hurried back to the Lettsom, giving him details of Samuel's condition as they went.

'You've come to save my life?' The boy's eyes brightened. 'I feel like I'm dyin'.'

'You are far from dying, young man. Let me have a look at you.' Doctor Clifton was very thorough, listening to Samuel's chest with his stethoscope while Hannah took off the dressing to reveal the marks left by the leech. The blood kept coming, until she wasn't sure if the boy had any left.

'I'm going to apply a tourniquet for a while. It won't hurt, although it might feel a little uncomfortable. By putting pressure at the top of your arm, I'll be able to slow the bleeding, giving it a chance to form a clot.'

'That was an 'orrid creature to do this to me,' Samuel observed.

'The leech has been a little overenthusiastic in its ministrations,' Doctor Clifton admitted. 'Sister, I'd be very grateful if you'd make some notes.'

Hannah stayed on until the bleeding stopped, and the doctor deemed that Samuel was out of immediate danger. He prescribed a tonic and a bottle of stout to be administered by the night staff, before he and Hannah made their way out of the ward.

'Shouldn't you have gone home by now?' he asked as she turned the lights down, watching the flames in the gasoliers die back.

'Officially, yes, but — '

'You should go.'

'What about you?'

'I'm on call all night. Everyone else is at this ball.' He paused before continuing, 'I'm going down to the kitchens to beg a coffee. Will you join me? Unless you're in a hurry . . . '

Ruby would be in bed by now, she thought, and she felt restless, so although she might regret it in the morning, she accepted his invitation. It was just coffee, a chance to catch up and perhaps find out why he was not out dancing with the great and good of Margate.

The kitchen maid, employed to serve refreshments to the night staff, served them coffee and eggs on toast at a table in the comer of the dining hall.

'I expect you're wondering why I didn't go to the ball tonight,' Doctor Clifton said. 'You don't have to pretend.'

'I did think it odd that you'd decided not to go,' she confessed. 'Especially with Mr Hunter inviting Nurse Finch — maybe there will be an announcement soon.'

'You think she will accept him?'

'Is he going to offer?'

'I've told him he'd be foolish not to. She's perfect for him, but perhaps she doesn't feel the same way.'

'She's fond of him, I believe, but I can't say whether or not she still has reservations about his character.'

'We'll see if he has the courage to ask her.' Doctor Clifton smiled.

He was diverting her, she realised, but it was fair enough. He took a lump of sugar from the bowl on the table and dropped it into his coffee cup, then picked up a spoon and stirred it.

'I'm sorry. I'm not very good company,' he said eventually. 'I was supposed to be going to the ball with Miss Osbourne-Cole.'

Hannah remembered how her world had fallen apart at the fête when she'd seen them together, even though she had no right to feel that way. 'I heard her playing the harp at the fête. It was very impressive.'

'She's very accomplished, and beautiful, but' — he shrugged — 'I've made a terrible mess of things. Her family are calling me a cad and sending me letters, threatening to sue me for breaking a promise, which I hasten to add I never made.' He fell silent as the maid came in to pour more coffee, then left the room. 'I shouldn't lay this on your shoulders.'

'You can say anything to me, Doctor Clifton. We are friends, I hope.'

'Thank you. I need someone in whom I can confide, who won't judge or mock me. My cousin is making a joke out of it.'

'What happened? Start from the beginning,' Hannah said.

'It began when I first set eyes on you.'

She stood up abruptly and turned to look through the window at the near darkness. 'You can't lay the blame for this at my door.'

'I know, but you wanted to hear it from the start . . . Perhaps I should have begun with Suzanna, my wife.' She heard the quaver in his voice. 'I thought I was ready to move on . . . with you . . . But when I learned that that was impossible, and having spoken to you, I convinced myself that I was ready to marry again.'

'And you chose Miss Osbourne-Cole.'

'Yes, a delightful young lady from a respectable family with links to the house, and all the right connections. We'd been introduced before and I'd thought nothing more of it, but when we met again recently at a musical evening to which my cousin had an invitation, we spoke at some length and she expressed a desire to spend more time in my company. She's most agreeable, and I thought I could grow to love her in time.'

'But?'

'I soon realised that I was wrong.'

'You made her a promise of an engagement?'

'No, but I can see how she might have misinterpreted my intentions.'

'You were walking out with her?'

'Not exactly. I invited her to play at the fête, thinking that she would enjoy showing off her talents for a good cause. I asked her father if it was permissible for me to do so before I spoke to her, and it all seemed perfectly acceptable. However, her father now says that I made her a promise of marriage, which isn't true, and I'm in deep water. I'm not even sure if I'll be able to continue to volunteer my services at the infirmary.'

'How can he stop you?'

'He's one of the governors, and he has influence throughout Margate. This could affect my private practice too, if he blackens my name.'

Hannah returned to her seat and rested her elbows on the table in a most unladylike manner, but she didn't care. She only cared about him. He was distraught and tired, and she wanted to take him in her arms and tell him that everything would be well.

'Apparently, Letitia is devastated because she was already thinking of the future we would have together: the wedding; the house . . . ' He ran his hands through his hair. 'I feel very guilty.'

'It seems to me that you didn't do anything wrong, although I do feel sorry for her.' She recalled Charlotte telling her how she had felt being jilted by the man who had gone on to marry her sister.

'I could have gone through with it — I could have made her my wife out of convenience, but that wouldn't have been fair on her. She would have suffered being married to a doctor, having to make sacrifices for my work.'

If a young lady truly loved you, she would make any sacrifice, Hannah thought, before realising, with a jolt of shock, that she was thinking of herself. She loved him, yet she hadn't been able give up her stubborn refusal to marry and sacrifice her vocation for him. Did that make her a hypocrite?

He took out a handkerchief and blew his nose.

'I'm overwrought. I've had a bad day — one of my private patients passed away. He was only twenty-six and married with three young children.'

Hannah nodded. There was nothing she could offer, except for the usual platitudes.

'All I can say is that I've learned a lesson — that although it might seem foolish, or greedy, I will marry only for love.' He sat back and placed his hands flat on the table. 'I will envy Henry if Charlotte accepts his proposal.'

'Perhaps we'll know tomorrow, if he has the courage to offer. It's getting late. I'd better be on my way.' She stood up to leave. 'I hope you have a peaceful night.'

'I'll see you tomorrow,' he said. 'Goodnight, Sister.'

Hannah walked home — it wasn't far and there were still plenty of people about, taking advantage of the taverns and dining rooms. She passed several couples: young newlyweds walking arm in arm or holding hands and even kissing on the street. Doctor Clifton had unsettled her again with his talk of love and marriage. She had managed to remain on an even keel for a while, but he had disturbed her peace of mind.

Accepting that he would marry Miss Osbourne-Cole would have been difficult, but not impossible, she reasoned, but now he was free again, there was no obstacle apart from her stubborn refusal to let go of her profession. She scolded herself inwardly for even imagining that he still felt the same way about her, after she'd rejected him in the past. He'd confided in her as a colleague and friend. He'd even emphasised the point that he saw her only as a nurse, not as someone whom he'd consider as his future wife, calling her Sister most definitely as he'd wished her goodnight.

* * *

'Nurse Finch, what time do you call this?' Hannah ambushed Charlotte when she arrived on the ward the following morning, having not turned up for breakfast.

Charlotte looked up at the clock. Her hair was in disarray and her cap askew.

'Um, it's five past eight. I'm so sorry . . . '

'I have three more leeches for you today.'

'No.' Charlotte's complexion paled. 'Is this an experiment of Doctor Clifton's?'

Hannah chuckled. 'I'm teasing.'

'That's very mean of you, Sister. I believed you . . . '

'How was the ball?'

'It was marvellous, more than I ever dreamed it would be. I danced all night — with Henry mostly, of course, and his friends, and once with Mr Anthony.' Charlotte had a beatific smile on her face. 'Oh, you'll never guess . . . '

'Mr Hunter's going to speak to your father.'

'How did you know?'

Hannah tipped her head to one side. 'I had an inkling.'

'Have you been talking to Doctor Clifton?'

'We had a problem with Samuel last night.'

'Is he all right?' Charlotte asked anxiously.

'He will be,' Hannah said. 'Congratulations anyway. I assume your father will give his consent?'

'I have no doubt. When I was jilted before, he was terribly upset and all he wanted was for me to find a decent man, but I wasn't ready then. He'll adore Henry — he'll say I've done very well for myself. Don't say anything until it's certain, though, will you?'

'Your secret's safe with me. Now, go and help Nurse May get our motley crew ready for the doctors.' Hannah watched her walk down the ward, her head held high as she greeted all the boys. She understood Mrs Knowles a little better — it was a shame to think that Charlotte would soon be leaving the house. She only wished that

259

Ruby was in a similar situation, safely engaged to a suitable gentleman, not under suspicion of encouraging a disreputable stranger's attentions.

She tried to put her worries aside and got on with her day. That afternoon, when he came in from the balcony, Samuel had some colour in his cheeks, and when Hannah re-dressed his wound, she found that the scrofulous swelling on his elbow had gone down a little.

The next morning, she kissed Ruby goodbye as she was sleeping, before she went to the house. During the morning, she found Alice taking a walk along the ward.

'Are you lost?' she called.

'I thought I'd see if there was anything I could do to help. I'm bored to tears.'

'You're supposed to be sunning yourself out on the balcony. Has Doctor Clifton authorised this? Has he told you that you can stop the treatment?'

'When I pressed him, he agreed that I could start taking a little exercise and volunteering with the little ones. I'll always regret wasting my time on Mr Fry. It was partly my fault — I was more in love with the idea of marriage than I was with him. Now I must accept that I'll never walk out with anyone again, that I'll never wed and bear children. Even though it appears that my condition has improved, there's no way of telling if the scrofula has gone completely. That's why I want to help. My greatest wish is to return to nursing.'

'Are you sure you're up to it?'

'To be honest, I've never felt better. Now, tell me what I can do.'

It was Hannah's afternoon off and she appreciated Alice's assistance because it meant she could get away on time. Often, she would stay on, but today she wanted to spend the afternoon with Ruby.

'Is everything all right?' Charlotte asked as she was leaving. 'You seem a little down.'

'I'm fine,' she said. 'It's just the extra work involved in being ward sister. I'll get used to it.'

'Make sure you get some rest then,' Charlotte smiled.

'Is there any more news?'

'Henry's calling on my father this weekend. Hannah, you will tell me if there's anything I can do to help, won't you?'

'Of course. Thank you. I'll see you tomorrow.'

★ ★ ★

'She's gone out,' Hannah heard Mrs Clovis say as she entered the lodging house. 'The gentleman I told you about came to collect her this morning, not long after you left. I thought you should know.'

'I'm very grateful for the information.' Hannah felt sick. 'Have you any idea where they went?'

'I asked Miss Ruby if she was all right, not knowing if she was leaving of her own accord or under duress, and she said she was very well, thank you. I'm afraid to tell you that she went of her own free will, which is why I didn't send word to the infirmary or speak to the police. You are acquainted with this gentleman?'

'I am indeed. He's a friend of ours,' Hannah said, 'a cousin.'

'I see,' Mrs Clovis said, gloating at Hannah's fabrication. 'Even so, she shouldn't have gone off with him like that, a young lady and a gentleman alone. You'd better go after her.'

'I shall,' Hannah said, turning to leave straight away. Would it be too late? Had Ruby already been ruined? She'd claimed that nothing untoward had happened during Mr Milani's visits to their rooms. Had he taken her elsewhere to seduce her? She didn't know what to believe any more.

She hurried to the Hall by the Sea.

'You must have a ticket, miss,' said the man at the entrance.

'I'm not here to see the sights. I wish to speak to Mr Milani about a private matter.'

'If I had a penny every time someone made up a cock-and-bull story to gain free entry, I'd be a rich man.'

'This isn't a ruse,' she said sharply, wishing she hadn't destroyed the tickets Mr Milani had given to Ruby.

'What business do you have with him, then?'

'I can't say,' she muttered, blushing with shame and embarrassment.

'Ah, he's told you that you can visit the cubs at any time. Well, it isn't possible. He doesn't own this place — it's Lord Sanger who gives out favours, not Mr Milani.'

'I'm sorry, but you compel me to reveal that I'm a nurse from the infirmary. Mr Milani has been attending and I have a message for him from one of the doctors.'

'You should have said.' The ticket man gave an exaggerated wink, his manner making her skin crawl. 'He has a dose of the French disease!'

'No, sir.'

'Go on. Go through. You'll find him with the big cats.'

'What's she doin' pushin' in?' someone in the queue behind her complained.

'It's a medical emergency,' the ticket seller said, and Hannah made her way through the turnstile and across the park in the sunshine to Mr Milani's lair, where the scent of cat assaulted her nostrils. Having passed a small crowd who were teasing the tigress with a feather on a stick, she saw a young boy scrubbing the floor of the lions' cage, whistling as he went.

'Excuse me,' she said.

The boy looked up, as something scratched at the other side of the door behind him.

'Please, can you tell me where I can find Mr Milani? It's urgent.'

'You 'aven't brought 'is money, 'ave you? 'E's expectin' Mr Allspice to pay 'im back today or tomorrer.'

'The matter I wish to see him about has nothing to do with Mr Allspice,' Hannah said impatiently.

'Well, 'e's out the back with the cubs. 'E said not to disturb 'im.'

'Does he have a young lady with him?'

'Yes' — the boy smirked — 'an' a very pretty one she is, too.'

'She's in a lot of trouble. I need to speak to

her.' In desperation, she took a shilling from her pocket and held it in front of him. 'This is yours, if you show me to her.'

'It'll cost yer more than that. He'll give me a good 'idin' for it.'

She held out two shillings and the boy came out of the cage and down the steps. He rattled the bars on the next one along. 'There's someone for you, Mr Milani,' he yelled. No one came and Hannah began to wonder if the boy had been mistaken. He slid the bolt on the cage and opened the door, letting himself in. Hannah followed close behind.

'You can't come in here, miss,' the boy said. 'It's too dangerous for the likes of you.'

'I'm not afraid,' she said, giving him his two shillings, sweeping past him and opening the door in the wall at the back to reveal Mr Milani with his arms wrapped around her sister. Ruby turned and stared at her, her cheeks pink, her hair awry and her eyes dark with lust.

'No!' Hannah exclaimed as Mr Milani released Ruby and she took a step back, her hand flying to hide her breast where her bodice was undone.

Hannah took off her cape and threw it at her. 'Cover yourself!'

'What's this all about?' Mr Milani said calmly as Ruby rearranged her dress and pulled the cape over her shoulders.

'It's Miss Bentley, my sister,' Ruby muttered coldly.

'I've come to take Ruby home before her reputation is completely destroyed,' Hannah said.

'I won't go,' Ruby proclaimed.

'Don't be too hasty, my love,' Mr Milani said. 'We'll soon be married — you said so.'

'I did, and we will be, but in the meantime, your sister is right. We should refrain from being alone together until that happy day when we are joined as husband and wife.'

'Ruby, you don't believe any of this, do you?' Hannah interrupted. 'This louse has no intention of marrying you, or he would have put a ring on your finger already.'

Ruby's face contorted with sorrow and doubt.

'Am I ruined, Antonio?' she whispered. 'Tell me I'm not.'

'This has to stop,' Hannah said. 'You must understand that my sister is a young — very young — lady who is set way above you. She appears to have developed an infatuation — '

'How can I help that?' He puffed himself up like a rooster.

'All I ask is that you leave her alone.'

'No, Hannah,' Ruby said.

'It isn't my fault if she comes preying on me, dropping her handkerchief so I'm obliged to return it, and leaving messages for me at the gate. She gets up to all sorts of tricks.'

'Mr Milani!' Hannah exclaimed. 'This is my sister you are speaking of.'

He inclined his head. 'Miss Bentley, Ruby is a sweet girl and generous to a fault. When she sends for me, looking for company, what can I do?'

'She will not send for you in the future. Good day, Mr Milani. Ruby, come with me.'

'I will stay here with you, Antonio,' she said with a stamp of her foot, reminding Hannah of when she was crossed as a small child, but Mr Milani shook his head.

'Go with your sister. I have much work to do to prepare my act for opening night,' he said.

'You will be in touch?' Ruby said, crestfallen.

'Of course. Now go, my love.' He took her trembling hands and kissed her cheek.

Hannah suppressed a wave of fury at his behaviour. She'd imagined that she could prevail on him to do the right thing, explain that their friendship or flirtation, whatever it was, couldn't continue, but it seemed that she'd been wrong. How was she to keep Ruby safe if Mr Milani wasn't prepared to play his part?

She turned to her sister. All she could do to prevent certain disaster for them both was to use any means possible — begging or shouting at her, if necessary — to prevail on Ruby to give the odious Mr Milani up. Taking her arm, she led her away, wincing as the cage door slammed shut behind them.

'You have much to explain, young lady,' she hissed as they walked back through the grounds. 'What did you think you were doing?'

'He came for me.'

'You sent for him!'

'And you embarrassed me by turning up out of the blue and making a scene! How could you?'

'I don't care. I'm glad I did. Who knows what would have happened if I hadn't come to find you? You have lied to me, gone against my wishes and put your reputation at risk yet again. If Mr

Milani had any affection for you, he would have spoken to me as your guardian — I've considered myself responsible for you since you broke with Pa — before offering his hand.'

'And you would have turned him away because you hate him so much!' Ruby spat. 'Anyway, we are as good as married — that's what he says.'

'Where is your ring? Your signature in the register? No, I thought not,' Hannah went on when Ruby fell silent. 'Your head might as well be stuffed with feathers, if you can't see that he's leading you on to ruin. This affects me too, and I'm very hurt at your lack of respect when I've only ever tried to do my best for you. What you've done today is scandalous. If anyone at the infirmary finds out, my reputation will be ruined by association. Ruby, I could lose my place over this. Apart from the shame of it, we'll have no money, no way of buying food or paying the rent. Do you understand now?'

'But I don't think I can go on living without him. Oh, Hannah, what am I going to do?'

'You'll promise me that you won't see him again — and you'll keep that promise.' Hannah's stony heart softened just a little at the sight of Ruby's distress. 'We have each other and much besides to be thankful for,' she continued. They walked along the front, passing the bathing rooms where a gentleman was waiting outside with his pipe, sending smoke rings curling into the air. Ruby kept her eyes to the sea.

15

The Circus

'Sister, are you busy?' she heard Doctor Clifton say, as she hurried along the corridor with the bottle of medicine that he'd prescribed for Samuel who was due to go home later in the day.

'I'm always busy,' she said, amused that he even needed to ask.

'May I have a word? In private?' She stopped and turned to find him holding the door of one of the examination rooms open. 'This won't take more than two minutes, I promise.'

Sighing with mock irritation, she slipped into the room with him.

'I didn't want to speak of this in front of our colleagues,' he said, closing the door behind them. 'I hope you don't think I'm being presumptuous, but I wonder if you'd like to accompany me to the circus this evening. Mrs Phillips has obtained two tickets for me and Henry, but my cousin isn't well enough to attend.'

'What's wrong with him?' she asked quickly, putting the brown glass bottle on the trolley just inside the door.

'I suspect that he couldn't bring himself to tell me that he'd prefer to sit up with his fiancée, so he's feigned illness. I don't mind — I see enough of him already. Will you come with me instead?'

She hesitated, and he went on, 'I don't think there'd be any harm in accepting, considering the circumstances. It isn't as if . . . ' His voice trailed off. 'I'm not asking you to walk out with me, nothing like that. You've made it perfectly clear that our interactions outside the house will always remain within the bounds of friendship. You'd be doing me a favour. I'd hate to see the ticket go to waste.'

'I'm not sure.' She was worried about leaving Ruby any longer than she had to after her escapade with Mr Milani, but then, she reasoned, he'd be preoccupied with his lion-taming act and therefore out of harm's way.

'I believe that Alan Allspice is performing.'

'I thought you didn't believe in patronising the circus, knowing the cruelty they inflict on the children.'

'In spite of my reservations, I'd like to see how Alan is.'

'Then it's more like a house call?' Hannah couldn't help smiling.

'You could say that,' he admitted.

'What about your patients? Who will look after them while you're out and about?'

'I have a colleague who will hold the fort for me at the clinic — it's rare for me to be called out after six. And I've told the junior physician to contact Mr Pyle or Mr Anthony if there's anything that can't wait at the house. We'll meet at the station and take the train, then I'll walk you home afterwards.'

'I've never been to the circus.' She'd wanted to go, ever since Pa had forbidden it and Nanny had taken them to watch the parade.

'Then come with me. What is life if not to be lived?'

'That's true. Yes, why not?'

'I'll see you at the station at six.' Beaming, he opened the door again and Hannah hurried away, passing Mr Mordikai who gave her an enquiring look.

'Good morning,' she said brightly.

'Sister Bentley. Sister!' Doctor Clifton came hurrying up behind her. 'You forgot this.'

'Thank you,' she said, blushing furiously as he handed her the bottle.

She returned to the ward and spent the time until the end of her shift in a ferment of anticipation. Hurrying home, she found Ruby in the sitting room, brushing her long, dark locks which gleamed in the slanting rays of the sun.

'I used the last bottle of beer on my hair. I hope you don't mind.'

Hannah did mind, but she didn't say so.

'I'm sorry, but I'm going to have to let you down today. I've been invited to the circus this evening.'

'You're going with Charlotte?'

'With Doctor Clifton.'

'I should have guessed,' Ruby smiled.

She explained that his cousin was indisposed, and that they were going to watch one of their former patients.

'You go and enjoy yourself,' Ruby said.

'You don't mind? You wouldn't prefer me to stay and keep you company?'

'No, I don't want to spoil it for you. But won't

people talk? They'll say you're walking out with him.'

'Well, I'm not.'

'It's rather hypocritical of you.'

'My situation bears no resemblance to yours.'

'As you've tried so eloquently to explain.' Ruby smiled again, all sweetness and light. For a young woman who could have been ruined by her recent escapade with the dreadful Mr Milani, she seemed remarkably lighthearted, showing no remorse or regret. 'You deserve an evening off. A change is as good as a rest, as Grandma used to say. You'd better hurry up and get changed. There's cold meat — ham and mustard — for supper if you aren't dining out.'

Thanking her, Hannah went to eat, then changed out of her day dress. She scrubbed her hands and face, but no matter how hard she tried to hide it with rose-scented soap, she always smelled of carbolic. She put on a dark green dress which set off her coppery hair, then returned to the sitting room.

'Ruby, may I borrow your brooch? The cameo?'

'I'm . . . I'm not sure where it is.'

Hannah collected her gloves from the shelf alongside her nursing books.

'Where are my shoes?'

'They're in the kitchen — I borrowed them to go shopping. You know how much mine make my feet ache.'

'That's because they're too small, even for your tiny feet.'

'They are the fashion — they say that a woman's social position can be judged by the appearance of the foot. A small, well-shod and prettily used foot adds charm to the appearance and indicates high standing.'

'You shouldn't allow yourself to be influenced by such claptrap.'

'You think me shallow, but . . . ' Ruby's face crumpled. 'I feel the loss of my status severely. At home, we had servants, tradesmen calling at the house, visits from our stepmother's friends and acquaintances . . . '

'Then go back to Canterbury,' Hannah said, hurt.

'How can I? Pa will only have me locked up again.'

'It's up to you, but surely there is some compensation: your sister's company; the fresh sea air; the entertainment. It costs nothing to stroll along the front and watch the world go by.'

'That's just it. I don't want the world to pass me by — I ache to be part of it. And even though I know I mustn't see him again, I miss Antonio . . . '

'Then we should consider finding something to fill the hours when I'm not here. We'll sit down and talk about it tomorrow.'

'Promise?'

Nodding, Hannah went to fetch her soft kid shoes. She slipped them on and fastened the straps across the front via the buttons at the side, then straightened the bows on the toes, before putting on her cape and bonnet.

'Make sure you tell me all about it,' Ruby said, as Hannah pulled on her gloves.

'I will, but don't wait up for me. I'm not sure

what time I'll be back.'

Ruby got up and walked across to give her a peck on the cheek. 'I'm sorry for being sharp with you.'

'Apology accepted,' Hannah said lightly. 'Goodnight, Ruby.'

She found Doctor Clifton waiting for her at the station. He greeted her with a smile, making her traitorous heart lurch.

'I've bought the train tickets.'

'That's very kind, but you must allow me to pay for mine.'

'Not when everyone knows that nurses are paid a pittance.'

'I should still pay my own way,' she said stiffly.

'We're friends — you're doing me a favour.'

'If you're sure,' she said, softening. 'I don't want there to be any misunderstanding between us.'

'We're friends,' he repeated, his voice tinged with regret.

She looked away. Did that mean he still harboured hopes of something more?

'I promise I won't try to kiss you,' he added gruffly, 'although I make no secret of the fact that I'd like to. I understand your ambition and the sacrifices you've made to get this far, and although I grieve that you prefer to be wedded to the house than married to me, I will have to live with it. And that's all I wish to say on the matter. Except that I wonder if you would permit me to address you as Hannah while we are away from the house?'

'Well, of course.'

'In return, you may call me James, if you like.'

'Thank you, James, although you must forgive me if I forget and revert to Doctor Clifton,' she smiled.

Smiling back, he looked past her. 'This is our train.'

They boarded and sat side by side on one of the upholstered benches in a first-class compartment. James asked after Ruby.

'Your sister is more settled in Margate now?'

'A little, thank you. She's finding it hard to fill her time.'

'It's said that the devil finds work for idle hands,' he ventured. 'Oh, I don't mean . . . Forgive me, but I wondered if all was well. You've seemed preoccupied recently, as if something is troubling you.'

'Ruby is a handful,' she admitted.

'You will let me know if there's ever anything I can do.'

'I'm very grateful for your kindness, but this is a family matter.'

'I won't press you, then, but remember that you're not alone.'

'I'm very fortunate,' she said, recalling how Charlotte had offered the same.

She gazed out of the window as the train rattled along the tracks. It stopped at Broadstairs then continued for some distance before sounding its whistle and entering a tunnel, making her jump.

James smiled. 'We'e almost there. From the station, it's only a ten-minute walk to the High Street.'

They disembarked at Ramsgate, not far from

the harbour, and found their way to their destination: the recently opened Sanger's Amphitheatre and Hotel, outside which stood several bronzes of barely dressed dancing ladies, holding lamps aloft. Joining the throng entering the building, they gave in their tickets and found their seats in the upper circle where the air was close and warm.

'We arrived just in time,' James said, as a fanfaronade of trumpets sounded, and the ringmaster in red tails and a top hat strode into the ring, cracking his long whip, and announced the start of the programme: a spectacle of equestrian skills in the manner of the Wild West; the story of Billy the Kid and a world where good conquered bad, and love won out. Next came the parade of freaks, the World's Tallest Man pushing a trolley, on which stood the World's Smallest Woman. Behind them came the 'Woman with Five Chins'.

'There has to be some trickery behind this,' James whispered. 'Look how the young lady is carrying a large bouquet of flowers to make her seem more diminutive than she really is. They advertise her as being twenty-one, but she can't be more than eleven. As for the tallest man, have you noticed how long his trousers are?'

She nodded.

'That's because his shoes have to be built up on platforms.'

'Keep yer voice down,' someone complained from behind them.

James muttered an apology as the freaks left the ring and a troupe of acrobats came tumbling in.

As they whirled and leapt through the air, Hannah began to understand Ruby's fascination with the lion tamer's showmanship. Her nostrils filled with the scent of pine, perfume and sherbet. The rainbow sparkle of a million sequins dazzled her, and the rhythm of drums and explosive cracks of the ringmaster's whip pounded her eardrums.

She turned to James who gave a sheepish smile, then looked back at the ring. She felt the slightest shift of his thigh against her skirt, and a shiver of longing ran up her spine while the acrobats posed and waved before running light-footed out of the ring.

'Ladies and gentlemen, give a big hand to . . . our masters of contortionism: the amazing India Rubber Brothers.' The ringmaster held out his arms, and two young men came into the ring with a table which they placed in the centre to roars of applause.

'It's Alan and his brother,' James whispered.

She hardly recognised their former patient, dressed in a close-fitting costume of blue, silver and white stripes, as he cartwheeled on to the table. He helped his brother spring up to join him, before they began to contort themselves into all kinds of impossible positions. Alan bent over backwards until the top of his head was pressed against the backs of his thighs, then he and his brother used each other as frames to balance on with one hand. Their finale was to make a great show of folding themselves up to fit into a tiny cardboard box before the 'World's Strongest Man' came to pick it up and carry it away.

Hannah could hardly believe her eyes, remembering how lame Alan had been when he was admitted to the infirmary. It was a miracle.

The India Rubber Brothers' act was followed by the lions which arrived in a trailer drawn by a pair of horses dressed as unicorns.

'Let's have a warm welcome for the Greatest Lion Tamer in the Universe, Antonio Milani,' the ringmaster announced, making Hannah feel sick at heart, because it wasn't fair that he'd gone unpunished for trying to seduce her sister. 'His bravery is beyond compare! Marvel as he subdues the king of the jungle and his queens.'

Mr Milani appeared, holding his hat and whip aloft.

'Open the cage,' he shouted. 'Release the beasts.'

At the sound of a drumroll, an assistant unlocked the cage and an elderly lion and two lionesses came lolloping out, growling, snarling and licking their lips.

With a twirl of his whip, the lion tamer directed the beasts to three brightly painted pedestals which had been placed in a row. They jumped up and sat on them, and the old lion turned and stared into the crowd with its yellow-brown eyes. What was it thinking? That one of them would make a good dinner? Hannah reached out for James's arm, a spontaneous impulse. He rested his hand on hers, and her heart beat even faster.

Mr Milani raised his whip and the lion struggled on to its hind legs, uttering a pathetic roar while the lionesses bowed at his feet. He called the lion to him, patted first one shoulder, then the other, to encourage it to jump up and place its giant paws on either side of his neck. He rubbed the lion's chest, then pushed it down again and flicked it away with his whip.

The crowd burst into applause, and Hannah caught sight of a young woman waiting at the entrance to the ring, her head uncovered. Her chest tightened as she recognised Ruby's dark shining hair and the familiar curve of her cheek. Mortified, she glanced towards James, but he didn't appear to have noticed anything was amiss, and that was the way it was going to stay if she had anything to do with it. How dare Ruby disobey her again! After all her promises that she wouldn't see Mr Milani! Having been dragged back into her web of lies and deceit, Hannah could quite cheerfully have thrown her to the lions.

'I'd advise you to see a doctor about your hearing,' she heard James say.

'I'm sorry?' she said, wondering what to do.

'I've asked you three times if you'd like a drink during the interval.'

'Oh yes, that would be lovely.' She glanced towards the spot where she'd seen Ruby, but she'd disappeared. She decided not to go after her, not wanting to ruin James's evening or reveal her sister's indiscretion, afraid that he'd judge her for it. The circus was in Ramsgate for at least another week, so she'd know where to find Mr Milani if she had to. She accompanied James to one of the anterooms to buy ginger beer at the bar, then they moved to a quiet corner.

'I was glad to see how well Alan looks,' she said.

'He's made a remarkable recovery, thanks to you.'

'You would have made sure he was admitted if I hadn't been there.'

'Well, maybe.'

'Of course you would — I know you too well. Thank you for inviting me this evening. It's been an education.'

'I think it's supposed to be fun as well,' he pointed out. 'I enjoyed the contortionists, but not watching the freaks who are people just like us.'

'Without the circus, they wouldn't be able to make a living. I don't think they can have a bad life,' Hannah observed.

'Then we'll have to agree to disagree on that one,' he said, adding quickly, 'It's a good thing — the world would be a very dull place if everyone held the same opinions.'

'The freaks have a choice. They can choose whether or not they display themselves in front of the public — '

'Are you sure about that? I'd have to be starving before I offered myself up to the curiosity and ridicule of this crowd for the sake of a few shillings.'

'I hadn't thought of it that way,' she admitted. 'I suppose they're exploited just like the animals, although the lion tamer, that ridiculous Mr Milani, says otherwise.'

'You've met him?'

'Ruby and I spoke to him when we visited the

menagerie.' She could hardly bear to speak of it because that was where her sister's infatuation with him had started. 'He took great pains to tell us that the lions were content with their lot, having protection, shelter and food in return for performing a few tricks, but they must pine for their freedom on the great plains of Africa, mustn't they?'

'He gives the illusion of cooperation and kindness, but he controls them with the whip. The poor creatures eye him with fear, not respect.'

'You can read the minds of animals?'

'At the risk of offending people who believe in the divine superiority of humans over the rest of God's creation, I have found there is little difference in the feelings that animals have — fear, joy, sadness — only in the ways that they express them.'

'When the animals were on the ward, the young ones playing with the boys and girls, there was joy on all their faces,' she remembered.

'There you go. As for our lion tamer, he's no more Italian than you or I. I wouldn't be surprised if he doesn't hail from London or Bognor Regis.' James checked his pocket watch. 'We'd better make our way back inside.'

'Prepare to be amazed, astounded, dumbfounded . . . ' bellowed the ringmaster when the audience had returned to their seats. Ruby was back beside the ring, Hannah noted. 'Let us welcome the Amazing Aerial Ajax whose audacity will confound, astonish . . . and amuse . . . '

Hannah looked up to the ceiling where the high wire and scaffolds had been prepared during the interval, then down at the safety net.

''E can't be all that amazin' if 'e needs somethin' to catch 'im,' someone grumbled, but a drumroll overwhelmed any reply.

Mr Allspice came striding into the ring, holding out his cloak to show off its golden lining. He whipped it off and flung it behind him where Mrs Allspice, wearing a sequinned tutu and a headdress laden with silk flowers, caught it. Her husband made the most of his ascent up the ladder, stopping now and again to pose on the way. When he reached the scaffold stage in the heights of the building, he stood with his arms outstretched, garnering further applause.

'He 'asn't done nothin' yet,' someone grumbled.

'Look at 'is assistant — mutton dressed as lamb.'

The audience fell silent and still, as Mr Allspice stepped out of the shadows on to the rope. He took a second step through the smoky haze of the gaslights and then another, and just as the crowd began to breathe again, he slipped.

At the collective gasp of horror, he caught hold of the rope with both hands and, with a surge of effort and a twist of his body, he was back on his feet.

'Bravo, bravo, sir!' someone shouted as the ropewalker stood on one leg, like a ballerina, his head to one side and his forefinger pressed to his cheek, as though he was wondering what to do next.

It had been a ruse to catch their attention, Hannah thought with relief.

'Ah, 'tis a comedy,' their neighbour said. 'I thought as much.'

'They call 'im the flyin' fool, so I've 'eard.'

'I've seen 'im before — I wa'n't going to say nothin' because I didn't want to spoil it for anyone.'

Hannah turned briefly to James, who grinned as Mr Allspice tipped into a handstand, his arms wobbling before he returned to an upright position, landing astride the rope and making much play of the pain that would have affected his nether regions, if it hadn't been part of the show.

'Ooh, I felt that,' someone commented as runnels of laughter spilled through the amphitheatre.

'Oh, how crude.'

The Amazing Ajax dropped to one side and crawled along the rope upside down, like a monkey. Clinging on with his legs, he released his grip with his hands, and caught an apple that came flying through the air, courtesy of Mrs Allspice. He bit into the fruit and tossed it away, then he was back on the rope, unfastening what appeared to be a skipping rope from his middle. He skipped a step, and another, then down he fell, tumbling through the air and landing on the safety net suspended beneath him.

The crowd roared with laughter as he pulled a funny face, bounced and fell down once more, spread-eagled on his back, but where he should have bounced up again, the net fell away beneath him, dropping him flat on the floor where he uttered a bloodcurdling scream.

'He's dead, sure as eggs is eggs,' somebody cried out.

'Please, ladies, do not be alarmed,' the ringmaster shouted, walking across to Mr Allspice and catching his boots in the net which was spread across the sawdust. 'It's all part of the act. Ajax, let me help you to your feet.'

'Can't you see I'm 'urt?' the ropewalker cried. 'Someone 'as nobbled me.'

'You can stand up?'

'I told yer, I'm injured — I can't move me legs.'

'You can't stop the Amazing Aerial Ajax — he's always clowning around.' The ringmaster nudged him in the arm with the toe of his boot. 'Ladies and gentlemen, boys and girls, there's no harm done, no harm at all. He'll be as right as rain in a couple of days.'

Some members of the audience were more sympathetic.

'Is there a doctor in the house?' one asked as Mrs Allspice came running across the ring and fell to her knees at her husband's side. She grasped his hand and broke into a terrible wail.

'Come quickly, Hannah,' James said.

As they made their way down the steps, she saw Alan, who was wearing grey trousers over his costume, calling for a stretcher.

'Don't move him. He mustn't be moved,' James bellowed.

'Doctor Clifton?' Alan recognised him straight away. 'Nurse Bentley.'

283

'It's Sister Bentley now,' James said.

'He has to be moved — the show must go on,' the ringmaster interrupted.

''E 'as to stay there. Doctor's orders,' Alan said. 'I trust these people — they're the ones who made me better.'

'I need to assess his injuries before he goes anywhere — it won't take long,' James said, taking charge.

'What can I do?' Hannah asked as he knelt in the sawdust beside the afflicted man.

'Go to the other side of him — take off his shoes.' She squatted down, untied his laces and removed his sweaty slippers which had holes in the soles.

'Send for a constable,' Mr Allspice gasped. 'I want 'im arrested and thrown in gaol.'

'Who?' Mrs Allspice said.

'That felon — your brother. 'E's the one who put the net up — 'e offered.'

'My brother would never 'urt you.'

'We will deal with this ourselves, within the family,' the ringmaster said, but Mr Allspice wasn't listening.

'Alan, fetch your brother and go after 'im. Catch that murderin' bastard and bring 'im back here so I can give 'im what for. He says I've defaulted on a loan, that I haven't paid 'im back yet. When he borrered me that money, 'e said it was a gift.'

Which was a lie, Hannah thought, recalling the conversation that Mr Milani and Mr Allspice had had in front of her and Ruby at the Hall by the Sea.

''E said I'd promised to make 'im top of the bill as well. Does 'e really think I'd put 'is act above mine?' He tried to drag himself up, but his legs were limp and his body shaking.

'Don't move,' James said. 'For your own sake, keep still until I say so.'

Alan acknowledged Hannah with a nod of his head, then disappeared.

'I can't afford to pay a quack.' Mr Allspice swore out loud, and Hannah heard the whispers and rustle of the ladies' dresses as they got up from their seats and began to make their way out of the theatre.

'Ladies and gentlemen, there's no need to hurry away,' the ringmaster insisted. 'The show will go on.'

'We've had more than enough entertainment for one evening,' one said. 'The poor man — this is most unfortunate.'

'We'll worry about payment later,' James said. 'Are you able to move your legs?'

'I don't think so . . . ' Mr Allspice grimaced. 'Are they movin', Doc?'

James shook his head as he moved round to his feet. 'Hannah, may I prevail on you for the use of a hat pin?'

She removed one from her bonnet and handed it to him.

He used it to scratch the patient's soles. 'Can you feel this? Or this?'

Mr Allspice shook his head, his eyes dark with misery as the impact of what had happened began to sink in. Sticking the hatpin through the flap of his waistcoat pocket, James asked him where he was feeling pain.

'All over . . . ' His teeth began to chatter.

'Is there anywhere where it feels worse?'

'My back and my legs — they're on fire.'

'You've suffered an injury to your spine and in view of my suspicion that the bone is fractured, you must remain completely still. Don't move. Do you understand?'

'Yes, Doc.' Mr Allspice's face was etched with fear.

'If we can immobilise you on a stretcher to get you to the infirmary in Margate, then we can look at putting you into a full body cast.'

'I can't 'ave that — we have shows booked for weeks in advance.'

' 'E's right. If 'e can't work, we can't feed our littluns,' Mrs Allspice contributed. 'They'll starve.'

'Mr Allspice, you are paralysed from the waist down. Without enforced rest, there is no route to recovery. Even then, there are no guarantees. I can't work miracles — all I can do is support the body in healing. The rest is in God's hands.'

'Will I be able to walk the rope again?'

'I don't know, sir.'

'If I can't be up there, bringin' exclamations of wonderment and tears of laughter to the public, I may as well be dead.'

'You are in good hands,' Hannah said.

'I know, I know. Then take me to the infirmary and the sooner the better — the show will go on.' He turned to his wife who was sitting on the floor, rocking back and forth, sobbing and crying. 'Stop snivellin' and get out there, cap in

286

'and before all these gen'rous people disappear. Call the papers, but don't let slip a word without agreein' payment in advance. Got that?'

She nodded.

'What am I supposed to say to 'em?'

'You'll tell 'em the truth — that your brother, your own flesh and blood, tried to murder your 'usband.'

'You can't ask me to squeal on 'im.'

'I'm tellin' yer to. It'll serve you well to remember where your loyalties lie.' The patient's eyes were bulging with anger and pain. 'Now, send the littluns their pa's love and tell 'em to behave or I'll 'ave their guts for garters when I get 'ome.'

Hannah and James travelled to the infirmary in one hansom cab, while Mr Allspice went strapped to a door in another. When they arrived, they woke the duty porter, and disturbed the night staff. Their patient was grunting and groaning with pain worse than an animal, and it was all they could do to transfer him to a trolley to convey him to one of the men's wards. Doctor Clifton prescribed opium, and Hannah and the night sister helped him strap Mr Allspice into a temporary cast which Hannah obtained from the splint workshop.

'It's quite a coincidence that you and Doctor Clifton were at the same performance in Ramsgate tonight,' the night sister said with a sly look, while Hannah waited for James to write up his notes.

'And a lucky one for Mr Allspice,' Hannah said. 'He would have been in even more of a predicament if we hadn't been there — the ringmaster was all for moving him so the next act could follow on.'

'Sister, you will permit me to walk you home,' James interrupted.

'Oh no, I can make my own way,' she said, flustered.

'I couldn't have it on my conscience to let a young lady wander the streets alone at this time of night.' Hannah wasn't sure if she was pleased that his chivalry extended to other young ladies, but she reminded herself that that had been her choice. At least, when she became a matron one day, she would have this evening to look back on. 'I'll drop by in the morning to look in on Mr Allspice,' he added aside to the night sister.

'Yes, Doctor. I wish you goodnight.'

'This escapade will be all over the house tomorrow,' Hannah observed as James offered his arm to cross the street outside. She took it, thinking to make the most of his company.

'It'll give the gossips plenty to talk about, but it'll soon blow over. Do you think that the lion tamer really tried to kill Mr Allspice? He must have known that he'd guess who the culprit was.'

'I know something about it — I was present during a conversation when Mr Allspice revealed that Mr Milani is his brother-in-law. Mrs Allspice is Mr Milani's sister.'

'I suppose it isn't surprising that they have a family connection — they're both showmen who spend time in each other's society.'

'What I heard would support Mr Allspice's allegation — I think I should go to the police.'

288

'I should sleep on it, if I were you, Hannah.'

'I want to do the right thing.'

'I know, but you don't want your name — and your sister's — to be dragged into something which doesn't concern you. If Mr Allspice can provide enough evidence to back up his accusation, there's no need for you to get involved.'

'That might be wise,' she concurred. If the story broke in the newspapers, would she not be accused of making false claims against Mr Milani as revenge for his pursuit of her sister?

'I imagine that the details will unfold naturally over the next few days,' James said. 'It's been a most unexpected and eventful evening, but I have to say that there's no one I'd rather have spent it with than you.'

'Thank you,' she said softly, her heartstrings taut with desire and regret as they walked on in silence to the lodging house. He stood waiting for her to go inside.

'Goodnight, dear Hannah,' she thought she heard him say as she closed the door behind her. A sweet yearning filled her breast. If only . . . She was a fool, she told herself. Love and lust were like opium — once tasted, one only wanted more. She should never have let him persuade her to go to Ramsgate. It had awakened the feelings she thought she had overcome.

16

The Rules of the House

Hannah threw off her cape and fumbled in the dark to find a stub of candle and a match. She struck the match and touched the flame to the wick which flared, flickered and died, expelling a whiff of tallow. She tried again, and the flame caught, illuminating a tiny pair of eyes under the kitchen table. A mouse! But she didn't chase it away. She had other fish to fry.

She went to the bedroom and pushed the door open, walked across to her sister's bed, pulled the coverlet back and shone the candle in Ruby's face.

'What are you doing? I was asleep!'

'Really? I'm surprised that your conscience allows you to rest. You lied to me. I saw you at the circus, gawping at the infamous Mr Milani.'

Ruby didn't attempt to deny it. She pulled herself up to sit on the edge of the bed.

'How is Mr Allspice? I heard him fall.'

'Doctor Clifton thinks that he's broken his back. He's at the infirmary, but he may never walk again.' She recalled his accusations against the lion tamer. 'How could you go against me yet again?'

'I don't know,' Ruby stammered. 'When you forbid me to do something, it's like a red rag to a bull. I just have to do it.'

'You have no modesty or self-restraint.'

'Whereas you have both of those virtues in buckets.'

Hannah straightened and stepped back, holding the candle as the wax dripped hot on to her fingers. She snuffed it out and put it on the washstand, before opening the curtains to let in the light from the moon.

'I can't help feeling more than you do,' Ruby went on. 'I'm not as good or as clever as you. All I want is to be loved.'

'Modesty and restraint can be learned,' Hannah said softly, thinking of how she had had to suppress her feelings for James. 'You don't think I feel anything?'

'There are times when you are as cold as ice.' Ruby's eyes glittered with tears.

'That's unkind. I feel at least as much as you do — I just don't show it.' There were occasions — she recalled Peter's demise — when she couldn't help revealing her emotions. 'And I don't let it rule my impulses.'

'I had to see him. Forgive me.'

'I'm not sure that I can this time.'

'Do keep the noise down!' Mrs Clovis banged on the floor upstairs, creating a small shower of plaster and whitewash in the corner of the room.

'Did Doctor Clifton see me?' Ruby asked, lowering her voice.

'I don't know,' Hannah said quietly. The last thing she wanted was to annoy their landlady when their position was already precarious, thanks to Ruby's behaviour. 'I don't think so. We got caught up in the accident, which' — she wouldn't spare her — 'apparently might not have been an accident at all, but attempted murder. Clearly, the ropes on the net hadn't been fastened properly . . . '

'I'm not entirely surprised,' Ruby said. 'Mr Allspice is regarded with little affection — he beats his wife and treats his children cruelly. There are many people who don't like him.'

'That's no reason to try to get rid of him. Please, tell me what you know.'

'There was an argument over the money that Antonio lent to Mr Allspice. Everyone heard them, not just me.'

Hannah sat down next to her sister, the bed creaking beneath her.

'Then it's all over between you and Mr Milani. Thank goodness for small mercies.'

'How can you say that? It'll never be over. I've told you before — I love him.'

Hannah grasped Ruby's hands and squeezed them tightly.

'You can't blame him for this,' her sister sobbed. 'He's from just outside Rome, you see. The people there are renowned for their hot blood and fiery tempers. It's the sunshine that does it.'

Mrs Clovis banged on the floor once more. 'Please! Have some consideration!'

'Have you any idea where he is?' Hannah murmured, refraining from offering her opinion on Ruby's beliefs.

'No, but if I did, I'd throw myself upon him and beg him to take me with him. I'd follow him to the ends of the Earth. He will send for me one day, I'm convinced of it.'

'I don't know what to do with you,' Hannah whispered angrily. 'I can't afford to lose my place at the infirmary. Your wayward conduct is pushing me into a corner.'

'I wish I could go and stay with Grandma for a few days.' Ruby broke down completely, her shoulders racked with sobs.

Hannah was about to snap back at her, but she took a breath. Grandma was gone and here they were arguing — she would have hated it.

'I'm sorry . . . She's looking down on us from Heaven,' Hannah said softly.

'On you, you mean? You were always her favourite.'

'That isn't true. She loved us both the same.'

'She lost Ma not long after I was born — she always blamed me.'

'She didn't say that, did she?'

'It was the way she looked at me sometimes.'

'With sadness and regret for what might have been, nothing else. I know that, because she talked about you and Ma when I was living with her. She adored you.'

'Did she?'

'You know she did.' Hannah despaired — Ruby's moods were like the clouds flitting across the sky: sometimes light, often dark, always changeable.

'I could always say, if anyone asks, that you were with me this evening, that we went to the circus together,' Ruby offered.

Hannah didn't deign to grace her with a reply. She would do what she thought was right, not get herself entangled any further in Ruby's lies. She was worried sick, though, about what the next few days would bring: what Ruby might do, and what James would think of her if he found out about her connections to the circus through her sister.

★ ★ ★

She kept busy the following morning, running the ward and looking after her patients. Doctor Clifton didn't turn up for rounds — Mr Hunter said that his appointments at the clinic were fully booked, thanks to the publicity surrounding his evening at the circus. He didn't say anything else, but Nurse Finch and Nurse May were itching to know exactly what had happened.

'Mr Allspice's accident is the talk of the house,' Charlotte said when they were taking lunch on the balcony with the patients.

'There isn't much to talk about. He fell from a great height and, by coincidence, Doctor Clifton was present to treat him and bring him back to the infirmary.'

'Where he lies, trussed up and unable to walk,' Charlotte added. 'There are rumours that someone tried to kill him.'

'I don't know anything about that — you'll have to ask him.'

'Oh no, I don't think so. He's giving Sister Trim and her nurses terrible trouble. In any event, I'm sure we'll find out the truth soon enough. The police inspector's been in to speak to him.'

'How are your plans for the wedding?' Hannah changed the subject.

'Everything is underway, ready for Christmas. I've chosen my dress and flowers, and the only issue that could thwart us is if Henry fails to gain his registration with the Royal College of Physicians in time.'

'I wish him luck,' Hannah said.

As she made her way back to the Lettsom after lunch, Matron called her into her office.

'You look as though you could use a tot of brandy and some sleep, Sister Bentley.' Mrs Knowles smiled as she offered her a seat. Hannah glanced down at the ale stains on her apron — she wasn't her usual pink of neatness today.

'You've heard about last night?' she said.

'Indeed. I'm delighted that you and Doctor Clifton were able to assist Mr Allspice in his hour of need yesterday evening, but I'd caution you against accepting any more invitations from him. We've come a long way recently in encouraging an atmosphere of mutual respect and cooperation between the doctors and nursing staff, and I'd hate to see our work go to waste. A personal relationship becomes a distraction to both the lady and gentleman involved, and to their colleagues.'

'I'm well aware of that.' Her eyes stung. 'Doctor Clifton and I are friends, that's all. There's no impropriety.'

'I wasn't suggesting for a moment that there was, but I wonder if it's fair to lead him on.'

'He knows of my intentions.' She didn't

enlighten Mrs Knowles about how she'd turned down his proposal some weeks ago.

'Just be careful. I can see the potential for this to turn out badly for one or both of you. His affection, I believe, runs deeper than you think, as does yours for him.'

'Thank you for your wisdom, but how can you have any idea — '

'When I am not married?' Matron cut in. 'I have walked in your shoes. When I was younger — much younger — I found myself fascinated by a visiting surgeon. The attraction was mutual, and I was tempted by his offer of marriage, but nothing came of it.'

'May I ask why?'

'There were too many things I wanted to do here — I had committed everything to this house. I would be lying if I said I never regretted it — I did. I've missed out on the mutual affection and support which come with marriage and I have no children to love and take pride in, but I've been rewarded ten times over. It's been a great pleasure to have helped alter the course of many lives. It's also been a trial at times, having to deal with the likes of Mr Cumberpatch, Mr Anthony and Mr Taylor, but there, I've said too much.' Matron changed the subject, leaving Hannah questioning if she was making the right decision by choosing nursing over marriage.

'This jaunt of yours and Doctor Clifton's appears to have been of benefit to the house. We've already had pledges of money and gifts of bandages, toys and jam, and I'm hopeful that the funds will pay for the extra nursing staff I've been lobbying for.' She paused for a moment. 'There's nothing further that I should know . . . ?'

'Only that I know of the man who's been accused of attempting to murder Mr Allspice,' Hannah said. 'Mr Allspice said that a gentleman tried to kill him last night. He named Mr Milani, a lion tamer. I've been thinking, and it's occurred to me that we should warn Mr Mordikai and the other porters to look out for him, in case he comes to the house to try to finish Mr Allspice off.'

'I don't think he'd dare come here, when the police are looking for him,' Mrs Knowles said, picking up a copy of the late edition of *Keble's Gazette* from her desk. 'Look. There's an article about Mr Allspice's fall. I'll read it to you . . . *Mr Allspice fell from a very great height to the horror of shocked onlookers. A spokesman for the circus and owner of the amphitheatre confirmed that the safety net had been improperly secured.*

'*The lion tamer, a Mr Milani whom the authorities wish to question over his failure to secure the safety net, has disappeared and is thought to be on the run. A keeper has been appointed to care for the lions.*'

'I have a very low opinion of him,' Hannah said. 'The very same gentleman took an unwanted interest in my sister when we visited the menagerie.' She couldn't bring herself to tell Mrs Knowles the truth of what had happened after that. Far from being brave and fearless, she felt that he'd turned out to be rather a coward, running away from the trouble he'd caused.

'She's very young, isn't she?'

'A few weeks short of her eighteenth birthday. In fact, I'd be very grateful if you'd let me know if there are any vacancies coming up for a maid or bathing attendant. She has my recommendation as to her good character.' Hannah pushed down the memory of Ruby's response to her earlier suggestion that she think about working as a maid at the house. It was time to get firm with her.

'She volunteered here before, but as I recall, she didn't stick at it,' Matron pointed out. 'What makes you think she'll apply herself if we offer her a place?'

That was a very good question, Hannah thought, annoyed that Ruby had jeopardised her prospects of employment because she'd preferred to meet with Mr Milani, but with him gone, she wouldn't do it again.

'She wants to work — I have no doubt about her commitment.'

'Is she in good health?'

'Yes. She is small of stature and not robust enough for a nurse, but she can certainly manage a full day's work.'

'What about her temperament? Do you think she can cope with our younger patients, their infirmities and tantrums? Does she have the patience to deal with the ones who hate getting into a bath, and the others who kick up a fuss when told to get out?'

'She loves children.' She didn't like to say that Ruby was like a child herself in many ways, recalling instead how she had cared for the twins.

Matron frowned. 'I have heard . . . oh, what does it matter? It's hearsay, not from the horse's mouth. There's a vacancy for a bathing attendant working alongside Mrs Merry. She can have a month's trial.'

'Thank you.' How much did Matron know, and who had told her?

'Remember that I know everything that goes on in my domain. Tell your sister to be here at seven o'clock sharp tomorrow morning.'

'I'm sure she'll be most grateful.'

'You haven't asked after Mr Allspice,' Matron said.

'No. How is he?'

'For your information, he's about the same and causing merry hell on the ward. You should go and see him on your way back. He wishes to thank you personally for helping him.'

Hannah raised one eyebrow. From what she knew of him, it seemed unlikely, but she dropped by to see Sister Trim en route back to the Lettsom.

'How's the new patient?' she asked.

'He's in a bad way. Mr Anthony is coming in to offer a second opinion later, but I've had patients like him before — he won't walk again.'

The thought crossed Hannah's mind that she didn't care, having heard that he was alleged to be a wife beater. He reminded her of her father, and she had to force herself to bring her reaction under control. She was a nurse and she would treat him like any other patient — without prejudice. At least, she'd do her best . . .

'I'll go and have a word with him.' She walked

across to his bedside where he was lying flat on his back in a cast and strapped to a board.

'Afternoon,' he said as her shadow fell across his face. 'Thanks for what you done for me, but look . . . I can't move anythin' except me arms.'

'My commiserations,' she said curtly.

'I'm in agony,' he went on, swearing aloud. 'My throat's as dry as a bone.'

'I'll fetch you a little ale.'

'A proper drink — some gin or a whisky — would be much appreciated.'

'Oh no, that's too strong for a man in your condition.'

She fetched a small glass of ale and found him a glass straw through which he could drink.

'Can you manage this yourself?' she asked.

'My arms are very weak. You hold it for me, Nurse.'

'It's Sister,' she said, leaning across to help him. He sucked on the end of the straw, but his eyes were elsewhere as the ale dribbled down his chin.

'You're a pretty one. Give us a bed bath, will you?'

She couldn't help it. She had to say something.

'You are a nasty little man, Mr Allspice,' she whispered. 'I know about the debt you failed to pay back to Mr Milani, and what you do to your wife.'

He frowned. 'You know nothing. I can do anythin' I want to my missus — it's my right.'

'I'd advise you to behave yourself while you're here. We nurses stick together, and we could make things very uncomfortable for you. Do you get my meaning?'

'Yes,' he muttered.

'Good. I'll leave you to it.' She straightened and left the ward, speaking briefly to Sister Trim on her way out.

'I've told Mr Allspice that you'll give him a paper copy of the rules of the house,' she said. 'I don't think he can see them up on the wall.' The rules were displayed on every adult ward: no smoking; no chewing of tobacco; no cursing, swearing, gambling or drinking. The patients weren't allowed to sit up after eight-thirty, and they had to rise at seven in the summer, or eight in the winter.

Sister Trim smiled. 'That's an excellent idea. Don't worry — I'll keep him in line.'

When she returned to the lodging house, she found Ruby sitting beside the fire which had almost burned out in the grate, the embers emitting a mere wisp of smoke.

'How are you?' Hannah asked, noticing how fragile her sister looked, her eyes dark from exhaustion and crying. She empathised with her. When love and desire were this powerful, how could anyone with Ruby's spontaneous and impulsive nature resist?

'I'm tired,' she said.

'I have some good news — '

'They've found him? Antonio?' Ruby got to her feet.

'Not as far as I've heard.'

'Mr Allspice has succumbed to his injuries?' Ruby said spitefully. 'This is all his fault.'

'He's still at the infirmary and likely to stay there for quite some while.'

'Then you have no good news for me.'

Ruby's face fell further, when Hannah went on, 'Matron's offered you a place as a bathing assistant. What do you think?'

'That wouldn't suit me at all — I can't swim,' Ruby said eventually.

Hannah tried not to laugh. 'All you need are strong arms, gentle hands and a listening ear.' And a lot of patience, she thought with regret. 'There are rules that you have to follow and Mrs Knowles will have your guts for garters if you're lazy.'

'It's kind of her to offer, but I don't think I can live up to her high standards.'

'Mrs Merry will train you up. There are other ladies there — it will be good for you to have companionship.'

'Oh, I don't know . . . ' Ruby bit her lip.

'You could at least show a little gratitude for my efforts — it wasn't that easy to persuade her to take you on. I don't think you realise how bad things are. We are very low on funds . . . ' Hannah walked across to the fireplace and picked up a folded piece of paper. 'What's this?'

'It's a letter from Mrs Clovis — she wants us gone before the week is up.'

'Why didn't you say?'

'I thought you'd find out soon enough.'

'Ruby, this is a disaster.'

'We can find other accommodation, a bigger place in a better part of town now you're on a sister's wage.'

'It doesn't make that much of a difference.' Her heart sank at the thought of having to find somewhere else to live. 'We can't pay much more in the way of rent than we do here.'

'What about Grandma's money? You can't have spent all of it.'

'It's all gone, every penny.' Hannah went out to fetch the box from under the bed. 'I have a little saved up — that might pay for the deposit.' She came back to the living room, shaking it. 'This is odd. It's as light as a feather,' she remarked as a few coins rattled about inside. She placed it on the mantelpiece, took the brass key from under the rug and unlocked the box. She opened it and peered inside, looking for the leather pouch in which she stored the crowns and shillings. All that was left were a few pennies and ha'pennies. She felt sick. 'It's gone! My savings!' She rushed back to the bedroom to check that she hadn't dropped the pouch, but there was no sign of it. 'Do you have anything to do with this?'

'I can only suggest that Mrs Clovis has been in here, nosing about,' Ruby said with complete confidence.

'She wouldn't touch anything,' Hannah countered. 'She isn't stupid, unlike somebody else who sits looking at me, wringing her hands and popping her eyes to feign innocence. Ruby, I'm disappointed, angry and very upset. How dare you steal from me and then lie about it? I've just given Matron a reference as to your good character!'

Ruby stared at her, her expression mutinous.

'What did you spend it on? Tell me.'

'I bought some shoes,' she confessed. 'I didn't

want to keep borrowing yours . . . Hannah, you said I couldn't have any money to buy nice things, so when I found your savings stashed away, I was tempted. I'm sorry, but those shoes have given me a lot of pleasure.'

'You bought a single pair of shoes with my hard-earned wages! How could you?'

'Now that I have work at the infirmary — '

'You'll pay me back, every penny.'

'I will, I promise,' Ruby said.

'Where are these shoes?'

'They're in a drawer in the dressing table. They need to be kept away from sunlight so they don't fade.'

'I can't believe how deceitful you've been!' Hannah exclaimed. 'What happened to the brooch I wanted to borrow?'

'I pawned it,' Ruby said in an almost inaudible voice. 'Antonio was short of money because his brother-in-law owes him a considerable sum. He'll pay me back as soon as he can . . . '

'Then you are even more stupid than I thought. I've been scrimping and saving, buying tallow instead of beeswax candles, and the cheapest soap, while you throw our money away.'

'You'd have done the same.'

Hannah glared at her. Ruby's shoulders sank as she buried her face in her hands.

'You're making yourself look ridiculous,' Hannah said without sympathy. 'The great Antonio has disappeared, along with our money, and you'll have to get used to the fact that you'll never see him again. Tomorrow, you'll come to the infirmary with me, you'll work hard and make a good impression. At the end of the week, you will give your wages straight to me. Is that understood?'

Snivelling, Ruby nodded.

'All your earnings will go to pay for food, rent and coal.' Hannah looked towards the grate. 'I don't know why you thought you needed to light the fire today. It isn't cold enough for it. Go to bed — we have an early start.'

Hannah sat up late, thinking, but there was no easy way out of their dire financial straits. All she could do was keep going, as she always did.

On her afternoon off a couple of days later while Ruby was working, Hannah found a room to rent in the part of town known as Buenos Ayres. It was a dark, damp attic room and there was barely space to swing a cat, but it would have to do. She paid the landlady, a Mrs Wells — who, like her property, had seen better days — and arranged to move their possessions in the following day.

'I don't like it,' Ruby said when they were unpacking their boxes. 'It smells.'

'It could be worse.'

'We have to share the privy.'

'Ah, Mrs Wells impressed on me that if we need to use the pot at night, we shouldn't leave it under the bed because it rusts the springs.'

'Really?' Ruby raised an eyebrow. 'I've never heard of that before.'

'That's what she thinks.' Hannah allowed herself a small smile. 'It isn't so bad — we have a sea view,' she pointed out as the wind rattled the window. She rubbed at the glass with her cuff to make a circle in the grime. A bedraggled gull sat on the sill, its feathers ruffling in the wind.

'I suppose so. I'm going to work really hard, so we can afford to move out of here as soon as possible.'

'I'm pleased to hear it,' Hannah said drily.

'Beckett splashed me this morning — he was being very difficult. And Mrs Knowles came to see how I was getting on — I don't like the way everyone compares us because we're sisters.'

'Unfortunately, you have to get on with it.'

'I shall until Antonio sends for me. I'm sure he will. He kept telling me how he couldn't live without me.'

Could she detect a hint of doubt in her sister's voice?

'Don't count on it. He's too much of a coward to risk coming back, even if he wanted to. If he's caught, he'll be tried for attempted murder,' Hannah said, at which Ruby burst into fresh tears.

Hannah worried about how the turmoil of uncertainty would affect Ruby's heart and mind, and her fears were confirmed when, the next morning, Ruby declared that she didn't want to go to the house.

'I'm aching all over,' she said, holding her hand to her brow.

'Get dressed. I'll brush your hair and then we'll walk together,' Hannah said quickly.

'It's all right for you,' Ruby grumbled. 'You're accustomed to early mornings.'

'And you will get used to them too.'

'There's cleaning and dusting to be done here.'

'Oh, Ruby, when did you ever take an interest in housework? We'll do it together when we come home.'

'Mrs Merry says that I'm lazy, but I'm only slow doing the baths because I'm new to it.'

'Then you'll keep trying until you are quicker than her,' Hannah said.

A week later and although Hannah was still cross with her sister, she had managed to keep her on the straight and narrow. Mrs Merry and Mrs Knowles were pleased, praising the way Ruby treated the children. She'd made friends with Nurse May, and the lady volunteers adored her, calling her a doll.

That evening, Hannah was late leaving for home, as she'd stayed on to catch up with some paperwork. It was late September by now, and as she left the house, she pulled the hood of her cape over her head against the distinctly autumnal chill, and trudged along the front where a single stallholder was selling tea and hot pies.

'Evenin', miss,' the pie seller said.

'Good evening,' she replied with a small smile.

''Ow about a pigeon pie, only a shillin' apiece? Or if that don't appeal, I have the steak and ale variety, only one left.'

'No, thank you. Another time.' Feeling sorry for him, she hurried on by. Most of the summer visitors and the hokey-pokey men had left Margate, making the town seem eerily quiet. Not wishing to draw any further attention to herself, she kept her head down.

'Sister Bentley? It is you.'

She looked up as a gentleman approached.

'Doctor Clifton? James, how lovely to see you, but what are you doing out here at this time of night?'

'I might ask the same of you.' He smiled and her pulse missed a beat. 'I've been looking for you.'

'You know where to find me,' she said, smiling back.

'That's just it. I don't. I want to give you something, but I don't want to embarrass you by doing it at the house, so I tried your lodgings, but the landlady — one of my patients, as it turns out — said that she'd had to ask you to leave. What's going on?'

'Mrs Clovis turfed us out, not wanting to be associated with the publicity in the papers.' She stopped beside one of the streetlamps and gazed up at the halo of light around his head. 'It wasn't just that — she accused my sister of entertaining a gentleman.'

'I see. That's unfortunate. Have you moved very far away?'

'It's along here; the house with the green door. It's cosy enough,' she added, not wanting to reveal their circumstances.

'I remembered that I borrowed your hatpin when I was examining Mr Allspice.' James pulled a small box out of his coat pocket. 'I've bought you this to replace it. I thought it wrong that you should wear it on your head after it had been in contact with his feet.'

'Thank you, but you didn't have to . . . '

'Hannah, I wanted to.' He took her hand and placed the box in her palm.

She opened it: an ornate gold flower mounted on a pin glinted from a nest of dark blue velvet.

'Oh, that's beautiful, but it's far too good . . . ' The one she'd lent him had been made from brass with a polished stone. 'James, I can't possibly accept it.'

'I give it to you freely and without any ulterior motive on my part, I promise you. I had thought to replace like for like, but when I went to look in the shop, this one caught my eye.'

Her head throbbed with indecision. She would enjoy wearing it, but whenever she looked at it, she would think of him.

'Please, take it. I can't return it and it's of no use to me.'

'I will treasure it then,' she said. 'I'm very grateful.'

'How are you anyway? You're still happy in your new role?'

'It's hard work, more challenging than I expected, but I find great joy in it. How about you? Are you well?'

'I'm a little tired, but that's nothing unusual. Have you heard that my cousin has set the date of his wedding?'

'Many times over.' She smiled, and he grinned back. 'Nurse Finch can't stop talking about it. I shall miss her, though. Nurse May will have to pull her socks up if she is ever to step into Charlotte's shoes.'

He collected himself. 'What am I thinking of? I mustn't keep you here in the cold. Goodnight.'

'Goodnight, James.' She closed the box and clasped it to her breast as he disappeared along the promenade. With a sigh of regret, she went to join Ruby in their dingy room, and put the hatpin away in a drawer with Charlie's picture of the stick people.

17

The Shell Grotto

It was a balmy October day three weeks after the incident at the circus, and Hannah was off, planning an afternoon out to see one of Margate's attractions. Ruby was at home as well, her free day coinciding with her sister's.

'You have a touch of the morbs again,' Hannah said that morning, having done some shopping and laundry. 'It's being stuck indoors on a day off that does it. Why don't you come for a walk with me and Alice? I've arranged to meet her in town at two o'clock.' Alice was still a patient at the house, but she was well enough now to manage a few outings.

Ruby was sitting on the bed with her feet up and a cup of ale in one hand.

'I don't want to go. It's kind of you to ask, but — '

'I know you're still sad about Mr Milani, but this grief will pass.'

'How do you know? What do you know of love?'

'More than you realise.' Hannah recalled the pain that came of being forced to reject James and his proposal. She loved him, and always would. 'I don't want to hear any more about it,' she went on. 'I won't change my mind. I have no need for marriage and children when my days are filled with — '

'Duties and obligations,' Ruby finished for her. 'How dull!'

'Have you eaten?'

'No, I'll wait until later. I'm feeling a little out of sorts.'

Hannah hoped she wasn't building up an excuse not to go to the house the following day.

'I think it was the bacon we had last night,' Ruby added.

'I had the same and I'm not ill,' Hannah said. 'Ruby, we can talk about anything, can't we?'

'What do you mean?'

'There's no chance that you're with child?' she ventured.

'Do you really have such a low opinion of me that you think I'd . . . ?' Ruby bit her lip and her eyes glazed with tears of hurt and outrage. 'How dare you suggest such a thing!'

'I had to ask. If you were and you didn't want it, I believe there are measures one can take at an early stage to prevent it.' She stopped abruptly, unable to carry on. It was illegal and dangerous for the mother. She couldn't possibly entertain it.

'I am innocent!'

'All right.' Hannah held her hands up. 'I'm sorry.'

'If it hadn't been for Mr Allspice, Antonio would be here with me in Margate, and we'd be making plans for our wedding,' Ruby maintained.

You're being ridiculous, Hannah wanted to

say, but she didn't want to upset her sister any further. She seemed fragile and distressed. When Ruby was sad, it seemed as though she was swimming in a sea of grief, and where Hannah would drag herself out of it and do something to take her mind off her sorrows, all Ruby could do was continue treading water. When Ruby was happy, she was excessively jolly and overexcited, talking loudly at nineteen to the dozen as if her mind had been taken over by a thousand thoughts at once. Hannah was never sure how she would be from one day to the next.

'You can't sit here all day, moping,' she said. 'Come with us. We're going to visit the grotto.'

'What do you want to go there for? It's only a hole in the ground.'

'I think it's more than that — you won't know unless you come with us.'

They met Alice in town later, and made their way to their destination, umbrellas at the ready as the clouds scudded above their heads, threatening rain.

'How are you enjoying your position as sea-bathing attendant?' Alice asked Ruby.

'It's better than I expected, but I don't know why Matron isn't keen on me bathing the gentlemen. Mrs Merry doesn't like doing it, so I offered, but no . . .'

'I prefer not to have anything to do with the men. I shouldn't gossip, but Sister Trim says that Mr Allspice is a menace to her nurses and the ladies in the ward next door. His wife called him a rancid old fool when he slapped her on the rump and told her she'd have to put her finery and feathers back on to support their children. When Sister Trim told him that she'd give him another enema, he backed down, saying he was well, thank you very much, but she gave it anyway.' Alice chuckled, and Ruby smiled back.

'He deserves it,' she said.

'He's no gentleman,' Hannah interrupted.

'Talking of gentlemen, where did you get that lovely hatpin?' Ruby said with a wicked twinkle in her eye. 'I haven't seen it before.'

Hannah wished she hadn't dared put it on, but when she'd looked in the slightly foxed mirror on the wall at their lodgings, it had looked so pretty against her navy plush Gainsborough that she hadn't been able to resist.

'It's a long story,' she said.

'You bought it? That seems unlikely. It was a gift. Alice, look at the way she colours up,' Ruby teased.

'You have spiked my curiosity,' Alice said.

'If you must know, Doctor Clifton appropriated my hatpin for a medical examination.'

'He is a hat doctor? Tell me, how were the bonnet's reflexes?'

'Ruby, don't be silly. This is a replacement for the one he used on a patient, not a gift.'

'There!' Ruby exclaimed. 'I knew it. It's a cut above the original.'

'I hope you don't go spreading scurrilous rumours amongst Mrs Merry's assistants,' Alice said. 'Doctor Clifton was right to replace the hatpin, although it was a little thoughtless perhaps to give Hannah one so elaborate and expensive.'

'It belonged to his wife,' Hannah lied, not wanting Ruby to continue with her line of speculation.

'Oh, I see.' Ruby seemed deflated as Hannah stopped to read the sign outside the grotto with the entrance fees and opening times. 'This is the place, I think.'

They paid their money and walked down the steps which were hewn into the chalk. Hannah and Alice walked along the underground passageway ahead of Ruby who loitered along behind them.

'Is your sister well?' Alice asked. 'She seems quite subdued.'

'She isn't herself,' Hannah admitted as they reached an arch where the shell mosaic began. She reached out and touched the mother of pearl, which shimmered splendidly by gaslight. 'Sometimes I worry about her.'

'Mrs Merry says she's been sick recently . . .' Alice paused, but Hannah didn't respond. 'Come on, Hannah, you're my best friend. We can talk about everything and anything. There's speculation among the staff at the house . . .'

'I know what you're saying, but it isn't true,' Hannah said stiffly, following Alice beneath the arch into the Rotunda, and then the Dome, a shaft rising to the surface where a hint of daylight came through.

'Are you sure? Only she talks often of a particular gentleman.'

'She doesn't?'

'Don't be cross — she's very young and I think she fancies herself in love.' Alice blushed. 'I remember how I was with Mr Fry, always talking of him. I must have driven you to distraction.'

'Yes, I suppose you did.' Hannah smiled ruefully. 'Has she mentioned this man's name?'

'Not as far as I know. Do you know who he is?'

'I'm afraid so. He's a showman, a lion tamer.'

'An acquaintance of Mr Allspice?'

Hannah nodded. 'It's a long story, but Ruby has seen him more than once behind my back. Alice, I'm responsible for her, and I feel as though I've let her down. What must you think of us now?'

'It isn't your fault. Look at what you've done for her, taking her in like this. Anyway, he's gone and there's no harm done.'

'Except that he's broken Ruby's heart.'

'It will mend. Her work at the house will keep her mind off this rogue.'

'Please don't say anything to her. I've already upset her today by asking her if she could be . . . you know what I'm saying.'

'What are you talking about?' she heard Ruby ask as they passed through another arch into the serpentine passage which was covered with more mosaics.

'Her reaction said it all — no case to answer. Just infirmary business,' Hannah said, turning to face Ruby. 'I attended a hearing with Mrs Knowles the other day.'

'I heard about that,' Ruby said, brightening. 'One of the maids was accused of stealing food from the kitchens, then let off.'

'That's right,' Alice said.

'Who do you think would have had the time to create these designs?' Hannah said, changing the subject as she gazed at the images on the walls: the tree of life, the stars of Perseus and a corn goddess.

'Not a nurse,' Alice said. 'It must have taken years to arrange all these shells.'

'What do the pictures mean?' Ruby asked.

'They represent the journey of life from conception to death. At least, that's what I think,' Hannah said, feeling awkward in front of her sister.

'Mrs Merry told me that the grotto was found by a workman who lost his spade through a hole in the ground. Why build it, then close it up, unless it was intended as a shrine to love?' Ruby said.

'That's a very romantic idea,' Alice observed, and Ruby smiled, more like her usual self.

In the last chamber, the mosaics were more geometric, the mussels, cockles, limpets, whelks, scallops and winkles laid out to form the shapes of stars and the sun, reminding Hannah of a calendar counting out the passing of the days.

Having left the grotto, she and Ruby bade farewell to Alice before walking back through the park where the leaves on the trees were turning bronze and some of the sweet chestnuts had fallen to the ground where they looked like prickly yellow hedgehogs.

'I have a vague memory of collecting sweet chestnuts with Ma and Grandma,' Hannah said. 'We can roast some of these on the fire.'

They crushed the seed cases underfoot to

reveal the nests of brown chestnuts inside them. They picked them out and filled their pockets to take them home, where they forgot to cut crosses in the tops, so the chestnuts exploded on the fire, making a terrible mess.

'Ouch, they're hot,' Ruby said, amused.

Hannah watched her peel off the tough shells and papery thin skin, then take off the bitter tan before they ate them with a little salt.

'I've enjoyed today.' Ruby smiled. 'It's been fun.'

'I'm glad,' Hannah said, relieved to hear some joy in her sister's voice. The question was, though, how long would it last?

★ ★ ★

The following day, Hannah and Ruby went to work as usual.

'Are you still feeling sick?' Hannah asked as they hurried to the dining hall for breakfast at the house.

'Only a little,' Ruby said. 'I don't like you watching me eat — it makes me lose my appetite.'

'I won't watch you then,' Hannah reassured her, but out of the corner of her eye, she was pleased to note that her sister managed a bowl of porridge and some dry toast. When she got up from the table with Charlotte and Alice, Sister Trim came over to speak to her, an unusual occurrence for someone who usually kept herself to herself.

'That dreadful patient of mine is being sent

home. The doctors say there's nothing more that they can do for him, which is what I've said all along. I've kept telling them how it's time he left to make space for one more deserving of our care. I can't wait to see the back of him.

'He has no appreciation for what we've done — Doctor Clifton arranged for him to receive the donation of a bath chair, so he can be pushed around, when he can find anyone willing to do so. I don't envy his wife when he gets home — he eats like a pig and pisses for England.'

'He must have raised your ire for you to speak of him like this. I have to say I'm surprised he hasn't been discharged for misconduct.'

'He would have been if it hadn't been for the risk of bad publicity. He's well-known — infamous, even — and it wouldn't go down too well if the house was seen to discharge a popular showman struck down with paralysis. No, it's better this way. Well, I must get going.'

'Have a good day,' Hannah said.

'I will do now.' Sister Trim stalked away, and Hannah went to the Lettsom for the handover from the night staff. As she left the sluice, having checked the room for cleanliness and found it wanting, she hesitated on hearing voices. Doctor Clifton and his cousin were making their way along the corridor.

'She turned you down. Why let yourself suffer any longer?' Mr Hunter was saying. She pulled the door up and hid behind it. 'You made an error of judgement with that other piece of muslin — '

'Don't talk of Miss Osbourne-Cole like that,'

Doctor Clifton hissed.

'There are plenty of others out there who would take you like a shot, but perhaps you are enamoured of the thrill of the chase?'

'Like you, you mean?'

'I've forsaken all others and settled on Nurse Finch. We come from different backgrounds, but we share the same values. She is a darling.'

'You'd better look after her or you'll have the other nurses to answer to,' Doctor Clifton said.

'I'm aware of that. Matron's staff are like an army, standing up for each other.'

'How are the studies going? If you don't achieve your registration, you won't be able to marry at Christmas.'

'You don't have to keep reminding me. I have every incentive I need to complete it . . . '

Their voices began to fade and Hannah dodged out of the sluice and followed them into the ward. She greeted Doctor Clifton as she always did, and he smiled as he always did, but she felt embarrassed, having heard the doctors talking about her. How dare Mr Hunter class her and Miss Osbourne-Cole as pieces of muslin!

'It still seems strange without Beckett,' Doctor Clifton said.

'He was quite a character.' Hannah had said farewell to him two days before when his parents had turned up to collect him.

'Have you been introduced to Ronald yet?'

'Not properly.' She knew which patient he was — he was standing beside his bed in his pyjamas, scratching his scalp and face. He was nine years old and small for his age like many of their patients. His hair was brown, his eyes blue and he had scars on his hands.

'He's suffering from scrofula of the skin, inflammation of the eyes and bloating,' Doctor Clifton said. 'It's of utmost importance that the bathing assistants attend to his hygiene and cleanliness.

'Unfortunately, his mother has been giving him decoctions of acorn and nettle and they've done more harm than good. I've prescribed Dover's powder — syrup of ipecac and opium together as a single dose — followed by copious amounts of warm fluids to drink.'

'What about his hands?' Hannah asked.

'There was an accident — his nanny let him too close to the fire . . . ' James shuddered visibly. 'I can't imagine — ' He stopped abruptly. 'Never mind — Ronald's scars have healed.'

He continued through the ward, examining every patient before he left. When he had gone, Hannah called for Nurse May and showed her how to bathe Ronald's eyes, after which he was sick, and Nurse May had to clear it up.

'It's another one of those rites of passage.' Hannah smiled kindly.

'I hope there aren't going to be too many more.' Holding the sick bowl and cloths at arm's length, Nurse May scurried away to the sluice as Ruby entered the ward.

Hannah called her sister to her and introduced their new patient.

'Shall I take him next?' Ruby asked.

'I don't need a bath,' Ronald said. 'I 'ad one last week.'

'This is no ordinary bath,' Ruby said, bending down to his level. 'The water comes straight from the sea.'

'Does it 'ave crabs in it? I don't like their pinchers.'

'There are no crabs, no fish, no monsters,' Ruby confirmed.

'What about shrimp?'

'I couldn't say,' she teased.

'I'm afraid we'll have to leave the bath for today. You'll have one tomorrow, Ronald.' Worried for him, Hannah sent for Doctor Clifton again later that morning.

'You were right to send for me,' he said. 'Delay giving the medicine until I've seen him again tomorrow.'

When midday came, Hannah excused herself and left the ward, passing Mr Allspice who was lying on a trolley on the balcony, bragging about his act to a tattooed sailor who'd lost his leg. Smoke from their pipes drifted into the air, spreading the sweet scent of tobacco.

'I expect you've 'eard I'm goin' 'ome today. I don't know 'ow I'm goin' to keep my littluns fed and watered, but the Amazin' Aerial Ajax will find a way.'

'I'd 'ave liked to 'ave seen you flyin' through the air,' the sailor said.

'Any chance of a house call, Sister Bentley?' Mr Allspice leered.

She said nothing. It was a shame he'd taken advantage of their goodwill.

She continued on to the boardroom and knocked on the door.

'Go on in,' Matron said from behind her. 'We're early. Mr Phillips has been delayed by a quarter of an hour.' They sat waiting until the meeting was convened with the chairman, Mr Cumberpatch and the treasurer in attendance.

'Mrs Knowles, I believe this meeting has been called to discuss funding for an extra nurse,' Mr Phillips said. 'How much money do we have available for this purpose?' He addressed the treasurer who slid a hefty book across the table and tapped at a figure halfway down the open pages. Mr Phillips put on his spectacles and raised his eyebrows. 'I see.'

'Mr Phillips, if I may speak,' Mr Cumberpatch said ponderously. 'Any extraneous funds have been earmarked for redecorating the offices and splint room where Mr Brightside is in need of shelves and cupboards.'

'When you say 'offices', you mean your office, don't you?' Mrs Knowles said.

'Matron, I refer to offices in general.' Mr Cumberpatch scowled, his cheeks florid and fat. 'You have more than enough staff — when I walk through the house with my clipboard, listing everything that requires my attention, I see nurses wandering back and forth as though they have all the time in the world. I hear chattering and laughter from the sluices, and on a sunny day, they are all out on the balcony, taking the air with the patients.'

Mrs Knowles stood up, leaning her hands on the table to berate him.

'You will take that back, Superintendent,' she snapped.

'I speak the truth!' Hannah noticed how the buttons on his brown coat were popping open one by one across his ample chest as his annoyance grew.

'My nurses work hard, much harder than you, sir. They're disciplined, responsible — '

'They take every chance to put their feet up while your back is turned.'

'That's nonsense and you know it. One nurse does the work of ten of you.'

'Ladies and gentlemen, this should be a simple case of allocating resources according to priority,' Mr Phillips sighed.

'That's correct,' Matron jumped in. 'The decoration of an office can wait, but an extra nurse — well, that is a matter of life and death.'

'You're exaggerating,' Mr Cumberpatch exclaimed.

'I would appreciate your silence while I ask Sister Bentley what she thinks,' Mr Phillips said. 'Sit down, Mrs Knowles.'

Hannah cleared her throat. 'The nurses on my ward — the Lettsom — are on their feet for more than twelve hours a day. Not only are they responsible for the care of our patients, some of whom are incapacitated and unable to do anything for themselves, but they liaise with the doctors — '

'I've heard about that,' the Superintendent cut in.

Mr Phillips banged his gavel against the table. 'Go on.'

'They keep the ward clean, scrubbing the floors every day, polishing the windows every week.'

'Woe is me.' Mr Cumberpatch yawned.

'If you interrupt once more, I will have to ask you to leave,' Mr Phillips frowned. 'Sister . . . '

'We've been very grateful for the staffing kindly given by the Board in response to the allocation of an extra bed, but we can always do with more.' Hannah looked towards Mrs Knowles who took over.

'You may be aware that Miss Huckstep, a patient here, has been volunteering on the wards, and it won't be long before she's looking for a place. We can't afford to lose such an experienced' — she glared at Mr Cumberpatch — 'and conscientious nurse to another establishment. Compared with the cost of running this house, a nurse's wage is a drop in the ocean.'

Mr Phillips turned to the treasurer, who nodded.

'Motion passed,' Mr Phillips said.

'But this must go before the whole Board. We haven't had a proper debate,' Mr Cumberpatch protested.

Mr Phillips looked down his nose. 'This house cannot exist without nurses. It will survive the want of a lick of paint and a few shelves.'

* * *

'That went well. I hope you were watching and learning, Sister,' Mrs Knowles said as they walked back along the corridor. 'I'll give Miss Huckstep the good news.'

They parted outside Matron's quarters, and Hannah headed for the dining hall. What had she meant about her watching and learning? Did that mean she was encouraging her in her ambition to progress? It was a promising sign.

18

An Ounce of Prevention is Better than a Pound of Cure

Ronald's condition stabilised and various other patients came and went. Ruby's sickness wore off and she settled into the routine, even going as far as expressing a wish that one day she would work in the splint room with Mr Brightside. Hannah was glad for quieter times, which lasted until the middle of December when the excitement on the ward grew to a fever pitch.

It was two days before Christmas when a brief flurry of snow settled on Margate. The cold pierced her bones and her face felt as if it might crack as she walked to work in the dark with Ruby. On the Lettsom, Ronald was still undergoing treatment and showing some improvement, although he had days when he fell silent and hadn't the energy even to smile. Doctor Clifton was worried that the scrofula had spread, forming tubercles in his lungs, but Hannah preferred to remain optimistic.

That morning, she sent the patients outside as usual.

'I don't want to go outside,' Ronald said. 'Ma says I'll get a chill and die of the pneumonia.'

'You have to sit out for the good of your health.' Even if she thought he'd be better off

327

indoors, Mrs Knowles wouldn't have it. 'Matron says that all our patients must be exposed to the four winds in all weathers.'

Ronald frowned and scratched his head. 'The only shelter is the veranda. How can I lie outside when there's snow falling on my blankets?'

'We'll shake it off,' she smiled. 'Don't worry, I'll find you a hot water bottle.'

Even so, after an hour, Nurse May came to inform her that Ronald was suffering, almost insensible and unable to speak, his nose and fingers blue with cold and his teeth chattering.

'Oh dear,' Hannah said. 'Then you must bring him inside, but say he's coming in for his medicine — I don't want a mutiny in the ranks.'

'It's a little ironic that we ask the patients to sit out in the cold, while Mr Cumberpatch has allowed the fitting of a double layer of glass in the windows facing the sea, and the wards to be heated by steam,' Nurse May observed.

'It is, but who are we to argue? Please deal with Ronald and carry on with your chores.' Hannah saw Doctor Clifton at the entrance to the ward with Mr Mordikai who was pushing a trolley. She waved them in.

'This is Master Jackson,' he said, introducing her to the boy on the trolley. 'Oliver is coming to stay with us for a while.'

Hannah looked down at the boy. He was about eight years old, tall and bony with his skin stretched taut over his cheekbones. His eyelids were drooping, and his blonde hair fell around his shoulders in ringlets.

'He has a marked curvature of the lower spine,

he's in constant pain and, although he can walk, his mobility is limited. His previous physician has had him on opium. I'm planning to wean him on to a lower dose. As you can see, he's half asleep.'

Mr Mordikai turned and left the ward.

'Good morning, Master Jackson,' Hannah said gently, but he made no response.

Doctor Clifton gave her an enquiring look. 'Will you be attending the wedding or are you on duty on Christmas Day?' he asked.

'I'm going to have an hour or two off — Charlotte will never forgive me if I miss it.'

'I'll be there, and I'll stay for as long as my patients allow. I'll see you tomorrow — I'll be here in the morning for rounds. Oh, I meant to tell you. I've admitted Mrs Phillips to the house — she's suffering from a mysterious malaise.'

'You mean she's still pursuing you.'

'There's no need to look so discombobulated — I thought I was a good catch.'

She couldn't help it — the more she tried not to blush, the hotter she felt. She had begun to think that she was cured of her infatuation, but it seemed that she'd had a relapse.

'Thank you, Doctor,' she said, before calling Nurse May over and asking her to take on Oliver's care.

'He'll be easy to manage if he sleeps all the time,' Nurse May observed.

'It's the opium,' Hannah explained. 'You'll need to keep him under close observation.'

The boy opened his eyes and sat up abruptly, muttering and waving his fists, as if he was suffering from night terrors. Nurse May took a step back and stared.

'No, no, that won't do. You must reassure him.'

'I haven't seen a patient do this before.'

'If it's upsetting for you, imagine how it feels for him,' Hannah said. 'He's lost in his own world, but if you speak kindly, he'll hear you and respond. Oliver, all is well. This is Nurse May who'll be looking after you.' The boy began to settle, and his breathing steadied.

'Where am I?' he said eventually, gazing around the ward.

'You're at the infirmary,' Hannah said. 'Nurse May will take you out to the balcony and show you the sea.'

'What about my chores?' she whispered. 'I'm overwhelmed . . . I don't know how I'll manage when Nurse Finch leaves.'

'Think of it as a chance to learn self-reliance, not depend on other people. Nurse May, you've done very well, but you're exhausted. It will do you good to go home for a while.'

She nodded through tears. 'I miss my family.'

'Will your father be there, or is he still at sea?' Hannah asked kindly.

'His ship returned to Folkestone last Tuesday. I can't wait to see him. My brothers and sisters are due to visit on Boxing Day, so we can all be together again.'

Hannah recalled family Christmases at home with Ruby and her half-brothers, the occasion when she had found the silver sixpence in the plum pudding and Pa had taken it away and given it to Christopher. Although she'd argued that the wealth and good luck afforded to the finder wouldn't necessarily travel with the coin, Pa had given her the iciest stare and told her she should be pleased to donate her good fortune to her half-brother. Since she'd been spending the festive season on the wards, she'd had much more fun.

'I hope you have a wonderful time,' she said.

'What about you, Sister? Don't you want to go home?'

'I have Ruby with me, and I count the staff and patients of this house as my family. I wouldn't want to be anywhere else on Christmas Day, and besides, who will look after the boys when you aren't here?' She changed the subject. 'It's Charlotte's last day today — I've arranged for Cook to send a cake to the ward and I've hidden a small gift in the cupboard in the sluice.'

That afternoon, having made sure that Ronald and Oliver were as comfortable as possible, sitting up in their adjacent beds, Hannah announced that they were having a small celebration to thank Nurse Finch for her contribution to the Lettsom during the past few years.

'Oh no.' Charlotte covered her face with her hands. 'I don't want a great send-off.'

'But you must have one,' Hannah said. 'We can't let this event go unmarked. Will one of you boys fetch a chair for Nurse Finch?'

Ronald put his hand up and slid out of bed. He collected a chair from the end of the ward and put it in the middle.

'Nurse Finch, please sit down,' Hannah said. 'Nurse May, would you kindly fetch our gift while I wheel in the cake?'

'Cake? There's goin' to be cake!' one of the boys cried.

'Hurrah!' Ronald shouted.

'Hush,' Hannah smiled. 'I don't want the whole infirmary to hear, otherwise we'll have to share . . .' She fetched the cake which the kitchen maid had left on a trolley in the corridor: a large fruit cake with marzipan and icing, and a message reading 'Good Luck!' By the time she reached the middle of the ward, all the boys who were able, were out of their beds, mobbing Nurse Finch. Ben, the littlest one, scrambled on to her lap.

'I'd like to say a few words,' Hannah said as Nurse May returned. 'Firstly, I'd like to thank Nurse Finch for her work on this ward. She's been a wonderful nurse to her patients, and a great friend and support to her colleagues. We've shared good, and not so good, times.' She remembered the patients who had left much improved, and Peter whom they had lost. 'I'm very sad that Doctor Hunter is taking her away from us, but I wish them every happiness.'

'Where's he takin' her?' Ronald asked.

'You mustn't interrupt while Sister's talking,' Nurse May cut in as she handed a small package to Oliver.

'It's all right,' Hannah smiled.

'We're getting married,' Charlotte said, with Ben clinging to her. 'I won't be going far away — in fact, I'll come and visit the infirmary as often as I can.'

'Here's a present for you.' Oliver offered the gift.

'Thank you. You shouldn't have.' Charlotte glanced towards Hannah and smiled.

'Open it,' Ronald said impatiently.

'I'm going to need scissors to cut that knot.'

Nurse May fetched them and handed them over, laying them flat in the palm of her hand. Charlotte snipped the string and opened the package.

'Fudge and peppermints, my favourites, and drawings.' She looked up at the boys. 'Did you do these?'

'We did,' Ronald said.

'Who is this?' Charlotte held up one of the drawings, a picture of a lady in a tiara and gown.

'It's you — because you're like a princess,' Ronald said.

The boys applauded as Charlotte thanked them and Hannah took a knife and sliced the cake into ragged pieces.

'You'd never make a surgeon,' Charlotte chuckled.

'I'm a nurse — I wouldn't want to be anything else,' Hannah said, handing her a plate.

'I'll miss the camaraderie on the ward, but I won't miss the bedpans — or the leeches.' Charlotte let Ben down and tucked in to her slice of cake.

'We'd better be getting on.' Hannah glanced at the clock. 'Look at all these crumbs. Nurse May, I'm afraid you'll have to do the floors again.'

'I won't miss all the sweeping and scrubbing either,' Charlotte said as Nurse May began to clear up, shooing the boys away.

'What will you do all day?' Hannah asked.

'I'll keep our housekeeper in order, look after my husband and enlist as a lady volunteer.' Her eyes twinkled with humour. 'I may even put my feet up for an hour or two. Imagine having time to read a book or go shopping!'

'Won't you find it rather quiet?'

'I'm going to take up sea bathing in the summer, and dancing in the winter. Seriously, though, I'm going to be the best wife I can be. Henry deserves that — he's worked very hard and against his natural inclination because studying isn't easy for him. To my shame, there were times when I doubted that he'd ever become a physician, but his cousin always had faith in him. Hannah, I wish . . . Oh, it doesn't matter. You have set your chosen course. Everyone says that one day you'll be matron of this house.'

⋆ ⋆ ⋆

On Christmas morning, Hannah and Ruby hurried to the infirmary in the dark, Hannah dressed in her uniform and Ruby in her Sunday best. There was no bathing to be done today, so Ruby was acting as a lady volunteer, having decided that she couldn't bear to be alone.

'It'll be like old times on the ward,' Hannah said. 'Alice and I are looking after the patients who can't go home to be with their families.'

'Why didn't Alice go to her mother's?' Ruby asked.

'Because she can't leave the lady she's looking after — she's too unwell.'

'That's dedication to duty.'

'When your patients are sick, you can't just walk away — '

'Oh, look,' Ruby exclaimed as they stepped into the reception hall where the scent of carbolic mingled with the aroma of pine. 'A tree!'

A spruce fir stood in the middle of the room, adorned with flags and ribbons.

Mr Mordikai stepped out from behind it. 'Merry Christmas, ladies.'

'And the same to you,' the sisters said in unison.

They ate breakfast in the dining hall, then exchanged greetings with the night nurse. The patients who were left had had a peaceful night, although some of them were already up and dressed, impatient for the celebrations to begin.

'Anyone would think it was a special day,' Doctor Clifton said, entering the ward for his round.

'It is special.' Ronald was skipping up and down the aisle between the rows of beds. 'It's Christmas and Nurse Finch is marrying Mr Hunter, and we're going to have plum pudding for dinner.'

'Well, I never knew.' Trying not to smile, Doctor Clifton glanced towards Hannah and their eyes locked.

'Happy Christmas,' she said as Ronald bent over and started coughing, his breath coming in sharp gasps. Hannah hurried over to him and grasped his heaving shoulders. 'Sit on the edge of the bed.' She sat down beside him and held his hand as the coughing began to subside and Doctor Clifton listened to his chest.

'May I venture an idea?' Hannah said.

'Go on.' Doctor Clifton looked up.

'When I was at the Hospital for Sick Children, one of the physicians used steam inhalation to clear the lungs — it helped some of our patients breathe more easily.'

'It's worth a try,' he smiled. 'I'll see if I can find some suitable apparatus to deliver the steam containing a few drops of Friar's balsam.'

'I think you're making it far too complicated. A kettle, bowl and towel to place over the head to trap the steam are perfectly adequate.'

'Thank you, Sister,' he said wryly. 'I can always rely on you to find a practical solution.'

'I can still go to church with the rest of them, and play games afterwards?' Ronald interrupted.

'I don't see any reason why not,' Doctor Clifton agreed, and after the patients had eaten breakfast and washed, they moved to the chapel where Hannah caught sight of James standing with Henry's family in the pews behind the patients' trolleys. The chaplain gave the Christmas sermon before the organist struck up a wedding march. Everyone's eyes turned towards the doors which opened to reveal Charlotte on her father's arm, and a gaggle of young bridesmaids.

'She looks beautiful,' Ronald whispered from where he was sitting beside Hannah.

'She does indeed.' A tear pricked her eye as she watched the bride, wearing a veil and pale blue gown trimmed with lace, walk down the aisle. Hannah noticed the pride and admiration on Henry's face as he turned to look at Charlotte when she reached the altar. The chaplain said a few words before James stepped up to hand over the ring. Hannah wondered how he was feeling — she prayed that he'd put her rejection firmly behind him.

'I now declare you husband and wife,' the chaplain said after the couple had exchanged their vows. 'You may kiss your bride.'

Henry lifted Charlotte's veil, smiled and gave her a chaste kiss on the cheek, making her blush, before taking her hand and walking her back down the aisle. Suppressing a frisson of envy, Hannah turned to Ruby who was sitting beside Oliver whom she'd brought in a bath chair. To her relief, her sister appeared cheerful.

They returned to the ward with Alice and the festivities began with a dinner of roast goose, potatoes, sprouts and gravy, followed by plum pudding and custard. Having cleared up and made sure that all the patients had taken their midday medicines, they pushed the beds to one side and prepared to play games, but before they could start, two ladies arrived on the ward: the Misses Osbourne-Cole.

'Good afternoon,' Letitia said, a ring glinting from her finger as she held up a flute. 'We've come to play for you — you can join in with the singing, if you wish.'

Letitia played while her sister sang — the children took up the strains of 'O, Little Town of Bethlehem' and 'Once in Royal David's City'. They didn't know all the words, but it didn't matter. They sang like angels.

'Can we play games now?' Ronald asked when they had gone.

'You're feeling better?'

'If we're playing games, then yes. A lot better.'

'You're too cheeky for your own good,' Hannah jested. 'What shall we play first, Nurse Huckstep? What do you think, Ruby?'

'How about 'Hide the Slipper'?' Alice said. 'No running, though.'

They played with one of Oliver's slippers, the game interrupted now and again by visitors, coming to see their loved ones or leave gifts of nuts, oranges and apples for the staff and patients.

'Hannah — I mean Sister — it's Doctor Clifton.' Alice nudged her as she was showing Ronald how to peel an orange and divide it into segments.

'I'm sure I've asked you this before, Doctor,' Hannah said archly, 'but don't you have a home to go to?'

'My housekeeper is away.' He looked flushed as if he'd partaken of a little too much wine. 'I left the wedding breakfast where I toasted the happy couple with champagne, then wondered what I should do next.'

'Weren't your family there?' Hannah asked.

'I'm meeting my parents and sisters for dinner at their hotel tonight. This might sound strange, but I couldn't suffer my mother's expressions of disappointment for a moment longer.'

'She's disappointed in you?' Hannah left Ronald with his orange and headed across to help Oliver deal with his. James accompanied her while Alice kept control of the nutcracker, breaking open nuts for each boy in turn, and Ruby peeled and cored apples with a sharp knife.

'In my situation,' he said. 'I hope you don't mind, but I came here on the promise there would be fun and games.'

Hannah couldn't help raising an eyebrow at the thought of their respected doctor running around with her patients. 'You wish to join in?'

'If you'll allow it.'

'I suppose so,' she said. 'It is Christmas, after all.'

They played charades until the boys asked to try another game.

'How about 'Squeak Piggy Squeak'?' James suggested.

'Use this.' Ronald fetched a pillow and thrust it into his hands.

'You've obviously played this before, young man,' James said.

'With my aunts and uncles. We need a blindfold as well.'

'I'll sacrifice a clean bandage, if I may, Sister,' Alice said, smiling as she collected one from the trolley and handed it to Hannah, who made to hand it to James.

'You'll have to help me put it on.' He grinned. 'I don't want anyone accusing me of cheating.' He held out his hand and helped her on to a chair. She stood behind him and wrapped the bandage around his head twice, making sure his eyes were covered, then secured it with a reef knot.

'No peeking.' Chuckling, she grasped him by the shoulders and spun him round several times, while the children took their places. She stepped down from the chair and led him to the middle of the circle of piggies.

'Where am I?' he laughed, making a play of staggering about.

Hannah guided him to the first piggy — Ronald — and helped him place the pillow on Ronald's lap.

'I realise that it's part of the game to sit on the piggy, but I don't want to squash anyone, so I'll just say, 'squeak piggy squeak'.'

Looking relieved, Ronald squeaked.

Doctor Clifton scratched his head. 'Who is it? Could it be Nurse Huckstep?'

'Noooo. It's — '

'Don't give it away,' Hannah said.

'Could it be Sister Bentley or Miss Bentley?'

'Noooo.' The boys screamed with laughter. 'Try again.'

Ronald was laughing so hard that he began to cough, giving himself away.

'Ah, it's Ronald,' Doctor Clifton said. 'It's your turn to be the farmer.'

They played until dusk fell outside, and the kitchen maid came in with their tea.

'I'd better go,' Doctor Clifton said. 'My mother will be waiting.'

'Thank you for entertaining us,' Hannah said. 'I think you went into the wrong profession — you should have been a clown. Merry Christmas, James.'

When he had gone and the patients were in bed, Hannah sat with Alice and Ruby, drinking glasses of mead while they waited for the night nurse to come on duty. It had to be one of the best Christmases ever, she thought, and it wasn't just because James had graced the ward with his presence. It had been an occasion of many 'firsts': her first as Sister; her first for a long time with Ruby; her first with Alice at the infirmary. She wondered what next Christmas would bring.

★   ★   ★

Storms heralded a freezing January when icicles formed on the railings on the balcony at the house, and showers of hailstones blustered across the patients' blankets when they were outside. Alice remained well, and Doctor Clifton managed to control Oliver's pain with the judicious use of opium and extract of willow bark. Ronald continued to have bouts of coughing, and Mr Piper came from St Pancras with more patients, and news of Charlie who sent his regards. With assistance from his sponsor who'd visited him at the poorhouse, he'd moved to private lodgings with his mother. He was doing well at school and had started working in his spare time for the ostler whom Doctor Clifton had mentioned.

Doctor Hunter joined his cousin as a visiting physician and they looked forward to seeing him on the ward, while Charlotte visited several times to read to the boys, revelling in her new status.

Hannah's only real concern, apart from the health of her patients, was Ruby, who was growing fat and fleshy on the good food at the house. Although her spirits had rallied over Christmas and into the New Year, she'd fallen into another spell of moping by February.

It was the fourteenth of the month and Ruby's day off. There was an icy draught gusting through a crack in the window at their lodgings. Having tried to seal it with paper and glue, Hannah lit the fire before she dressed for work. Ruby stirred when she knocked the poker against the grate.

'Morning, sleepyhead,' Hannah said brightly.

'I don't think you realise how annoying you are,' Ruby sighed. 'How can you be as cheerful as a lark at this unearthly hour?'

'I like mornings.' Hannah tipped her head to one side, catching sight of her reflection in the mirror. She looked very well — even her freckles had faded a little. 'In fact, I like afternoons, and evenings too.'

Ruby rolled on to her side. 'It's too much,' she muttered.

'You can always find something to be happy about.'

'It's Valentine's Day. Is that why you're so chirpy? Have you sent a card to Doctor Clifton?'

'Of course not.'

'Then you are expecting to receive one?'

'It's never crossed my mind.' Hannah placed her hands on her hips. 'I suppose the sight of cards in the shops has reminded you of what passed between you and Mr Milani.'

'Antonio, yes, but he's never out of my thoughts. I bought him a card, but I don't know where to send it. Even Mrs Allspice doesn't know where he is.'

'You're still in touch with her?'

'I meet with her occasionally — '

'When? When did you last meet her?'

'Last week. You're frowning at me. It's none of your business what I do on my afternoons off. I don't have to tell you everything!'

'Oh, Ruby, you mustn't associate with the likes of Mrs Allspice,' Hannah said hotly.

'I shall do as I please. She's kind to me. She understands my suffering, and I know something of hers. Mr Allspice has much in common with our father and his controlling ways.'

'That's all the more reason for you and his wife not to be acquainted. How long has this been going on for?'

'Antonio introduced us, and then I talked to her a few times when she was visiting her husband at the house. Since he went home, I've called on her two or three times at their lodgings in Ramsgate.'

'You can't have anything in common with that poor woman. You're only befriending her so you can find out if she's heard from her brother. I'm not stupid!' Except that she was, Hannah thought with regret. Having assumed that Ruby's connection to Mr Milani had been broken, she'd lapsed into a false sense of security. This revelation that she was visiting Mr Milani's sister made her vulnerable to further scandal. 'Why don't you drop into the Lettsom today?' she went on. 'You can read to the children or take them for a walk along the beach.'

'What would I want to do that for? It's my day of rest and it's the middle of winter, and I'm not standing around in the cold, minding those naughty boys.'

'All right.' Hannah was sorry for suggesting it. 'There's some sewing you can do to while the time away.'

'I don't feel like doing anything — I caught myself with the needle last time.'

'You must try. Occupation is good for the mind and spirit.' Hannah couldn't help offering advice, despite having promised herself not to try to jolly her sister out of her gloomy mood. It was against her instincts to leave her alone.

'Please don't tell me to pull myself together — it doesn't work. There's nothing you or anyone can do . . . '

'Why don't I have a quiet word with Doctor Clifton?'

From the pit of her bed, Ruby stared at her in abject misery. 'He treats children with scrofula — he can't cure the mind. Nobody can.'

'I wish I could stay and keep you company.'

'So you can spy on me? I'm not going anywhere today, I promise.'

'Can I trust you?'

'Yes. Now go. You're driving me to distraction. I know myself — this will pass.' Ruby forced a tearful smile. 'I'll feel better tomorrow. I'll see you later.'

Hurrying to the house, Hannah fretted over her sister's state of mind. Over the past few months, she'd watched Ruby's mood fluctuate from high spirits to the deepest despair, and she was at a loss as to how to help her. As for this strange friendship with Mrs Allspice, it had to stop, whether Ruby liked it or not. She resolved to keep a closer eye on her in future.

When she arrived on the ward and the night nurse had left, she looked along the rows of beds. All was well. Everything was in its place, except Ronald.

'Where is Ronald?' she said crossly.

The boys peered out from under their blankets. Somebody sniggered, which was reassuring, she thought.

'You must think I was born yesterday . . .' She hastened towards one of the long windows and turned the handle to raise the blind. A set of toes, then a pair of ankles came into view. She lowered the blind again and walked away. 'If Ronald isn't here, he'll miss breakfast,' she said out loud.

'He's there, behind you,' Oliver said with glee, pointing towards the window. Hannah turned and made a show of looking.

'I can't see anyone.'

'He's there.' Another boy joined in.

'No, he isn't.'

'Yes, he is. On the windowsill.'

'Surely not?' Hannah went over to raise the blind. 'Oh, there he is!'

'I'm not goin' to miss breakfast, am I, Sister?' Ronald stammered.

'Not if you get down straight away, and promise you'll never play tricks on me again.' She tried to keep a straight face, but it was impossible. Grinning, she took his hand and helped him down. 'Back to bed, young man. The doctors will be here soon.'

'Do you know what day it is?' Ronald asked.

'I do have an idea,' she said.

'*The rose is red, the violet's blue, the honey's sweet and so are you.*' Blushing, he gave her a small bow and returned to his bed, pulling his covers up over his face.

'Thank you,' she said solemnly.

'I know the rest of it,' she heard Doctor Clifton say from behind her, the sound of his voice like Cupid's arrow piercing her heart. '*Thou art my love and I am thine; I drew thee to my Valentine: The lot was cast and then I drew, and Fortune said it should be you.*'

'You're a better physician than a poet, and that's saying something,' Mr Anthony commented.

'It's a traditional verse,' Doctor Hunter joined in. 'He hasn't the imagination to create his own rhymes. What do you think, Sister? Did he deliver it like Romeo speaking to his Juliet?'

'I have no idea,' she said dismissively. 'I'd be very grateful if we stopped wasting time. Some of us have a busy day ahead of us.'

'I'm sorry,' Doctor Hunter said. 'We won't hold you up any longer.'

'I'm glad to hear it.'

The doctors agreed that Ronald should continue his treatment, but they were still concerned about the state of his lungs, while Oliver's spine was growing more curved every day. They took Hannah aside.

'He will have to go into a whole-body cast,' Doctor Clifton said. 'We've put it off for long enough.'

'The poor boy will hate it,' Hannah said.

'It's a better option than surgery,' Mr Anthony

346

said. 'Putting him under the knife would be a last resort.'

'Who will tell him?' Doctor Clifton asked.

'I will.'

'Thank you, Sister,' he said, sounding relieved.

She went to speak to Oliver. 'I have good news and bad news. Which would you like to hear first?

He frowned. 'Is the bad terribly bad?'

'Fairly.'

'Then I'll hear that first.'

'The doctors have said that you need complete bed rest while your body is held in a cast to encourage your spine to grow straight.'

'I don't like the thought of lying in bed all day. Tell me the good news.'

'I remember you telling me how you wish to work on the ships one day.'

He nodded. 'If I do this, my back will end up straight? I'll be taller than my sister?'

'It has a good chance of turning out right,' she said, not wanting to make false promises. 'What do you think?'

'I'll do it,' he said bravely.

However, when Mr Brightside fitted the cast, assisted by Nurse May, Oliver fell silent, realising he was trussed up like a goose and expected to spend half his time on his front.

'I don't like it,' he grumbled when Hannah and Nurse May turned him on to his stomach. 'I can't see anything.'

'You'll soon get used to it,' Hannah said. 'It's important that we turn you regularly. Why is that, Nurse May?'

'To prevent sores,' she replied. 'It's easier to stop them in the first place than it is to treat them.'

'That's right,' Hannah said, her mind darting from the subject of bedsores to Ruby's problems and her longing for James. 'It's the same for many other situations in life. Prevention is better than cure.'

19

A Dose of Godfrey's Cordial

One morning at the end of March, when the sun was emerging meekly through the mist outside their grimy window, Hannah caught sight of the unmistakeable swell of Ruby's stomach and the veiny fullness of her breasts as she changed out of her nightgown. There had been times when she'd wondered if her sister was suffering from dropsy, with her bloated stomach and thick ankles, but she was the picture of health. She could have cried.

Taking a deep breath, she waited for her to finish dressing.

'Sit down,' she said sharply. 'I need to speak to you.'

'We'll be late.' Ruby studiously avoided Hannah's gaze.

'This can't wait any longer.' She stood with her arms crossed as Ruby perched on the sagging armchair with a woollen shawl arranged to hide her belly. 'I know why you go around padded out with petticoats while the boilers are roaring in the house. You're with child.'

'It isn't true.' Ruby's lip quivered and her beautiful eyes glazed with tears as she looked up.

'If you'd only confided in me before . . . ' Hannah wasn't sure what difference that would have made, but at least she could have been prepared.

'I'm not with child.'

'After all I've done for you, you can't bring yourself to tell me the truth. Why?' Her heart went out to her poor deluded sister. She saw what ruination meant now. Ruby was broken.

'I will not confess to anything,' she said, her voice tremulous.

'I'm sorry for what happened with Mr Milani. I say that sincerely — I would have treated him as my brother, if he'd faced up to what he'd done and seen fit to marry you.' Hannah chose her words carefully, not wanting to add to Ruby's distress. 'You aren't going to work today.'

'I'm expected — I can't just cry off.'

'I'll square it with Mrs Knowles.'

'I'm so sorry — I've let you down.'

'You need to face up to it, Ruby. The child will be here in what . . . a month? Two months?'

'Soon.' She nodded, her face etched with misery.

'You won't be going to work again until after the infant's born, and then you'll have to find something you can do from home, because you won't be able to go back to the infirmary.' Hannah stared at the few coals that were left in the basket beside the fireplace. 'How are we going to manage to bring it up?'

'A babe doesn't need much.'

'A mother's love isn't enough. Children can be a blessing, but they're also a means of keeping their parents poor. I see it every day.' It crossed her mind that she might be able to persuade

James to give her some hours at his private clinic, but that would mean having to tell him of their predicament.

'I hope I haven't ruined everything for you,' Ruby said quietly.

'I'm afraid that you've ruined everything for both of us. We'll talk some more when I get back.' When Hannah went to the door in her shoes and cape, Ruby let her out.

'I know you think I don't appreciate what you've done for me, but I do,' she said.

Hannah forced a smile. 'Then you will prove it by doing as I ask.'

Matron was unavailable that morning, attending meetings with the chief superintendent and the governors, which was a relief to Hannah who informed Mrs Merry instead that Ruby was indisposed and wouldn't be at work that day. Having bought time before she would have to tell her and Mrs Knowles that the situation was permanent, Hannah went to help little Oliver whose blonde ringlets fell over the shoulders of his plaster cast as he tried in vain to escape its restraint. He was used to lying on his front, but he still didn't like it when Hannah and Nurse May moved him in the turning plaster, or when Hannah gave him his dose of Godfrey's cordial, a mixture of treacle, opium and sassafras to help him lie still.

'Sister, Oliver seems worse this morning,' Nurse May said, giving her his vital signs.

'Thank you for letting me know. I'll have a word with him.'

'You've had your medicine?' she asked him.

He nodded weakly.

'Have you managed to eat your breakfast?' Hannah knew very well that his porridge was sitting untouched on the tray at the end of his bed. 'Let me help you,' she said, picking up the bowl and spoon and giving the porridge a stir. She spooned some up and offered it to her young charge who shook his head.

'I don't want it.'

'Just taste it — that's all I ask.'

Wrinkling his nose, he took a little porridge from the spoon.

'Is it sweet enough?'

'Yes, Sister.'

She offered him a fresh spoonful and he ate that, and another, after which he pushed the bowl away.

'Let me find one of the lady volunteers to read you a story while you're out in the sunshine,' Hannah suggested. 'It won't be long before you're better, and Mr Anthony will say you're ready to sit up.' Unsure how much hope there was for the poor lad, she fastened the forehead rest to keep his head still.

'Where is Ruby today? Mrs Merry is missing her,' Alice said.

'Oh, she's unwell. I didn't think it wise that she should come here and mix with the patients.'

'There's much talk, Hannah. People had their suspicions before, but now some dare to say that it's certain.'

'I know.'

'What's the truth of it?'

Hannah shook her head.

'Later, then. Come on, Oliver. Let's dry your tears,' Alice said breezily.

The day went on, and Doctor Clifton arrived on his ward rounds with Mr Anthony. Hannah tried to avoid him, speaking only when spoken to, because she felt she might break down and give herself away. Had Oliver had a good night? Had he eaten all the food offered? Had he expressed any sensation of pain or tingling in his limbs?

When she answered, he tried to catch her eye, but she dropped her gaze, unable to face him. Alice suspected the truth. How long would it be before everyone knew that her sister was having a child out of wedlock? She was in almost as much trouble as Ruby, her reputation tainted by association. How would that affect her standing at the infirmary? Worse, though, was wondering what opinion James would have of her when he found out. He would think he'd had a lucky escape, not marrying her.

At the end of her shift, she hurried back through the dark to the lodging house. Entering their room where the air was cold and still, the lamps unlit and the ashes in the grate barely glowing, she hurried straight to the bed.

'Wake up,' she called, seeing the outline of Ruby's figure lying down with her hair flared across the pillow. She didn't stir. Hannah stood over her, her eyes gradually making out the grey strands of the mop, the handle under the coverlet padded out with bolsters, and at the end of the mattress, Hannah's best shoes.

Shaking with anger and panic, she checked the

dressing table. Several of Ruby's personal effects had gone: the necklace Grandma had left her; the hairbrush and mirror set with the silver and mother-of-pearl backs; her dressing case and carpet bag. Hannah went into the sitting room where there was a note on the side table: a few scrawled words on a scrap of headed paper that Ruby must have filched from the hospital.

Dear Hannah,

Please don't worry. I've gone away for a while. Don't try to find me.
  Your devoted sister,
  Ruby x

Overcome, Hannah sat down, the words blurring in front of her eyes. It was a shock when Ruby had seemed so calm and controlled that morning. After a while, she got up to check the box under the bed. It was — as she'd expected — empty. Now she would be short for the rest of the week, but that didn't matter. At least Ruby had thought to take some money with her.

Where would she have gone? She ran through a list of their family, friends and acquaintances; the Foundling Hospital . . . or was it possible that Mr Milani had sent for her? Ruby hadn't mentioned Mrs Allspice for several weeks, but Hannah couldn't discount the possibility that she'd gone to stay with her in Ramsgate.

Still wearing her cape and shoes, she went to see their landlady who lived on the ground floor.

'Done a runner, 'as she?' Mrs Wells said,

answering the door in her slippers.

Hannah's instinct was to deny it for appearances' sake, before realising that that approach wasn't going to get her anywhere. It was a private matter, but she had to reveal some of the details if she was going to find Ruby.

'Is it possible that you noticed her go out today?'

'I 'ave better things to do than mind your sister, but let me think.' She scratched her chin, dislodging a crust of dried egg yolk, before gazing up at the sky as if the arrangement of stars might nudge her memory. 'I did see her go, matter of fact. It was at about midday — she left, carrying a couple of bags and boxes.'

'Did you speak to her?'

'No, but I did think it a little odd that she should leave the 'ouse at that time when she's been goin' out with you early in the mornin's. Look at you. You've 'ad a shock. Come indoors and 'ave a little gin.'

'I'm very grateful, but no thank you.' Needing to keep a clear head, Hannah excused herself. Her expectations of her and Ruby living happily together in Margate had been turned upside down. She could only console herself with the fact that Ruby had left voluntarily, leaving a note and taking some of her belongings, indicating that she'd had a plan in mind, rather than running away on a whim.

Hannah had no choice but to go to work the next morning — she had a ward to run, patients and staff depending on her. Sick at heart and weary from waiting all night in the hope of hearing Ruby's knock at the door or the sound of her voice, she washed and dressed and made her way to the infirmary where she found that Oliver's condition had gone downhill.

He was in bed, crying.

'Sweetheart, what's wrong?' she asked.

'My back is burning.' His voice was panicky. 'I can't feel my legs.'

'Let's ask Doctor Clifton what medicine you can have when he turns up on his rounds. He'll be here very soon.'

It wasn't long before Doctor Clifton turned up with Doctor Hunter and the junior physician. Hannah gave them a summary of her observations.

'How is little Oliver today?' Doctor Clifton said with a smile.

'I'm not little,' he replied.

'In view of Sister's report, I'm going to check your reflexes.'

Hannah and Alice held a sheet in front of Oliver's eyes, so he couldn't see what the doctor was doing.

'Can you feel anything?' he asked as the boy squeezed his eyelids shut, deep in concentration.

'How about now?' Doctor Clifton pinched his big toe.

'I think I can feel something like a feather.'

'And now?' The doctor used a needle.

'Nothing,' he said in a shrill voice. 'What's happening to me?'

'There's some pressure on your spine. I'm going to speak to Mr Anthony to see what he can do.'

'I need the use of my legs,' Oliver said. 'I'm going to build ships like my pa, and his pa before him.'

'It's important to keep looking towards the future. Perhaps one of the ladies will find a book about ships for you to look at,' Doctor Clifton suggested before walking further along the ward to speak to Hannah and his colleagues.

'I'd hoped to avoid surgery. This patient has been doing well with thalassotherapy, but it seems that it was a temporary state of affairs. I'm sorry to see that his condition is turning into a classic case of Pott's disease. I'll arrange for Mr Anthony to remove some of the diseased tissue that's pressing on the spine, but the prognosis is . . . well, poor.'

The doctors nodded sagely and moved on, but later when the children were on the balcony, wrapped in blankets against the fierce March winds, Mr Anthony turned up to examine Oliver and arrange for him to have surgery the following day.

As soon as he had gone, Hannah rushed off to the sluice to shed a few tears — for Oliver whose time was running out, and for Ruby. When she emerged minutes later with a clean bedpan, Doctor Clifton ambushed her in the corridor.

'I see you're upset,' he said.

'It's the wind,' she responded. 'It stings my eyes.'

'I keep asking myself if it's fair to put Oliver through an operation, but Mr Anthony and I agree that this is the only way to proceed. The alternative is for him to live out the rest of his days — and there won't be many of those — confined to a cast and dosed up with morphia.'

'I trust your opinion, James,' she said, knowing that it was a case of kill or cure.

'You seem on edge. Is there something wrong? You look gaunt . . . ' His eyes were filled with concern. 'Are you having any aches and pains, any fevers?'

'Oh no, goodness no.'

'Thank God for that.'

'I'm well.' She forced a smile. She was good at that, but Doctor Clifton gave her a knowing look and she realised that she hadn't succeeded in pulling the wool over his eyes.

'Don't forget that you have to look after yourself so that you're fit to care for others,' he said sternly. 'Make sure you go and have something to eat. You're as white as a sheet.'

Not only was she worried about her sister's welfare, she was growing angrier by the minute. As soon as her shift ended, she walked to the Hall by the Sea to ask if anyone had any idea of Ruby's whereabouts, but it was closed for the winter season. There was a caretaker at the main entrance beneath the sign reading, *Beasts, Birds and Reptiles from All Parts of the Universe*, but he was no help.

'Lord Sanger has taken on new staff to look after the big cats,' he said. 'We do have plenty of young ladies who visit the menagerie during the year, offering to assist with the animals, but I don't recall a lady of that description.'

'What about Mr Allspice? Do you know of his address?'

'I know of the gentleman, but not his where-abouts. Did you know he met with an accident? Terrible, it was,' he went on.

'Thank you for your time, sir,' she said, wondering what she could do next.

★ ★ ★

The next morning, Hannah was up before dawn, so that she could spend an hour or so searching the streets for Ruby, but there was no sign of her anywhere. Arriving late at the infirmary, she missed breakfast and went straight to the ward to prepare Oliver for surgery.

'You seem happy today.' She unfastened his cast and bathed his back.

'It's being so cheerful that keeps me going. That's what Ma says. She's coming in to see me this afternoon.'

'I hope you'll be awake by the time she gets here. The chloroform makes one very drowsy.'

'They're going to saw you in half,' Ronald said from beside him.

'That isn't right — Mr Anthony is going to remove the parts that have gone bad, that's all,' Hannah said.

'You won't leave me, will you, Sister?'

'Nurse Huckstep will sit with you for now, but I'll make sure that I've finished my duties in time to accompany you to theatre. How about that?'

'That's good.' He smiled.

'You aren't yourself, Hannah,' Alice said when she went to find her. 'What's wrong? I wanted to talk to you last night, but you disappeared off home without a word.'

'I wasn't going to worry anyone else with it, but I can't keep it to myself any longer. Ruby's gone missing.'

'Missing?' Alice raised her eyebrows. 'She has vanished, or run away?'

'She left me a note to say she was leaving.'

'She's gone home?'

'This is her home. No, she has got herself into a bit of a — '

'Ah, I thought as much.'

'I'm so angry and upset. I've done my best to help her, and she's let me down. I've been looking for her all over Margate, but I can't find her. I've written to my stepmother and uncle in Canterbury, and I've tried to find out the Allspices' address in case she's gone there. I don't know what else to do.'

'Have you looked at the patient records? Mr Allspice would have had to give his address when he was admitted.' Hannah's spirits lifted a little as Alice continued, 'Let me do that for you later. Have you reported her missing to the police? They're perfectly acquainted with all parts of the town — I think you should notify them, so they can keep an eye out for her.'

'That's a good idea. I'll call at the police station at lunchtime. You won't say anything, will you?'

'My lips are sealed.'

Hannah turned and looked back down the ward. 'Will you sit with Oliver for me until Mr Anthony sends for him?'

Later, Hannah took Oliver to theatre where

Mr Anthony's assistant put him to sleep with a chloroform mask. As his hand relaxed in hers, she whispered him good luck and let him go, watching the pretty theatre nurse wheel the trolley away into the next room with its panorama of Westbrook Bay, where the surgeon would carry out the procedure. Having left her patient, she took advantage of her break to visit the police station after she'd had a quick word with Mrs Knowles to say that Ruby was still unwell. The police sergeant was sympathetic, but unhelpful. Ruby had left home of her own accord. There was no evidence of coercion or kidnap, so he could do nothing. As for finding the Allspices' address, Alice had no better luck. The address given in the patient records didn't exist — she'd checked discreetly with one of the maids who knew Ramsgate well — which meant that Hannah was no further forward in her search.

Despondent, she returned to the ward, to find that Oliver was back from surgery, in a half-cast with a dressing over the wound on his spine, and fast asleep.

'Dear boy,' she murmured, checking his toes, which were cold, and covering him with an extra blanket before his mother arrived at visiting time, bringing a small bag of his favourite sweets.

'He's too sleepy to eat anything yet,' Hannah said, guiding her to her son. 'He's doing as well as can be expected, though. Why don't you sit and hold his hand?'

The sight of mother and son together reminded her of Ruby, who had never had the chance of having her ma sit with her when she was ill or upset. Hannah swallowed hard, knowing she had to keep going, no matter how much she wanted to get away from the house to look for her.

In the evening, when she'd checked that Nurse May had cleaned the floors properly, the patients were settled in their beds and the ward was ready for the night staff, Doctor Clifton dropped by.

'It's been a long day, but I had to come and see one of my favourite patients before I went home,' he said. 'How are you, Oliver? Ah, I see you're sleeping. I'll leave instructions for the night staff and they can administer more morphia if necessary, after midnight. The wound is clean?'

Hannah nodded, having checked several times during the day for fly eggs that might turn into maggots, a not uncommon occurrence after surgery.

'When do you finish, Nurse Bentley?'

She looked up at the clock. 'In half an hour — I have some paperwork to complete and then I'm done.'

'I'll wait for you. I haven't dined yet. Have you?'

She shook her head.

'We can dine together.'

'Oh no, that isn't necessary. I'm not hungry.'

'Don't argue. It's doctor's orders.' He smiled again, and her heart lurched. 'It's been a tough day, and I could do with the company.' Suddenly, his face fell. 'Oh, your sister. I'm sorry, I forgot. You have to get back to her.'

Hannah's eyes stung with tears.

'What is it? You can trust me — you know that by now.'

'I'm very grateful, but I don't deserve your consideration in this matter in which I've been unwillingly caught up.'

'You deserve every consideration. You go beyond the call of duty with the patients and staff of this house. You're an angel — look at the way you've helped little Oliver today.'

'I'm not little,' Oliver muttered, and despite her tears, Hannah smiled.

'Somebody is earwigging,' she said.

'Then we'll speak in private over dinner. I'll be back in half an hour to take you to the dining rooms off Cecil Square.'

'I'm hardly dressed for the occasion.'

'In my opinion, you look beautiful whatever you're wearing,' he said. 'I won't apologise or retract my words because I speak the truth. I'll see you soon.'

'I have things to do this evening, though.'

'The service is prompt and I won't keep you.'

Hannah gave in, and an hour later, they were ensconced in a private alcove in the dining rooms, ordering eel pie and mash, and hot chocolate.

'My housekeeper has given up cooking for me — Henry's moved out now he's a married man, and I'm rarely at home, so the dinner usually spoils.' James looked her straight in the eye as they waited to be served. 'I have an idea that your sister is the cause of your troubles. Is that right?' He went on, 'Mrs Merry was grumbling that she's had to do most of the bathing herself recently. If Ruby's unwell, I'm happy to make a house call — '

'I've told Alice, and everyone else is bound to know soon enough. Ruby left home without telling me where she was going. I have no idea where she is.'

'You must be out of your mind with worry.' He paused, waiting for her to speak. 'You know you can rely on my discretion,'

She gazed back at him, deflated.

'Where do you think a young girl would go to give birth to her child?' she said quietly.

A query flashed across his eyes, but to her surprise, no condemnation.

'There are a few options. Would she have gone to other relatives, or taken lodgings elsewhere and employed a private nurse for her lying in?'

'She has very little money. Only what she earns as a bathing attendant and what I give her. Unless I get my hands on her wages first, she spends them like water.'

'I see. You support your sister?'

'Ruby had this idea that she would marry a man with an income of several thousand pounds a year, but she's thrown away any chance of that.'

'May I ask the identity of her lover?'

'You know of him — Mr Milani.'

'The b — ' James swore out loud, then quickly apologised. 'He hypnotises young ladies as well as lions,' he muttered. 'I'm not a violent man, but if I ever set eyes on him again, I'll give him what for. You don't think she's gone off with him?'

'I doubt it. He's on the run.'

'Have you spoken to the police?'

'I've given them her details, but all they could say was that they would keep the information on record, in case someone found her and reported back to them. They didn't take me seriously — they said that young women who'd got themselves into a pickle often went missing. That's how the constable described it, 'in a pickle'.'

'Does she have friends in Margate?'

'I don't know. She can be very secretive, revealing only what she thinks will please me. There's a possibility that she's gone to the Allspices'. Mrs Allspice befriended her a while ago.'

'Then it's a simple matter to rule that one in or out.'

'It should have been, but the address the Allspices gave when Alan and his father were admitted here is false.'

'I should have guessed that was the case,' James sighed.

'Of course, she might be out on the street.' She thought of her sister cold, frightened, hungry and even in labour. 'Oh my goodness, what if I can't find her?'

'We'll find her,' he said firmly.

'Sometimes I think I was too harsh with her, too keen to criticise — a bit like my father was — and she ended up too scared to tell me the truth. I can't believe I did that. I didn't look at anything from her point of view. What kind of nurse am I? What kind of sister?'

'You're the best kind,' James said gently. 'You wouldn't have spoken your mind if you didn't care. Now, eat your pie and we'll make a plan. What is that adage? Two heads are better than one.'

After dinner, they asked around at some of the local inns without success, then knocked on the doors of a few of Margate's lodging houses.

'This is hopeless,' Hannah said eventually.

'Don't despair. Tomorrow, I'll send my man, Dobbs, out — on the quiet, of course — to see what he can find out. In the meantime, you should get some rest. I'll walk you home.'

She wanted to keep going, but she could hardly put one foot in front of the other and her spirits were drained, so she let him see her back to her lodgings, wondering if she'd ever see Ruby again.

20

On the Side of the Angels

Mr Mordikai came to the Lettsom to speak to Hannah just before she took her break for lunch the next day.

'There's a young man — one of your former patients — asking for you. I asked him to wait in reception.'

'Thank you.' She hurried away to find Alan sitting on one of the benches with his arms twisted around his head. He straightened himself out and, apologising for delaying her with his antics, walked across the new Turkish rug to join her. 'Master Allspice, what are you doing here? Are you well?'

'I've never felt better.' He was a little taller than she remembered, and his voice gruffer. 'I need to 'ave a word with you, in private.'

'My sister? You have news?' Her heart beating faster, she guided him outside where they stood in the shadow of one of the giant columns.

'Pa will kill me if 'e finds out it's me who grassed, but I owe you a favour. That's why I'm 'ere — to tell you that Miss Ruby's at our lodgin's in Ramsgate.' He gave the address. 'I thought you should know, for your peace of mind. She's bein' looked after, but if you want to check on her yourself . . . '

'I won't say anything to your father, but I will go to her. Are you going back to Ramsgate now?'

'That's my intention.'

'Please give her a message: that I will meet with her as soon as I can. I have a day off tomorrow.' She thought for a moment. 'No, don't say anything. I don't want to alarm her.'

'Understood,' he said.

'Allow me to pay you for your trouble.'

'It isn't necessary,' he said, but he let her press a shilling into his hand before he left.

How could Ruby entertain living in the same house as the dreadful Mr Allspice? She went to tell Alice, and then Doctor Clifton who was holding a clinic for the outpatients.

He offered the use of his brougham to cover the six miles to Ramsgate the next day, but she declined, saying she would take the train.

He smiled gently. 'By tomorrow evening, you'll have your sister back with you where she belongs.'

'I hope so,' she said.

★　★　★

The lodging house was in the middle of the town. It looked rundown, with peeling paint and arched windows of different shapes and sizes, as though the builder hadn't been able to afford matching ones. Having rung the doorbell, Hannah had to wait until a young girl holding a toddler on her hip opened the door. Both had runny noses and tangled hair.

'What do you want?' the girl asked.

368

'I'm here to see my sister, Miss Ruby Bentley.'

'She i'n't here.'

'So you do know her?'

The girl nodded. 'I'm not allowed to say where she is,' she added fiercely.

Hannah sidled past her, putting her hand across her nostrils to block out the scent of cold cream, musk and cesspool.

''Ey, missus, you can't come in 'ere.' The child sounded terrified, but Hannah had no choice.

'Where's your ma?' She followed the girl's anxious gaze, darting nervously to and from an open door with stairs leading down to what she assumed was the cellar. At the sound of voices and a sharp cry of pain, Hannah hurried down the steps into the gloom, with the girl close behind her.

'I told 'er not to come in, but she didn't take no notice.'

'Who is it?' Hannah heard Mr Allspice bark, as she stepped across a heap of dirty laundry towards the middle of a windowless underground cavern. The walls were black with mould, matching the colour of the mattress on which several of the Allspice offspring were playing, rolling around and scrapping over an old bonnet. 'Oh, it's you,' he went on. ''Ow did you find your way 'ere?'

'I spoke to one of the staff at the Hall by the Sea,' she lied. 'They told me your address. I'm looking for my sister.'

'Oh yes.' Mr Allspice leaned back in his bath chair and sucked on his pipe. 'The one who played fast and loose with that murderin' — '

'You can't talk,' she snapped back, the hairs on her neck standing up on end at the sight of him. 'You are as evil and dissolute as each other. Where is she?' Hannah moved towards the corner of the room where a pale, wet snout appeared between the slats of a pallet. One of the children tossed a cabbage leaf into the pen and the pig gobbled it up.

A muffled cry came from behind a curtain further along into the bowels of the house.

'She i'n't here. I don't know what gave yer the impression — oi, leave that alone — it's my property,' Mr Allspice warned, as Hannah yanked the curtain aside to find her sister lying on a makeshift bed, her face pinched with pain, with Mrs Allspice perched beside her.

'I don't want you here. Go away,' Ruby gasped.

'You 'eard what she said.' Mrs Allspice dabbed at Ruby's forehead with a damp rag.

'I'm not leaving. She needs a doctor. We must send for a physician straight away.'

'Oh, she don't need a quack. The babe's on its way, that's all.'

'How long has she been like this?' Hannah pushed in and grasped Ruby's hand — she didn't protest. 'Half an hour? An hour?'

'Since about six last night.'

'It feels like an awful lot longer,' Mr Allspice sighed.

'That's too long, surely . . . ' Hannah began to doubt herself. She had never nursed a woman in childbirth.

'It took over a day and two nights for my first.

The others were quicker.'

'The last one just fell out, didn't it?' Mr Allspice said crudely. 'It isn't a good sign that it's takin' so long. A tiny infant would 'ave been born by now.'

'Remember that everythin' is in proportion,' Mrs Allspice said. 'If both mother and infant are small, then it'll take the same time as if both mother and infant are large.'

'Why, wife, never 'as a truer word been spoken.' Mr Allspice sounded surprised. 'Then we must keep the faith — the bottle is 'alf full.'

Ruby cried out again.

'If you won't send for a doctor, let me take her to see one,' Hannah said in desperation, wishing she had James at her side with access to chloroform like Queen Victoria had had for her confinements.

'It's too late to move 'er — she isn't going anywhere until this babe is born,' Mrs Allspice said. 'Pull the curtain across. I need to 'ave a look at what's goin' on down below. Open your legs, girl.'

This was no time for modesty, Hannah thought, tugging at the curtain to hide her sister's nakedness from Mr Allspice's stare.

'Ah, it's comin'. I can see the top of the littlun's 'ead. Ruby, I want you to strain with the next pain. Are you ready?'

'Listen to Mrs Allspice. Do exactly as she tells you!' Hannah said.

Ruby's face contorted as she took a deep breath and strained to get the baby out.

'It's almost there. 'Ere are the shoulders . . . '

Hannah felt her hand being squeezed even tighter . . .

'It's 'ere.' Mrs Allspice swept the infant into the air — she couldn't have sounded more delighted than if it had been one of her own. In contrast, Ruby sank back ashen and exhausted, and the child opened its mouth and began to whimper.

'Well done,' Hannah whispered, stroking a tress of Ruby's hair from her cheek.

'Put it straight to the breast.' Mrs Allspice dangled the baby and lowered it on to Ruby's chest.

'What is it, Mrs Allspice?' called her husband.

'It's a little girl, my dear.'

'Is she as we expected?'

'Oh yes. She's perfectly formed, a babe in miniature.'

'Excellent. Miss, you have done well, very well,' Mr Allspice chuckled. 'Don't let 'er suck for too long.'

Hannah was grateful for his consideration of her sister's health, but a little perturbed by the extent of his interest. She supposed he must find life very dull, confined to his bath chair and dependent on help to get him out of the cellar, because there seemed to be no exit apart from the steep steps.

'Fetch the gin to wet the baby's 'ead,' he ordered. 'And stout for the mother, and sweet tea . . . '

'All in good time.' Mrs Allspice gazed down proudly at the child. Ruby managed a smile, her hand cupping the baby's head as she nuzzled at her breast.

'Isn't she beautiful?' Hannah could hardly speak. This was her niece, her own flesh and blood, and the sight of her brought out all her protective instincts. 'As soon as you can get to your feet, we must go.'

Ruby looked at her, astonished. 'I'm not going anywhere. I don't want to sit indoors all day on my own while you're at the infirmary. Mr and Mrs Allspice have kindly offered to look after us.'

'Why?' was Hannah's reaction. 'They owe you nothing.'

'We're doin' it out of the kindness of our 'earts,' Mrs Allspice said, and Hannah stared at her in disbelief.

'I told you before — Mrs Allspice has been very kind to me since Antonio disappeared,' Ruby said. 'I'm delighted to consider her a friend of mine.'

How could she? Hannah wanted to say, but she bit her tongue. How could Ruby lower herself to stay in a cramped and filthy place with a wife beater and the woman whose brother — a criminal, no less — had left her with a child born out of wedlock and with no hope of regaining respectability in the eyes of society?

'We're on the side of the angels,' Mr Allspice went on from the other side of the curtain. 'Your sister was wronged by one of our own kind — my wife's brother and a member of our circus family — and, as a gentleman with a conscience, it's my duty to make up for what 'e done to 'er. Oh, you might think I'm touched . . . but my 'eart has softened over the years, and I 'ate to see a young lady brought down by misfortune, and

373

an innocent child disadvantaged.'

'I can't bear to think of you losing your place on my account, Hannah,' Ruby said. 'I know how much it means to you, especially now you're a sister — although I suspect that Doctor Clifton's regard means just as much, if not more.'

'Ruby, I'm begging you to come home with me.'

'How can I?' Ruby's voice quavered as Mrs Allspice covered her with a blanket and opened the curtain. 'You don't want us getting under your feet.'

'Look at this place — it isn't healthy.'

'You can't frighten me. It's all right, really it is. Look at all the children Mr Allspice and his wife have brought up.'

'It's at least twelve and countin',' Mr Allspice cut in, from a veil of pipe smoke.

'Mr Allspice, it's thirteen . . . ' his wife corrected him. 'You've forgotten one of the littluns again.'

'What am I going to tell Matron? I've told her you've been indisposed . . . '

'Tell her I've moved away, gone back to Canterbury.'

'Think of the baby, your daughter. We can care for her between us. I'll support you. I'll do anything to have you back at home . . . safe . . . '

'I'm sorry.' Ruby's eyes filled with tears.

'She's made up 'er mind,' Mrs Allspice said. 'I reckon you should go now. They need to rest, both of the little darlin's.' Hannah had softened slightly towards Mrs Allspice. She was a devoted, fierce mother if not a gentle one. 'Don't you worry about 'em. We won't let 'em out of our sight.'

Hannah gave in. She pressed her fingers to her lips then touched them to the baby's forehead, before leaning across to kiss Ruby's cheek.

'I'll be back soon. Take care of yourself and the child. Send word as soon as you decide to come home and I'll be here to collect you. I love you, Ruby.'

'I love you too . . . ' she whispered.

Wishing her goodbye, Hannah left the house in Ramsgate.

Ruby was in good health and the child, although small and frail in appearance, was feeding. Call it her nurse's instinct, but she wasn't unduly worried for them at this stage.

However, when she returned to Margate, the more she thought about it, the more her fears began to grow. Why would the Allspices want to look after Ruby and her child when they had so many of their own? They lived in poverty and squalor — more mouths to feed would only drag them down further.

It wasn't her only concern. In the morning, she would have to see Matron and tell her that Ruby wouldn't be returning to her post. She couldn't keep her sister's shame a secret any longer.

★ ★ ★

The next day, she went in to the house early and knocked on the door of Matron's apartment.

'Good morning, Sister,' Matron said as she opened the door.

'I'm sorry to disturb you at this hour.'

'I've been up and dressed for a while — life is not a bed of roses, more's the pity. I have a meeting with the Board to attend later. I'm glad you've come to find me. I wanted to speak with you last night, but you'd already gone home. This is about your sister, is it not? I presume she's indisposed yet again ... Mrs Merry is short-handed and pressing me to take on a replacement. With patients needing to be bathed daily, her absence is most inconvenient.' Mrs Knowles paused for a moment. 'Oh dear. You'd better come in.'

It was the first time Hannah had seen inside Matron's private rooms. The parlour was well-appointed, decorated in pale blue and cream, with likenesses of people she assumed were family members, along with some of the dignitaries who had honoured the infirmary over the years.

'Do sit down.' Matron looked towards the carriage clock which ticked quietly but insistently on the mantel. There were twenty minutes before Hannah needed to be on the ward. 'Would you like some tea?'

Hannah declined, but Matron poured two cups from the pot on the tray beside her anyway. She added milk from the jug, along with a lump of sugar, stirred it and handed it to her. The cup rattled on the saucer as Hannah held it on her lap.

'My sister won't be returning to the house,' she began.

'She has left Margate?'

The truth spilled out: Ruby had confessed that she was with child.

'I'll write my letter of resignation later . . . '

'Why would you want to do that?'

'I haven't been able to give my patients my full attention over the past few days, and of course, my sister's reputation . . . well, it's mine by association.'

'You've hidden your concerns well. I wouldn't have known if Doc — ' Matron broke off abruptly, then went on, 'if someone hadn't mentioned that you seemed out of sorts. How is your sister?'

'She's staying with a family . . . you know of them: the Allspices.'

'The potty-mouthed parents, and the incontinent rope-walker with the incurable case of the wandering hands?'

'The very same.'

'That is very unfortunate.' Matron raised one eyebrow which continued to hover as Hannah told her a little more of the story.

'I found her confined at their home. I begged her to come back with me, but she refused, so I left Mrs Allspice attending to her and the infant. Now I don't know what to do.'

Hannah sipped at the tea.

'I suspected there was something wrong — we all did, but what a fall from grace!' Matron exclaimed. 'I think you must let her make up her own mind — she'll be back in her own sweet time.'

'You don't know my sister. She's hot-headed, stubborn and easily led. The Allspices seem to have a hold on her.'

'That's obvious, isn't it? I didn't think he had

an ounce of good in him, but Mr Allspice has taken responsibility for his child and its mother at least.'

'Oh . . . ' Hannah almost blurted out the truth, that he wasn't the father, but Mrs Knowles went on, 'One has to hope that a man with such an injury won't be able to father any more children. I know that Mr Allspice's harem is a rather unconventional arrangement, but under the circumstances, it isn't a bad thing. It leaves you free to continue working here — the last thing I want is to lose a sister of your calibre.'

'People will point fingers,' Hannah said.

'Without doubt. They'll gossip about your sister's fall from grace and they'll examine your conduct more closely for a while, and then they'll move on to another topic of scandal.'

Hannah couldn't help flinching at the word.

'Why don't you move back into the nurses' home? There's no reason for you to go on living out.'

Only that she had grown used to her new-found independence, having time away from the hospital, and being able to go wherever she liked — and with whom — without scrutiny, she thought.

'I'll give it a little while, in case Ruby does decide to come back,' she stated. 'I'll have to give my landlady notice anyway.'

'Of course. In the meantime, if there's anything I can do . . . '

'Thank you. I'm very grateful for your understanding.'

'Just remember, these troubles will pass.' Matron looked out towards Westbrook Bay. 'Worse things happen at sea.'

Hannah left for the ward, wondering if she should have enlightened Matron about the identity of the father of Ruby's child. She felt bad for not telling her the whole story — half the truth was often a whole lie.

21

Enough to Make the Angels Weep

Sitting up after work in front of the fire at her lodgings, Hannah read and reread the letter which had arrived while she'd been out that day. It was dated the eighth of April, with the Allspices' Ramsgate address in the top corner written in Ruby's neat copperplate hand. There was a single blot of ink, nothing in particular to indicate the writer's state of mind.

Dear Hannah,

I hope this letter finds you well. Mercy is a little doll — I called her Mercy after Ma.
I have little else to say, except to beg your forgiveness for what I have done.
Your loving sister,
Ruby

Hannah was disappointed that it hadn't been a message imploring her to come and collect Ruby and the infant and bring them home, but at least she'd been in touch. Hannah planned to call on her on Friday afternoon, but in the meantime, she sat back on the chair and stared into the flames, wondering how they had come to this. Following one's vocation left one open to loneliness: she could see that now.

It was past ten when a knock at the door disturbed her reverie.

'Ruby? Is it you?' She leapt up and flung the door open, to find Alice standing there. Her expression filled her with dread.

'You must come quickly,' Alice said. 'It's your sister.'

'Where is she?' Hannah exclaimed, grabbing her cape from the hook and throwing it over her shoulders. 'Tell me. Where is little Mercy?'

'I have no news of her, I'm afraid. Here. Take my arm.'

Hannah hurried along with Alice, clinging on to her for dear life. Having seen her sister with the baby, she'd thought that Ruby was on an even keel, but knowing how her moods swung from one extreme to the other, changing direction like the wind and blowing her off course, she chastised herself for not having called on her again sooner.

'Doctor Clifton and Mr Rose — the night porter — are with her. A couple walking along the beach found her. They sent for help, but . . . ' Alice struggled to catch her breath, unable to walk and talk at the same time.

As they hurried along the front, Hannah caught sight of a group of shadowy figures milling around at the edge of one of the seawater reservoirs with lanterns and matches. She let go of Alice's arm, picked up her skirts and ran, pushing her way through the crowd.

'No, miss, you can't go there.' Somebody pulled her back. 'There's a drowned girl — it's no sight for a lady's eyes.'

'She's my sister,' Hannah hissed. 'Let me pass.'

'Then you have my every sympathy,' the man said, releasing his grip. 'Let the lady through.'

The moonlight glinted across the water, illuminating two more figures who were kneeling over a body clothed in sodden garments.

'Ruby! Whatever's happened, whatever's been going on in that mind of yours, there's nothing that can't be resolved.' Hannah sank to her knees and chafed Ruby's hand, trying to bring the blood back into it, while James checked for a pulse at the side of her neck, and the night porter sat back on his heels, his head in his hands. 'Please, my darling sister, wake up.' She could hear breathing, but it was only the sea. She turned to James. 'Why is she so cold?'

Slowly, he shook his head.

'Do something!' she urged as the tears began to flow. 'There must be something you can do to save her.'

'I've tried,' he said softly. 'I'm sorry. When I arrived, I thought I could feel the weakest of pulses, but it soon faded. Believe me, Hannah, I have tried my best, but her lungs were filled with water and her spirit already flown.'

She watched him gently close her sister's eyes and rest her head on his coat, folded into a makeshift pillow. She leaned across and lifted the damp tresses of Ruby's hair away from her face, as she'd done on the day that she'd given birth to her child. She looked more beautiful than ever, and for the first time in a long while, she appeared at peace. Hannah bent over and pressed her lips to her sister's cheek.

'I love you,' she whispered.

' 'Tis such a pity — she's only a girl, a tiny little thing. Can't be more than twelve or thirteen,' someone muttered.

'Oh, Hannah.' She felt Alice's hand on her shoulder.

'What was she doing here?' Hannah said, kneeling up. 'Where is the child?' She pressed her hand to her mouth to quell a wave of nausea as she looked across the reservoir, the sand and the black sea. 'Ruby, what have you done?' Remembering the letter, she turned to Alice. 'She asked me to forgive her. I thought she meant she was sorry for running away to the Allspices, but no, she was asking me to forgive her for this . . . ' Hannah sobbed as she got to her feet. 'I have to find the child — I have to find Mercy.'

'I'll come with you,' Alice offered.

'Miss Huckstep, let me go with Hannah,' James cut in. 'You and Mr Rose stay here to oversee the arrangements for transferring the deceased to the mortuary at the house. And send someone to knock on the doors of the men who can work the pumps to drain the reservoir. Any expenses are to go on my account.'

'Should we contact the coroner?' Mr Rose asked in a low voice.

'I'll write the death certificate — I hope that will be enough.' James bowed his head out of respect, before standing up and walking to Hannah's side. 'At least we might be able to save the child . . . ' he said, but she knew what he was thinking: that Ruby had done away with her too.

Glancing along the tideline, she caught sight of a small, dark mound being lapped by the waves. Her heart in her mouth, she ran down to look, but it was only seaweed, torn up and tossed around by the sea.

'We can't run around like headless chickens,' she heard James say. 'We must have a plan.'

'Where do we start?' she said miserably. 'She could be anywhere.'

'When did you last see your sister?'

'It was over a week ago. She gave birth to her child, a girl, whilst staying with the Allspices in Ramsgate.'

'I know — I pressed Mrs Knowles to tell me what was going on.'

'I begged her to come home, but she refused.'

'We should retrace her steps, heading back in the direction of Ramsgate, then,' he said. 'Would she have taken the train?'

'I doubt that she'd have had the money for the fare.'

'Then she would have walked. Someone would have seen her on the road.'

'James, it's dark. Everyone will be abed.'

'That's true. I'll call for my carriage — we'll go straight to Ramsgate, and keep our eyes peeled while we're on the road. When dawn breaks, we can walk the route and interview any possible witnesses who may have seen your sister.' James sounded confident, but she didn't share his optimism. 'We should send word to your father and family as soon as we can.'

'Finding Mercy has to come first,' she said. Everything else could wait.

Within the hour, they were travelling in James's brougham, sitting side by side, staring out into the darkness, the bushes on either side of the road illuminated by the carriage lamps. The horse was reluctant to step out at night time, and the driver had to keep sending it on.

'This feels hopeless,' Hannah said, straining her eyes as the carriage stopped and started, lurching about. 'It's like looking for a needle in a haystack.' James reached out and squeezed her hand. 'Why didn't Ruby come home? We would have managed. We would have found a way. What must you think of us?'

'My respect and admiration for you remain the same as they ever were. It's me who feels ashamed.'

'Why? You have no reason —'

'I should have gone with my instincts, but I didn't want to make you feel uncomfortable by insisting that I made a house call to check on your sister and the child.'

'What good would that have done? You'd never have convinced her that she needed help. When she's happy, she has the most beautiful smile and contagious sense of joy. She's brave, adventurous and light-hearted, but when the sadness — hopelessness, call it what you will — comes over her, she becomes a different person. Her mind plays tricks, deluding her into thinking that no one cares, and the sunshine disappears behind a cloud of misery, self-doubt and stubbornness.

'I'm talking as if she's still here, but she's gone. How will I ever get used to it?' Recalling how Ruby had once claimed that she couldn't go on living without her lover, Hannah picked at a loose thread on her cape — the material ruckled beneath her fingers then flattened out as the stitches unravelled. 'I have no doubt that she followed in our mother's footsteps and took her own life.'

'Dear Hannah, you have suffered greatly,' James began after a long pause.

'I'm not the only person to have experienced tragedy,' she murmured.

'Don't you think it possible that Ruby was coming back to Margate to find you, took a wrong turn and fell into the reservoir?'

'Who knows what was going on in her head?'

'Her illness caused her to act irrationally,' James said. 'There's no proof of her state of mind, so I'm willing to sign a certificate, stating death by drowning, circumstances unknown. That way, we might avoid the need for a public inquest and exposure in the newspapers, which have a fascination for a sensational story. What's more, you'll be able to give her a proper burial in consecrated ground.'

She wasn't sure she could bear the same outcome for Ruby as there had been for Ma, to have no place to take Mercy — if they found her — to sit quietly in her mama's presence, to leave flowers and reflect.

'Are you sure about this? Doctors are obliged to be completely honest. You'd be risking your reputation.'

'I have to go on the facts. Ruby was walking by the sea, wanting to clear her head, having recently given birth to a child. Weakened by the burden of her maternal duties, she fainted face down into the water and drowned. I'm sorry for spelling it out, but this has implications beyond the next few days. It is better for a child to believe that their mother died by accident, not through choice.'

'I don't know . . . I don't understand how a mother could be so selfish as to abandon her child, a helpless infant, and take her own life.'

'On the surface, it doesn't make sense,' James agreed, 'but we can't know what goes on in another person's deepest thoughts.'

'It might be that Mercy died of sickness and Ruby, overcome with grief, couldn't go on . . . ' Her voice broke. Tears began to flow.

'Oh Hannah. Come here.' James turned to her, put his arms around her and pulled her close. 'Let me hold you. Don't worry about what others will think — we're alone.'

Why was he being so understanding towards her sister, Hannah wondered, when he was entirely at liberty to condemn her for taking her own life?

Torn between propriety and instinct, she sank against him and rested her head on his shoulder, as she cried for her sister and the lost child. She felt his fingers tangling in her hair at the nape of her neck, and the warm whisper of his breath against her cheek.

Eventually, the jolting of the carriage stopped. The horse's hooves clattered on the road and the brougham's wheels swished along as they entered Ramsgate, where the driver pulled up to ask for the address.

Hannah gave it.

'Dobbs, do you know of it?' James said.

'Yes, sir. I know Ramsgate like the back of my 'and. It's in the direction of West Cliff.'

It wasn't long before they were standing on the pavement in front of the Falstaff Inn, looking along the row of cottages in Addington Street. Hannah recognised number 8 by its decrepitude, even in the moonlight.

'It's that one,' she said, pointing.

James stepped past her and rapped at the door with the end of his cane.

'Open up,' he shouted, at which the door came flying open, the wood splintering on the hinges.

'Not you again!' The man who answered James's knock swore furiously and spat at their feet.

'I'm Doctor Clifton from Margate.' James introduced himself, his voice calm, the muscle in his cheek taut.

'A doctor? Oh dear, then I'm sorry for my mistake.'

'I wish to speak to Mr Allspice — I believe he's one of your lodgers.'

'Oh, 'im? 'E's been nothin' but trouble, 'im and 'is nearest and dearest.'

'I need to speak to him, urgently. Is he here?'

''E's here all right, more's the pity. 'E had a caller earlier this evening, just before closin' time across the road. There was fisticuffs and the constable came, but 'e'd been in the alehouse as

388

well and could 'ardly walk, let alone talk. Anyway, the gentleman concerned got away and now old Allspice and 'is missus won't let up. Listen to 'em.'

From the bowels of the house, Hannah could hear a man and woman shouting at each other, and a child bawling its eyes out. Ignoring James's protestations to be careful, she pushed past the landlord and headed down the stairs to the dingy cellar to find Mr and Mrs Allspice positioned at each end of the windowless room, yelling across their gaggle of children who were lying top-to-tail under a sheet on the mattress. It was one of the boys who was crying, not Mercy. There was no sign of her.

'What are you doin' 'ere, pokin' your nose into our business? Can't you see we're 'avin' a barney?' Mr Allspice snapped from his bath chair.

'Where's my niece? Where is my sister's child?'

'She's gorn, thanks to my wife who is even more stupid than I was led to believe.' The room began to spin as he went on, 'I don't know 'ow many times I told you not to let 'er out of your sight — '

'I 'aven't got eyes in the back of my 'ead. Mr Allspice, you expect too much. I run back and forth and side to side, lookin' after you and our littluns, and givin' the infant 'er medicine — '

'The babe is sick?' Hannah cut in, but the Allspices ignored her. 'Where is she? Where is little Mercy?' She raised her voice in desperation.

'They've gorn, both of 'em,' Mr Allspice confirmed, dashing her hopes. 'And good riddance to the girl because she was eatin' us out of 'ouse and 'ome, and I caught 'er drinkin' our gin — that's why the bottle was goin' down so quick.'

'This young lady's sister, Ruby, has met with an accident,' James said.

'What's 'appened to 'er?' Mrs Allspice turned to him.

'She drowned.' James kept his voice low.

'Drowned?' one of the children exclaimed.

'Hush,' said one of the others, and they all sat up on the mattress, several sets of eyes shining from the filthy darkness. Even the pig was silent, as though overwhelmed by the news.

'Oh, my poor child!' Mrs Allspice pressed her hand to her mouth.

'You mean the infant? Mercy?' Hannah urged, wishing her nightmare to be over, one way or the other. It was the not knowing . . .

'I mean Ruby. I was fond of 'er, even though she could be a pain in the — '

'Where is the child?' James interrupted. 'Did Ruby take her with her?'

'It's none of your business. She's my property,' Mr Allspice said.

'She isn't an asset to be bought and sold,' Hannah exclaimed. 'A child belongs with its mother.'

'Your sister gave 'er to me. It was 'er express wish — '

'She'd never have done that. I don't believe you.'

'I 'ave the paperwork to prove it.' Mr Allspice clicked his fingers and his wife, who seemed to be in a state of shock, went rummaging around under a pile of laundry and dragged out a metal box. She opened the lid and took out a scroll of paper which she handed to her husband. He unrolled it across his knees.

'That's 'er signature and there's my mark,' he said in triumph. 'The child is mine.'

Hannah had to read it twice before reality slid like a block of ice down the back of her neck. Ruby had begged her forgiveness for signing little Mercy away to the Allspices.

'Why do you want another child when you have so many already?'

'We're doin' it entirely out of the goodness of our 'earts. We plan to rear 'er as our own, feed 'er, wind 'er and wipe 'er bum. She'll be put above all our other little tykes — that's right, isn't it, Mrs Allspice?'

'Don't you keep calling 'em tykes, they're our littluns.'

'They're tykes as soon as they fall out of the womb,' he said. 'Little Mercy is our princess and the key to our fortune. She's small — very small — and fine-featured, thanks to her parents. A freak of nature. With daily baths in gin and the same spirit diluted in milk, she'll maintain 'er stature, and as soon as she can walk, we'll show 'er off in New York and Los Angeles. When she's of childbearin' age, we'll marry 'er off to the world's smallest man, and breed from 'er.'

'You can't do that,' Hannah shouted.

'She'll be eternally grateful for the way we 'elped her to fame and fortune,' Mr Allspice went on.

'The gin will burn holes in her gullet,' Hannah protested. 'It'll kill her.'

'It's a tried and tested means of keepin' a person small,' Mr Allspice opined. 'She'll be feted and adored, and in return, she'll favour us with a gen'rous pension. Why should I 'ave to scrimp and save when she's been sent to me as a gift from God to make up for my sufferin'? I won't give 'er up to anyone else, least of all 'im.'

'Who, Mr Allspice?' James interrupted.

'That rotten, murderin' scoundrel who turned up out of the blue and stole 'er from us.'

'Mr Milani?' Hannah said. 'When was this? When did he take her?'

'This evenin',' Mr Allspice said.

'Then we're wasting time. We must go after him,' Hannah exclaimed.

'My boys are on 'is tail,' Mr Allspice said. 'All is not lost. They'll bring the infant back and beat the livin' daylights out of 'im for good measure.'

'You're deluded if you think I'll let you take the child back.'

'You'll 'ave 'er over my dead body!'

'Have some compassion for the child's aunt,' James interrupted.

'I appreciate what you done for me, Doctor Clifton, but this is none of your business. Go and poke your nose in somewhere else.' Mr Allspice flashed a glance at his wife. 'You and the doc will lift me up the steps in the chair, so I can go and look for the boys.'

'Oh no, never again, Mr Allspice. I won't help you. You're a wicked, vile man, the lowest of the low,' Mrs Allspice said.

Her husband's brow furrowed. 'I beg your pardon?'

'You 'eard me. I won't 'ave anythin' more to do with you after this. You can stay and rot in this basement. I'm leavin' you.'

'You mean you've double-crossed me?' he roared. 'How dare you! I'll 'ave you 'ung, drawn and quartered. I'll tear yer hair out!'

'Mr Allspice,' James shouted. 'That's enough!'

'Don't you come between husband and wife. This woman — she's been lyin' to me for weeks.' He turned to Mrs Allspice. 'It was you! It was you who told 'im to come.'

She began to tremble and shake. 'I did it for the girl — for Ruby — and my brother. I wanted somethin' good to come out of this terrible mess. A babe should be with its mother and father.'

''E tried to kill me!'

''E 'ad 'is reasons — and not just because you broke every promise you ever made to 'im. No, 'e did it for me, because 'e couldn't stand by and watch you treat me badly any longer. Why do you think he lent you the money? It was to 'elp me and the children, not you, Mr Allspice.'

''Ow did you know where 'e was?'

'I didn't. 'E didn't want you torturin' me, thinkin' I'd give 'im up. No, a mutual friend of ours at the 'All by the Sea sent notes back and forth on our behalf.' She broke into sobs. 'I didn't tell Ruby either — I wish I 'ad, but I thought I was keeping 'er safe until 'e came to get 'er and Mercy. I didn't know she was goin' to leave like that. If I'd 'ad any idea, I'd 'ave said something to 'er. I'd 'ave let 'er know 'e was coming for 'er.'

'Why didn't he come back before?' Hannah

asked, horrified at the way events had unfolded, when they could have gone so differently.

'I didn't 'ear anythin' from 'im for a while — 'e was lyin' low. But knowin' of my situation, 'e's never out of touch for long. I admit 'e done wrong, but when 'e 'eard your sister was with child, he chose to come back for 'em.'

'It was too late,' Hannah said bitterly. 'He'd already ruined her.'

'I should 'ave taken more notice of what Ruby was sayin' — she's been low since the babe arrived. Very low. I stopped her walking out of 'ere the other day. It was freezing and she wasn't wearing any shoes, but she didn't care. She said she was ready to end it . . . ' Mrs Allspice shuddered. 'I told her not to be so silly. If only I'd said my brother was on 'is way . . . I'll regret it for the rest of my days.'

'What about the boys?' Mr Allspice said suddenly. 'Are they in on this too?'

'I wish that they were, but you sent them off after 'im before I 'ad a chance to explain. When 'e saw Ruby wasn't 'ere, 'e thought e'd been set up — that's why 'e made 'imself scarce.'

'Hannah, come with me.' James took her hand and they ran up the stairs and out on to the street to the waiting brougham with the sound of the Allspices' voices fading behind them.

'What would you do if you were in his shoes? A man in hiding, with a child in tow? Where would you go?' James said, having briefly explained the situation to Dobbs who was waiting patiently at the horse's head.

'If I were him, I'd make my way abroad — to

the Continent or America perhaps,' Dobbs said. 'Unless he has friends here who will give him shelter.'

Hannah racked her brain for any clue that Ruby might have dropped in the past about her lover's other connections, but she couldn't think of any.

As Dobbs helped her into the carriage, he said, 'The person in question would have to wait till later this morning to take the coach to London or Dover. If he's in a hurry, he'll head for the harbour and make his getaway by boat. The Ramsgate Packets sail every other day to France and there are other steamers that leave the Pier Head for London. It would be unusual for a gentleman to travel unaccompanied with an infant — someone will have seen him.'

'Then we will go to the harbour forthwith.' James jumped in beside her and Dobbs closed the door, stepped up into his seat and flicked the whip across the horse's rump, sending it on into a jolting trot.

'What if he's decided to travel by hoy? We'll never find him,' Hannah said, frantic at the thought of Mercy disappearing without trace.

'We have to,' James said. 'The infant is too sick to travel — she needs proper medical care before anyone can make a decision about her future. This Mr Milani is her father by blood, but he can't possibly look after her. He's on the run, a wanted criminal who treated your sister most cruelly, seducing her, then abandoning her. I can't allow it. It's too late for him to make amends.'

'I'm not sure what to believe,' Hannah said. 'I'd like to think he came back for Ruby — out of guilt, or love maybe — but knowing a little of his character and not having the same faith in his goodness as Mrs Allspice has, I suspect that he returned to retrieve the child to rear her as a freak for money and fame. Or, fearing arrest, to sell her to somebody else.'

'It's no use speculating,' James said. 'We just need to find her.'

A misty dawn was breaking when Dobbs dropped them at the wharf in the Royal Harbour.

'It's best that you go on foot from here. Try that way.' Dobbs pointed his whip towards the ships and smaller boats that were moored alongside. James grabbed Hannah's hand.

'We must think logically,' he said gently. 'Where might they be?'

Hannah looked along the wharf at the stacks of cargo, the people milling about, and a steam packet which was berthed ready for boarding. The passengers were waiting in an orderly queue at the foot of one gangway, while a group of porters were loading boxes and trunks via a second.

'This is hopeless. They could be anywhere,' she said above the sound of fluttering flags and water slapping against the stones, but then she heard shouting from behind them, and the pounding of feet heading in their direction.

'Stop 'im. Stop that man! 'E's a murderer!' Two men were chasing another, who was carrying a bundle under one arm and trying to keep his flamboyant hat on his head as he ran past them.

'James, that's him!' Hannah cried out.

'Let me through — I have a ticket.' One of the ladies in the queue started screaming when Mr Milani pushed his way through and on to the foot of the gangway with the Allspice boys right behind him. He turned sharply, lifted the bundle by a knot in the swaddling and let it swing above his head, while he bellowed at his pursuers, 'Lay one finger on me, and the child will get it!'

The Allspice boys backed down, the whites of their eyes gleaming in the ship's shadow.

'Just give us the child and we'll leave you to make your escape,' Alan said.

'I'm not falling for that one. Do you think I was born yesterday?'

James stepped up behind the Allspice boys. 'Give me the child and I'll restore her to her mother's sister where she rightfully belongs.'

'She's mine. She's the fruit of my loins!' Mr Milani hissed, as he reversed two steps up the gangway. 'Keep back!' The bundle dangled precariously over the black water as he stared at his audience, his hat dropped back behind his shoulders and his hair streaming in the breeze.

Hannah moved up between the Allspice brothers, aware that James had slipped away.

'How will you care for your daughter while you're on the run? Let me look after her. You have my word that we will let you go, if you will just hand her over to me. For Ruby's sake . . . '

'This is a trick,' he said scornfully, glancing over his shoulder where two of the crew were standing, waiting to pounce. His voice was filled with bravado, but his actions were those of a cornered man. 'I'm not falling for it — this little one is my insurance.'

'She's sick,' Hannah said, fighting the tremor in her voice. 'If your daughter, this innocent babe, dies, then you will be charged twice over — for cruelty, as well as attempted murder.'

She heard the passengers' gasps from behind her and a thud as some poor lady fainted, followed by muttering as her fellows tried to rouse her.

'Why would I give you the child? You'll only give her to her mother who'll hand her back to that dirty rat, Allspice.'

'Her mother is dead,' Hannah said bluntly. 'Drowned!'

Mr Milani's mouth dropped open. 'No . . . I never thought . . . My sister said she'd run away.' He snatched the bundle close to his body and cradled it in his arms.

'I blame you!' Hannah snapped, her self-restraint entirely vanishing into the morning mist which was clearing into a blood-red sky. 'You killed her! This is all your fault and I'll never forgive you! Give the babe to me!'

'Or else?' he mocked. 'What can you do, a mere woman? One look from your sour face and the cream would turn. You drove your sister to it — she went mad with boredom.'

'Give up the child and take me with you instead,' she suggested. 'Let me be your insurance.'

'She is mine! My flesh and blood,' he

repeated, looking over his shoulder to where the crewmen had shuffled a little closer. 'I said, keep your distance!' He held the bundle back over the water.

'Abel, I'm goin' to do you for this — we 'ad 'im and you let 'im go.'

Hannah heard Alan duck back behind her, then a sickening crunch of knuckle hitting bone.

'What did you do that for?'

'You've been lookin' for a fight all day, and now you're goin' to get one.'

As Mr Milani was distracted by the scuffle going on behind her, she spotted a figure emerge from between the two crewmen. It was James, who leapt on to the lion tamer's back and grabbed him around the neck.

'Take the child,' he shouted above Mr Milani's howl of anger as he let go of the bundle. Hannah dived forwards, catching it in her hands and pressing it to her breast.

'James! Be careful,' she cried as he clung on to Mr Milani, half strangling him as he pulled him back. Mr Milani's face was turning purple, but somehow he managed to reverse, slamming his adversary into the handrail and knocking him to the ground. Having let go, James got up again and before Mr Milani could get away, he tripped him up and pinned him down. The Allspice brothers joined in, sitting on his legs to stop him thrashing around, as one of the crewmen brought ropes to bind his wrists and ankles.

'Tie him to the railings,' someone suggested as the crowd cheered.

Hannah checked on the precious bundle,

moving the cloth away from the infant's face to reveal her blotchy cheeks and cracked lips. Her eyes were closed and sunken into her skull, but she was still breathing, albeit in short, sharp gasps.

'He should be made to walk the plank.'

'Drown the man — it's no more than he deserves for puttin' an innocent child in danger.'

'No, 'e should 'ang for this.'

Hannah turned and walked away, not caring what happened to Mr Milani, her only concern being her niece.

'Hello, darling,' she murmured, her heart throbbing with relief and renewed fear. 'Don't give up, I beg you.' She looked for James and saw him walking towards her, having removed his coat and rolled up his shirtsleeves. He was supporting his right arm with his left. 'She needs milk and medicine,' she told him.

'We'll find Dobbs and get her to the house.'

'You're hurt!' There was a scratch across his forearm and his elbow was at an unnatural angle.

'It's nothing, just a flesh wound.'

'Really? You're a doctor — you know it's broken.'

'I'm fine.' James turned to face the Allspice brothers. Alan had a black eye, and Abel's nose was bleeding.

'Pa will kill us if we go home empty-handed,' Abel moaned.

'You can't take her,' Hannah said abruptly. 'Alan, you know that.'

He nodded. 'I can't 'ave it on my conscience to take the littlun back to 'im. You know what 'e wants to do with 'er and it isn't right. It's what 'e did to us — bent us into shape, so to speak — for 'is own ends. Look at 'im, sitting there, smoking baccy and drinkin' all day while Ma runs 'erself ragged, tending to 'is every need. And 'e takes our 'ard-earned money off of us.'

'I'm not riskin' it,' Abel said.

'These are good people — they saved my leg. I won't go against 'em. Besides, what can Pa do when 'e's an invalid, stuck in that chair for the rest of 'is time on earth?'

''E could 'ave someone do us in.'

''E isn't the bigwig 'e used to be. There's nobody left who owes 'im a favour,' Alan said. 'We don't have to go 'ome at all. We'll start our own act, somethin' new that no one's ever seen before. We'll go to America and make our fortune.'

'What about Ma — she's makin' good money as the oldest acrobat on the circuit,' Abel said.

'The audiences love 'er, but they're laughing at 'er. We'll take 'er and the littluns with us, so she doesn't 'ave to work again. Let's do this — the world is waitin'. I can feel it in my bones.' Alan turned to Hannah. 'You take the babe. We won't give you no trouble.'

'Thank you,' she said, stepping back. 'And good luck.'

'I wish you all the best in your new venture,' James said. 'Don't shake my hand,' he added quickly.

'I 'ope your arm's better soon,' Alan said.

'So do I, young sir.' James and Hannah slipped away as the passengers and crew congratulated the brothers on their bravery and stared at the prisoner, pointing at him like the lion in its cage at the Hall by the Sea. By the time they found Dobbs, James could barely speak for the pain and Hannah was completely distracted by her worries for the infant in her arms, unable to tell whether she was dead or alive.

It wasn't until she was seated safely in the carriage that she could look at her properly.

'How is she?' James asked from beside her as the horse trotted along.

'The same,' she said flatly. 'Her breathing is shallow and fast.' Mercy's tiny fingers had escaped from the dirty swaddling and were blue with cold. 'I'm afraid they have done for her as well as my sister.'

She felt James's arm sliding around her back and his hand coming to rest on the curve of her waist.

'We'll do our best, but her fate is in God's hands. The Allspices' regime is likely to have caused permanent harm: stunting of the mind and body, injury to the stomach and intestines.'

'It's so unfair . . . ' The baby whined, opened her mouth and spilled a little brown liquid. Hannah wiped it from her chin with the corner of her handkerchief, then kissed her forehead.

'I think you should be prepared . . . '

'There, there, sweetheart,' she whispered, her heart shattering into a thousand pieces as she thought of Mercy joining her mother.

22

Fools Rush In Where Angels Fear to Tread

Mr Mordikai was in the reception hall at the infirmary. There was no comment, no odd look when she carried Mercy to the desk with Doctor Clifton walking behind her. Everyone had heard the news. They knew that her sister had met with an accident and drowned, and that there was more to her story than met the eye.

'Please, call the duty physician,' she said.

'I'll deal with this. Mercy is my patient,' James cut in.

'You need treatment as well.'

'The child comes first,' James said. 'Mr Mordikai, I need to speak to Mr Anthony when he comes in and I'd be grateful if you can find someone to organise a cot on the girls' ward. Perhaps Matron can be persuaded to allow Nurse Huckstep to provide one-to-one care for as long as it's necessary.'

'Of course, Doctor Clifton. I'll give her the message.'

Hannah followed James to an unoccupied examination room where she placed Mercy on the trolley and began to unwrap her from the swaddling, removing two safety pins, then unknotting an extra band of material which had been tied around the baby's middle.

'She's very tightly bound,' she observed. 'Oh my goodness, you don't think . . . ? James, look how the cotton has chafed her skin. They have deliberately bound her like this to keep her small. How cruel . . . '

'What with that and the gin, they have done everything they can to turn her into a freak of nature,' James agreed. 'We'll tube-feed her and then we'll make urgent enquiries to find a wet nurse. After that, I'll find out what's going on . . . '

'With Ruby?' she finished for him.

He nodded.

'What about your arm?'

'That can wait.'

'I don't think so. You should have those bones set as soon as possible — your patients need you. Promise me that you'll speak to Mr Anthony this morning.'

'Anything you say, Sister.' He gave a small smile. 'Let's give this little one a dose of glucose and water, then get her on to the ward.'

Hannah wrapped her in a clean cotton cloth, wishing she had proper clothes for her: a pretty knitted barracoat or bootees trimmed with lace like her brothers had worn. Suppressing a wave of grief, she picked her up and carried her to the girls' ward where she found Alice waiting.

'Matron's asked me to look after her. She's moved one of Sister Trim's nurses across to the Lettsom,' she said. 'Hannah, how are you? I've been thinking of you.'

'Please, don't speak kindly to me. I don't think I can bear it.'

'Let me take the baby . . . '

'Keep fighting, little one.' Hannah touched Mercy's cheek and laid her in Alice's arms before giving her the paperwork which James had put together. Having summarised his plans for Mercy's care, she forced herself to continue, 'Doctor Clifton says that the prognosis is poor. The likelihood is that she will join her mother in Heaven within the next couple of days.'

'The poor little mite,' Alice murmured.

'I have to go, before my nurses take advantage of my absence. Promise me you'll let me know if there's any change in her condition.'

'You know I will. How is Doctor Clifton?'

'He's a hero — he ended up in a fight, saving Mercy from her father who'd snatched her away from the Allspices. I dread to think what would have happened if we hadn't found him in time — he would have left the country with her. Thanks to Mr Milani, Doctor Clifton has broken his arm. I feel terribly guilty.'

'Sister Bentley, to my office.' Hannah turned to face Matron who was standing at the entrance to the ward, her hands on her hips and her chin jutting forward, reminding her of a bulldog. 'I've put Nurse May in charge of the Lettsom until I can find someone with more experience.'

'It's my ward,' Hannah said quickly.

'I've relieved you of all responsibility for now. We have much to discuss. Follow me.'

The rest of their encounter continued in Mrs Knowles's office with the door firmly shut.

'First of all, I'm sorry for what has happened to your sister. She's been a good worker and an asset to the infirmary. Secondly, I wish you'd felt able to tell me what was going on — I'm not sure what I could have done, but there might have been some way to mitigate the situation before it came to this.'

Hannah stared at her apron where grey blots began to appear in the white cotton.

'I'm not saying that your sister's course of action could have been altered, just that the revelations could have been handled differently. I'm not going to suspend you as such, but you'll take a week's compassionate leave while we decide how to proceed.'

'What about my patients? Oliver will be expecting me.'

'I'll find some way of covering your absence.'

'Am I going to lose my place?' Hannah said, looking up.

'I'll be raising it at the next meeting of the Board. Don't worry — I'm on your side, but I fear that I'll struggle to win the governors over if this episode is deemed to have brought our work here into disrepute. It'll be in all the newspapers.'

Hannah felt sick. 'They will drag my sister's name through the mud.'

'Inevitably, I think. Go home and rest.'

'My niece requires intensive treatment — I can at least do that to relieve the burden on the other nurses.'

'I understand your motives, but I can't allow it. There must be no room for speculation and questions. It's never a good idea for a family member to be nursed by another, particularly when we're under siege from the press.'

Hannah frowned.

'Mr Mordikai has already seen off several reporters, and we're expecting to have to keep them at bay when they come in later, pretending to be outpatients.' Matron's manner softened. 'Use this time to make the arrangements to bury your sister and I'll be in touch as soon as I have news of our decision. You may, of course, spend time with the child.'

'Thank you, Matron.' Hannah hesitated. 'May I visit the boys on the Lettsom?'

'I don't think it's a good idea. I'll ask Nurse May to speak to them — she can tell them that you're indisposed.'

'They'll be worried about me.'

'I'll tell her to make light of it.'

'What if they see me when I'm visiting the child?'

'You'll be discreet,' Matron said firmly, and she had to be content with that.

Hannah left the office and dropped by at the mortuary where she watched over Ruby who looked for all the world as if she was sleeping.

'Dear sister,' she whispered hoarsely. 'Why did you do it? Why didn't you come to me?' She prayed for Ruby's soul, for the miracle of Mercy's recovery and for James, that he would recover his strength so he could continue to practise without disability and pain. 'I promise you, my darling, that out of love for you and little Mercy, I'll do the right thing by her, whatever that may be. Rest in peace.'

After she'd spoken to the chaplain and the

mortuary assistant about Ruby's funeral, she made her way towards the reception hall. In the corridor, she ran into Sister Trim, who took one look at her and turned away, muttering to her companion, one of the dispensary nurses.

'There's no way she'll be allowed to work here again, not after what's happened with her sister,' she heard her say.

'What was that?' Hannah turned sharply and Sister Trim stopped with her back to her.

'You heard. What class of parent is going to allow someone like you to look after their child?' Sister Trim spun round and glared at her.

'My sister's misfortunes have no bearing on my ability to do my work.'

'Misfortunes? I'm sorry for your loss, but having a child out of wedlock is a terrible sin. Ruby was a pretty girl, lacking in morals — I was forever chasing her off my ward.'

'Take that back. I won't hear you speaking badly of my sister.'

'I won't take it back — it's the truth. You're no better than she is, throwing yourself in Doctor Clifton's way all the time.'

Hannah's face burned as she watched Sister Trim continue along the corridor with the dispensary nurse. Was this how it was going to be from now on?

She left the house. Once she'd sent telegrams to her father and uncle, she returned to their lodgings, feeling a cold draught of loneliness as she entered their old room. Mrs Wells offered her tea but little sympathy, as well she might, Hannah thought, sensing that their comforting little chat was turning into an interrogation.

'I was thinkin' of turfin' you out on your ear'ole, but I've seen there's no sense in that. You need a roof over your 'ead at this sad time.'

'Thank you — I'm very grateful,' Hannah said.

'The gen'lemen from the papers 'ave called 'ere today.'

'I hope you didn't say anything.'

'I told nothin' but the truth as I see it. I couldn't believe my ears when they said there was money in it. How about that then? There's financial reward to be found in gossip and 'earsay, as well as the satisfaction of spreadin' news of folks' misfortunes. They said I should 'ave a reg'lar column in the newspaper. 'Ow about that?'

'I should go,' Hannah said, feeling sick at the thought of her private business being embellished by Mrs Wells's imagination.

'If there's anythin' you need — within reason — you only 'ave to ask.'

Hannah couldn't stay at their lodgings. She put her hat and cape back on, and returned to the house where she went to find Alice who was on the girls' ward, rocking Mercy in her arms.

'How is she?' Hannah said abruptly.

'She's about the same, according to Doctor Clifton.'

'He's been to see her? I thought he'd gone home to rest.'

'Him, rest?' Alice uttered a hollow laugh. 'He never stops. He's been in four or five times to give her glucose water by tube, and there's a wet nurse arriving early this evening. Even so, I've

409

been praying for her all day. Here. Take a seat. You hold her for a while.' Hannah sat down, and Alice bundled the infant into her arms.

'She's beautiful, isn't she?' Alice said.

'Like a little doll.' The air caught in Hannah's throat, thick like treacle, as she reached out and touched Mercy's cheek. The baby stirred slightly, her eyes shut and her skin sallow. Hannah unwrapped her arms from the swaddling and reached for one of her tiny hands, but her fingers remained unfurled. She wrapped her up again and held her close, wishing she could breathe more life into her.

'You might not have heard,' Alice said, 'Doctor Clifton has signed the death certificate so there's no need for a public inquest, but the whole escapade is in the later editions of the papers. Mr Mordikai showed them to me.'

Hannah bit her lip. The press could assassinate Ruby's character, but she wouldn't let them change her opinion of her lovely, flawed sister who'd felt more passion than she would ever know in her lifetime.

'There are rumours that you've been suspended . . . '

'I've been given compassionate leave, although my future here is in the balance, depending on what the Board decides.'

'We've had a whip round. There's a few shillings waiting for you to use as you wish — perhaps for clothes for Mercy or a contribution towards your sister's funeral. I'll bring it round to you later.'

'I can't accept — '

'You'll take it without argument,' Alice said sternly. 'People around here think you've been hard done by. After all you've done for them, they want to give something back. Be grateful and take it.'

'I don't know how to thank you all . . . '

'Oh, Hannah, sometimes even an angel needs help to find her wings again. You've helped so many people, it's time you accepted some help yourself.'

'How is Doctor Clifton?'

'Mr Anthony told him he shouldn't have interfered, that he was a fool to rush in where angels fear to tread, but that's only to be expected, the way they bicker. Anyway, he gave him chloroform and put his arm in traction to line up the ends of the bone, then Mr Brightside made a cast to fit. He's gone home now to let the plaster of Paris set. You should have heard him arguing about it — he's a terrible patient. Anyway, Doctor Hunter's going to step in and help out here for a few days. Mrs Hunter sends her kind wishes too.'

'I'm mortified that James got dragged into this,' she said.

'He made the choice to do it. He could have gone to the police, but he wanted to be there for you.' Gently, Alice took Mercy back. 'Go home and get some sleep while you can.'

How could she do that? Grieving for her sister and worried about her niece's future, she didn't think she'd ever sleep again.

Hannah walked along the empty seafront, gazing out at the cold grey sea, and wishing that

411

she could turn back time to the summer when she and Ruby had bought ice cream from the hokey-pokey men, and life had tasted sweet and full of promise.

★ ★ ★

Alice came to the lodging house in the morning. Mrs Wells let her in and showed her up to the room that Hannah and Ruby had shared.

'A visitor for you, miss,' she said. 'Oh, you poor thing. You look as if you've hardly slept a wink.'

'Thank you, Mrs Wells.' Hannah pushed the door closed.

'She has a nose like the parish pick-axe,' Alice observed, taking off her cape and hanging it on the hook. 'She's right, though — you look dreadful. Here, I've brought you some breakfast — cold beef, bread and ale.'

Hannah gazed around the room, looking for somewhere to put it, but every surface was cluttered with Ruby's bits and pieces: her sewing kit; a stray cotton-reel with its thread unwound across the bare floorboards; a grubby stocking; a bottle of scent. She picked up the bottle and removed the glass stopper, then held it to her nostrils and took a deep breath, as if by inhaling it she could bring her sister back to life.

'You should wear it,' Alice said gently. 'This is Ruby's day, after all.'

Hannah dabbed a dot of scent on each of her wrists and rubbed them together, as Alice made the bed and cleared a space on the washstand for the food, some pieces of black crape and pins. It wasn't right. It should have been Ruby who was standing there.

'This is too much,' Hannah exclaimed suddenly. 'I can't bear it.'

'Come here,' Alice said, turning and holding out her arms. 'Let me give you a hug.'

'I feel such a fool,' Hannah sobbed. 'I can't stop crying.'

'It's only natural to feel this way. Let's have something to eat, then I'll help you braid your hair.'

Hannah took a step back. 'I don't know what I'd do without you.'

'You'd do the same for me.' Alice dashed a tear from her face with the back of her hand. 'Would you like me to help you tidy up a little?'

'I don't know.' The presence of Ruby's belongings was a comfort in a way, but also a reminder that she'd gone for good. 'I don't think I'm ready.'

'Then we'll leave it. There's no hurry.'

'I'm glad to see you have your appetite back,' Hannah said, nibbling at some bread while Alice tucked into her breakfast.

Alice smiled briefly. 'I'm making the most of it.' She got up and washed her hands, then put Hannah's hair up in gleaming copper braids. Hannah dressed, putting on her dark dress, cape and black shoes, and her navy hat to which she'd attached a band of black crape.

'Thank you for coming, Alice.'

'You aren't obliged to go, you know. Ladies aren't expected to attend burials.'

'I have to go — no one else will be there and I can't bear to think of her being alone. I've written to everyone, and those who've replied have declined to attend for various reasons. I don't blame them.' She fiddled with her hatpin, then put it back in its box, deciding that it wasn't appropriate for a funeral.

She and Alice walked to the cemetery on Manston Road where a cart drew up with Ruby's coffin, a simple wooden box, adorned with a single red rose. The sexton, four paid bearers and the chaplain from the infirmary turned up a few minutes later, followed by three carriages which halted at the wrought-iron gates.

Hannah turned away.

'Wait. I believe they're people who've come to pay their respects to your sister.' Alice squeezed her hand.

'I'm not expecting anyone,' she said, as the bearers lifted the coffin from the cart and began to walk along the pathway between the yews and gravestones, none of them more than thirty years old. Keeping her eyes on the box containing her sister's mortal remains, she followed with the chaplain and sexton behind her. Why should anyone turn up, when Ruby's behaviour had gone against the accepted view of maternal conduct and feeling?

They made their way to a corner of the burial ground where a hole had been freshly dug. Hannah could smell the scent of the earth, and then the fragrance of cologne as the breeze ruffled the crape on her hat. She turned slowly to find herself face to face with a small procession

414

of mourners: James who was supporting her stepmother; Doctor Hunter and Charlotte; Mrs Merry and Mrs Wells.

'Did you know they were coming?' she asked Alice through a veil of fresh tears. Alice nodded.

'Nurse May wanted to be here too, but Matron couldn't give her the time off. Your sister was loved, Hannah.'

Doctor Clifton and his cousin offered their condolences and the mourners stood at the graveside to say one last farewell. Hannah picked up a handful of earth and dropped it on the coffin as the chaplain said his final words, 'Ashes to ashes, dust to dust.'

One by one, she thanked everyone for turning up, then whispered to Alice that she would like to go home.

'Allow me to give you a lift,' James said. 'This is rather an imposition and you may, of course, choose to be alone, but I've arranged a small reception at the Cliftonville Hotel. Your step-mother has travelled from Canterbury and wishes to rest for a while before making the journey back. The invitation is open to everyone. Will Mrs Knowles miss you for another hour or two, Nurse Huckstep?'

'Matron's expecting me back, I'm afraid,' Alice said.

'Thank you for helping me this morning,' Hannah said. 'And, James, thank you for everything you've done. I'll join you at the hotel — out of respect for my sister.'

James helped her into the carriage and they set off for the wake.

'How did you come to meet my stepmother?'
she asked.

'She turned up at the house looking for you
this morning — Mr Mordikai introduced us,
knowing that I'd be attending the funeral.'

'I haven't thanked you properly for what
you've done for me and Mercy.'

'I would have done the same for any child, and
for you, of course. Hannah, I would do anything
for you — you should know that by now.'

'Did you see her this morning?'

'She's doing as well as can be expected.'

'You mean, she's still in danger.'

He nodded, as the brougham whisked them
along the street.

'She seemed a little better last night, but this
morning . . . ' He said no more. He didn't need
to, Hannah thought, her heart filled with dread.
'There was some blood . . . '

'She's still spewing up?'

He didn't respond.

'What can we do for her?' Hannah was crying
again. To have rescued her, only to lose her
. . . Don't give up now, little one. Don't you
dare, she prayed inwardly. Your ma would have
wished you a long life of health and happiness.
The angels aren't ready to receive you yet.

'I haven't used thalassotherapy in one so
young — we can but try,' James said. 'I'd suggest
boiling the water for a while to bring the salt out,
then let it cool before offering it mixed with a
little warm milk.'

'Do you think it will have side effects?'
Hannah asked.

416

'We'll monitor her very closely. At the first sign of a problem, we'll stop.'

'I can't leave her at the house for much longer without a ticket. I haven't the funds to pay for her stay.' She felt ashamed to admit it.

'Don't worry about the money — I earn more than I need.'

'I can't impose on you any more than I already have. You know that. People are talking — '

'Let them,' he said.

She went on, blushing, 'They think that we've formed an intimate association. They say that you've gone beyond the call of duty There's even talk that Mercy is yours . . . '

'Why are you so upset about the rumour-mongering? Of course,' he frowned, 'you still aspire to become matron. I'm sorry for causing you grief in this matter, but I fear that it's too late for me to take a step back — unless I hand over her care to Doctor Hunter.'

'I'd rather you didn't. You've been looking after Mercy — you know all about her.'

'Then I will carry on. Don't worry about me, Hannah. There was a time when I took gossip to heart.' He lowered his voice. 'I'm talking about the insinuations and accusations I heard when Suzanna lay dying. There were people who should have known better — Mr Anthony, for example, who suggested that my wife was a lunatic. I was livid, but in the end, I forgave him for it. Loose talk doesn't bother me any more.' He shrugged.

'I'm sorry about the publicity,' she said softly.

'It's fine. I've had new patients queuing at my

door to see the hero doctor who tackled Mr Milani without a thought for his own safety. It's been keeping me and Henry busy, which is a good thing. Have you kept up with the news?'

'No.' She'd stopped reading the papers when she'd spotted the headlines about how her sister had sold her infant to the ropewalker.

'Mr Milani was dragged in front of the magistrates and committed for trial at the next assizes. He languishes in Canterbury gaol, accused of grievous bodily harm and attempted murder. It seems that Mr Allspice convinced the magistrate that there was a case to answer. There is a chance he will be hanged for his crime.'

'I have faith that God will exact the appropriate punishment. What he did to my sister is many times worse than what he did to that blackguard, Allspice.' She didn't want to think of Mr Milani again. 'How are you? How is your arm?'

He turned to her, smiling wryly. 'It hurts, but it will mend. Bones repair more quickly than hearts, I think. I wanted to ask you — if you need occupation, something to take your mind off your troubles while you're waiting for the Board's decision, I'd be delighted if you'd come and work for me at the clinic.'

'Haven't you got staff already?'

'I have Mrs Bellows who's in her sixties and rather a dragon. While I'm somewhat incapacitated, I could do with some extra help. You don't have to give me an answer straight away.'

'No, I'd like to.' She owed him.

'I'll pay you, of course.'

'But I feel responsible for your injury —'

'I can't let you work for nothing. Mrs Bellows won't admit it, but she's struggling to keep up. With you there, she might realise that it's time she retired, or at least reduce her hours.'

'When can I start?'

'Tomorrow, if you like.'

She thanked him. She had rent and bills to pay, and she wanted to buy a memorial for Ruby, a simple tribute to mark her grave — this would be her salvation.

'Are you able to give me any news on the boys on the Lettsom? I miss them terribly.'

'They're missing you too. Oliver and Ronald ask after you every time. Ronald's chest has cleared, thanks to your suggestion that we try daily steam inhalation for his lungs. As for Oliver, the news isn't so good. I've warned his poor parents that he hasn't got long left, and they've decided to take him home as soon as they've found a private nurse who can look after him. He wants to sleep in his own bed and have his family around him. I'm sorry — I wouldn't have been so insensitive as to speak of him if you hadn't asked.'

'It's all right. As long as he's comfortable . . .' Hannah's voice faded as she thought of the boy with the bright eyes and blonde ringlets. He'd put up quite a fight, but now it seemed that God had chosen to give him his wings as he had done with Peter.

'You must think of Ronald and how you've helped him,' James said, reaching out to touch her hand. It was the briefest contact, but more

419

comforting than any words. 'I'll be sending him home soon and he'll have every chance of living a healthy and happy life.'

When they arrived at the wake, they drank a little sherry to toast Ruby's memory before James excused himself, leaving Hannah to talk to her stepmother, who was dressed smartly in black with jet beads around her neck. She was approaching forty, yet she could pass as much younger with her slender figure and bright blonde hair.

'I appreciate your coming, Stepmother,' Hannah said, 'but where is Pa?'

Her stepmother couldn't bring herself to meet her eye. 'I'm afraid he had a prior engagement at the office, a meeting he couldn't possibly postpone. He allowed me to attend instead, wanting to keep up appearances.'

'What can be so important that he can't put aside one day to bury his daughter?'

'He sends his regards, and regrets. Those are his exact words.'

'What about Christopher?'

'We haven't told him yet — he's away at school until Easter, and your father felt that his studies shouldn't be disturbed. He's doing very well — we're very proud of him. Hannah, what happened?'

'I'm sure you've seen the papers,' Hannah said, recalling how Pa used to read them every day at breakfast.

'I want to hear it from you.' A tear like a diamond formed in the corner of her stepmother's eye and rolled down her cheek. 'When I married your father, I was very young — I resented having to take on you and Ruby and I'll always regret not trying harder to befriend you. I couldn't be a mother to you — I didn't know how.

'After you left home, Ruby and I spent more time together, sharing our interests in reading and fashion. I grew rather fond of her, so I was terribly upset when she ran away. I begged your father to fetch her back, but he said she'd made her bed and she'd have to lie in it. Believe me, I did try. I wanted her to be happy, but she had this self-destructive, wilful streak. Did she tell you that Cook found her in an embrace with the butcher's boy?'

'She always denied it,' Hannah said.

'I asked your father to send her away for a while so the whole sorry episode could be forgotten, but he locked her indoors instead and kept her prisoner. Hannah, I wrote to you about this several times to warn you to keep a close eye on her.'

'I didn't receive any letters.' Hannah frowned, then began to wonder. Ruby must have intercepted them and thrown them on the fire. It was just what she would have done to hide her shame.

'I wondered why you didn't write back. Oh dear, your sister became very secretive. I wish I'd come to warn you in person.'

'It's no use,' Hannah said. 'I have to look forward now, for Ruby's daughter.'

'How is she? The doctor told me that she was at the infirmary.'

Hannah shook her head, hardly able to speak.

'I see.' Stepmother took her hand. 'If there's anything I can do, let me know.'

It was a platitude, Hannah realised. Her stepmother might have professed her affection for Ruby, but she had no interest in her illegitimate child. Admitting one had a bastard in the family was like announcing one had the plague.

23

On the Horns of a Dilemma

The next morning, she washed and dressed, putting on her nurse's cap, clean cuffs and apron. If she'd been married she would have been in deep mourning, not her work clothes, she thought, wearing black crape as an outward expression of her love for her sister, and a shield against unwanted curiosity. She recalled how when Theo had died, Stepmother had consulted with her copy of Cassell's to decide what they should wear, and arranged for a London dressmaker to call, bringing ready-made clothes and patterns.

She knew it was useless speculating, but she couldn't stop asking herself if Ruby would still be alive if she'd obeyed their father and stayed in Canterbury; if Hannah had kept a closer eye on her; if she'd been stricter, or less strict . . .

Bracing herself, she put a few of Ruby's precious possessions into a box for safekeeping, then made her way to the clinic on Cecil Square. She gazed up at the house, feeling a pang of regret. If she'd accepted James's hand in marriage, she could have been living there as his wife, not coming to work to scrape a living from the hours he could offer, which were nowhere near as long as those she'd had at the infirmary.

Eyeing the brass plaque outside the door, to which Doctor Hunter's name and qualifications had been added, Hannah rang the bell. An elderly woman answered.

'Good morning. You must be Sister Bentley.'

'Good day, Mrs Bellows.'

'Do come in. Doctor Clifton is expecting you.'

She waited in the reception area where the walls were decorated in cool blues and greys with a patterned wallpaper above the dado rail. The floor was carpeted and there were several over-stuffed chairs for the use of the paying patients, who could read the magazines and books left on the side table.

'Sister Bentley, I'm so glad to see you.' She turned at the sound of James's voice as he emerged at the foot of the stairs. 'I've been in to the house this morning, and Mercy is a little better, having taken to the breast. Now that she's feeding on milk, I've been able to stop tube-feeding her. She's still terribly underweight and sleeping most of the time, but she hasn't been sick since yesterday.'

'That's a relief,' Hannah said.

'I'm crossing my fingers for her.' He smiled briefly. 'The ones on my left hand, anyway. We have a busy surgery this morning. Mrs Bellows will welcome the patients at reception while you assist in the examination room. You may hang your cape in the cloakroom through there.'

Within a few minutes, Hannah was working alongside him, looking after their first patient, a young boy with bellyache. The second patient was a familiar face.

'Oh, it's you?' Mrs Phillips said, looking down her nose at her as she entered the room.

'Sister Bentley is assisting me while my arm mends,' James said jovially.

'I see . . .'

'If you wish to consult with another doctor, I won't stand in your way,' James went on.

'I will trust your judgement,' she said quickly. 'I have this rash, a few pimples across my chest. I would describe them to you, but it's far better that you see them for yourself.'

'Sister Bentley, help Mrs Phillips into a gown,' James said, leaving the room for a while before returning to look at his patient at great length and with even greater ceremony.

'Have you been taking blood purifiers recently?'

'My friend recommended a course of iodide of potassium.'

'You would listen to an acquaintance rather than your doctor?' James made a pretence of looking aghast, and Mrs Phillips had the grace to look rather ashamed.

'I don't like to bother you all the time,' she said.

'It's well known that blood purifiers can cause an eruption of pimples on the skin.'

'I'm confused — the apothecary never mentioned it.'

'You really should have come to me first. I advise you to stop them and return to taking a half-pint of seawater daily.'

'Isn't there some sweeter medicine? I'd rather take champagne.'

'I'm afraid not. There are occasions when one must feel worse before one feels better.'

'I see. Oh dear, it sounds like purgatory.'

When she had gone, they saw several more patients before James excused himself to attend to his messages. Hannah cleaned the examination room from top to bottom, making it smell of carbolic and lemon. When she was ready to leave, James met her in reception.

'You must stop for luncheon. We can go to the inn nearby for refreshment. It's my housekeeper's half-day — she won't be at home to cook for me.' He glanced at his cast. 'I'm not much good at making anything for myself. What do you think?'

'It's very kind of you, James, but — '

'You want to rush back to the house to sit with Mercy?'

She nodded. She didn't like to waste a minute.

'Nurse Huckstep is with her, and visiting doesn't start for half an hour. We've had this conversation before — you have to keep yourself healthy, for the infant's sake. Come with me — we'll be less than one hour, I promise.'

They went to one of the local hotel dining rooms where they ordered a light lunch of cold meats and potatoes, the waiter serving James's meat pre-cut.

'He seems particularly attentive,' Hannah observed.

'They know me well here. How are you, Hannah?'

'I've felt better,' she admitted. 'I can't sleep for nightmares. I keep thinking I should have done

426

something to save my sister.'

'I noticed your father didn't come to the funeral.'

'He's a bad-tempered and brutal man, and I wish I wasn't his flesh and blood. I think that was part of the problem — Ruby was looking for a man's approval, something he never gave. If it hadn't been Mr Milani, she would have thrown herself in the way of somebody else.'

'She must have been terrified when she found out she was with child, not just for herself but for the effect it would have on you.'

'Why didn't she turn to me? I should have been kinder, more understanding.'

'She wanted to protect you for as long as she could. I'm sorry that I couldn't see what was going on.'

'How could you have done? She put on a front while she was at work — it was only when she was at home that she would slip into a slough of despond. I wish I'd been able to share my concerns for her, but how could I when she had broken the rules of polite society by consorting with Mr Milani? And then there is the stigma of it — a mother is supposed to be loving and protective of her infant.'

'I'm just as guilty for not raising the subject of disorders of the mind. My wife — Suzanna — she didn't blunder into the fire and catch her nightgown alight. I walked into the parlour to find her standing beside the grate, pouring lamp oil down her gown and holding a lighted match. As I shouted at her to stop, she touched the match to the oil and — it was too late. The flames engulfed her . . . '

'I'm so sorry.'

'I've never told anyone of this before. It took a long time for me to forgive her. I was angry with her, very angry. And ashamed for feeling that way as I watched her endure a lingering death from her burns. I understand your suffering, Hannah. I let the coroner interpret the situation as he wished. I regret that I lied — or rather kept the truth to myself at the inquest — but I wanted to protect her reputation, her family and myself. I couldn't forgive her at first, but now I know there was nothing I could do to save her. One day, she would have tried again and succeeded.'

'As I've said before, Ruby followed in my mother's footsteps,' Hannah said. 'She took her own life soon after Ruby was born, and my family kept that a secret too.'

'It appears that these disorders can be passed down through families from one generation to the next. I'm making it part of my life's work to investigate how to treat the afflicted to prevent further suffering. That's why I see the likes of Mrs Phillips at my clinic. One day, we'll find a cure for these ills which cause as much difficulty to patients and their loved ones as physical disorders. I hope that as my cousin develops his practice, I'll be able to take on fewer of the routine cases and concentrate on conditions of mood and mental distress.'

'It's an admirable ambition, and I hope you make progress quickly.'

'What Ruby did, I'm sure she did out of love. She would have hoped for a better future for her daughter and wanted you to carry on nursing, unfettered by the responsibility and financial cost of looking after your niece.'

It was a reasonable explanation, she thought, biting back a fresh attack of tears.

'I'm very grateful for your friendship,' she said eventually. 'There are some who won't give me the time of day.'

'Then that is their loss,' he smiled gently. 'I'm sure you've thought about the future. Have you any plans for Mercy when she's well enough to leave the house?'

'I've done little but think,' she admitted.

'She'll remain on the ward for at least another couple of weeks.'

'The wet nurse . . . ?' she began.

'It's all right. She's all paid for — '

'I don't like accepting charity, but I have no choice in this instance. I'm exceedingly grateful, but I intend to pay you back every penny.'

'Let's not worry about that now,' James said. 'Have you heard anything from Mrs Knowles?'

Hannah shook her head.

'She's informed me that the meeting has been put back by a few days.'

'It makes no difference,' Hannah said wearily. 'I have little hope of being restored to my place.'

'I think there is some room for optimism,' James insisted. 'The infirmary has received many donations of food, bandages and money since the publicity in the newspapers. I shall advise that it doesn't make a good impression, dismissing a valued member of staff in these circumstances.'

'Thank you for trying, but I know my future there is precarious. The people of Margate are donating to the house to honour the heroic Doctor Clifton, not to help Ruby's child.'

'There are some who've been touched by your sister's story . . . '

'You don't have to dress it up to make me feel better. They blame her for the situation, for allowing Mr Milani to lead her astray and for selling her child to the Allspices to be paraded as a freak. I am Ruby's sister. In the eyes of society, I am tarred with the same brush.' She couldn't restrain herself any longer. It was all too much. The tears flowed. 'I don't know why you continue to risk your reputation by standing by me.'

'You know very well,' he said gruffly, handing her a handkerchief. 'You've helped me — unknowingly, perhaps — find renewed joy in my work as a physician. You have restored my faith in God, and . . . ' He fell silent. 'Before we met, I was dying from grief, but you healed me with your friendship. It's my turn to make you better, if I can. You deserve to stay on the wards at the house, and I will do my utmost to make sure that happens, and one day, when you are matron, we will look back and say, look what we've achieved.'

It was kind of him to stand up for her, she thought, but with her worries for Mercy's future, her ambition to become matron didn't seem quite as important as it had been before.

★ ★ ★

In the days that followed, Hannah visited Mercy morning and evening, and assisted both Doctor Clifton and Doctor Hunter at the private clinic. At last the time arrived for the special meeting of the Board, to decide on Hannah's future at the infirmary. It was convened in private with Mr Phillips, Mr Osbourne-Cole and two other governors, Doctor Clifton, Mr Anthony and Matron in attendance.

'What chance do I have of being allowed to continue at the infirmary when these gentlemen are sitting in judgement?' Hannah whispered aside to Mrs Knowles as they were shown to their seats in the boardroom.

'Hush,' she said. 'Sit down.'

Flanked by Mrs Knowles and Doctor Clifton, Hannah sat opposite the Chairman of the Board, who banged his gavel to call for their attention.

'Good day, ladies and gentlemen. We are met here to discuss the possible suspension or dismissal of Sister Bentley. For what crime, may I ask?' Mr Phillips peered over his half-moon spectacles, his head tremoring before his gaze settled on Mrs Knowles. 'Matron?'

'Sister Bentley is currently on compassionate leave from this house,' she said. 'As far as I'm aware, no crime has been committed.'

'May I speak?' Doctor Clifton said.

'I should speak first,' Mr Anthony interrupted. 'I'm a busy man with patients queued up outside theatre waiting to go under the knife.'

'I appreciate that, but — '

'You have no idea, Mr Phillips,' Mr Anthony said acidly. 'I'm up to my elbows in blood and

431

gore every day. Thanks to your cuts, my scalpels are blunt and my forceps are falling apart.'

'This isn't the time to be talking about finance,' Mr Phillips said crossly.

'Then I insist on it being noted down for consideration at the next full meeting of the Board.'

'Consider it done. What did you wish to say? Doctor Clifton, I will come to you later.'

'Whatever you decide, our visiting physician should not be allowed to influence proceedings.' Mr Anthony cast him a glare as he opened his mouth to argue. James sat back. 'I don't know the truth of it, and I don't wish to, but I would suggest that his friendship with Sister Bentley leaves him open to accusations of bias. I'm the one person who can offer a frank and fair judgement on this matter.'

Hannah's heart sank, any hope she'd had dismissed in an instant. Mr Anthony didn't like her. He never had.

'Sister Bentley and I didn't see eye to eye at first,' he went on, 'but I've come to appreciate her competence and complete devotion to duty. In a nutshell, why should a valued member of staff be dismissed because of her sister's sins? Since when has sin been a contagion?'

'This is about the reputation of the infirmary,' Mr Phillips responded. 'As in any family, one is forced to make unpleasant decisions on occasion to keep up appearances.' He paused, and Hannah wondered if he was thinking of his wife.

'As in any family, we should look after our own,' Mr Anthony insisted. 'Mrs Knowles, what is your opinion?'

'She should stay on. I'm sure we all have a skeleton or two in our cupboards, so to speak, yet we are all in positions of responsibility and influence.'

'Really, Matron.' Mr Phillips frowned. 'What proof do you have of this? How do you back up that accusation?'

'It's my job to know everything that goes on within this hospital. I see who comes and goes, whose wife attends frequently to consult with a particular doctor, like a bee to a honeypot. I hear the sounds of . . . intimate connection . . . going on in theatre late at night.' Hannah noticed her glance towards Mr Anthony, whose shoulders shrank a little. 'I believe that we should take the path of forgiveness and charity and let Sister Bentley continue in her place. I feel sure that you agree with me, gentlemen.'

There were general murmurings of assent before Mr Phillips declared that Hannah could remain as Sister of the Lettsom without a stain on her character.

'Thank you for speaking up for me, Mr Anthony,' she said, as they left the boardroom and entered the corridor.

'I spoke my mind. Don't you dare prove me wrong on this or I'll make sure you never work again.' A twinkle appeared in his eye. 'And there's absolutely no truth in what Matron said.'

'Of course,' she said, thinking of his wife and the nurse who worked with him in theatre.

'That went better than I expected,' James said, joining them. 'It's a shame in a way — Mrs Bellows will miss your help at the clinic. Perhaps you could drop by later to collect your wages.'

She nodded — she needed time to think about the implications of being allowed to return to work.

'Welcome back,' Mrs Knowles said, letting the gentlemen pass. 'You see how a little knowledge is never a bad thing. When can you start? I realise that you'll have to make provision for the child, so I'm willing to be flexible.'

'I'm not sure. I haven't decided what to do.'

'It's a heavy burden. I have an acquaintance who farms her son out to her family — she hardly sees him, perhaps only once or twice a year. Unfortunately, the boy is a distraction — she's always worrying about him. It's probably better all round to put the little one up for adoption. I'll make some enquiries.'

'Thank you, Matron.' Hannah bit her lip to suppress a wave of renewed resentment at poor Ruby for putting her into an impossible quandary.

'I'll assume that you'll be back within the month. If not, I'll have to advertise for a replacement. In the meantime, I'm going to transfer Nurse Huckstep to the Lettsom as acting Sister. The infant is much improved, and the doctors have agreed that she doesn't require intensive nursing any longer.'

'I'm sorry for putting you to all this trouble.'

'Let me know of your intentions as soon as possible,' Matron said. 'I don't want to be forced by urgency to take on a slatternly widow or runaway wife in your stead.'

'I will, I promise.'

'Come with me and we'll give Nurse Huckstep the news.'

When they arrived, Hannah could see through to the balcony where the wet nurse was suckling Mercy. She suppressed her desire to rush across to see her niece as Alice came over to greet her and Mrs Knowles.

'Good morning, Matron and Sister Bentley,' she said.

'Is all well?' Matron asked.

'Everything's shipshape and Bristol fashion, thank you.' Eyebrows raised, Alice glanced from Matron to Hannah and back.

'How is Mercy? What have the doctors said today?'

'That Doctor Clifton's modifications to the saltwater treatment have given her much benefit during the past week. Her pulse, breathing and temperature are all normal for an infant of her age, and she's feeding well. However, Doctor Hunter has expressed his continuing reservations about the likely extent of her recovery from the effects of strong spirits on her brain and liver.'

'Then it is a case of 'wait and see',' Matron said. 'Nurse Huckstep, Doctor Clifton has said that the child no longer requires individual nursing.'

'That's right,' Alice said.

'In that case, I must ask you to hand over her care to Sister Riley. After lunch, you'll join the staff on the Lettsom, where you are to take over the role of acting Sister until Sister Bentley returns to work.'

'I'm honoured,' Alice said, touching her

throat. She flashed Hannah a smile before she went to speak to Sister Riley, who seemed a little upset to be losing her to one of the boys' wards.

'You've been a boon, and I hope to have you back very soon,' Hannah heard her say.

'Is there anything I need to finish before I take my break?' Alice asked.

'You can go now, if you like. It's almost twelve.'

'Thank you. I'd like one last cuddle with Mercy and I'm sure Hannah — I mean, Sister Bentley — wants to see her too.'

Alice took the baby from the wet nurse who fastened the buttons on her blouse, pulled her shawl over her shoulders, and hurried off.

'There, there, little one,' she murmured as Mercy started to sob. 'Here's your Auntie Hannah.'

'I find it strange being addressed as such,' Hannah said, holding Mercy against her shoulder and patting her back. She belched and her sobbing subsided.

'Ah, it was a touch of wind,' Alice said. 'She'll be fine now. She's had the most terrible gripes.'

'Hello, sweetheart.' Her heart melting, Hannah held Mercy a few inches from her face and gazed into her eyes. Mercy stuffed her fist into her mouth and stared back, cross-eyed. 'She seems all there. What do you think, Alice?'

'She still sleeps a lot, but when she's awake, she's as bright as a button. Sometimes, I think the doctors are worrying unnecessarily about her development, but I suppose they're wary of giving a good prognosis, in case they turn out to be wrong.' Alice winked. 'There's more kudos to be gained that way. I'm so glad you've kept your place, but I hope you don't think I'm treading on your toes, taking over the Lettsom. It's only temporary.'

'I can't think of anyone better to do it.'

'What are you going to do about Mercy?'

'I don't know.' Hannah held her close, breathing in her scent of milk and soap. The choice was stark. 'I promised Ruby I'd look after her and I'll do my best, even if that means putting her up for adoption, or farming her out. I have a cousin on my mother's side who might be prevailed upon to take her.'

'Can't you have a girl to look after her while you work a few hours a day for someone like Doctor Clifton?' Alice suggested.

'I've thought of that, but how will I make ends meet? How can I pay for a child's care out of a nurse's wage?'

She was under no illusion that the first option would cause her great pain — like having a surgeon cut out her heart without anaesthetic. The second option was easier to contemplate but would lead to a life of penury and struggle.

'I could help you,' Alice said. 'I have a little money put by.'

'I couldn't possibly,' Hannah said. 'You never know when you might need that yourself.'

'I could mind her for you from time to time.'

'I'm very grateful, but you have enough to deal with. Are you sure that you're recovered enough to manage a ward?'

'I like to work to keep my mind off what might happen to me in the future. I feel better than ever, but I'll never be able to say that I'm cured, only that my symptoms have abated. There's no need for you to feel sorry for me. I've never been happier.'

'Do you think you'll ever go back to London?'

'Doctor Clifton says that for the benefit of my health, I should stay in Margate, which suits me very well.' Alice changed the subject. 'Have you heard? Mr Allspice has tried to gain readmittance to the house because he's destitute and wants to avoid the poorhouse.'

'What's happened to his wife and children?'

'Alan and his brother came into some money and took the whole family, apart from their invalid father, to America. They've gone and left him to fend for himself, an impossible task for a grumpy old man in a bath chair. Anyway, he's come to a sad end now. As Mr Taylor was turning him away for the third time of asking, he suffered an apoplectic fit.'

'I haven't any sympathy for him, I'm afraid.'

'It seems that Mr Taylor has — he's admitted him, knowing he hasn't got long for this world and that he's too far gone to be any trouble to Sister Trim and her nurses.' The infirmary clock chimed — one, two . . .

'That's midday — you're due your break. I'll change Mercy and sit with her in the sunshine for a while.' Exhausted, Hannah fell asleep on the balcony and it wasn't until Sister Riley came to take Mercy from her that she woke.

'I thought you were going to drop her then,' she chuckled. 'Come on, little one, it's feeding time again. Can I get you anything?'

'No, thank you.' Hannah struggled to her feet. 'I'm going home via the Lettsom.'

'You're going to check up on Nurse Huckstep and make sure she's doing everything right. I would, if that was my ward. Good luck, Sister. I don't envy you one little bit.'

As she stepped on to the Lettsom, Hannah sensed a change. Only a couple of weeks had gone by, but it seemed like a lifetime. The patients had changed — other boys had taken over Oliver's and Ronald's beds. Ben was still there — he waved from where he was sitting at the table, turning the pages of a picture book with one of the lady volunteers who studiously ignored her.

'Hello, Sister Bentley,' Ben called.

'Hello,' she said. 'How are you?'

'I have dots.' He lifted his pyjama shirt and showed her the rash on his belly.

'Oh dear,' she said.

'It's time we put some more lotion on those,' Nurse May said, walking across to him. 'Come along. Good afternoon, Sister.'

'I'll let you get on,' Hannah said, turning to see Alice trying to persuade one of the new patients to drink his medicine. Another boy was helping, perched on the edge of the bed.

'Jim, you 'ave to 'old yer nose and swaller,' he said, sounding like an old hand. 'It'll do yer the world o' good.'

'Since when have you been so keen on taking your medicine, Eric?' Alice said, amused.

'Pinch yer nose like this, then you can't taste the stuff,' the boy ordered.

The boy called Jim did as he was told. He opened his mouth and Alice administered the offending potion on a spoon. Having swallowed, the boy gagged and fell back against his pillow.

'You're a liar, Eric,' he cried.

'I'm not!'

'Boys, not on my ward,' Alice said, pulling the two boys apart as they rained fisticuffs on each other. 'Eric, go and sit out on the balcony.'

'It's rainin',' he said, aghast.

'It'll cool your temper. Go on.'

Head down, Eric shuffled away. 'As for you, Jim, you can sit here in silence. I don't want to hear a word.' She turned to Hannah, a smile on her face. 'It won't be long before I've knocked them into shape. Can I help you? Is it the baby? Is she all right?'

'I came to wish you well,' she said, regretting that she'd dropped by. It didn't feel like her ward any more and she wasn't sure if it ever would be again. 'I should go.' She turned on her heels and fled, feeling like a spare part.

On leaving the infirmary, she remembered to call at the clinic.

'I've come to collect my wages,' she said to Mrs Bellows.

'Ah yes, Doctor Clifton has company. I'll ask him to come down.'

'Oh no. Please don't bother him,' she said, but Mrs Bellows was already on her way up the stairs. She returned shortly afterwards.

'He says to go up and join them.'

'Thank you.' With some trepidation, Hannah went to find him, wondering if she was about to discover that he was keeping company with a lady.

'Is that you, Sister?' she heard him say from a room at the top of the first flight of stairs. 'Do come in.'

She stepped inside a high-ceilinged room, decorated in deep reds and creams with leather chairs and a brass-faced longcase clock. The carpet was patterned and springy underfoot. Her surprise at its opulence was surpassed when she saw Charlotte, sitting drinking tea. She'd lost the ruddiness of her complexion and looked thinner than she remembered, but she was wearing the most beautiful tea dress made from ochre satin, trimmed with lace, with a bustle at the back and pleats along the front.

'Greetings,' James said, standing up. 'Come and take the weight off your feet.'

'It's very kind, but I don't like to intrude.'

'Sit down,' he insisted. 'I'll call for more tea.'

She accepted and took a seat beside the window. There were oils on the walls — too many to count and all in gold frames.

'You are wondering about the paintings?' he smiled.

She nodded.

'I collect them, not so much as an investment, but because I like to look at them. Anyway, I'll leave you two ladies to talk — I have a patient due at four. I'll be back as soon as I've finished with them. Hannah, I hope you don't mind waiting.'

'Not at all.' She hadn't got anywhere else to go, except back to her lodgings. James left as his housekeeper came in with a fresh pot of tea. Charlotte offered to pour.

'If you're sure?' the housekeeper said, leaving the tray on the low table which stood in the centre of the room.

'I don't think I've had the chance to say how sorry I am,' Charlotte began, having handed Hannah a cup of tea. 'It was a shame that I didn't get to speak to you properly at the funeral. How is the baby? James says she's doing better.'

'I've been to the house to see her,' Hannah said. 'She's a sweetheart.'

'You're going back to work on the Lettsom?'

'Yes, once I've decided what to do about Mercy. Oh, Charlotte, I'm at a complete loss.'

'It can't be easy being on the horns of such a dilemma.'

'I don't know which way to turn.'

'It would be a shame to have to give up nursing, but there's a poor innocent child to consider. I'm sorry — I'm not helping, am I?'

'I'm grateful for any advice you can offer,' Hannah said. 'Since Ruby . . . since she died, I've felt rather alone.'

'James has been helping you?'

'He's gone out of his way . . . '

'I wish I could do something, but Henry and I — well, that's one of the reasons I'm here. I've had a consultation with Doctor Clifton. I've been very sick recently, barely able to keep anything down. He's diagnosed me with hy-per-em-esis gra-vi-da-rum,' she said speaking slowly. 'I'm with child.'

'Oh, that's wonderful news.'

442

'James says that I might lose the infant prematurely. He's prescribed the seawater treatment and said that he'll re-examine me in two months. You won't mention this to anyone, will you?'

'I won't say a word. If you need anything, let me know.'

'And vice versa. Look at us. How times have changed! Less than a year ago, we were Nurses Finch and Bentley with hardly a care in the world.'

'Except for having to watch out for Trimmie,' Hannah smiled. 'How is married life?'

'Apart from this terrible sickness, it's been better than I could have imagined. Despite our differences, Henry is the best husband — he's kind, considerate and loving. He's helped me overcome my fear of not making the right impression in society, and I'm beginning to enjoy entertaining. Giving up nursing was the right choice for me.' She smiled. 'It still seems odd, though, getting out of bed every morning and choosing which dress to wear. As for those horrid flat shoes — I've given them away.'

'I'm done,' James said, entering the room with his stethoscope around his neck. 'Hannah, if you'll come with me. Mrs Hunter, will you excuse us for a moment?'

She followed him downstairs, where he showed her into one of the examination rooms and closed the door.

'I hope you don't mind — I wanted a quick word.' He passed her an envelope. 'These are your wages. If you'd like to work here again, let me know. I can always find you some hours.

Henry's list is lengthening far more quickly than I imagined it would. He's very popular.'

'He learned his bedside manner from you,' Hannah dared to say, making him smile.

'You've seen Mercy?'

'I have. Nurse Huckstep mentioned that Doctor Hunter suspects that she has damage to the brain and liver.'

'The immediate danger has passed, but she isn't out of the woods yet. As for the hindrance to her development, we won't know the extent of it for a long time. However, I recommend that you remove her from the house as soon as you're able to.'

'Why?' Hannah began to panic. 'I thought she'd have to stay on the ward for weeks, if not months.'

'We've managed to stabilise her condition with the modified thalassotherapy treatment, but, being so young, she's vulnerable to other diseases . . . '

'Like scrofula?'

'That's right. Thanks to Dr Koch and his microscope, we've learned that the tuberculous conditions are infectious, not hereditary, or caused by foul air as the medical profession once thought.'

'Then I'll take her immediately,' Hannah said.

'Let me examine her once more on my rounds. If I'm happy, you can collect her tomorrow morning. I understand from Mrs Knowles that you're taking another week off from the infirmary, so you can organise care for the child . . . ' He paused for a moment before continuing, 'I'll arrange for the wet nurse to continue her visits three times a day — I have your address. Is that all right with you?'

It had to be, she thought as she hurried back to her lodgings. She'd promised Ruby that she'd do the right thing by Mercy, and that's what she intended to do.

24

More Than Anything in the World

It was the most nerve-racking thing she'd ever done, taking a sickly infant home to nurse. Having cleaned the room from top to bottom and cleared the washstand so there was room to change her, she collected Mercy from the hospital, carrying her in her arms and wrapped in a shawl to protect her from the April showers. It was Alice's day off and she helped by carrying the small bag of clothes, donations to the infirmary that were too small to fit the other patients. Mrs Wells brought round a pale lemon-yellow sheet and blanket she'd been given by one of her neighbours, saying they were too good for rags, and then when Hannah tried to pay her rent, she said that it had already been paid.

'By whom?' Hannah asked.

'A person who wished to remain anonymous,' was all Mrs Wells would say.

If she'd known, Hannah felt sure she would have been able to winkle a name out of her.

That evening, after the wet nurse had gone, Hannah stood alone in her room, rocking Mercy back and forth, trying to get her to sleep, but she wouldn't settle. She checked her nappy — it was dry. Was she drinking enough? She gave her a little water that she'd boiled in a pot over the fire and left to cool, and after a while, Mercy fell asleep.

She tiptoed across to the middle drawer of the chest that she was using as a makeshift cot and lowered the sleeping baby on to the sheet, at which Mercy's eyes opened, her face crumpled, and she started to cry again. It was the longest night of Hannah's life. By the morning, when Mercy finally dropped off, she could hardly think straight.

★   ★   ★

Within two days, she found that she was beginning to manage looking after a baby. Mercy was asleep in the drawer, snug and warm under a blanket. Every so often, she would wrinkle her nose and twitch, then smile as though she was dreaming.

'Ah,' Hannah sighed as she forgave her for the sleepless nights and the smell of dirty nappies which she soaked in a bucket of carbolic before washing them. 'What am I going to do with you? I promised your ma that I'd do what's best for you . . . ' The problem was that she was growing mighty fond of her. How could she possibly give her up? It would break her heart.

Glancing through the window, she noticed a carriage draw up and drop off a gentleman in a grey coat, top hat and leather bag. What was James doing here? Why had he not warned her of his visit, so that she had time to clear up the dirty dishes and sweep the floor? Thinking to intercept him, she went out on to the landing, running her fingers through her hair which she'd left down, having washed it that morning.

'Good day, Mrs . . . ?' she heard him say as she leaned across the banister.

'Mrs Wells,' her landlady said, aquiver with curiosity.

'Thank you,' Hannah interrupted. 'Doctor, I wasn't expecting you . . . '

He was frowning as she walked halfway down the stairs.

'You asked me to make a house call this afternoon at two.' He looked at his pocket watch. 'It's two o'clock precisely.'

'Oh yes. Of course. Silly me. I forgot, which is one of the reasons I wished to see you.'

'I'm glad you invited me to give my opinion on your health.'

'Mr Anthony at the infirmary recommended you as being a physician with a special interest in memory lapses.' Despite everything, she suppressed a giggle at the sight of her landlady's expression. James coughed as though disguising a chuckle.

'May I?' he said, regaining his composure.

'Come this way.'

'You can leave the door open, Miss Bentley,' Mrs Wells said.

'Please, don't worry about me,' Hannah said, as James followed her upstairs. 'I trust Doctor Clifton implicitly.' She closed the door firmly but quietly behind them.

'How's Mercy? Where is she?' he said, glancing around the room.

'She's over there.' Hannah nodded towards the chest of drawers.

'You haven't got a cot for her?'

'Not yet.' It was a matter of pride to pretend that all was well, but it was obvious that she was suffering from impecunious circumstances. 'I'm sorry about — '

'No need to apologise. You have a lovely room — you've made it feel very homely,' he interrupted, moving across to the window. 'And it has a sea view.'

Hannah smiled ruefully. 'Just as Ruby wanted.' She had cleaned it thoroughly before moving Mercy in, and added some extra touches: a spray of dried lavender in a pot and a shell Ruby had found on the beach placed on the mantelpiece. There was a wooden rattle that Nurse May had given her for Mercy, as well as a cushion that one of the kitchen maids had made for the chair.

'Will you permit me to stay awhile or are you in a rush to get rid of me?'

'I'm sorry for being remiss. Let me take your coat.'

'I'll need some assistance,' he frowned. 'Henry had to help me put it on.'

'How is your arm? Is it still as painful?' she said as she took hold of the lapel of his coat and lifted it gently off his shoulder, then tugged the other sleeve down his arm.

'It's getting better. Another three or four weeks and I can have this dratted plaster taken off. I miss bathing in the sea — one can't let it get wet.'

'Do you bathe at this time of year?' She laid

his coat across the bed. 'The sea is freezing.'

'I swim all year round. It's chilly, I grant you that, but it's most invigorating and excellent for the constitution.'

'You can't be of sound mind,' she smiled, then fell serious. 'I shouldn't have said that. It reminds me of Ruby . . . '

'She would want you to be happy,' he said.

'I know. Take a seat.' She gestured to the rickety wooden chair. 'Can I make you some tea? Or would you prefer ale?'

'Neither, thank you. You must have the chair. I'll stand.'

'No, it's all right. I'll perch here.' Before he could argue, she sat down on the edge of the mattress.

She watched him pace back and forth in front of the fireplace before stopping and clearing his throat. 'I've come to you today with a proposition,' he said.

'Oh? What is it?'

'I've always wanted children. Suzanna and I used to laugh and say we wanted ten, but having seen the Allspices, I'm all for having one or two. I've grown attached to little Mercy since she's been at the infirmary and I'm keen to provide her with a home and all the advantages I can offer: a nanny, medical treatment, education . . . the love and guidance that a father figure can bestow.'

Hannah opened her mouth to speak, but he gave her a stern stare.

'Let me finish. I need to explain the two options I can offer in full. If I adopt Mercy as my ward, you'll be free to progress in your profession as a nurse.'

'You wouldn't have her put away in a home, if she does turn out to be backward or odd in any way?' Hannah didn't think he would, but she had to ask.

'You know me better than that,' he said.

'I'm sorry.'

'It's all right. Ruby wouldn't have wanted that for her, and neither do I. Mercy would stay at my house with all the help that she needed. You would, of course, be welcome to visit her and take her out whenever you wanted to.

'The alternative is that you accept my hand in marriage and we adopt Mercy as our own,' he went on. 'Your kindness, my seaside angel, has healed my wounds — your refusal would undoubtedly inflict them afresh, but I would understand. I am a man. I have ambition and society allows me to do as I please. It is different for women. I wouldn't judge you for putting your profession before wedlock.'

'Oh, James.' He had put her into a predicament.

'When I say that I offer marriage, I do it out of love, not convenience — not for Mercy and your sister's memory, but for you, because you mean everything to me. I would do anything for you — give you up, if I had to. This is your decision.'

Hannah thought of the wards and how the Lettsom didn't feel like hers any more. She thought of the giant behemoth of the infirmary, the challenge and satisfaction of keeping it running smoothly, the conflicts with the doctors and the governors, the minutiae of keeping the bathing attendants happy, and the patients adequately fed. She recalled Matron once talking of how she had missed out on marriage.

James's love was selfless, thoughtful . . . he'd said he loved her. And if she was honest with herself, she loved him too, deeply. Their affection for each other had been tested, and not found wanting.

'I realise that it's a lot to think about,' he said eventually. 'You can have as much time as you need.'

'I have some questions,' she said.

'Ask me anything you like.'

'I have a reputation, thanks to what's happened. You will lose patients.'

'That is up to them. I will always have enough work — it's the nature of the job. I know I've talked of this before, but I have no doubt that Suzanna would give her blessing to my marrying again. She wouldn't have wanted me to grow old alone . . . and childless.' His voice was taut with suspense. 'Neither of us will forget those we've loved and lost, but we must move on, honouring their memory and the parts they played in shaping us. Hannah, does this mean that you're reconsidering my offer?'

'I have one more question, an obstacle which is harder to overcome than anything else we've encountered,' she said. 'What if I should turn out to be like my mother?'

He smiled. 'Don't all daughters turn out like their mothers?'

'I mean, what if I develop the same tendencies as her, the melancholia and insanity, like Ruby?'

A brief frown crossed his eyes.

'We would cross that bridge if we came to it. When you marry, it's for better, for worse, in sickness and in health. There's no suggestion in your attitude or character that you would exhibit these signs. Is that all?'

'Not quite. Are you sure you're willing to take on an infant who was born out of wedlock?'

'To be honest, I adore her already. Who could fail to love an innocent child like little Mercy? But these are all side issues.'

Hannah's heart beat faster. She didn't care any more. She could hear Alice saying, I told you so, and Charlotte's expressions of disbelief, that she would give up her vocation for love.

'What do you say?' he said. 'You've gone remarkably quiet.'

'In this situation, I believe it's the custom for the gentleman to go down on one knee.'

'You mean?' A flicker of a smile crossed his face.

'Ask me,' she said softly, and he raised himself from the chair — awkwardly with his arm still encased in plaster — and knelt in front of her. 'You might have to help me up afterwards,' he chuckled. 'Take my hand. I'm sorry I can't give you both.'

Smiling, she reached out and caught his fingers in hers.

'You're trembling,' she whispered.

'So are you . . . ' He gazed up at her. 'My dear Hannah, I've loved you since I first set eyes on you. You took my breath away and stole my heart when you turned up at the house that day with the boys from St Pancras. You've impressed me with your courage in speaking out when you see something is wrong, and the way you care for our patients as if they were part of your family. You have also infuriated me at times with your stubborn refusal to acknowledge our feelings for each other, but I admire your determination and grit in going forward with your ambitions, staying true to yourself. You are the most caring person I've ever met, selfless, compassionate and kind.

'When I met you, I was a deeply dejected man — grieving for my wife, stuck, in a way, but your friendship has healed my broken heart.'

'Oh, James . . . '

'Will you do me the honour of becoming my wife?'

A tear rolled down her cheek. He released her hand and reached up to wipe it away, his touch like fire against her skin.

'I was hoping to make you happy,' he said, half smiling.

'I am happy,' she exclaimed. 'Oh, let me help you up. The answer's yes, my love, my dearest man.' Her eyes stung and her heart ached with a joy she had never experienced before.

'I thought you would turn me down,' he said as she helped him to his feet. 'May I kiss you?'

Boldly, she put her arms around his neck, inclining her face towards his. He bowed his head and pressed his lips to hers, the contact making her giddy with delight and desire.

Eventually, she tore herself away. 'When will we be married?'

He smiled again, as though reading her mind. 'As soon as possible, if you're happy with that.'

'I'll write my letter of resignation to Matron.'

'I realise how much I'm asking of you, but I've wished for a long time to have you at my side — ' There was a cry from the chest and he frowned. 'I'd almost forgotten . . . Go on. She's calling for her aunt.'

'She's quite demanding, much like her mother,' Hannah smiled.

'Is she hungry or thirsty?' he asked as he accompanied her to the makeshift crib. 'Does the wet nurse still attend to her as arranged?'

'Dear Effie comes three times a day, but that isn't enough for a hungry infant, so I supplement her diet with pap and goat's milk. I have a bottle ready for her. I keep it outside in the box on the windowledge.'

'Let me get it.' He hauled the window open and fetched the bottle, while Hannah collected Mercy who was squalling pitifully. 'It needs warming.' She nodded towards the iron pot she'd rigged up over the fire. 'If you place it in the water, it'll heat up quite quickly.'

'Perhaps not fast enough to save our eardrums,' James smiled. 'Hannah, you can't live like this. It isn't right.'

'It's the best I can do. Mercy has clean clothes, warmth, fresh air, food and more love than I thought capable of bestowing on a single human being.'

'What I said wasn't an insult. I admire what you're doing, but I find it painful to see you in a place like this when, in my mind, you deserve nothing less than a palace — '

'Will yer keep that racket down? Either feed the child or put it out of its misery. I 'ave a piller that'll do the job very well.' The words were accompanied by a hammering at the door.

'Oh dear. That's one of the other lodgers.'

'Then something must be done. I'll go and — '

'No, James. You would be at a considerable disadvantage — Mr Garling is twice your size and has the use of both arms.'

'You mean, he would enter into a fight with me?'

'I wouldn't put it past him. Pass me the bottle — take it out of the pot with the tongs, then wrap it in the cloth. That's right.'

He handed the bottle to her. She sucked on the teat to unblock the hole, then turned it upside down, pouring a couple of drops of milk on to her wrist.

'That's perfect.' She offered Mercy the teat, and after a moment or two of crying and snuffling, she took it. 'Silence is golden. Are you sure you still want us after that?' she asked when the only sounds she could hear were the baby sucking, and the air bubbling back through the milk as she drained the bottle.

'More than anything in the world,' James said.

★ ★ ★

On the first Wednesday in June, Alice was with Hannah at the lodgings James had found for her, having decided that Mrs Wells's rooms weren't suitable for his fiancée and an infant.

'You'll have to put her down soon, you know,' Alice chuckled as Hannah walked up and down the bedroom, rocking Mercy gently in her arms.

'I know.' Breathing in her sweet, milky scent, Hannah kissed Mercy's forehead. 'I'm getting married! I can't believe it.'

'Neither can I, when I look back to all the times when you said you'd never wed.' Alice went to answer the doorbell. 'Miss Gold is here,' she said, returning with a young woman who was dressed modestly in a navy coat and hat.

'You've come to take Mercy,' Hannah sighed. 'I'm not sure I can give her up.'

'You'll see her after the wedding, no doubt.' Miss Gold smiled and, reluctantly, Hannah handed Mercy over and watched as the baby settled contentedly in her arms, confirming what she already knew: that she and James had chosen well. She couldn't wish for a better nanny. 'I'll look after her, Miss Bentley,' she said. 'Oh, I'll have to get used to calling you Mrs Clifton very soon.'

'We all will,' Alice said.

'I'll take her downstairs — I have the pram waiting.' Miss Gold gave Hannah a small curtsey. 'I hope you have a lovely day.'

Hannah thanked her, and within the hour, having put aside her mourning dress she was wearing her silk wedding gown with a train and veil, satin shoes and a gift from James, a necklace of pearls.

'Marry in white, you've chosen right.' Alice fastened the clasp at the back of her neck. 'I'd be lying if I said I wasn't even the tiniest bit envious.'

'I have a present for you.' Hannah opened the drawer in the dressing table and pulled out a small velvet box.

'Oh, you shouldn't have.'

'It's a token to say how much we appreciate your friendship.' She turned to face her. 'It's never wavered, no matter what.'

'Well, of course it hasn't — it wouldn't be friendship if it had.'

'Open it.' Hannah pressed the box into her hand and watched Alice's eyes light up as she took out the brooch, a knot forged from silver.

'It's delightful. More than delightful. I don't know what to say, except thank you.'

'It's our pleasure.' Hannah heard the sound of a carriage pulling up outside. 'I think it's time for us to leave.'

She took one last look around the rooms that she'd shared with Mercy for the past few weeks. Tonight, she would be staying in a hotel with her husband, and after that, she would be moving into the house in Cecil Square. 'Alice, look at my hands.'

'They're shaking,' she said.

'I'm nervous . . . and excited at the same time.'

'I believe it's quite normal for a bride to be a bag of nerves on her wedding day,' Alice said. 'Come along now. We don't want to keep everyone waiting.'

Outside Holy Trinity Church, they were united with the flower girls, James's nieces, wearing white dresses with blue sashes which matched the colour of the groom's frock coat.

'Where is my bride?' Her heart missed a beat when she saw James come striding towards her. 'Hannah, you look radiant. Isn't she the most beautiful lady in the whole world?' he said, turning to the flower girls, of which there were six, all under ten.

'Yes, Uncle James,' they said, giggling and skipping in circles around him.

'It's time for you to calm down, young ladies,' Alice said. 'We have an important job to do. Can you remember what it is? One at a time.'

James drew Hannah aside while Alice arranged the flower girls in pairs, preparing them to walk into the church.

'Are you ready?' he whispered, offering his arm.

Smiling, she nodded and rested her gloved hand on his sleeve, and together they followed Alice and the flower girls along the aisle to the altar where they were married in front of a huge crowd of well-wishers — James's family, Charlotte and Henry, Mrs Knowles and their friends from the infirmary, and many of James's patients. Hannah had invited Stepmother out of politeness, but she had declined to attend, giving no reason for her absence. She thought of Ruby who would have loved the occasion, and of her mother who had missed out, but this was no time for regrets.

Tears pricked her eyes as they said their vows — for better, for worse, in sickness and in health — and, after Alice had removed Hannah's glove, James slid the wedding ring on to her finger. It was a new beginning, the first step into a golden future with the man she loved at her side.

25

Trust Me, I'm a Doctor

On a warm August morning, James walked into the dining room on the first floor of the house in Cecil Square where Hannah had been waiting impatiently for him, a newspaper on the table beside her.

'You look worn out, my dear,' she said as he came across and kissed her on the cheek. 'What time did you come home last night? I didn't hear you.'

'It was in the early hours — I didn't like to disturb you. The poor man had only just been discharged from the house where he'd been treated for a growth on his leg. Rather foolishly, he decided to celebrate his recovery with a few measures of whisky at one of the taverns. On his way home, he was run over by a carriage.' James sat down, and Hannah got up to pour his coffee: black with one lump of sugar, just as he liked it. 'Thank you.'

'How is he?' Her rings glinted in the sunshine which streamed in through the long windows, the sapphire in the engagement ring being the colour of a summer sky over Margate, the gold sparkling like freshly washed sand.

'The driver, who was in shock, dropped him off at home. His wife sent for me because he

461

wasn't making sense, but having seen him, I put it down to drink. I've given him some opium — he can sleep it off.' He took the lid off his plate and picked up his knife and fork. 'I'm sorry to rush, but I have appointments from half past eight.'

'I know,' she said. 'You're fully booked.'

'Henry is at the infirmary, doing rounds with Mr Anthony today.'

'I'll go tomorrow morning to read to the boys.' Hannah was enjoying being a lady volunteer: part of the house but without the responsibility. She missed nursing, but not as much as she'd imagined she would. She did find it hard to bite her tongue if she saw anything was amiss, though — not that that happened often, because Alice was a surprisingly strict sister. 'I have some news of interest — let me read it to you,' she said as he tucked into bacon and sausages. 'It's about' — she would always struggle to say his name — 'Mr Milani, no less.'

'This is what happened at the summer assizes?'

'He was released from gaol because there was inadequate evidence to charge him with attempted murder, both men being liars.'

'He would have been sentenced for hard bed, hard board and hard labour, if I'd had my way,' James said, glancing down at his arm. It had healed, but still gave him pain at times.

'I'm less forgiving than you are — I'd have seen him hanged.'

'You don't mean that.'

'Imprisoned then, for life. It doesn't matter

anyway. He's gone back to lion-taming and the lion has taken its revenge.' She carried on. '*The lion tripped Mr Milani with its paw. As he fell, it leapt on top of him and, having caught him by the throat with its jaws, it closed its mouth and shook its head with a violent passion.*'

'My goodness. It killed him?' James interrupted.

'Let me finish,' Hannah said with humour. 'You are always in a rush.'

'I know. I'm sorry. Do go on.'

'*The aggressor inflicted frightful injuries on to Mr Milani's throat before dragging him like a rag doll to the rear of the cage ... where it proceeded to engage in eating Mr Milani's flesh until it could be persuaded away.*' She'd read it before, but this time, she felt sick. She put the paper down, pushed her plate away and held a napkin to her mouth.

'Are you all right? I thought you had a stronger constitution than this.'

'I'm fine, thank you ... it was the thought of the lion ... and the ... oh dear.'

'Can you manage a little dry toast?' he said anxiously. 'No? Perhaps we should abandon our plans for this evening.'

'We're going, come hell or high water. We have tickets.' She was determined to be there — to dance with her husband, to help raise money for the house, and to honour Ruby's memory. Hannah had promised to take her to the ball, and it had been too late, but she felt sure that her sister would be looking down on them; an angel in Heaven. Although unsure that she

463

should be thinking of dancing when she was still in deep mourning, she knew that's what Ruby would have wanted.

'Then you must take a nap during the day.' James stood up and walked round behind her. He rested his hands on her shoulders and kissed her again, this time on the nape of her neck. 'Promise me you won't run yourself ragged.'

She touched his hand. 'I'll be careful,' she said. She did feel out of sorts.

'I'll see you later, my darling.'

When he had gone downstairs, Hannah went to speak to their housekeeper who cooked and cleaned for them with the help of one maid. They both lived out, leaving room for the nanny to stay in the attic next door to Mercy's nursery, while Dobbs occupied rooms above the stables a short distance away. Although James sometimes wished that they had space for more servants, Hannah was happy with the arrangements.

'Will you be dining at home tonight?' the housekeeper asked.

'We'll dine at the hotel, thank you, Mrs Tapp.'

'Are you taking the littlun out today?'

'I will, I think.'

Mrs Tapp smiled. 'The fresh air will put a little colour in your cheeks. I've told the master not to wear you out, dancing all night.'

Hannah thanked her again and, having spoken to Miss Gold, she took Mercy out along the promenade. She would take her to visit her mother's grave on another day to see the headstone she and James had chosen to mark Ruby's resting place.

'What do you think, my little angel?' Hannah said as she wheeled the pram through the crowds of visitors: ladies dressed in their straw bonnets and elaborate dresses with layers of overskirts; gentlemen perspiring in their coats; children skipping along in summer clothes and sailors' outfits.

Mercy cooed and smiled from beneath her white lace bonnet. Hannah stopped to tie the ribbons under her chin, and tuck back a lock of her hair which was growing dark and lustrous like Ruby's. She was doing well, putting on weight and developing slowly but surely. Hannah and James watched her closely, monitoring every milestone and panicking over every cough and sneeze.

'It's marvellous to see a loving mother with her child,' an elderly gentleman said as he walked by. 'Good day, young lady.'

'Good day, sir,' she said, moving on, pausing now and again to listen to the silver band, and show Mercy the man and his singing dog which her mother had liked so much. 'Your ma loved you more than you will ever know,' she went on softly, a lump in her throat.

On returning home to Cecil Square to find that James had been called away on a house visit, she left Nanny to feed Mercy with goat's milk and pap, while she checked her gown. A frisson of excitement and anticipation drove her grief and weariness away, as she admired the lilac satin and brocade — six yards of it trimmed with black lace, and draped with satin ribbons and flowers, along with a pair of shoes that Ruby would have coveted.

Later, when they were ready to leave, she put on her coat and kissed Mercy goodnight, and James counted the freckles on her little nose, before they set out in the brougham, arriving at the Cliftonville Hotel on Ethelbert Street in good time to meet Doctor and Mrs Hunter for dinner. Hannah and Charlotte left their coats in the ladies' cloakroom.

'You're feeling well now?' Hannah asked, noting the drapery folded strategically across Charlotte's stomach. 'You certainly look well — blooming, in fact.'

'I'm six months gone. James has confirmed it — Henry already knew, but he wanted a second opinion.'

'Congratulations . . . '

'I'm already the size of an omnibus.' Charlotte smiled ruefully. 'I wouldn't be surprised if I'm carrying twins.'

'Are you sure you should be out dancing?'

Charlotte held out her arm. 'Of course. I've had plenty of practice now — do you remember how you caught me out in the sluice?'

'I found it hard to be cross with you.' Hannah giggled at the memory. 'Let's go and find our husbands before they send out a search party.'

'Here are our beautiful wives,' she heard Henry say as they walked towards them in the reception hall. 'Look at them.'

Hannah released Charlotte's arm and walked over to James who stared at her, his eyes raking her figure.

'You look wonderful, my darling,' he said. 'In

466

fact, you take my breath away.'

'The doctor needs a doctor to revive him,' Henry jested. 'Come along, Mrs Hunter. Lead the way to the dining room — I'm famished.'

Hannah followed the Hunters with James at her side, wondering if they would ever reach their table as her husband's well-wishers, friends and acquaintances crowded in on them to greet him. Even the Osbourne-Coles greeted him cordially, although her father took great pleasure in introducing Miss Osbourne-Cole's fiancé, the son of a top-hat at a London bank.

'If I didn't know better, I'd think you a god, Doctor Clifton,' Hannah said wickedly as they finally sat down to dine, sharing a table with the Hunters, Mr and Mrs Phillips and the Anthonys.

'Can I order you some champagne?' James asked her as she surveyed the food being served: coronation chicken; cold salmon served with cucumber and a horseradish cream; ham glazed with honey. It looked delicious, but she had no appetite. She nibbled a little ham, but she might as well have licked a flat-iron.

'A little lemonade would be acceptable, thank you,' she said, and he looked to their waiter to fill her glass as the party made small talk. At least, some of them did. Charlotte and Doctor Hunter discussed the price of madeira with the Anthonys, while Mr Phillips stared at Hannah as if he was trying to recall where he'd met her before.

'You remember Sister Bentley?' James asked him.

'Ah, I thought there was something familiar

about her . . . You've married her, then, made a decent woman of her.'

'You know that, Mr Phillips. I told you beforehand, so you wouldn't embarrass yourself,' Mrs Phillips said. 'It's lovely to see you so happy, Doctor Clifton. I really do mean that,' she added, making Hannah wonder if she meant it at all. Dripping with jewels, she was one of the wealthiest, most privileged ladies she knew, yet she was oozing envy from every pore. 'Your husband is a marvel — I think it's fair to say that he has saved my life with his new treatment.'

Hannah noticed how James turned quickly to the Anthonys to add his ha'penny-worth on the topic under discussion, which she found odd because he never drank madeira. It wasn't to his taste.

As Mrs Phillips began to tell her about her previous physician and the one before that, Hannah felt faint. She gave James's arm a gentle nudge.

'What is it? Oh, you look like you could do with some fresh air. Allow me.' He stood up and escorted her outside to the balcony overlooking the gardens. 'I thought perhaps you were swooning from boredom. Mrs Phillips does rather go on about her ailments. Would you like to sit down?'

'I'm all right.' She leaned against the stone balustrade and took a few deep breaths.

'Something's been bothering me for the past few days. I knew something wasn't right, but I couldn't put my finger on it.' He lowered his voice to a whisper. 'Hannah, you're with child.'

'Do you think so?' She touched her flat stomach, delighted and apprehensive at the same time.

'All the signs are there.' He took her hand and linked his fingers with hers. 'You mustn't worry about a thing. I'll look after you. Whatever happens, we will get through it together, I promise, and in the fullness of time, this child will become an addition to our family and a playmate for Mercy. I can see them in my mind's eye, a boy and girl, or two girls — I don't mind which — paddling and splashing around in the sea on a hot summer's afternoon.'

She smiled. 'I like the sound of that.'

'It will happen. Trust me' — he grinned suddenly, his teeth gleaming in the evening light — 'I'm a doctor. Shall we return inside?'

'Before we go, there's something I'd like to know — confidentially, of course. How did you cure Mrs Phillips of her ills?'

'She spoke to one of her friends who suffers from hysteria and diagnosed herself. It's what I suspected a long time ago but hadn't been able to confirm to my satisfaction. Who am I to argue with a lay person when I'm merely a physician who's studied medicine for many years? Anyway, the term covers a multitude of ailments and symptoms, including insomnia, irritability, loss of appetite and a tendency to cause trouble.'

'She has the latter in spades.'

'This condition is thought to be linked with the womb.' He quickly changed the subject, 'Are you up to dancing?'

'Of course I am.'

They found their way to the ballroom where James led her on to the floor to dance a quadrille, before Henry requested the next dance, Charlotte having chosen to sit it out. After that, Hannah danced a waltz with her husband, moving in perfect time with him and the music, as they spun their way around the ballroom. Amongst the sparkling gems and colourful gowns, Hannah caught sight of a girl — a young woman — in a scarlet dress, with her dark hair put up and adorned with fresh roses. She was smiling, gazing up into the eyes of an adoring young gentleman, who seemed to carry her around the floor, faster and faster until they blurred into the whirl of dancers and disappeared.

Ruby? she thought, tears springing to her eyes.

'I thought I saw my sister,' she said, when the final note of the music died away.

'Perhaps you did,' James said softly. 'The spirits of those whom we've lost live on long after in our hearts. Come here, my love.' She breathed in his scent of cologne and musk, and the tiniest hint of carbolic as he held her close. 'We will always hold them dear in our memories, and we will go on, making the most of every day, as they would have wished.'

'I must look a mess,' she said, wiping away a tear. 'I'm sorry.'

'Don't apologise. You're the most beautiful woman I've ever set eyes on, inside and out, and I still have to pinch myself sometimes to prove that we really are married. I used to see you on the ward, caring for your patients with kindness and grace, and I used to say to myself, how I wish that seaside angel could be mine — and now you are.'

Welcome to

Penny Street

where your favourite authors and stories live.

Meet casts of characters you'll never forget,
create memories you'll treasure forever,
and discover places that will stay with
you long after the last page.

turn the page to step into the home of

EVIE GRACE

and discover more about

The Seaside
Angel

Dear Reader,

When I decided to set Hannah's story in Margate, I had little idea of the town's history as a nineteenth century sea bathing resort. The arrival of the railway made it accessible to day trippers from London, some of whom let their hair down in the most brazen manner, shocking Margate's residents. Although there were horse-drawn bathing machines designed with hoods to protect the modesty of the Victorian ladies, many of the men bathed in view of the beach, forgoing their bathing drawers. Couples would walk hand in hand along the seafront, something they would never have done at home.

My grandparents took me to Margate when I was about seven years old — rather longer ago than I care to remember! I recall a sleepy seaside town with amusement arcades, fish and chip shops, and ice cream parlours. I paddled in the sea and built sandcastles, but the highlight of my day was a ride on a donkey, hanging on to the hoop on the saddle and marvelling at the big grey furry ears in front of me.

There are no donkeys on Margate Beach now, but there are other attractions, including Dreamland, home to the oldest rollercoaster in Britain. Dreamland was built on the site of the Hall by the Sea, the Victorian pleasure-ground that plays a part in *The Seaside Angel*.

The Royal Sea Bathing Infirmary where Hannah works as a children's nurse, treating her patients with sunshine, fresh air and sea bathing, has been converted into luxury apartments.

I hope you enjoy getting to know Victorian Margate as much as I did.

Evie x

The Penny Lick:
A Dangerous Treat

While I was researching Margate's history for *The Seaside Angel*, I discovered that Hannah would have seen hokey-pokey men selling ice cream on the seafront, and probably have been tempted to buy a penny lick now and again. A little more digging on my part revealed a horrifying link between this Victorian treat and Hannah's work as a nurse at the Royal Sea Bathing Infirmary.

The ice cream sellers came from Italy and the name 'hokey-pokey' is thought to have come from a corruption of 'O che poco!' meaning 'try a little'. A hokey-pokey man would keep his ice cream cold with ice from Norway and salt from Cheshire, a good start when it came to food hygiene.

When Hannah paid her penny, he would take a glass from his stall, dip a wooden paddle into the ice cream container and take out a lump which he would press into the top of the glass, a small glass with a wide base and conical opening, designed to give the optical illusion of there being more ice-cream inside than there actually was.

Hannah would lick the ice-cream from the glass and hand it back. The hokey pokey man would wipe it with a grubby cloth and put it backon the stall for the next person without washing it, thus encouraging the spread of germs between complete strangers.

To be fair, the Victorians didn't understand the role of germs and hygiene at this time, and it wouldn't have occurred to Hannah that by treating herself to a penny lick, she was putting herself at risk of catching the very same disease that her patients were suffering from on the wards of the infirmary.

Margate's Royal Sea Bathing Infirmary had been set up to treat cases of scrofula, a form of tuberculosis, in which the patient would develop fevers and swellings of the glands in the neck. It was thought to be a hereditary disease because tuberculosis would often strike down whole families, the Bronte siblings being just one example. Consumption was another form of tuberculosis, affecting the lungs and causing the patient to cough up blood and waste away. Both scrofula and consumption were generally fatal in Victorian times, there being no treatment apart from surgery, but some cases were improved by the sunshine, fresh air and sea bathing treatments recommended by the doctors at the infirmary.

It wasn't until 1882 that the German bacteriologist, Heinrich Robert Koch identified the infectious agent, the tubercle bacillus. It took time for the medical establishment to accept that tuberculosis was spread from person to person through microscopic droplets released into the air by coughing and spitting, or through direct contact with an infected person's saliva. It took even longer before effective drugs were developed to treat it.

Hannah's role as a nurse would include making sure her patients spent as much time as possible outside, rain or shine, that they bathed daily in seawater, and ate a plentiful diet. She would have been involved in cleaning the ward, changing dressings and monitoring her patients after surgery. Although the surgeons would have used carbolic acid, surgical wounds would usually become infected or colonised by maggots, resulting in a poor infected or colonised by maggots, resulting in a poor outcome for the patient.

It wasn't only tuberculosis that could be spread by the penny lick. In 1879, a medical report blamed an outbreak of cholera on dirty glassware and the penny lick was eventually banned and replaced by edible cones, an innovation I'm very thankful for today!

I hope you enjoyed reading Hannah's story and come to admire the dedicated staff of the infirmary as much as I did.

We do hope that you have enjoyed reading this large print book.

Did you know that all of our titles are available for purchase?

We publish a wide range of high quality large print books including:
Romances, Mysteries, Classics
General Fiction
Non Fiction and Westerns

Special interest titles available in large print are:
The Little Oxford Dictionary
Music Book
Song Book
Hymn Book
Service Book

Also available from us courtesy of Oxford University Press:
Young Readers' Dictionary
(large print edition)
Young Readers' Thesaurus
(large print edition)

For further information or a free brochure, please contact us at:
Ulverscroft Large Print Books Ltd.,
The Green, Bradgate Road, Anstey,
Leicester, LE7 7FU, England.
Tel: (00 44) 0116 236 4325
Fax: (00 44) 0116 234 0205

Other titles published by Ulverscroft:

A THIMBLEFUL OF HOPE

Evie Grace

Dover, 1864: Violet Rayfield leads a happy life with her family in a beautiful terrace on Camden Crescent. But Violet's seemingly perfect world is shattered when her father makes a decision that costs her family everything. Now Violet must sacrifice all she holds dear, as a series of shocking revelations leaves her feeling even more alone. But where one door closes, another opens, and the embroidery skills Violet perfected while a young woman of leisure win her vital work. If she can find the strength to stitch the remnants of her family back together, there might just be a little hope after all . . .

HALF A SIXPENCE

Evie Grace

East Kent, 1830. Catherine Rook takes her peaceful life for granted. Her days are spent at the village school and lending a hand on her family's farm. Life is run by the seasons, and there's little time for worry. But rural unrest begins sweeping through Kent, and when Pa Rook buys a threshing machine it brings turbulence and tragedy to Wanstall Farm. With the Rooks' fortunes forever changed, Catherine must struggle to hold her family together. She turns to her childhood companion, Matty Carter, for comfort. With the threat of destitution nipping at her heels, Catherine must forge a way out of ruin . . .